The Grail

Relic of an Ancient Religion

The Grail

Relic of an Ancient Religion

Simon Andrew Stirling
With illustrations by Lloyd Canning

MOON BOOKS

Winchester, UK
Washington, USA

First published by Moon Books, 2015
Moon Books is an imprint of John Hunt Publishing Ltd., Laurel House, Station Approach, Alresford, Hants, SO24 9JH, UK
office1@jhpbooks.net
www.johnhuntpublishing.com
www.moon-books.net

For distributor details and how to order please visit the 'Ordering' section on our website.

ISBN: 978 1 78279 725 8

A CIP catalogue record for this book is available from the British Library.

Design: Stuart Davies
Cover image: Lloyd Canning 2013

Printed and bound by CPI Group (UK) Ltd, Croydon, CR0 4YY, UK

CONTENTS

To Kiri,
γνώθι σεαυτόν,
with love

An ART & WILL Book

By the same author

The King Arthur Conspiracy:
How a Scottish Prince Became a Mythical Hero

Who Killed William Shakespeare?
The Murderer, The Motive, The Means

To the man who has no magic in his blood the cavern of Keltic profundity is for ever sealed. He who approaches it must, I feel, not alone be of the ancient stock of the first culture-bringers of this island, but he must also have heard since childhood the deep and repeated call of ancestral voices urging him to the task of the exploration of the mysteries of his people.
Lewis Spence, *The Mysteries of Britain*

Here is the Book of thy Descent,
Here begins the Book of the Sangreal,
Here begin the terrors,
Here begin the miracles.
Perlesvaus

AUTHOR'S NOTE

This book is the result of an experiment. As is fitting for an exploration of the history, mythology and science of the 'Holy Grail', it grew out of a challenge – to write a book in 12 instalments, with each new chapter being published at the end of each month on the Moon Books blog. Compiling a book in this manner was a new experience, and I am indebted to Trevor Greenfield of Moon Books for initiating the quest and accepting me as the fool who would be a knight.

Thanks must also go to my two principle collaborators: to John M. Gist, who happily read through and gave me supremely useful feedback on every chapter as it began to take shape, and whose intelligence, discernment, enthusiasm and knowledge of philosophy and religion were invaluable; and to Lloyd Canning, whose fascinating illustrations helped me to visualise the themes of each chapter, and with whom I enjoyed many an evening of tea and talk as we sketched out our ideas. Thanks also to Hugh McArthur, Clan Arthur *Seannachie*, and to Andrew Sinclair, who gave my career a very early boost. But as always, the biggest thanks go to my long-suffering helpmate and life partner, Kim.

Finally, there is a system at work in this book. Those who seek the key will find it in so many clear concise lucid words, repeated by degrees, with a free life entailed and an eye that initially leaps from the page.

Simon Andrew Stirling

CAVTES

1

The Waste Land

... there is an Unknown Country lying beneath the places that we know, and appearing only in moments of revelation.
Hilaire Belloc

THE YEAR is 1984. A-Level French. We're reading *Tueur sans Gages*.

Bérenger, a nondescript Everyman, is being shown around the Radiant City by the Architect, who also happens to be the Superintendent of Police. The Radiant City fills Bérenger with amazement: everything is suffused with a brilliant light, and it never rains. He is reminded of an old memory, of a time when 'there was a blazing fire inside me ...'

> Everything was virgin, purified, discovered anew ... I felt I was there at the gates, at the very centre of the universe ... I walked and ran and cried: I *am*, I *am*, *everything* is, everything *is*!

But the glorious feeling had passed, replaced by a 'chaotic vacuum', the 'immense sadness you feel at a moment of tragic and intolerable separation.'

'And since then, it's been perpetual November ... The light of dawn has gone! And to think we call this civilisation!'

The Architect is hardly listening to him. A telephone keeps ringing, which the Architect keeps in his pocket, taking it out to answer it. He is both out of the office and still at work.

When Eugène Ionesco wrote *Tueur sans Gages* in 1957, the idea that a municipal functionary would carry a phone in his pocket was absurd. It still seemed pretty surreal in 1984. But ten years later, I had a phone I could keep in my pocket so that, like the Architect, I was never entirely out of the office.

Looking back, Ionesco's absurdist drama – usually entitled *The Killer* in English – reads like a snapshot of the 20th century: a time when the absurd became commonplace.

Bérenger is astonished to discover that nobody wants to live in the ideal city. There is a killer on the loose. And no one, it seems, can be bothered to catch him. The police are too busy directing traffic and menacing the public. A Schoolmaster teaches nonsensical history and a political agitator promises to change everything by changing nothing – 'If an ideology doesn't apply to real life, we'll say it does and it'll be perfect ... We'll replace the myths ... by slogans ... and the latest platitudes!' Finally, Bérenger finds himself on an echoing street, desperately trying to reason with the chuckling Killer. The play ends on a note of despair as Bérenger sinks to his knees and moans:

> 'Oh God! There's nothing we can do. What can we do ... What can we do ...'

This, you could say, was the 20th century in a nutshell. We were continually promising to build the city of the future, but the Killer still lurked in the suburbs and the subways.

For all our technological advances – from bombs that could wipe out whole cities to phones you could carry in your pocket – there was something fundamental missing. Bérenger understood this: 'What I'm suffering from doesn't show, it's theoretical, spiritual.' Another word would be 'existential'. The problem was one of *existence*.

T.S. Eliot put a name to it in a poem published in the wake of the First World War. Western society seemed zombified, fragmented, morally adrift:

> Unreal City,

Under the brown fog of a winter dawn,
A crowd flowed over London Bridge, so many,
I had not thought death had undone so many.

Little had changed in the 35 years which separated the Unreal City of Eliot's *The Waste Land* from Ionesco's Radiant City on the outskirts of a damp, grey Paris. The need for escape – through sex, drugs, consumerism, political extremism or Eastern mysticism – increased as the century wore on. Television came as a narcotic, the new opiate of the people. But the dis-ease remained: the essential, existential problem would not go away.

The Grail castle

In a series of talks given in 1969 in San Diego, California, a Jungian analyst named Robert A. Johnson approached the problem – much as T.S. Eliot had done in *The Waste Land* – from the direction of myth, arguing that the medieval legend of Perceval could be interpreted as an essay on modern man. The burden of these lectures was published in *He: Understanding Masculine Psychology* (1974).

Robert A. Johnson had turned to a 12th century myth to elucidate a 20th century predicament. Like Ionesco's Bérenger, Johnson's Perceval is an Everyman figure. Raised in seclusion by his mother, Perceval encounters five knights in the forest and assumes that they are angels. When he learns that they are in fact knights, he resolves to become a knight himself. His mother dies of a broken heart when Perceval rides off.

During the course of his adventures, Perceval happens upon the Grail Castle, where he sits down to dine with the Fisher King. A mute procession passes in front of him. First, a squire enters the chamber, carrying a lance which bleeds from the tip. The squire is followed by two youths bearing golden candle-holders. With them is a maiden; beautiful, noble and richly-attired, she carries in her two hands a 'grail' which lights up the room.

Perceval had previously been advised not to be too talkative, and so he refrains from enquiring about this strange ritual. He goes to bed and wakes up to find the castle deserted. As he rides out, the drawbridge snaps shut behind him. He soon finds himself being criticised for his failure to ask the crucial question.

Robert A. Johnson considered Perceval's experience in the Fisher King's castle to be typical of young men. At some point during adolescence, every youth stumbles into a Grail Castle. The world suddenly appears different: magical, full of promise, as if his consciousness has been raised. He senses that the universe holds possibilities beyond anything he had imagined.

William Wordsworth expressed a similar feeling, softly and succinctly, in his *Intimations of Immortality from Recollections of Early Childhood*:

There was a time when meadow, grove, and stream,
The earth, and every common sight,
To me did seem
Apparell'd in celestial light,
The glory and the freshness of a dream.

The experience also compares with Bérenger's memories in *Tueur sans Gages* of his adolescent awakening: 'I was deeply aware of the unique joy of being alive ... Suddenly the joy became more intense, breaking all bounds! And then, oh what indescribable bliss took hold of me!'

Robert Johnson believed that this moment 'usually happens around fifteen or sixteen years of age' (Bérenger recalls that he had last experienced 'that dazzling radiance, that glowing feeling' when he was seventeen or eighteen). It is not just in early childhood that the world can appear apparelled in celestial light; even in mid-to-late adolescence a young man can be pleasantly surprised by a moment of transcendence, a glimpse of the Grail.

What this moment consists of – and how it might be recreated

– will be part of the subject of this study. For now, we might simply observe that the 'Grail Castle' experience which, Johnson claimed, is shared by every young male (though the experience is invariably a solitary one) comprises a brief interlude in which the youth ceases to be governed by *thinking* and succumbs to *being*. It is as if the boundaries of the ego (still forming in adolescence) are dissolved. The barrier between the inner 'subjective' realm and the outer 'objective' reality collapses, and the young man is suddenly immersed in the world – a participant, rather than a detached spectator.

Plato's cave

For most of our waking hours we inhabit a world of hard surfaces, which we apprehend from the viewpoint of an isolated, self-enclosed 'I'. Thus, I see a rock and recognise it as something solid and immobile. There is a distance, a gulf between me and the rock, even as I reach out to touch it, because 'I' am the subject and the rock is the object. We are separate things.

Modern man assumes that this is the only reality there is. The Celtic imagination, however, regards certain places as 'thin', which is as much as to say that the seemingly impenetrable veil between realities – the inner 'I-ness' and the outer 'Other-ness' – can become flimsy and permeable.

The Greek philosopher Plato described, in *The Republic*, a group of prisoners chained to the floor of a cave, watching shadows on the wall. Because they can see nothing else, the prisoners believe that they are observing reality. But this perception is false. What the prisoners see are merely the silhouettes of things which exist beyond the limits of their vision.

Our everyday reality is something of a shadow-play. We see forms but seldom suspect that they might be manifestations of a deeper reality. If we could but loosen our chains and swivel round we would discover – after our eyes had adjusted to the unaccustomed light – something more substantial than the shadows we had been viewing before. This, argued Plato (or rather his mouthpiece, Socrates), is how liberated philosophers perceive the world. It is also what the Celt meant by a 'thin' place, for it is possible that the walls of the cave can shimmer and fade, and for the immanent reality which underscores the apparent world to reveal itself.

This can only happen when we abandon the ego habit and abolish the artificial distinction between subject and object, the 'I' and the 'Other' – that is, when we stop *thinking* and start *being*.

If Robert Johnson's interpretation of the Grail myth is correct, and if Eugène Ionesco's drama is anything to go by, the experience of a contented and awakened state of being is not uncommon, at least in adolescence. It struck Bérenger as he was walking along a narrow street in a little country town and Perceval as he sat down to dine with the Fisher King. In both instances, a dominant theme is *light*: the 'celestial light' which, as Wordsworth recalled from his childhood, vouchsafed him a vague sense, an intimation or presentiment, of immortality. Bérenger remembers that the 'light grew more and more brilliant ... It's as if there were four suns in the sky'. Perceval beholds the Grail, borne by a beautiful maiden: 'After she had entered the hall carrying the grail the room was so brightly illumined that the candles lost their brilliance like stars and the moon when the sun rises.'

Returning to Plato's parable of the cave, we can posit that the peak experience which occurs during childhood and/or adolescence happens because the metaphorical chains which hold us down are loosened and we find ourselves facing, not the wall of the cave, but the entrance, where the things which cast their shadows on the wall are brightly illuminated. Dazzled at first, we enjoy a momentary glimpse of the world *as it really is* – apparelled in celestial light,

The glory and the freshness of a dream.

But the moment passes. The vision crumbles, the radiant light fades, and we are thrust back into Bérenger's 'perpetual November, perpetual twilight, twilight in the morning, twilight at midnight, at noon.' Perceval awakes to find the castle deserted. The gates slam shut and the hidden retreat of the Fisher King disappears from view.

THE QUEST BEGINS

In his analysis of the Perceval legend, Robert A. Johnson put this sudden, crushing return to everyday reality down to immaturity. The adolescent male who experiences the Grail moment has yet to acquire the spiritual or psychological resources to make the most of it. Perceval remains tongue-tied in the presence of the 'grail' and this, we soon learn, is a grave error – had he asked the appropriate questions, the Fisher King would have been restored to health. Such reticence, though, is understandable: who can know what questions are to be asked of the moment of transcendence, the vision of radiance, when it occurs during the teen years?

Johnson cited an old proverb from the Middle Ages which held that 'a person has a chance at the splendour of God, at the golden world, twice in his life – once early in adolescence and again when he is forty-five or fifty.' The first visit to the Grail Castle is a kind of preparatory experience, a transitory glimpse of a reality which exists beyond the narrow bounds of ego-consciousness. The opportunity will arise again, later in life, when hopefully we are better prepared for it.

Without that initial Grail experience life would be pretty meaningless, a brutish struggle for survival consisting of little more than 'getting and spending', in Wordsworth's words ('The world is too much with us; late and soon, / Getting and spending, we lay waste our powers'). Bérenger admits that 'It's only the memory of what happened that's helped me to go on living in this grey city.' But the memory also turns Bérenger into an alienated outsider, surrounded by human robots and dead souls.

And this, one might say, is the very definition of the Waste Land. The land seems barren, the city 'unreal'. The Grail experience – always a solitary one – shows us the reality behind appearances. After that, nothing in our daily lives seems really real.

The young man who dimly remembers his moment of awakening, the dawning of a sort of super-consciousness, can never be truly at peace. Life outside the Grail Castle is painfully empty. Endless amounts of energy will be expended – and much money spent – in trying to rediscover the entrance to the 'hidden retreat' or to compensate for the loss of the vision, often with disastrous consequences. The cost to the individual, his relationships, and society in general can be colossal.

It would help if we could only avoid falling into the trap of believing the Grail to be a thing. Such thinking is typical of a materialistic age and leads only to wild-goose chases and disillusionment. The advertising industry thrives by dandling the promise of the Grail before our glassy eyes, but the Grail is not for sale. Anyone who tells you otherwise saw you coming.

By placing too much emphasis on the Grail as an artefact, a material object, the storytellers have overlooked its primary function. It was not a *thing* but a *process*, and in later chapters we will examine what this process might have involved, both in terms of the outer rituals and the inner workings of the brain (for this investigation will have no real value unless its conclusions are grounded in science and applicable to the physical universe we inhabit). Furthermore, as we shall see in the next chapter, an understanding of the process is both timely and necessary. The Grail has eluded us for too long, and we have made a terrible mess – a veritable Waste Land of our planetary home – while flailing about in a facile and costly search for the wrong thing.

Nevertheless, if we are to come anywhere near an appreciation of the Grail experience we must determine what form the Grail took. In other words, we must recognise what the Grail *was* before we can grapple with what it was *for*.

The wise fool

The earliest mention of the Grail occurs in a poem written in the 1180s by a French troubadour named Chrétien de Troyes. *Perceval, le Conte du Graal* runs to about 9,000 lines. Chrétien almost certainly never completed it, and a succession of poets attempted to round off the story. In addition to the total of 54,000 lines contributed by the four 'Continuations' of the poem there is also a short prologue or *Elucidation*, which names the source of the material as one 'Master Blihis', of whom more anon.

The hero of Chrétien's poem is Perceval le Gallois – 'Perceval the Welshman'. The term is potentially misleading; 'Welsh' derives from a Germanic word meaning 'foreign' and would have referred initially to the native inhabitants of Britain: especially those parts of Britain which, between the 1st and 5th centuries AD, had come under Roman rule. Perceval was not necessarily Welsh in the familiar sense of the word. He belonged to the *Cymry* ('fellow-countrymen') who were eventually driven out of their tribal lands and into modern-day Wales by the incoming English in what has been aptly described as 'an ethnic cleansing event'.

Perceval is the naïve son of 'the widow lady of the Waste Forest'. His father was 'wounded through his thighs and his body maimed' in the manner of the Fisher King, and both his elder brothers died in combat, their father then dying of grief, which explains his mother's neurotically over-protective behaviour towards her son. But when Perceval encounters five knights riding through the forest he is overawed and eager to attain the status of knighthood. His heartbroken mother gives him some advice – always come to the aid of a maiden in distress, and if a lady offers you a ring you may take it. She then faints dead away when Perceval takes his leave of her.

He soon comes across a fine tent in a clearing. A damsel is alone and asleep inside. Perceval rushes in and kisses her ('He who kisses a maiden gains much,' his mother had told him). Naturally, the woman is terrified, both of the mad youth and of her jealous lover, who is not far away. The boy takes a ring from her finger by force and then helps himself to some refreshments before leaving the maiden in tears.

By displaying such youthful insensitivity – and storing up trouble for the unfortunate damsel – Perceval establishes himself as an archetypal young man, rash, brash and rude. There is more to the tent scene, however, than a mere study of juvenile manners, although it will be a while before we can spot what it is.

Onwards he rides, seeking directions to King Arthur's castle at Carduel (unidentified, though frequently assumed to be Carlisle). As he approaches the castle he meets an armed knight, all in red, bearing in his hand a golden cup which he snatched from King Arthur's table 'with his wine still in it'. The Red Knight's seizure of the golden cup seems to correspond to Perceval's forcible removal of the ring 'set with a shining emerald' from the maiden's finger. The Grail adventure – though we do not know it yet – is underway.

Perceval enters the castle to find Arthur downcast, 'disheartened and silent'. When he finally speaks, Arthur explains that the Red Knight – 'the greatest enemy I have, who hates and distresses me most' – has laid claim to the land. None of Arthur's knights rose up to challenge the king's greatest enemy, not even when the Red Knight snatched up the golden cup, spilling its contents all over the queen. Arthur seems to doubt that his queen will survive this awful insult.

The Fisher King

Perceval desires only to be made a knight, and a 'red knight', no less. He offers to take the red armour of Arthur's enemy, the knight who snatched the golden cup.

A 'fair and noble' maiden who had not been heard to laugh in 'six full years or more' greets Perceval with a laugh, telling him 'if you live long enough, I think and believe in my heart that in this whole world there will never be, nor will anyone ever acknowledge, a better knight than yourself.' This earns her a slap from Arthur's thuggish steward, Kay. Perceval rides out, confronts the Red Knight and kills him. He takes the Red Knight's armour and sends the golden cup back to Arthur's court.

Perceval is now a knight, both in name and deed, but he has much to learn. He receives some training from a gentleman who persuades him to relinquish his coarse homespun garb (the lad is growing up) but whose sage advice – 'He who talks too much commits a sin' – will have dire repercussions. Perceval again rides forth and comes to the aid of an impoverished maiden whose castle is under siege (the Waste Land seems to be all around). But Perceval is anxious to return to his mother – he does not know that she died when he left her – and so he sets out to find his way home. Seeking shelter for the night, he spies a boat drifting on a river with two men inside it. One of these men is the noble Fisher King, who directs Perceval to his 'hidden retreat'.

The Fisher King lives in agony. He was struck by a javelin through both thighs during a battle, and now the only activity he can bear to engage in is fishing. As Perceval sits down beside the Fisher King a squire enters, bearing a sword 'made of such good steel that it could not be broken except in one singularly perilous circumstance known only to him who had forged and tempered it' (Perceval will later be told precisely where this sword can be 'rehammered, retempered, and repaired'). The Fisher King presents the sword to Perceval, since it was 'ordained and destined' for him.

Then, as Perceval and the Fisher King prepare to dine, the Grail procession makes its first appearance. A youth enters the chamber carrying a white lance which drips blood from its tip, followed by two handsome squires bearing golden candelabra 'with enamel inlays'. With them walks an exquisite maiden clutching a *graal* (Chrétien's word) in both hands. Behind her comes another maiden who carries a silver carving platter.

The *graal,* Chrétien tells us, was made of 'fine pure gold' and set with a multitude of precious stones, 'the best and costliest to be found in earth or sea'. So brightly illumined was this wondrous item that it outshone the candles as the rising sun transcends the softer light of the moon and the stars.

The procession passes before him several times during the course of the meal but at no point does Perceval venture to ask who is served from the *graal,* and the Fisher King does not volunteer this information. Having been told that 'He who talks too much commits a sin', Perceval watches it all and says nothing. Chrétien assures us that Perceval had wanted to know who was served from the *graal,* but the question was put off.

A bed is prepared for him. He awakes in the morning to find the castle deserted. And soon he is castigated by a maiden – his first cousin, in fact – for neglecting to ask the meaning of the procession. His failure has only prolonged the Fisher King's suffering. The land will remain waste.

PEREDUR FAB EFROG

A good half-century before Chrétien composed his Grail romance a Welsh *latimer* or 'translator' brought certain tales of Arthur and his companions to France, recounting them to the Count of Poitou – most likely William VII, the grandfather of the remarkable Eleanor of Aquitaine. French poets referred to this 'translator' as 'Bleheris', later 'Blihis' and finally 'Blaise', the so-called 'master of Merlin'. No one, it seems, told the old tales better: it was said that this *latimer* knew 'the history of all the counts and all the kings of Britain'.

Giraldus Cambrensis or 'Gerald of Wales' (*c* 1146 – *c* 1222) would later write of a 'well-known story-teller' named Bleddri. This storyteller can be identified as Bleddri latimer ap Kadifor, a 'translator' from the Carmarthen area of Wales, who served under the Norman king Henry I. The Priory of St John was founded at Carmarthen as a cell of the abbey at Battle in Sussex by King Henry I in *circa* 1110; Bleddri made a gift to the priory about twenty years later. He was around during the lifetime of William, Duke of Aquitaine and Count of Poitou, nicknamed 'The Troubadour', who died in 1126, and to whom 'Bleheris' or 'Master Blihis' told his Arthurian tales.

At about the same time as the Norman-Welsh *latimer* took the old tales of Arthur and his knights to France, a marble archivolt was carved and installed over the north portal of the Romanesque cathedral at Modena in Italy. The Modena Archivolt depicts a battle scene: 'Artus de Bretania' (Arthur of Britain) is seen attacking a fortress in which his wife is being held. Evidently, the Arthurian legends had spread through mainland Europe by the second quarter of the 12th century.

The stories circulated among the minstrels and jongleurs of medieval France, finally coming to the attention of Chrétien de Troyes. Chrétien enjoyed the patronage of Marie de France, Countess of Champagne and daughter of Eleanor of Aquitaine, the wife of Henry II of England (grandson of King Henry I). He duly created his own versions of the legends, including *Yvain, le Chevalier au Lion* and *Le Chevalier de la Charette*, which introduced the world to Sir Lancelot.

If the original tales which inspired Chrétien's romances existed in written form at the time, those manuscripts have been lost. The earliest surviving transcriptions of Welsh poetry pertaining to the heroes of 'The Old North' – *Yr Hen Ogledd* – are found in the Black Book of Carmarthen (*Llyfr Du Caerfyrddin*). Compiled in about 1250, the Black Book, so-called because of its binding, is now housed in the National Library of Wales, where it is catalogued as Peniarth MS 1. It can hardly be a coincidence that the oldest collection of traditional Welsh literature should have been transcribed at the very priory in Carmarthen with which the 'well-known story-teller', Bleddri latimer ap Kadifor, was connected.

The stories which had most influenced Chrétien de Troyes

were not written down until even later; they were preserved in the White Book of Rhydderch (also known as Peniarth MS 4 and Peniarth MS 5), which dates from the middle of the 14th century, and the Red Book of Hergest (Jesus College MS 111), compiled in about 1400. Both contain native Welsh versions of Chrétien's *Conte du Graal*, in which the hero is known as Peredur.

After the elegance of Chrétien's courtly verse the Welsh versions can seem crude in comparison. Arguably, the less refined quality of the Welsh tales betrays their antiquity, in that they drew on authentic traditions passed down from bard to bard before they were transcribed by medieval monks. Moreover, the Peredur tales name certain individuals – such as Owain, the model for Chrétien's Yvain, *Le Chevalier au Lion* – who will help us to identify the historical Arthur.

Flower of knighthood

The Welsh accounts present Peredur as the son of Efrog 'who owned the Earldom of the North'. Instantly, we are provided with a location outside the modern principality of Wales, *Caer Efrog* being the Welsh name for the English city of York, once the principal military garrison of the Roman province of *Britannia Secunda* or, as the Britons came to think of it, 'The Old North'.

In about AD 559, Eliffer of the Great Army died defending York against the Angles. One of his sons, who became the chief of *Caer Efrog*, was named Peredur. As 'Peredur son of York' (*Peredur fab Efrog*), this historical prince was the inspiration behind Chrétien's romanticised *Perceval*.

According to the tale, Peredur's father and brothers had perished in combat, and so his mother brought him up far from the madding crowd and dreams of knighthood. All the same, the boy meets three knights in the forest, one of them being Owain son of Urien (a contemporary of Peredur of York). Peredur questions them and then returns to his mother, who swoons at the very mention of 'knights'.

Peredur sets off for Arthur's court, pausing only to take a large ring from a 'lovely auburn-haired maiden'. Approaching Arthur's citadel, he encounters the knight who snatched a golden goblet from Arthur's queen, poured the contents over her and struck her a blow across the face. The knight had challenged Arthur's courtiers to retrieve the goblet and avenge the insult done to Gwenhwyfar, but not one of them had moved. Peredur enters Arthur's hall – where it is not a maiden who breaks her silence to greet him but a dwarf and his wife who, having been mute for a year, hail Peredur as the 'chief of warriors, and flower of knighthood', for which they are both beaten senseless. Peredur is told that he will receive the order of knighthood if he overthrows the churlish knight and returns the golden cup, which he does. He refuses, however, to receive the order of knighthood until he has avenged the injuries done to Mr and Mrs Dwarf.

Onward he journeys, defeating one knight after another, until he comes to a lake on the edge of a vast wood. A 'venerable, hoary-headed man' rises from a cushion to greet him. The man is lame. He is also Peredur's uncle, his mother's brother. He instructs Peredur in the ways of knighthood, admonishing him: 'If thou seest aught to cause thee wonder, ask not the meaning of it'.

Peredur soon finds himself in another castle, the guest of another 'hoary-headed' old uncle. This one invites Peredur to strike an iron staple with a sword. The sword snaps in two. His uncle tells him to 'Place the two parts together, and reunite them.' Peredur does so. The sword is entire again. Peredur succeeds in fixing the sword twice; the third time, the sword remains broken.

Two youths enter the hall bearing 'a spear of mighty size, with three streams of blood flowing from the point to the ground.' The appearance of this spear causes an outbreak of wailing and lamentation.

Two maidens then enter the chamber, carrying 'a large salver between them, in which was a man's head, surrounded by a profusion of blood.' There is another anguished outcry. Peredur goes to bed, and in the morning, with his uncle's permission, he rides forth again.

There is no mention of a 'grail' in the Peredur story – a striking omission, given that Chrétien's account had been around for some 200 years by the time the Welsh versions of the tale were written down. Chrétien had stressed that Perceval's 'failure to have asked what is done with the grail' only prolonged the Fisher King's agony. The Welsh accounts ignore this altogether.

Peredur vs. Perceval

Many scholars have presumed that the romance of *Peredur fab Efrog* is but an inferior imitation of Chrétien's *Perceval*, supposing that the Frenchman's *Conte du Graal* came first and was then mangled and garbled by Welsh bards. But we should not be too hasty here – for a start, the Welsh versions point to a distinct timescale (late-6th century) and geographical region (North Britain) for the setting of the legend, guiding us towards the true realm and era of Arthur and his 'knights'. Still, the Welsh storytellers did not include a Grail in their accounts, implying that they might not have realised what the story was really about.

We could of course spin this around to suggest that, by placing undue emphasis on an object which he called a *graal*, it was Chrétien who missed the point. Other elements, such as the sword which breaks but can be repaired and the spear that drips blood, are present in the Welsh story, and whereas Chrétien followed the 'grail' with a silver carving platter, the Welsh account comes up with something more startling: a large salver with a man's head 'surrounded by a profusion of blood'. It may be that the native tradition of Britain recalled that the central mystery was contained in the breakable sword, the blood-dripping lance and the head on its platter, in which case there was no need for a *graal* of 'fine pure gold'. Perhaps Chrétien's courtly sensibilities recoiled from the image of the blood-soaked head and so he replaced it with something more seemly: a 'grail' which lights up the room.

This takes us to the heart of the conundrum, for if it was Chrétien de Troyes who helped to shift the focus away from the assorted objects – sword, spear, salver – and onto a single item, which he termed a *graal*, then he set a hare running. In short, Chrétien altered the nature of the problem. The mystery of the Grail became the Grail itself: What is it? Whom does it serve?

What if these questions are the wrong ones? Or rather – what if they are perfectly good questions asked in the wrong context? (In the next chapter we shall consider some of the wrong answers which have come from asking the wrong questions about the Grail.)

Peredur is not reproached for his failure to quiz his uncle about the strange procession of the bleeding lance and the severed head. No explanation is forthcoming, but this does not reflect badly on the 'flower of knighthood'. This raises the possibility that the procession *was not meant to be questioned* – or not by Peredur at any rate – which in turn suggests that Chrétien was telling a slightly different story.

In the third chapter, we shall return to the traditions of Britain to discover what the 'grail' might have looked like before Chrétien got hold of the tale.

But we are not yet finished with Peredur/Perceval. We should recall Robert A. Johnson's argument that the Waste Land is a spiritual or psychological condition caused by a momentary glimpse of the Grail (for which we might read the awakened consciousness, the vision of eternal delight or the state of pure Being) which is lost through ignorance and immaturity. The Waste Land would therefore be an objective correlative or metaphor for the existential agony of being *unable to forget* the peak experience which occurred, once upon a time, in youth.

This interpretation arises from Chrétien's retelling of the story, with its insistence that something called a *graal* is the key to the mystery and the inference that failure to ask the question = suffering = the Waste Land. But the Waste Land already exists, and the Welsh accounts let the bleeding lance and the bloody head pass by without comment, leaving us to draw our own conclusions.

PARZIVAL

The Waste Land is not caused by Perceval's diffidence: the land was already in chaos before he set foot in the Fisher King's hidden retreat. The debilitating wound 'through both thighs' had been sustained by Perceval's father, or Peredur's uncle, many years earlier. Arthur is morose, effectively moribund, when the boy arrives at his court. Queen Gwenhwyfar has been insulted and might not survive. Knights lay siege to damsels in their castles. It would take more than a question to put everything right.

So why did Chrétien de Troyes make such a fuss of the 'grail' and the questions which should have been asked: what is done with the Grail and where is it carried? More to the point, why is there no mention of a 'grail' in the Welsh tale and no suggestion that Peredur was at fault for not asking the question? Either the Grail mattered or it didn't – and if it didn't, then we have been duped into seeking a worthless item.

What exactly did Chrétien mean by a *graal*?

The word is an Old French one. *Graal* seems to have derived from the Old Provençal *grazal* – a cup or bowl made of earth, wood or metal; the alternative spelling, *greal*, can be traced back to the Old Catalan *gresal*, which meant the same thing. Chrétien's *graal* would appear to have been just such a cup or bowl of 'fine pure gold' which was 'completely uncovered' every time the maiden carried it past Perceval, who neglected to ask who was served from it.

The idea that the Grail was a container squares with what Hélinand of Froidment, a French minstrel-turned-Cistercian monk, had to say in his *Chronicon,* written between 1211 and 1223. Hélinand claimed that a British hermit of the 8th century received a miraculous vision of Joseph of Arimathea and the 'basin' (*catino*) in which the Last Supper was served. Another word for this 'basin' was *gradale*. Hélinand described a *gradale* as a pan or saucer, 'wide and fairly deep' (*scutella lata et aliquantulum profunda – scutella* being related to *scutum*, a 'shield'), in which fine foods were served to the wealthy, 'one morsel after another in different rows'.

Hélinand's description of a *gradale* would appear to indicate an ornamented, shield-shaped receptacle for use at banquets or a deep dish used as a stand for other vessels, a sort of Lazy Susan for the über-rich. He added that 'the common people' called it 'greal' because those who ate from it were 'thankful' (*grata*).

It is possible – nay, probable – that Hélinand was actually describing the Eucharist, and that he conflated *gradale* with the Gradual, a part of the Mass which was sung on the church steps. Hélinand remarked that the privileged were served from the *gradale* in step-by-step fashion (*gradatim*), one delicacy after another. This interpretation would appear to derive *gradale* from the Latin *gradus*, a 'step', and to have equated the *gradale* with the Eucharistic Sacrifice or Mass, which was celebrated 'by degrees', one step at a time.

A more likely derivation of *gradale* is from the Latin *gradalis* and its earlier form, *cratalis,* a variant of *crater*. This was a Latin loanword from Ancient Greece. At a Greek symposium or drinking party a two-handled bowl (*krater*) was placed in the centre of the room. Wine was mixed with water in the *krater* and served to the assembled guests in smaller vessels.

The maiden who passed before Perceval carrying a *graal* 'with her two hands' might well have been bearing a two-handled *krater*. As we shall discover, images of two-handled cups or bowls can be found throughout the realm of the historical King Arthur.

But not everyone saw the Grail in these terms.

"Elaborate volute-style krater dating from the 4th century BC. Discovered in a tomb at Derveni, near Thessaloniki in Greece."

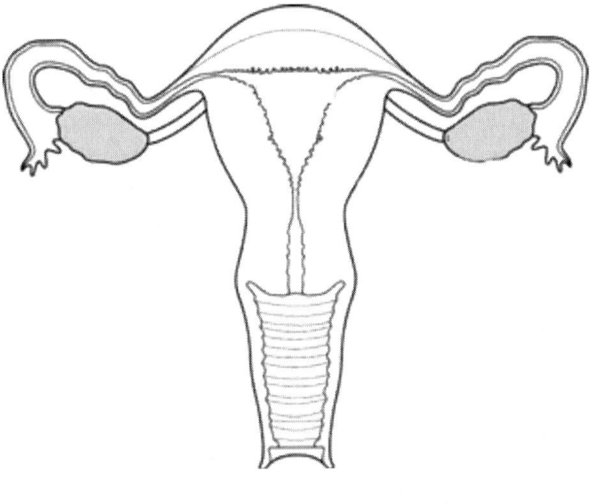

"Human uterus – the shape of which compares with the two-handled krater or mixing bowl."

Lapsit exillis

Early in the 13th century, a Bavarian *Minnesinger* composed an elaborate version of the Grail legend. Wolfram von Eschenbach's *Parzival* was no straightforward attempt to complete Chrétien's unfinished *Perceval*. Indeed, Wolfram accused 'Master Christian of Troyes' of misrepresenting the original story.

Wolfram claimed to have access to the authentic Grail tradition, preserved in an Arabic manuscript, which had reached him by way of a Provençal author called 'Kyot'. This might not be true. Undeniably, though, Wolfram's account is riddled with hermetic and alchemical symbolism.

The existence of the Grail, so Wolfram informs us, was revealed to one Flegetanis, a pagan astronomer whose knowledge of 'the recession of each planet and its return' allowed him to see 'hidden secrets' in the stars (maybe he had been studying the Crater constellation). The Grail had been brought down to earth by neutral angels when war broke out in heaven. Since then, it had been guarded by 'a Christian progeny bred to a pure life'. Wolfram identified these 'formidable fighting-men' as the Knights Templar:

> They live from a Stone whose essence is most pure ... It is called 'Lapsit exillis'. By virtue of this Stone the Phoenix is burned to ashes, in which he is reborn ... Which done, it shines dazzling bright and lovely as before!

Furthermore, the Stone had the ability to forestall sickness and even death – 'Such powers does the Stone confer on mortal men that their flesh and bones are soon made young again.' This Stone, wrote Wolfram, 'is also called "The Gral".'

The Stone, which is also the 'Gral', compares with the Philosopher's Stone of the alchemists: it is 'forever incorruptible', 'paradisal', 'transcending all earthly perfection!' The maiden who carried it was perforce required to be 'of perfect chastity and to have renounced all things false.' The Stone would dispense whatever food and drink a man desired. 'As to those who are appointed to the Gral, hear how they are made known.'

Under the top edge of the Stone an inscription announces the name and lineage of the one summoned to make the glad journey. Whether it concern girls or boys, there is no need to erase their names, for as soon as a name has been read it vanishes from sight!

These children, the chosen ones, are 'fetched from many countries and forever after are immune from the shame of sin ... When they die here in this world, Paradise is theirs in the next.'

There is much that is esoteric here. Wolfram's explanation – what the Grail was (a Stone) and where it came from (Heaven) – is clearly more fulsome, and indeed exotic, than anything we get from Chrétien de Troyes. The Stone was originally associated with Lucifer, otherwise the Morning Star or the planet Venus. Those angels who had refused to take sides when Lucifer rebelled against the Almighty carried the Stone down to earth, where a 'warlike company' of men (and women) received its bounty. It had something in common with the *gradale,* in that it would provide whatever nourishment was required, and yet it does not appear to have been a dish or bowl. The alternative name for the 'Gral' – *Lapsit exillis* – has no obvious meaning.

It is quite a leap from Chrétien's innocent-sounding *graal* – absent from the Welsh accounts – to Wolfram's extraordinary Stone, and it is tempting to feel that Wolfram was toying with us, or that he was perhaps alluding to some arcane ritual practised by the powerful and enigmatic order of the Templar knights. However, hidden away in Chrétien's tale is a 'dark stone' which – whether Chrétien realised it or not – might be germane to the matter of the Grail.

Lai du cor

Just outside Arthur's castle, the immature Perceval encounters the Red Knight who laid claim to Arthur's lands and then snatched up a golden cup, tipping its contents all over the queen. In Wolfram's *Parzival*, the 'finely-chased goblet' is 'entirely of red gold'. The Red Knight waits in a meadow nearby for somebody to come and challenge him. Perceval – formerly Peredur of York – wishes to become a knight and covets the Red Knight's armour. He rides out to face the Red Knight in combat.

While he prepares to do battle, the Red Knight places the golden cup on a 'block of dark stone'.

Perceval kills the Red Knight. He strips him of his red armour (Peredur receiving a little help here from his near-neighbour and historical contemporary, Owain son of Urien) and sends the golden cup back to King Arthur.

Chrétien's reference to a 'block of dark stone' passes by in the blink of an eye. Writing a few years later, Wolfram von Eschenbach insisted that the Grail itself was a heavenly Stone. 'She whom the Gral suffered to carry itself', wrote Wolfram, had to be 'of perfect chastity'.

We shall soon see that the Grail in its original form was frequently found resting on a stone slab. For now, the mention of 'perfect chastity' recalls a short and amusing 'lay' – a poem, usually meant to be sung – composed by a French minstrel, Robert Biket, two decades before Chrétien wrote his 'Story of the Grail'.

Biket's *Lai du cor* concerns a magical drinking horn which is introduced to Arthur's court at Carduel or 'Carlion'. The property of this horn is that it will spill its contents over a man whose wife has been unfaithful. Arthur drinks from the horn and – yes – gets covered in the liquor! His queen then admits that she once gave her ring to another man. The other knights drink from the horn and, with one exception, discover that their wives have been disloyal. The knight whose wife has remained true is rewarded, and there endeth the 'Lay of the Horn'.

The drinking horn of *Lai du cor* was a form of test. The

Arthurian landscape is dotted with secret places in which horns are hidden away, often with swords, waiting to test the seeker. Perceval's first test comes when he faces the Red Knight, whose theft of the golden cup compares with Perceval's removal of a ring from a maiden's finger. The youth had burst into a tent (which he mistook for a chapel) and prized a 'thick gold ring' set with a shining emerald from a lone maiden's hand. The woman was frightened out of her wits by Perceval's behaviour and terrified that her jealous lover would punish them both. In the Welsh account, the auburn-haired maiden happily hands over her 'large gold ring', though she suffers for this when her lover returns.

Perceval's unintended insult to the maiden – forcing kisses on her and seizing her ring – corresponds to the insult to Arthur's queen: the Red Knight had snatched up a goblet, poured its wine over the queen's face and breast and then boxed her ears. Perceval challenges the knight, who puts the golden cup down on a 'block of dark stone'.

A separate tradition, pre-dating Chrétien's Grail romance, tells of a drinking horn which spilled its liquor over Arthur. Why did it do this? Because his queen had given her ring to another man.

Like the 'Gral' in *Parzival*, the marvellous vessel would not suffer itself to be held by any but the pure and chaste.

The adventure begins with a ring – forcibly commandeered or freely donated – and a cup or horn or bowl or stone which can distinguish the virtuous from the base, the true from the false. The next step is to find the Grail, wherein lie the secrets of the soul.

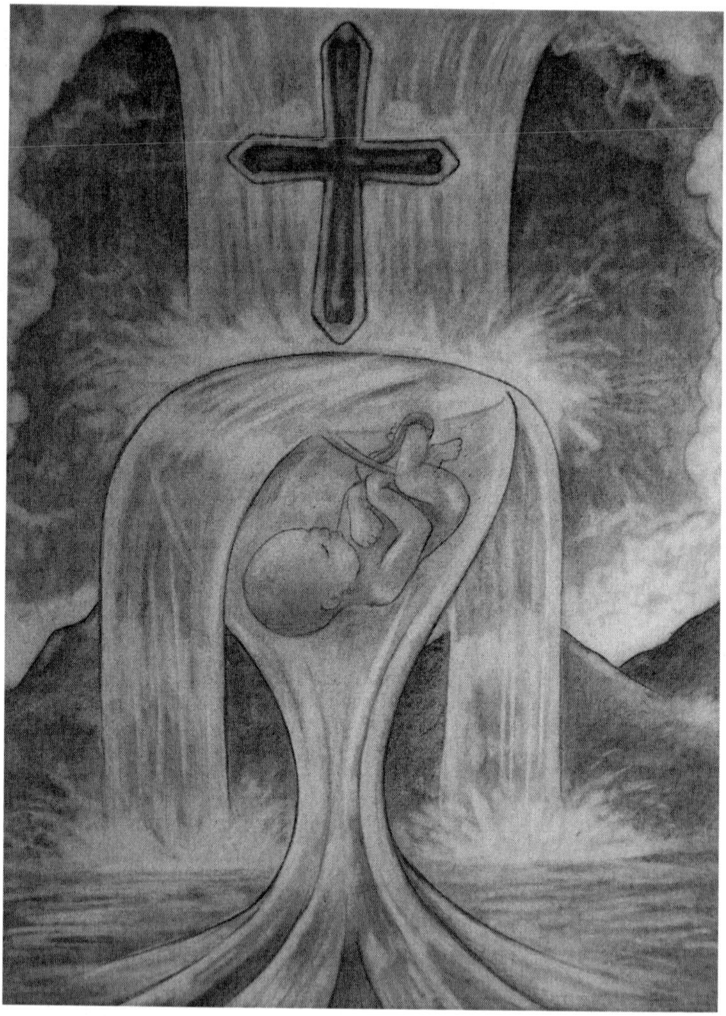

2

False Trails

The picture we frame of the past changes continually and grows every day less similar to the original experience which it purports to describe.
George Santayana

THE HEYDAY of the Grail romance lasted half-a-century. Beginning in the 1180s with Chrétien's *Perceval, le Conte du Graal,* the craze culminated in the 1230s with the anonymous *Estoire del Saint Graal* ('History of the Holy Grail').

That was not the end of the Grail story. Sir Thomas Malory and Alfred, Lord Tennyson would return to the tale in the 15th and 19th centuries, respectively, and today the Grail is as much a source of inspiration and speculation as ever.

But there was something about the late-1100s, early-1200s that was conducive to the spread of Grail romances. Wherever the idea had come from – the native tales of Britain, we should remember, did not mention a 'grail' – it found rich soil in Western Europe around the turn of the 13th century.

The very nature of the Grail, as it was depicted in the literary sources, underwent a significant change during that period. What had started out as a serving dish or *graal* became the *Saint Graal* or *sangréal,* and two myths were formed: one of its time and one for the future (the word 'myth' here is used, not in the traditional meaning of a story of origins, but in the familiar sense of a popular misconception).

This chapter will examine the background to the twin myths of the 'Holy Grail' (*san gréal*) and the 'Blood Royal' (*sang réal*) in order to show that they are both ingenious perversions of the Grail tradition. By placing these myths in the context of history and the changing outlooks which accompany successive phases in the evolution of society, we should reach an understanding of why these myths – compelling as they are – have little or nothing to do with the Grail itself. At the end of the chapter a short supplement or coda explores an extreme example of the attempted abuse of the Grail for political purposes.

Let us remind ourselves of the story so far.

The Grail first hoves into view in the unfinished *Conte du Graal*, composed by Chrétien de Troyes in the late-12th century. It was, so far as we can make out, a richly-ornamented serving vessel, like the *gradale* described by Hélinand of Froidment (early-13th century). A little later, Wolfram von Eschenbach declared that the 'Gral' was in fact a Stone which fell from heaven.

In time, what we might think of as the indigenous British accounts of the Perceval story were written down. The Peredur of York legend had presumably been transmitted orally by generations of Welsh bards before it was transcribed in the mid-to-late 14th century. But there is no reference to a 'grail' in *Peredur fab Efrog*.

When the hero of Wolfram's *Parzival* first beholds the 'perfection of Paradise' – the 'Gral' – it is being carried on *einem grüenen achmardî*, a green silk fabric from Arabia. This seems to have contributed to the notion that the Grail was a green stone or even the emerald which Lucifer placed in his crown and which was later incorporated into a chalice after it had fallen to earth. The only thing that matches this in the earlier account of Chrétien de Troyes is the gold ring 'set with a shining emerald' which Perceval takes from the woman in the tent at the start of his adventure.

Chrétien's *Perceval* breaks off suddenly, mid-sentence. We shall never know where he was going with his 'Story of the Grail'.

Within a few years, however, the *graal* had become decidedly holy.

Joseph d'Arimathie

Robert de Boron, a clerk from eastern France, produced more than one Arthurian romance around the turn of the 13th century. Only a fragment of his *Merlin* survives, but it is his *Joseph d'Arimathie*, otherwise known as the *Roman de l'estoire dou Graal*, which is most pertinent to our study.

In *Joseph d'Arimathie*, Robert claimed that the Grail was the cup used by Christ at the Last Supper. This cup was then given by Pontius Pilate to Joseph of Arimathea, a wealthy man whose relationship to Jesus is unclear. Joseph collected Christ's blood in the cup when Jesus was taken down from the Cross and interred in the rock tomb, which Joseph had prepared.

According to Robert, Joseph was later visited in prison by an apparition of Jesus bearing the Grail. Joseph was instructed to perpetuate the celebration of the Last Supper in memory of Christ's sacrifice (*Eucharist* = 'good-giving'). The sacred cup or 'vessel of the sacrament' would serve as a reminder of the stone tomb in which Christ's body was laid.

Joseph was eventually reunited with his sister and brother-in-law, Bron or Hebron, who became the first 'Fisher King'. They all went into exile, Bron and his offspring finally transporting the Grail to the *vaus d'Avaron* ('vales of Avalon') in the West.

The tradition invented by Robert de Boron in the 1190s – that the 'Holy Grail' was the Cup of the Last Supper – quickly took root. The *Gospel of John* had stated that while Christ was on the Cross, 'one of the soldiers with a spear pierced his side, and forthwith there came out blood and water', and so, like the Greek *krater*, the cup was a vessel in which water and wine (the symbolic 'wine' of Christ's blood) mingled. The spear which pierced Christ's side naturally became the Bleeding Lance of the Grail procession.

The *Estoire del Saint Graal*, written in the 1230s, elaborated on Robert's account, making Josephes – the son of Joseph of Arimathea – the Keeper of the Grail and leader of the exiles who found their way to Britain. The unknown author of the *Estoire* also remarked that Joseph was buried in Scotland (*escoce*), at an Abbey of the Holy Cross (*labeie de la seinte croiz*). The body of Joseph's son was also taken to Scotland, where it helped to end a terrible famine and was laid to rest in an *abeie de glay* ('Abbey of Glay'). Later interpreters removed all references to Scotland and stated that Joseph of Arimathea was buried at the English abbey of Glastonbury.

Glastonbury Abbey had been destroyed by fire in 1184. Money was urgently needed to pay for the construction of a new and more durable church. The monks began to excavate in 1191 and straightaway uncovered what they insisted was the grave of King Arthur and his 'second wife'. The leaden cross found in the grave, though, was inscribed in Medieval Latin: it could not have come from the time of Arthur. All mention of 'Guenevere his second wife' was swiftly dropped.

Every effort was made to publicise the dubious find. Giraldus Cambrensis ('Gerald of Wales') wrote an account of the excavation in 1193, falsely stating that Glastonbury 'was, in antiquity, called the Isle of Avalon'. At the same time, Robert de Boron was spinning his yarn about the descendants of Bron carrying the Grail westwards to the 'vales of Avalon'.

With a little tinkering, subsequent writers were able to pinpoint the resting place of Joseph of Arimathea, King Arthur and the 'Holy Grail' itself as Glastonbury – an abbey which, even if it had existed before the 10th century, had never previously been associated with the Grail and had only a spurious connection to Arthur.

The crusades

The idea that Glastonbury might have been the site of Arthur's burial was mooted by Henry II, husband to the redoubtable Eleanor of Aquitaine. The actual dig was instigated under Henry's son, Richard the Lionheart, who was both Count of

Poitou and King of England. In addition to raising funds for the reconstruction of Glastonbury Abbey, the timely discovery of King Arthur's grave helped to pay for King Richard's involvement in the Third Crusade.

The First Crusade had been launched in 1096. It resulted in the capture of Jerusalem and the massacre of its Muslim inhabitants in July 1099. The crusaders then established the Kingdom of Jerusalem, choosing as its first secular leader the French knight Godefroy de Bouillon, whose younger brother, Baudouin de Boulogne, had already founded the County of Edessa as a Crusader state. Baudouin succeeded Godefroy as the first King of Jerusalem in 1100.

The Mesopotamian city of Edessa fell to the Muslim Turks on 24 December 1144. The following year, Pope Eugenius III issued a bull calling on Louis VII of France (the first husband of Eleanor of Aquitaine) to launch a military expedition. Bernard of Clairvaux was commissioned to preach this Second Crusade.

St Bernard had been admitted to the Cistercian order, based at the French abbey of Cîteaux, in 1113 (the reforming Cistercians reinstated the Strict Rule of St Benedict, which had grown lax in the monasteries of their Benedictine rivals). At the Council of Troyes in 1128, Bernard drew up the Rule of the Poor Fellow-Soldiers of Christ and the Temple of Solomon – better known as the Knights Templar – whose enthusiastic patron he became. Wolfram von Eschenbach would later imply that the Templars were the 'chivalric Brotherhood' of the Grail.

The Second Crusade was a disaster. It culminated in a failed assault on Damascus and the breakdown of King Louis's marriage to Queen Eleanor, who went on to marry Henry II of England. St Bernard was particularly humiliated by the outcome of the crusade which he had so fervently preached – 'Cursed be he who does not stain his sword with blood!' – and for which he was held responsible. He tried desperately to distance himself from the Second Crusade, blaming its failure on the sins of the crusaders, and died in 1153.

Jerusalem fell to the Muslim Turks in 1187. The English king, Henry II, patched up his differences with King Philip of France in order to launch a new crusade. On the death of King Henry in 1189 command of the English contingent, along with the crown, passed to his son by Eleanor of Aquitaine, Richard *Coeur de Lion*, whose crusading activities were part-funded by pilgrims visiting the supposed grave of King Arthur at Glastonbury.

The Third Crusade failed to recapture Jerusalem. Richard struck a deal with Saladin in September 1192 which left the Holy City in Muslim hands.

A decade later, the Fourth Crusade set out to retake Jerusalem but got sidetracked, resulting in a hugely destructive attack on Constantinople. The Fifth Crusade (1213-1221) also failed to recover Jerusalem. The excommunicated Holy Roman Emperor, Frederick II, succeeded in negotiating the surrender of Jerusalem in 1229, but the truce expired after ten years. The city was besieged and completely ruined by the Turks in 1244.

It is no coincidence that the Grail romances flourished between the 1180s and the 1230s: a period during which repeated attempts were made to reclaim Jerusalem for Western Christendom; nor that the Cistercians, who had advocated the use of military force in the Holy Land, should have converted Chrétien's innocuous-sounding *graal* into the mystical *Saint Graal*, the cup of the blood of Christ from the city of his Crucifixion – the selfsame city which the crusaders, egged on by Cistercian monks, had so signally failed to recapture.

THE WHITE MONKS

The development of the Grail romances between *c* 1190 and *c* 1240 should be seen as a public relations exercise. The Cistercians, and especially their foremost orator, St Bernard of Clairvaux, had preached a holy war, the outcome of which had been profoundly disappointing. In an attempt to push the case for more crusades the White Monks took the Arthurian legend of the *graal* from Chrétien of Troyes – the city in northern France where St Bernard devised the Rule of the Templar Knights – and transformed it into the quest for God's grace.

St Bernard had attributed the fiasco of the Second Crusade to the crusaders' moral shortcomings. Consequently, the Cistercians began to weave tales about the Grail's fabulous provenance and the need for spiritual purity if Jerusalem was to be reclaimed.

The references in the *Estoire del Saint Graal* of the 1230s to the burials of Joseph of Arimathea and his son in Scotland point to a Cistercian influence at work. Hugues de Payens, the original Grand Master of the Knights Templar, had visited Scotland at around the time of the Council of Troyes in 1128. King David I of Scotland granted him the Barony of Balantradoch (now the village of Temple in Midlothian) where a Templar Preceptory of St Bernard of Clairvaux was established. Newbattle Abbey was founded nearby in 1140 by Cistercian monks from Melrose Abbey. The latter, founded in 1136, was but two steps removed from St Bernard's own abbey at Clairvaux and was possibly the inspiration for the 'Abbey of the Holy Cross' and the 'Abbey of Glay' mentioned in the *Estoire del Saint Graal*. Built in the form of a Maltese or St John's Cross, Melrose Abbey was the beneficiary of several bequests witnessed in the late 1100s by a *perambulator* or surveyor named Glay or Glai.

Scotland was also the setting for one of the lesser-known derivatives of Chrétien's *Perceval*. Written early in the 1200s by one Guillaume le Clerc ('William the Clerk'), the *Roman de Fergus* opens with King Arthur and his knights setting out in pursuit of a white stag. Perceval captures the stag in Galloway, south-west Scotland, where the impressionable Fergus is inspired by the sight of Arthur's retinue to seek knighthood. Mocked (like Perceval before him) by Kay, Fergus is charged with acquiring a marvellous horn from Arthur's bitter enemy, the Black Knight, for which purpose Fergus is given a sword by Perceval.

The adventures of Fergus take him across Scotland. He falls in love with the Queen of Lothian and vanquishes the Black Knight; he also travels to Dunottar Castle on the Aberdeenshire coast, where he takes a Shining Shield from a fearsome hag whose husband later attacks him at Melrose. The shield, painted with a red cross in the blood of Joseph of Arimathea's son, soon found its way into the anonymous *Queste del Saint Graal*, written in French shortly after 1215.

The Cistercian presence in medieval Scotland can only partly account for the Scottish locations of the *Fergus* romance, which were recreated in such detail that the 20th century historian Nikolai Tolstoy could use them to trace the hideaway where Merlin dwelt in his madness. Like other references to Scotland in the early Arthurian tales, however, these were obscured when English authors began to assert that Glastonbury, many miles to the south, was the Grail's resting place.

The Cistercians had converted the *graal* into the Cup of Christ. A subsequent campaign, focussed on the Benedictine abbey at Glastonbury, drew attention away from the Cistercian centres in Scotland and the militant message which the White Monks had grafted onto the 'Holy Grail'. The elusive Grail became the exclusive property of Glastonbury's booming pilgrimage industry and a source of income for the Black Monks of the English abbey.

The Albigensian crusade

Just four months before the Turks razed Jerusalem in July 1244, another crusade came to a bloody end.

The Languedoc region of France was effectively an independent state nestling between Provence and the Pyrenees. Compared with much of medieval Europe, the area was culturally rich, literate and sophisticated. The cult of *amour courtois* – 'courtly love' – had blossomed in this tolerant clime.

The established Church was not highly regarded there. Instead, the spiritual life of the Languedoc was dominated by a number of sects which came to be known as *Cathari* (from the Greek *katharos,* meaning 'pure'). After the Cathars were condemned as heretics during a Church Council held near the city of Albi they were also known as *Albigenses.*

The Cathars believed that there were two gods, roughly equal in power. Their 'God of Love' was pure spirit. This good god would never have dirtied himself with matter, and so the creation of the material world was deemed to have been the work of a diabolical deity. The Cathars referred to this other god as *Rex Mundi,* the 'King of the World'.

Man's objective in this life was to renounce material things and the lust for power which attends them. The Cathars rejected the 'King of the World' in the hope of achieving the unadulterated spirituality of the 'God of Love'. This alone set them in opposition to the increasingly materialistic Church of Rome.

The Cathars also argued that the discarnate 'God of Love' could not have manifested himself in the physical body of Jesus. The physical realm belonged to *Rex Mundi.* It followed that if Jesus was not a being of pure spirit (in which case he could not have suffered physical death on the Cross), then he must have been a mortal prophet (in which case he could not have been resurrected). In this, they concurred with the Muslims, who denied the Crucifixion whilst recognising Christ as a prophet.

St Bernard of Clairvaux had set out to denounce the Cathars in 1145, only to discover that their piety put the mainstream Church to shame. 'No sermons are more Christian than theirs', he declared, 'and their morals are pure.' But as Cathar thinking began to spread into Germany, Flanders and Champagne, the Church decided to act.

Pope Innocent III ordered a crusade against the Albigensians in 1208. A huge army was assembled under the command of the Abbot of Cîteaux, the home of the Cistercian order. Thousands of men, women and children were slaughtered – at least 15,000 in the town of Béziers alone. When the leader of the papal forces was asked how his troops were to tell the heretics from the true believers, the answer came: 'Slay them all. God will know which are His.'

The last redoubt of the Cathars was their mountaintop stronghold of Montségur. This was besieged by a 10,000-strong army in 1243. The inhabitants, numbering just a few hundred, held out for ten months.

On 1 March 1244, the surviving Cathars and their attendants negotiated a two-week truce. When the truce expired, some 200 *bonhommes* or *parfaits* were dragged down the mountainside and burned alive on a massive pyre.

That night, according to legend, four Cathar *parfaits* escaped from Montségur, taking with them a great treasure. Quite what this treasure was is unknown – most of the Cathar treasury had already been smuggled away. Tradition avers that the precious item which was spirited away from Montségur at the last minute had been used in the Manisola ceremony in which the Cathars took their holiest vow, the *Consolamentum* or devotion to chastity.

The object, it was alleged, was the Grail in the form of an emerald stone.

The hidden stream

The remark about Catholic soldiers being empowered to massacre everybody – '*Caedite eos. Novit enim Dominus qui sunt eius.*' – was recorded by Caesarius, a Cistercian monk from Heisterbach in Germany. Caesarius also wrote down an anecdote concerning Gervard, the abbot of his Heisterbach monastery.

Abbot Gervard was preaching one day when he noticed that his monks were dozing. Gervard suddenly exclaimed: 'Listen! I have something new and wonderful to tell you.

'There was once a king whose name was Arthur ...'

The monks all sat up, rapt with attention.

This cute story, written down by Caesarius of Heisterbach in about 1220, reveals that the Cistercians had a problem. Their order had been founded at the time of the First Crusade with the intent of revitalising the strictest principles of monastic life. But the White Monks were being outperformed in their pursuit of spiritual discipline and purity by such movements as the Cathars.

As Abbot Gervard of Heisterbach had demonstrated, the legends of Arthur held an appeal – even to his own monks – greater than that of the Scriptures. There was more to this than mere romanticism. The legends hinted at an alternative spiritual tradition, distinct from, and in many ways inimical to, the mainstream Church. This tradition had become associated with something called a 'Grail' (*graal, gréal, Gral*), variously described as a cup, a bowl or a stone, and the challenges it represented.

There were (and still are) suspicions that Chrétien de Troyes incorporated elements of this alternative tradition into his Arthurian romances. Even more so, Wolfram von Eschenbach implied that the 'Gral' was part of this esoteric underground heritage. Not only had Wolfram suggested that the guardians of the Grail were the Templar Knights – who, like the Cathars, would eventually stand accused of blasphemy, heresy and 'unnatural sexual practices' – but he indicated that the Cathars themselves were privy to the Grail's secrets.

Wolfram stated that the Grail Castle was known as Munsalväsche, otherwise Montsalvat, which researchers have identified with Montségur, the 'safe mountain' of the Cathars in southern France. Wolfram named the lord of the Grail Castle 'Perilla'. The Cathar fortress which was besieged by the papal army in 1243 had been rebuilt forty years earlier by the lord of Montségur, Raymond de Péreille – the Catalan form of his name was Ramon de Perella.

While the crusading armies of Christendom were failing to recover Jerusalem and, simultaneously, wiping out the

Albigensian 'Pure Ones' – who, as St Bernard had acknowledged, were in some ways more Christian than the Church – the Cistercians were rewriting the Grail romances in order to reclaim the tradition for orthodox Christianity.

Chrétien and Wolfram had envisioned a serving dish or a heavenly Stone, the latter having fallen from Lucifer's brow: Lucifer being another name for the Cathars' debased 'King of the World'.

Lucifer, the 'Light-Bringer', was also the green planet, Venus. The Emerald Stone of Grail lore was perhaps an aspect of Venus, the brightest object in the night sky (after the Moon). If the Cathars had honoured 'Heavenly Venus', the 'Purifier' and mother-goddess – *Venus Genetrix* – of Rome, this might account for the sexual equality they practised. Their religion of 'purity' steered them towards worship of the feminine, much to the chagrin of the male-dominated and misogynistic Church.

The Cistercians wrested the Grail, or at least the *idea* of the Grail, away from the 'heretics' and turned it into the cup in which Christ's blood had been collected *at the Crucifixion* (which the Cathars did not believe in) – a cup, moreover, that could only be apprehended by the most perfect holy warrior or crusader.

When Montségur fell and Jerusalem was lost, both in 1244, the Grail romances dried up. The 'Holy Grail' had served its purpose.

The one positive contribution made by the Cistercians – the association of the Grail mysteries with Scotland – was forgotten when opportunistic commentators tugged the Grail's centre of gravity south towards Glastonbury.

THE ROYAL BLOOD

Not far from the Cathar stronghold of Montségur stands the tiny hilltop village of Rennes-le-Château. Something peculiar happened there late in the 19th century.

A new priest took up his post at the Church of Saint Mary Magdalene in 1885. Bérenger Saunière initially led the quiet life of a country curé. Then, in 1891, he began the restoration of the age-old church. Before long, the humble priest was in Paris, where he was fêted by the cultural elite of his day. He also started spending money at a staggering rate.

His restoration of the church at Rennes-le-Château took a bizarre turn. A demonic statue was placed inside the entrance and an unusual set of panels depicting the Stations of the Cross was commissioned: one of these (Station 8 – Jesus meeting the women of Jerusalem) included the image of a child wrapped in a Scottish tartan plaid.

Saunière never revealed the source of his newfound wealth. He entertained notable guests, including the French Secretary of State for Culture, and died suddenly of a stroke on 17 January 1917, having ordered himself a coffin five days earlier.

Rennes-le-Château and its mysterious priest have received a great deal of attention since then, mostly from New Age enthusiasts. Things came to a head with the publication in 1982 of *The Holy Blood and the Holy Grail*. Throughout the 1970s Henry Lincoln, a BBC researcher, had made a series of television documentaries about the 'accursed treasure' of Rennes-le-Château. Joining forces with the novelist Richard Leigh and the photo-journalist Michael Baigent, Lincoln began work on what was to become a controversial bestseller.

Lincoln's interest in Rennes-le-Château led him to a shadowy organisation called the *Prieuré de Sion* ('Priory of Sion'). Beginning in 1956, a raft of books, articles and pamphlets had been appearing across France. These documents alluded to curious links between Saunière and Rennes-le-Château, the Cathars and the Albigensian crusade, the Knights Templar, the Order of the Rose-Croix and the ancient Merovingian dynasty of Frankish kings whose rule had come to an end with the assassination of Dagobert II in 679.

The researchers met the enigmatic Pierre Plantard and became convinced that the *Prieuré de Sion*, which M. Plantard fronted, had existed since around the time that the Order of the Knights Templar was established; that the Priory of Sion was the driving force behind the Templars and the Cistercians, and that such historical luminaries as Leonardo da Vinci, Sir Isaac Newton, Victor Hugo and Claude Debussy had served as Grand Masters of the influential Priory.

Baigent, Leigh and Lincoln arrived at an astonishing conclusion. Not only had the Merovingian line survived (Pierre Plantard claimed to be descended from King Dagobert II) but the Merovingian priest-kings were themselves the lineal descendants of none other than Jesus and his well-born wife, Mary of Magdala.

The 'Holy Grail' or *San gréal* – treasured by the Cathars, guarded by the Templars – was not a sacred chalice. It was, rather, the 'Blood Royal' or *Sang réal*, the living bloodline of the Messiah and the Magdalene.

This theory received a tremendous boost when it formed the basis of Dan Brown's all-conquering thriller, *The Da Vinci Code* (2003). Brown's novel opens with the murder of Jacques Saunière, curator of the Louvre Museum and Grand Master of the Priory of Sion, and ends up pretty much where it started, with its hero, Harvard Professor Robert Langdon, realising that the bones of Mary Magdalene are preserved inside the Louvre. The frenetic chase leads Langdon and his accomplice, Sophie Neveu, who happens to be Jacques Saunière's granddaughter, to the Temple Church in London and the grave of Sir Isaac Newton in Westminster Abbey, before they head off to Rosslyn Chapel, near Edinburgh, for the novel's climax.

The Eternal Feminine

The Grail-as-Bloodline theory was very much of its time.

The ground had been prepared: Robert A. Johnson, in his Jungian analysis of the Perceval legend (see Chapter 1), described the Grail as 'the highest feminine symbol, the holy of holies in its feminine expression.' In their study of 'Menstruation and Everywoman', *The Wise Wound,* published in 1978, Penelope Shuttle and Peter Redgrove held the Grail to have been 'the buried feminine secret' – the cup of magical blood which is also 'the uterus of the mother goddess'.

The word 'pelvis' does in fact come from the Latin word for a shallow bowl. Part of the pelvis is called the *os sacrum* or 'holy bone', and so there is some similarity between the pelvis and the *krater* or *graal,* especially when it comes to the mixing of substances (blood and water, 'spirit' or semen) in the pelvic 'basin'.

The notion that the Grail is or was the female reproductive organ – the cup-shaped uterus with its two Fallopian handles – is well-suited to the Age of Aquarius, the astrological Water-Carrier. It is but a short, if rather literal, step from the 'uterus of the mother goddess' to the womb of Mary Magdalene. Thus, in *The Da Vinci Code,* the Grail is 'literally the ancient symbol for womanhood'. The Holy Grail is 'symbolic of the lost goddess'. Both, it would seem, are metaphors for Goethe's 'Eternal Feminine' and the fruitful womb of the Bride of Christ.

This idea was vigorously expounded by Laurence Gardner in his *Bloodline of the Holy Grail,* subtitled 'The Hidden Lineage of Jesus Revealed' (1996). Drawing on ancient texts (the Dead Sea Scrolls, the Nag Hammadi codices, the New Testament apocrypha) Gardner reappraised the circumstances surrounding the birth, life and mission of Jesus, covering such now familiar topics as the likelihood that Jesus would have married and the inevitable suppression of this information in the orthodox accounts.

Like the Cathars before him, Gardner challenged the veracity of the Crucifixion, pointing out the discrepancies and contradictions in the biblical testimonies, and argued that Jesus survived while Mary Magdalene fled to Provence, giving birth to their second child in Marseilles in AD 44. Thereafter, Gardner traced the bloodline of Christ and the Magdalene, bringing in the usual suspects – the Merovingian kings, the Albigenses, the Templars, Rosicrucians, Freemasons and the 'Prieuré Notre Dame de Sion' – up to and including the Stuart kings of Scotland.

The Holy Grail, of course, represents the secret history of Christ's mortal descendants, the very thing which is most disturbing – and threatening – to the established Church. One noteworthy member of this royal bloodline was King Arthur.

To his credit, Laurence Gardner correctly identified the historical Arthur. In order to meet the criteria demanded by his theory, however, he made Arthur a Christian – indeed, a Roman Catholic who betrayed his own Celtic Church. The reasons why Arthur was almost certainly not a Christian (and why so many scholars refuse to recognise the original Arthur) are a matter for a later chapter. Suffice it to say that the inclusion of Arthur in Gardner's bloodline of Jesus and Mary required him to become a Christian – embarrassing if he wasn't! – and a custodian of the Grail insofar as the 'Blood Royal' flowed in his veins.

Engaging as it is, the *Sang réal* (Holy Blood) and the *San gréal* (Holy Grail) theory is a conspiracy theory. And like so many conspiracy theories it suffers from a fatal flaw.

The flaw in this instance is the *Prieuré de Sion*. Dan Brown claimed in *The Da Vinci Code* that the 'Priory of Sion – a European secret society founded in 1099 – is a real organisation.'

But it isn't. The Priory of Sion was an elaborate hoax.

The Great Monarch

Pierre Plantard was born in Paris in 1920, the son of a butler and a concierge. By the age of 21 he had formed two ultranationalist associations; both were profoundly anti-Semitic.

Fearing a 'terrible Masonic and Jewish conspiracy', Plantard offered to collaborate with Maréchal Pétain's Nazi-backed Vichy government. He later became an active supporter of General Charles de Gaulle, founder of the French Fifth Republic, and established a Committee of Public Safety in Paris during the Algerian Crisis of May 1958.

Plantard and his confederate, André Bonhomme, legally registered the *Prieuré de Sion* as a new association in June 1956 (the association had dissolved by December of that year). From then onwards, Plantard deposited documents in the Bibliothèque Nationale in Paris and concocted false genealogies in support of his claim to be descended from the last Merovingian king, Dagobert II. By the time the authors of *The Holy Blood and the Holy Grail* met him, Plantard was calling himself 'Comte de Saint-Clair' and 'Comte de Rhédae'.

In 1993, a French judge investigating a high-level scandal heard that the multi-millionaire Roger-Patrice Pelat might have been a Grand Master of the Priory of Sion. The judge ordered a search of Plantard's home, where forged documents were found, some of them indicating that Pierre Plantard was the true King of France. Plantard eventually admitted under oath that he had fabricated the entire history of the *Prieuré* [*de Notre Dame*] *de Sion*.

The Priory of Sion – a cornerstone of *The Holy Blood and the Holy Grail* and *The Da Vinci Code* – had turned out to be one man's fantasy, part of Pierre Plantard's attempt to present himself as something akin to the 'Great Monarch' prophesied by Nostradamus.

Laurence Gardner's *Bloodline of the Holy Grail* appears to have been motivated by a similar impulse. Gardner's biography describes him as the 'Presidential Attaché to the European Council of Princes' and 'the appointed Jacobite Historiographer Royal'. He certainly cut the Stuart kings of Britain a good deal of slack in his account of their reigns. And, according to Gardner, the Stuart line is alive and well. In November 1782, Charles Edward Stuart – then in exile in Florence – was supposedly approached by four envoys sent by George Washington, who offered him the title 'King of the Americans'.

Gardner identified Michael James Alexander Stewart (real

name, Michel Roger Lafosse) as the leading Jacobite claimant to the Scottish throne – and, naturally, a descendant of Jesus Christ, King Arthur, and others by way of the 'holy' bloodline. Among the many questionable titles vaunted by Lafosse was 'President of the European Council of Princes', to whom Gardner claimed to be an attaché. But Archduke Otto von Habsburg, whom Lafosse alleged was his immediate predecessor in the post, stated that he had never heard of any such 'European Council of Princes'.

Bloodline of the Holy Grail ends with a plea for an 'operative Guardian of the Realm'. Unlike the British monarch, whose rule is constrained by an elected Parliament, Gardner's ideal monarch would defend the Constitution, thereby holding the political class to account. The historical model for this is the 'eternal Precept of the *Sangréal*'. The answer to the question, 'Whom does the Grail serve?' is, in Gardner's eyes, 'The Community of the Realm', a.k.a. 'The People'.

The Grail-as-Bloodline myth grew out of an atavistic desire for a pan-European monarchy, a new 'King of the World'. Whether this Great Monarch is the son of a Parisian butler or a self-styled 'Count of Albany' from Brussels, the political saviour, it would appear, is a king who claims descent from an ancient line of priestly kings.

No matter that the genealogies are made up. There is an agenda here – a reactionary ideology which seeks to misconstrue the Grail for its own purposes.

NEW SCIENCE

The Grail is the cup of the Last Supper.
The Grail held the blood of Jesus.
The Grail was taken to Glastonbury in England by Joseph of Arimathea.
The Grail can only be attained by the most perfect Christian knight.

> The Grail is the womb of the goddess. It is the womb of Mary Magdalene.
>
> It is the bloodline of Christ.

None of these myths has any real substance. They arose in specific circumstances – Cistercians looking to justify their holy wars; Benedictines seeking to fill the coffers of an English abbey; well-meaning efforts to reintegrate the feminine principle after centuries of patriarchal control; misguided attempts to uncover a historical conspiracy; post-war angst; self-aggrandisement and crypto-fascism – and they are all distractions, dead ends.

What we need, if we are to avoid the trap of proclaiming a non-Grail as the thing itself, is a system – a litmus test which will separate the false trails from the promising leads.

Fortunately, a useful template exists. It will help us to understand how the familiar Grail myths came into being and provide us with a guide to what the original exponents of the Grail might have been thinking.

Life was tough for Giambattista Vico; he was underpaid, underappreciated and ahead of his time. Over a thirty-year period, until his death in 1744, he wrote and revised his magnum opus, but it was not until the birth of Romanticism in the late-18th century that his *Scienza Nuovo* began to be taken seriously. Today, the Neapolitan's 'New Science' is considered one of the most influential books ever written.

Vico's ideas can be summed up in the words of L.P. Hartley – 'The past is a foreign country: they do things differently there.' History, that is to say, cannot be properly understood from the perspective of the present.

In his early lecture, *On the Study Methods of Our Time*, Vico glanced back at Francis Bacon's theories on the past. 'Every epoch is dominated by a "spirit", a genius, of its own,' he said. Over the course of history many ideas have come and gone – wildly popular one moment, derided and neglected the next –

and if we want to comprehend our forebears we have to recreate their thoughts, understanding the ideas they espoused and how (and why) they espoused them.

The *New Science* approached human history from two directions: the *philosophical* (literally, 'love of wisdom') and the *philological* ('love of learning', philology essentially being the study of language). The classical Roman scholar Varro had broken history down into three phases – the 'chaotic', the 'mythical' and the 'historical'. Vico followed Varro's lead in devising his own three-part model of history.

In the beginning, men and gods walked together. Vico believed that early mankind was divided into two groups: the Jews, who were of normal stature, and the 'pagans', who were giants ('There were giants in the earth in those days', states the *Book of Genesis*). The term 'giants' will return to haunt us; perhaps it is better to think of them in the figurative sense: they were 'mighty men ... men of renown', as *Genesis* described the gigantic *nephilim*.

These giants were the 'sons of God'. They spoke the 'language of the gods'. But they lusted after the 'daughters of men' and copulated with them freely. Dispersed across the Earth, they occupied mountain lairs and wallowed in their own filth (Vico amusingly attributed their massive proportions to the fecund properties of faeces). Then, when Zeus began to hurl his terrifying thunderbolts at them, the giants calmed down. They curbed their sexual appetites by adopting the institution of marriage and, no longer inclined to bask in their own excrement, they returned to their natural size.

Three ages

Marriage introduced the concept of the family. This in turn gave rise to the territorial imperative – the sense of belonging to and in some way 'owning' a certain patch of land. Some families were more successful (or more ruthless) than others. The high-achievers remembered their divine ancestry and, taking their names from their tribal domains, became the nobility. Those families which had been eclipsed by the emergent aristocracy were enslaved. The nobles then went on to found the first cities.

But even the slave is aware of his own humanity. As society grows more complex – especially in cities – the demand for equal rights becomes overwhelming. In time, the exercise of power shifts from the privileged elite to the populace as a whole. We call this democracy (Greek *demos* – 'the people').

Vico's philosophical model of human history falls into three distinct phases of social development. The Egyptians, he wrote, had recognised these phases 'in their earliest history'. They were: the age of gods, the age of heroes, and the age of men (compare Varro's 'chaotic', 'mythical' and 'historical' eras). All civilisations evolve through these successive stages, which we might call the Divine age, the Heroic age and the Human age.

And here's the rub. All civilisations collapse eventually. Vico argued that the progression through the three social ages (Divine – Heroic – Human) is an endless and recurrent cycle; his word was *ricorso*. Sooner or later, society implodes. We return to the age of the gods and start again.

We will consider why civilisations fall asunder in a moment. First, though, we should explore Vico's *philological* map of history. For at each stage in the development of human society we see and interpret the world differently, expressing our thoughts *in a different way* each time.

When we walk with the gods, all power is in the hands of the gods. Everything – as Thales of Miletus observed – is full of gods. We speak the 'language of the gods'.

This can be illustrated by a primitive prayer of the Chenchu people of south-east India, as quoted by A.C. Bouquet in his *Sacred Books of the World*. After a successful hunt, the Chenchus roasted a choice piece of meat and threw it into the jungle, uttering the words:

Memu, tinturam, niwu tinu.
['Mother, we eat, you eat.']

At a later stage of development, power is wielded by those aristocrats who lay claim to a divine origin or bloodline; the myth of the *Sang réal* is clearly a 'Heroic' paradigm, in that it is a siren call for the return of a divinely-ordained aristocracy. Finally, before we are plunged back into the 'Golden Age' of the gods, power in the Human era is assumed by the electorate ('We the People ...').

To go with the three distinct ages, Giambattista Vico identified 'three kinds of language.'

The 'giants' of the first age lived in terror of the gods. Their ceremonies were 'wordless religious acts'. Early men then developed a 'divine and conceptual' sign language based on simple comparisons and correspondences. Thus, the hieroglyph or sacred symbol was born.

Vico stressed that the earliest wisdom was 'poetic' in nature, which is as much as to say it is *metaphorical*. One thing is like another. The image reflects and in some ways embodies the thing it represents. To the Chenchu hunters, the forest was 'Mother'. Like a parent, it sheltered and nourished them.

It is a very different kind of forest in which the Heroic age poet Dante finds himself at the start of his *Divine Comedy*. This 'gloomy wood' – 'how robust and rough its growth' – is symptomatic of a mid-life crisis, a soul gone astray. The symbol has become an emblem, as in the medieval art of heraldry. It is based, not on perceived similarity, but on an agreed *association of ideas*.

Barbarism of reflection

The Heroic age idealises ('idolises') noble individuals. The qualities associated with these individuals come to symbolise, in emblematic form, the individuals themselves. Linguistically, this is known as *metonymy* (literally, a 'change of name'). A thing, person or idea can be represented by something else which it does not resemble but with which it is thought to share certain attributes. Closely related to metonymy is *synecdoche* ('simultaneous understanding'), a figure of speech which uses a part of something to refer to the whole.

In the Heroic age, the Grail ceases to be a concrete object – a *graal* – and becomes an emblem (a cup of Christ's blood) which is itself a symbol of the quest for spiritual perfection.

The major characteristic of language in the subsequent Human age is *irony*. Whereas the primitive metaphor relied on congruity – the likeness of one thing to another – modern speech is incongruous. The literal meaning (what is said) and the implied meaning (what is meant) are not necessarily the same.

When we say 'It's a jungle out there', we don't mean it literally. And when we talk of the Holy Grail these days, we are not thinking of a serving bowl or the grace of God – we're referring to something that doesn't exist yet. That, or the reference is tongue-in-cheek (as Joe Orton quipped: 'My wife is a nymphomaniac. Consequently, like the Holy Grail, she's ardently sought after by young men.') Either way, we are being ironic.

George Orwell was not the first to appreciate the problem of irony or, as he called it, 'Doublethink' – the ability to hold contradictory beliefs in our heads and simultaneously to accept them as equally correct: a famous example being the US major in Vietnam who said, 'It became necessary to destroy the town to save it'. Excessive, habitual, cynical irony impairs language and suffocates meaning. This – as Giambattista Vico foresaw – leads to 'barbarism of reflection' (*barbarie della reflessione*), and pretty soon we are back in the 'primitive' age.

It may be that a return to the Divine age is unavoidable. With the human population growing at an unsustainable rate and mean global temperatures predicted to rise by several degrees above pre-industrial levels, we should be preparing for an imminent crash. But technological progress alone will not be our undoing. Our greatest enemy is maladaptive thinking.

First, we are ruled by multiple gods. Our thinking is essentially magical; sympathetic magic, such as the use of Voodoo dolls, works on the same principles of imitation and correspondence as the metaphors of Divine age communication.

In the next age we are ruled by one God in the form of His anointed: the militaristic aristocracy and the monotheistic Church. Everything is assigned a place in the cosmic hierarchy which – being God's great scheme – cannot be disputed.

The Divine age is magical; the Heroic age, religious. With the development of democracy in the Human age, rationalism supersedes religion. Scientific materialism becomes the prevailing wisdom, the voice of authority. (The neuropsychological preconditions for these different ways of thinking will be considered in due course.)

What will ensure the demise of our civilisation is the wrong kind of thinking – wrong, as in 'out-of-time'. This is precisely what has been happening in recent decades. The religious-aristocratic outlook of the Heroic age has been reasserting itself, shouting down science and democracy and abusing the methodologies of both to redefine reality.

The resurgence of religious-aristocratic thinking explains the 'Blood Royal' theory of the Grail, just as the original Heroic age reinvented the Grail as a Christian chalice.

But Arthur and his comrades belonged to another era altogether.

It is only by approaching the quest in the magical, polytheistic spirit of the Divine age that we can hope to find the Grail.

CODA

Like any scientific model, Vico's theory simplifies in order to clarify. The divisions between the three ages of mankind are in reality seldom clear-cut. Magical thinking still occurs, and the dogmatic religious-aristocratic mindset continues to oppose the empirical democrat. This is not a simple matter of right versus left (the terms 'left wing' and 'right wing' arose out of the French Revolution; they relate only to the Human age). The current crisis is brewing because a culture rooted in the past is seeking to subvert the systems of the present.

If history teaches us anything, it's that two ages can barely co-exist. Bundle all three together and you have the makings of a disaster.

What follows is a cautionary tale which will lead us, however disconcertingly, towards the Grail.

Otto Rahn was born in Michelstadt, Germany, in 1904. He was introduced to the Grail romances at an early age. They struck a deep chord – especially the *Parzival* of Wolfram von Eschenbach, which was written near Rahn's birthplace. Studying Philology at Heidelberg in the 1920s, he entitled his doctoral thesis *On the Research of Master Kyot of Wolfram von Eschenbach* and dedicated it to Wolfram, Richard Wagner and the medieval troubadours.

Rahn was also fascinated by the Cathars, whom he believed to have been related to the ancient Druids. The Cathar fortress at Montségur, which the Church had branded the 'Synagogue of Satan', was for Rahn the 'Golgotha of Occitania' – the Calvary of the West. He became convinced that Wolfram von Eschenbach had left clues regarding the location of the Grail Castle, the Munsalväsche of *Parzival* clearly being the Montségur of the Cathars. Rahn spent several months in the early 1930s exploring the Montségur region and its network of caves and published his first book, *Kreuzzug gegen den Gral* ('Crusade against the Grail'), in 1933. This brought him to the attention of Heinrich Himmler.

Himmler was obsessed with Grail lore. The Bavarian chicken-farmer who became Reichsführer of the *Schutzstaffel* thought of his SS troops as a 'knightly order' and determined that their cult centre would be the castle of Wewelsburg in Westphalia. His intention in restoring the Renaissance castle was to turn it into a 'Centre of the World' and a 'Leadership School' for his Reich SS. Study rooms there were given such names as *Gral* ('Grail'), *König*

Artus ('King Arthur'), *Runen* ('Runes') and *Deutscher Orden* ('Teutonic Order'). The triangular castle became a retreat for the highest-ranking SS officers, where they formed a secretive Round Table of their own.

A fixation on the magical mythic past ran like a vein through Nazi ideology. Adolf Hitler had been portrayed in the 1930s as a silver-clad Grail Knight in Lanzinger's *The Standard Bearer*, although this image was quickly withdrawn. It was, quite simply, too revealing of the Third Reich mentality.

Nazism was a historical anomaly. On the one hand, it was a product of the Human age – calling themselves a 'Socialist' Workers' Party (NSDAP) the Nazis promoted science and technology and exploited mass communication with superlative irony. Nazism also harked back to the age of religion (Hitler as Messianic idol) and aristocracy (the nobles rather liked it): its apocalyptic vision, appeals to 'destiny' and reliance on slave labour were typical Heroic age traits.

But what really marked Nazism out as a dastardly hybrid was its infusion of pagan elements direct from the Divine age. An ancient Indo-European symbol, the *swastika* (a Sanskrit word meaning 'lucky charm'), became the ubiquitous insignia of the movement. And, under Himmler, *Die Ahnenerbe* – a 'study society for Intellectual Ancient History' – began searching far and wide for such fabled objects of power as the Ark of the Covenant, the Spear of Destiny (supposedly the lance which pierced Christ's side) and the Holy Grail.

Otto Rahn gave the impression that he had made significant headway in his hunt for the Grail. He joined Himmler's staff, becoming an *Obersturmführer* of the SS in 1936. His researches were now ineluctably tied in with Himmler's occult obsessions. Rahn's second book, *Luzifers Hofgesind* – 'Lucifer's Court' – was published in 1937.

Rahn was a heavy drinker and a homosexual. He was sent to a special training programme at Dachau in 1937 as punishment for a misdemeanour. A stint at Buchenwald followed in 1938. At the end of February 1939 he sought urgently to resign from the SS. Within two weeks, he had apparently committed suicide on an Austrian mountain.

Rumours that Otto Rahn did not freeze to death in March 1939 have persisted ever since. Nigel Graddon – who, in his study of Rahn, described the German Grail-hunter as 'the real Indiana Jones' – noted a newspaper article printed in 2003 which referred to the presence of a German submarine, U33, in the Clyde estuary, near Glasgow, in early 1940. The piece touched on the Holy Grail and the theory that Otto Rahn had been onboard the stricken U-Boat. Rahn had visited Edinburgh in 1937, climbing Arthur's Seat, and it could be that he was following up his investigations into the Knights Templar in Scotland. Hitler's deputy, Rudolf Hess, fled Germany in May 1940, crash landing his fighter plane near Glasgow. There may be more to all this than meets the eye.

After the war, Rudolf Mund, an occultist and former member of the SS, wrote to Rahn's first publisher. Had Rahn, Mund wondered, ever mentioned a connection between the Chiemsee – the largest lake in Bavaria – and the Grail?

This query would mean little were it not for the discovery by two local divers in 2001 of a golden pot, about 200 metres from the shore of Lake Chiemsee. The cauldron – 30 centimetres high, with a diameter of 50 cm – was made of 10.5 kg of 18 carat gold. The Bavarian State Archaeological Collection in Munich described it as 'the Celtic discovery of the century'. A Swiss collector later attempted to sell it to investors from Kazakhstan for several million euros, claiming that 'this piece of world cultural heritage' was nothing less than the Holy Grail.

In fact, it had been made by the same silversmith who crafted the silver 'death's head' rings for the SS. With the help of a goldsmith named Alfred Notz, the 'golden cauldron weighing more than 10 kilograms, with a figurative ornament and manufactured by means of the paddle and anvil technique' had been created in a Munich workshop. This was seemingly confirmed when Nazi documents were found in a German attic in 2011. Dated 'April 1945', the papers had once belonged to Heinrich Himmler. Among the precious items listed was a 'gold cauldron/celtic' with the name of the manufacturer and the word 'Munich'.

The Chiemsee cauldron is, without doubt, an ersatz copy of a much older artefact. As *Der Spiegel* reported in 2007, the Nazis had planned an 'Elite NSDAP School' near the Chiemsee – just 50 kilometres from Hitler's Berghof retreat at Berchtesgaden – where the cauldron would perhaps have been used in consecration ceremonies.

The earlier cauldron upon which the Chiemsee cauldron was so obviously modelled is, as we shall discover, the closest thing in existence to the Grail.

It's chilling to think that Otto Rahn's researches, assiduously followed up after his demise by Himmler's agents, might have revealed the original form of the Grail, thereby enabling the Nazis to fashion their very own version of the sacred vessel for their dark satanic purposes.

For, if the Grail does hold any intrinsic power, surely the last people who should have been entrusted with it were the fanatics of Hitler's infernal regime.

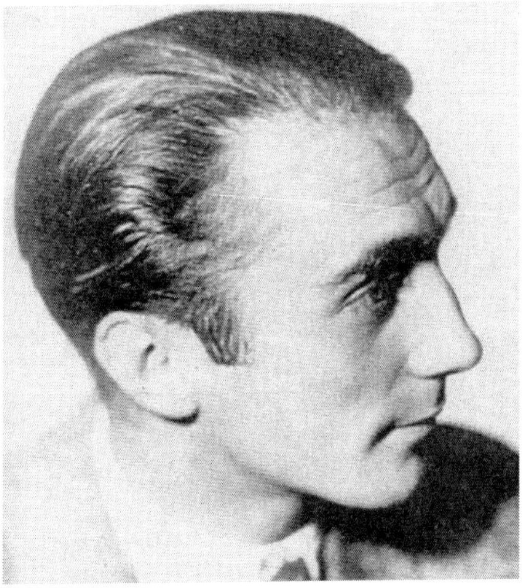

"Otto Wilhelm Rahn (1904-1939), notorious Grail-hunter and the 'real Indiana Jones'."

"The Chiemsee Cauldron."

The Grail

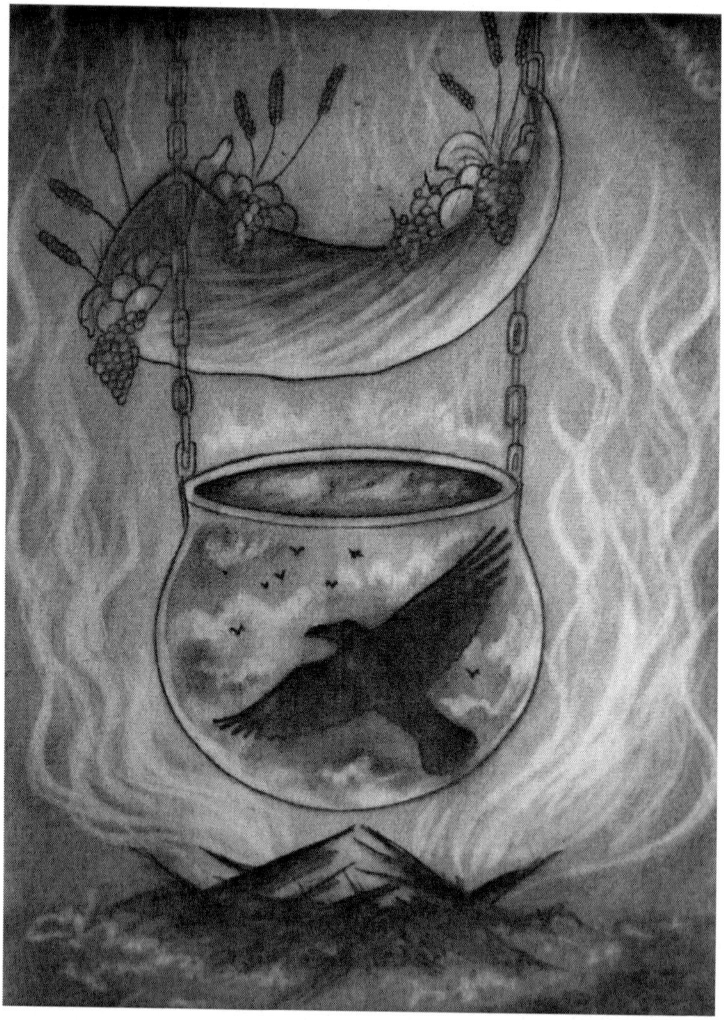

3

The Hallows

> À l'horizon lointain *is paradise,*
> abest silentium, le cor éclate -
> - et meurt, *Columba mused, but Kentigern*
> *replied,* renaît et se prolonge.
> Edwin Morgan

LANGUAGE HAD evolved as a form of social communication by about 250,000 years ago. Our closest living relatives – the apes – maintain their relationships by grooming. But this takes time. Sooner or later, groups become so large that it is no longer practical or cost-effective in time terms to cultivate allies and placate antagonists by patiently picking ticks out of their fur. Verbal communication solves this problem: it's quicker, and you can 'groom' more of your fellows at once.

The use of language in non-social contexts (e.g. tool-making, or describing the environment) probably came later. Starting about 60,000 years ago, a huge change came in the way early humans thought about the world. The first signs of art and religion began to appear. The change seems to have occurred when different areas of intelligence became joined-up. It was now possible to think of non-human things, such as animals, in human terms ('anthropomorphism') and vice versa ('totemism'), or of technical things, e.g. tools, as having a social function ('art').

Early art – such as the cave paintings of Lascaux and Altamira, which date back to the Late Stone Age – was effectively an extension of language. That is, it was a form of communication which married the social intelligence required for language to the study of natural history (observing animals) and the exercise of technical skills (reproducing them in visual form). The cave paintings of the Upper Palaeolithic share the same metaphorical basis as the 'primitive' language of the Divine age: the images resemble what they represent.

The next great leap came about 5,000 years ago with invention of writing. Again, the driving force seems to have been increasing social complexity.

Writing emerged from the first cities in Mesopotamia, between the Tigris and Euphrates rivers, and especially from Sumer (modern Iraq). The earliest examples were essentially bureaucratic: tallies and accounts necessary for the administration of burgeoning communities. But with the development of cuneiform (wedge-shaped impressions made in clay) more complex records became possible. The Sumerian *Gilgamesh* epic, one of the world's oldest literary works, survives on clay tablets dating from the 2nd millennium BC.

Major developments in writing and the transmission of the written word can help us to differentiate between the successive phases of social evolution which we have termed the Divine ('magical'), Heroic ('religious-aristocratic') and Human ('democratic') ages.

It is often claimed that those Divine age intellectuals known as the Druids wrote little if anything down. To counter this argument we have the testimony of Julius Caesar (100-44 BC). Caesar studied the Druids in Gaul and observed that 'in their public and private transactions, they use Greek characters.' The Druids had mastered the Greek alphabet, although they declined to commit their secrets to writing so as not to 'relax their diligence in learning thoroughly, and their employment of the memory' (*De Bello Gallico* 6:14).

The Heroic age was never so coy. The era of religion and aristocracy is predominantly the age of the Word.

Whereas the Druids preferred to keep their knowledge secret, the Church grew by distributing copies of its sacred texts. The book or scroll (Greek *biblion*, whence 'Bible') became the repository of all wisdom, fiercely guarded by the priesthood.

For upwards of 1,000 years the Church maintained its stranglehold on learning by monopolising the written word. It was during this period that the first Grail romances appeared. Naturally, the medieval Grail legends were written under the auspices of the Church and were therefore imbued with Christian thought. Whatever the Grail had been beforehand, it was reinvented – principally by the Cistercians – to serve a Christian purpose.

(Re)writing the past

The Church lost its iron grip on the written word when Johannes Gutenberg (*c* 1395-1468) invented his process of moveable type printing. This ushered in the Human age by allowing knowledge and ideas to be published widely, thereby undermining the authority of those hierarchical institutions (the Church, the nobility) which had governed the Heroic age.

Significantly, perhaps, one of the first works published in England using this new printing method was Caxton's 1485 edition of Sir Thomas Malory's *Le Morte d'Arthur*, which duly became the 'authorised' version of the Arthurian legends.

In 1970, Arthur C. Clarke predicted that satellites would 'bring the accumulated knowledge of the world to your fingertips'. Two decades later, this prediction came true with Tim Berners-Lee's invention of the World Wide Web.

Now, nothing is secret. The written word has become thoroughly democratised. Knowledge is available to all.

It is also unregulated, of course. The internet offers proof of Nietzsche's dictum, 'There are no truths, only interpretations'. We should also be aware of the religious-aristocratic backlash which impairs the search for knowledge. Just as the scientific discoveries of the Human age – Darwin's theory of evolution, for instance – have been denounced by believers in the absolute authority of the Bible, so the study of history is suffering from the revisionist tendencies of conservative thinkers.

History begins with the written record. But for most of our history, the written word was rigorously censored. All forms of learning which were not approved by the Church were ruthlessly suppressed – as we saw with the example of the Cathars. Those who seek to reinforce a religious-aristocratic view of the past start with a considerable advantage: their Heroic age predecessors controlled the written accounts.

The Heroic age mindset strives to restrict the admissible evidence to whatever supports its case and angrily dismisses all other sources. It does so in the pretence that it is obeying scientific principles (only selected archive materials are valid resources) but it is deluding itself. Its unspoken aim is to restore the religious-aristocratic outlook of the past, and this can only be achieved through the methods of the Heroic age: dogmatism, belligerence and censorship.

Nowhere is this more apparent than in the study of Arthur and the Grail.

How, then, are we to battle our way through the fog of obfuscation which was conjured up by the medieval Church – and has been reconstituted by the latter-day champions of religious-aristocratic thinking – in order to recover the original form of the Grail?

First, we need to remember how people thought, and how they expressed their thoughts, in the spirit-haunted universe of the Divine age.

This means that we must approach the existing written sources with the awareness that traces of magical Divine age thinking might still be detectable, even though they were glossed over by Heroic age hands. The process requires us to sift the nuggets of authentic tradition from the silt of later matter, rather as if we were panning for gold.

We should also be on the lookout for information which is not to be found in the early literature.

To the Divine age mind, the landscape itself is a record of the past: we might think of the Australian aborigine revisiting the events of the Dreamtime in his 'songlines'. Place-names tell their own stories. Legends often preserve a link with remote antiquity. One could even argue that folklore is a Divine age record held in the local memory – which is why so many historians of a Heroic age bent really don't like it.

There is a third source of information, distinct from the living language of the landscape and the glimmerings of genuine tradition in later literature. This additional resource is art: specifically, art which has survived because it was rendered in stone.

The land of the Grail

But it is one thing to know what to look out for. It is another thing altogether to know where to look.

A quick survey of the sources we have considered thus far reveals a recurring theme – one which is routinely smothered by those scholars whose thinking is blinkered by imperialistic Heroic age obsessions. That persistent theme is the connection between Arthur and his heroes, and the Grail and its mysteries, and Scotland.

In *Perceval, le Conte du Graal* (*c* 1180), Chrétien de Troyes described the sword which was presented to Perceval the Welshman by the Fisher King. This sword 'could not be broken except in one singularly perilous circumstance known only to him who had forged and tempered it' (a similar sword is broken three times, and twice repaired, by Peredur of York in the British version of the tale).

Perceval is then told that the sword could only be 'rehammered, retempered, and repaired' at the 'lake beyond Cotouatre'. The notes to the Penguin edition of Chrétien's *Arthurian Romances* state that:

> Cotouatre apparently derives from *Scottewatre*, i.e., the Firth of Forth.

This 'Scottish water' once marked the northernmost border of Britain.

The Cistercian author of *L'Estoire del Saint Graal* claimed in the 1230s that Joseph of Arimathea and his son, Josephus, were both buried in Scotland (*escoce*), possibly at Melrose Abbey in the Scottish Borders, although this was later altered to benefit the Benedictine monks of Glastonbury in England. The Cistercian-influenced *Queste del Saint Graal* (*c* 1230) also remarked that one Celydoine, an ancestor of the Grail knights, Lancelot and Galahad, was 'the first Christian king to hold sway over Scotland.'

These stories also feature a sword – 'the richest and most marvellous sword ever forged' – which is found by Galahad and called the Sword of Strange Hangings. Its hilt 'had two sides, and these two sides were of different beasts.' On one side was depicted 'a manner of serpent which frequents Calidoine [Scotland] more than any other land'; on the other, 'a fish which frequents the River Euphrates and no other water'. A curious link between Scottish serpents and fish from Mesopotamia will be considered later.

The Arthurian *Roman de Fergus*, written by Guillaume le Clerc, is set almost exclusively in Scotland, with especial emphasis on Galloway, Lothian, Aberdeenshire and Melrose. At much the same time – *circa* 1200 – a French poet named Béroul composed his romance of *Tristan*, in which King Arthur and his Round Table of chivalrous knights are located at Stirling, on the River Forth.

Before all of these, in about AD 1120, one Lambert, Canon of St Omer in Brittany, produced his encyclopaedic *Liber Floridus* ('Book of Flowers'). Lambert wrote:

> There is in Britain a palace of the warrior Arthur [*Artuir*

> *militis*], built with marvellous art and variety, in which the history of all his exploits and wars is to be seen in sculpture.

Lambert of St Omer then amended 'in Britain' to 'in the land of the Picts', indicating that Arthur's palace was to be found in the Pictish realms of northern Scotland, beyond the River Forth.

There are also the more recent examples of Otto Rahn, Grail-hunter extraordinaire, who considered himself to be 'in Arthur's bosom' when he climbed the volcanic outcrop of Arthur's Seat in Edinburgh, and Dan Brown who, in *The Da Vinci Code*, led his protagonists on an elaborate trail to the chapel at Rosslyn, south of Edinburgh, with the words:

> The Holy Grail 'neath ancient Roslin waits.

We can choose to ignore such clues, as so many self-professed experts have done, in which case we will never find the original Grail.

Or we can follow them – as the proper study of history requires us to do.

THE CAULDRON

We start with Welsh literature.

One of the oldest languages in Europe, Welsh had achieved its modern form by the 6th century AD: the time of Arthur. It was spoken throughout North Britain, including what is now southern Scotland.

As we saw in Chapter 1, the story of Peredur, whose father 'owned the Earldom of the North', was preserved in two medieval manuscripts, the White Book of Rhydderch and the Red Book of Hergest. It was one of several native tales which were translated in the 19th century by Lady Charlotte Guest and published as *The Mabinogion* ('Tales of Youth' or 'Fables of the Early Age').

The Peredur legend sees Owain son of Urien talking with Peredur in the forest and later helping him to remove the armour of the knight who had stolen the golden cup from Gwenhwyfar. Owain ap Urien has his own romance in the *Mabinogion* collection. It is entitled, *Owain, or the Countess of the Fountain*.

The story opens with Arthur relaxing in the company of his loyal servant, Cai. Owain is also there, as is Cynon son of Clydno (Clydno Eidyn ruled in Edinburgh in the mid-500s; his son Cynon was, like Owain and Peredur, a 6th-century prince of North Britain). While Arthur snoozes, Cynon tells Owain and Cai about an adventure that once befell him.

In search of a challenge, Cynon was directed to a mound in a forest. On the middle of the mound was a gigantic black man with one foot, one eye in the middle of his forehead, and an iron club; he was the keeper of the forest and its animals. He sent Cynon to a vale 'like a great waterway' with a tree in its midst. Beneath the tree was a fountain, and beside the spring a marble slab. On the slab was a silver bowl fastened by a silver chain. By throwing water from the bowl onto the slab, Cynon whipped up a fiendish storm and was then attacked by a black knight on a black horse.

Cynon failed to defeat the black knight and has heard no more about the mound, the tree, the fountain or the bowl. He cannot tell 'how the root of this tale is in the dominions of the emperor Arthur without its being hit upon'.

Owain decides to retrace Cynon's steps. He finds the tree with the fountain, casts water from the bowl onto the slab, weathers the storm, does battle with the black knight and pursues him to a 'great shining city'. There, he marries the Lady of the Fountain, whose lord he killed, and then guards the spring 'with spear and sword'. After three years Arthur sets out to find him, accompanied by his servant Cai and his nephew Gwalchmai (the 'Gawain' of the later romances). They too find the bowl, create the storm, and do battle with Owain in his new guise as the black knight.

The silver bowl on the marble slab has its counterpart in another of the *Mabinogion* tales. In *Manawydan son of Llyr*, Pryderi ('Anxiety') is out hunting with his stepfather, Manawydan. They chase a 'wild boar of shining white' into a strange new castle. Manawydan is suspicious, but Pryderi ventures into the fortress, which appears to be empty apart from 'a fountain with marble work around it, and on the edge of the fountain a golden bowl fastened to four chains, and that upon a marble slab.'

Pryderi is struck by the 'great beauty of the gold and with the exceeding good workmanship of the bowl'. He touches it, and his hands stick to the bowl, his feet stick to the slab, and 'all his power of speech forsook him so that he could not utter one word.'

Thirteen treasures

Manawydan tells Pryderi's mother about the boar-hunt. She sets out to find the mysterious castle and, alongside Pryderi, becomes stuck fast to the golden bowl and the marble slab. 'And with that, as soon as it was night, lo, a peal of thunder over them, and a fall of mist, and thereupon the castle [*caer*] vanished, and away with them too.'

The whole thing turns out to have been a trap set by a 'bishop' named Llwyd ap Cil Coed ('Grey/Holy son of the Hermitage of the Wood') as a punishment for Pryderi's mother.

This is not Llwyd's only appearance in *The Mabinogion*. In *Culhwch and Olwen*, probably the oldest of the tales, he is named as 'Arthur's chief huntsman'.

Culhwch is the grandson of Celydon Wledig, the 'Ruler' of southern Scotland. He is also 'first cousin to Arthur'. In order to marry Olwen, the daughter of the 'Chief Giant' Yspaddaden, Culhwch seeks the help of Arthur and a host of extraordinary warriors. Reluctantly, the 'Chief Giant' sets the heroes a series of daunting tasks, one of which is to acquire the cauldron of

Diwrnach the Irishman, the 'steward of Odgar son of Aedd king of Ireland', to boil the meat for the wedding.

Arthur and his men seize the cauldron by force and bring it back 'full of the treasures of Ireland'. They disembark at the house of Llwyd son of Cil Coed – 'And Mesur-y-peir ['Measure-of-the-cauldron'] is there.'

Among the old manuscripts held in the National Library of Wales is one – Peniarth 51 – which lists thirteen remarkable treasures. Other manuscripts of the 15th and 16th centuries provide more information about these 'Thirteen Treasures of the Island of Britain' (*Tri Thlws ar Ddeg Ynys Prydain*), the earliest sources referring to them as the treasures 'which were in the North'.

Most of the treasures do indeed have a northern provenance. The first is a white-hilted sword owned by Rhydderch the Generous, who governed Strathclyde from his chief seat at Dumbarton, near Glasgow, in the late-6th and early-7th centuries. His father, Tudwal, was associated with another of the treasures: a whetstone which would only sharpen the blade of a brave warrior.

Other treasures came from the ruling dynasty of Strathclyde – the Hamper of Gwyddno Garanhir, which could supply food for 100 men (Gwyddno was a cousin of Rhydderch), and the Halter of Clydno Eidyn, which would harness any horse the rider wished for (Clydno was the father of Cynon). The Chariot of Morgan the Wealthy, which could take a person wherever he wanted to be, was likewise associated with the North; Morgan supplanted Clydno Eidyn as the chieftain of Lothian in about 559.

Arthur is named in connection with one of the treasures: a cloak of invisibility known as the Mantle of Arthur in Cernyw (usually translated as 'Cornwall', although this is misleading). Another treasure – the Coat of Padarn Red-Coat – probably had a northern origin, being named after Paternus, a warlord who defending the Stirling region in the last days of the Roman occupation of Britain. There is also the golden 'Chessboard' (*gwyddbwyll*) of Gwenddolau son of Ceidio, who led the Selgovae warriors of the Scottish Borders and was killed at the Battle of Arderydd in *circa* 573, when 'Merlin went mad'.

The Cauldron of Dyrnwch the Giant (*Pair Dyrnwch Gawr*) is another of the Thirteen Treasures: 'if meat for a coward were put in it to boil, it would never boil; but if meat for a brave man were put in it, it would boil quickly'.

There can be little doubt that this cauldron was pretty much the same as the Cauldron of Diwrnach, which Arthur and his men brought back from Ireland to boil the meat for the wedding of Arthur's first cousin.

Primary chief bard

The Cauldron of Diwrnach the Irishman – or Dyrnwch the Giant – was captured and deposited, 'full of the treasures of Ireland', in the care of Arthur's 'chief huntsman', Llwyd son of Cil Coed. In the tale of *Manawydan son of Llyr* it is Llwyd son of Cil Coed who traps Pryderi and his mother by means of a golden bowl on a marble slab, which fixes them to the spot and deprives them of the power of speech. The story of *Owain* tells of a silver bowl, attached to a marble slab, which – like the golden bowl in *Manawydan* – is able to conjure up a storm, after which the challenger does battle with a fearsome knight clad all in black.

In his poem *Preiddeu Annwn* ('Treasures of Annwn'), the 'Primary Chief Bard' Taliesin described the 'cauldron of lofty utterance':

> By the breath of nine maidens it is warmed:
> It is the cauldron of the Lord of Annwn, whosoever desires it;
> A band about the rim, around the edge,
> It will not boil the meat of a coward, it will not avail him.

Taliesin's *Preiddeu Annwn* is often interpreted along the lines of

Arthur's cauldron-raid into Ireland, as recounted in *Culhwch and Olwen*, but it is wrong to do so. The common assumption is that Annwn (pronounced 'an-noon') was some sort of Otherworldly realm, and so *Preiddeu Annwn* is taken to be an account of a voyage led by Arthur into a parallel dimension in search of the cauldron. In fact, Annwn was an actual place. Later poets thought of it as 'Avalon'.

The *Book of Taliesin* (Peniarth MS 2) dates from the first half of the 14th century, although many of its 56 poems belong to an earlier period. Some of the verses were written in praise of Urien, a prince of North Britain, and his son Owain. Other poems praise Gwallog the Battle-Horseman and his father Lleënog, a 6th-century prince associated with Loch Lomond and the Lennox region north of Glasgow (Lleënog and Gwallog were probably the historical models for Lancelot of the Lake and his son, Galahad). There are also ample references to Arthur – not as a legendary hero of yore, but as a man whom Taliesin knew.

The story of Taliesin is inseparable from that of the cauldron. The early part of the Chief Bard's career is related in the 16th-century *Hanes Taliesin*.

The tale starts with a supernatural couple, Tegid the Bald and his wife Ceridwen, who lived at Llyn Tegid (Bala Lake) in North Wales. They had two children: an ugly boy named Morfrân and a beautiful daughter called Creirwy.

To compensate Morfrân for his hideous looks – he was also known as *Afagddu* or 'Black water-beast' – Ceridwen resolved to provide him with the gifts of verse and vision. She prepared the cauldron of inspiration and science, which would boil for a year and a day before three precious drops of its liquor could be extracted. A young lad named Gwion Bach was tasked with stirring the cauldron.

While Ceridwen's back was turned, three hot droplets splashed onto little Gwion's hand. He thrust his fingers into his mouth and instantly received the enlightenment which had been meant for Morfrân. The cauldron gave a shriek and broke apart, spilling its dregs into a stream and poisoning the horses of Gwyddno Garanhir.

As Ceridwen came lumbering after him, Gwion turned himself into a hare. She chased him in the form of a greyhound. He leapt into a river, becoming a fish, but she kept up her pursuit as an otter-bitch. Gwion took to the air as a bird; Ceridwen flew after him in hawk-form.

Finally, Gwion transformed himself into a grain of wheat.

Ceridwen became a hen and swallowed him whole.

INSPIRATION AND REBIRTH

The long freshwater lake of Llyn Tegid in North Wales is reputedly the home of a water-monster affectionately known as 'Teggie'. This was presumably the inspiration for the figure of Tegid the Bald (the name comes from Tacitus, the 'Silent' one) who was said to have his dwelling in the middle of the lake. The 'wife' of this lake-spirit was apparently the mistress of the cauldron. Her name – Ceridwen – meant 'Blessed Song'.

Morfrân ('Sea-Crow') appears elsewhere in Welsh literature. He is named in *Culhwch and Olwen* as one of the handful of survivors of Arthur's last battle ('so exceedingly ugly was he; all thought he was a devil helping'), and a medieval list of the Twenty-Four Horsemen of Arthur's Court identifies Morfrân as one of the three 'Offensive Knights'. He also seems to have been the father of a poet who went mad and became known as the 'crazy man' or *myrddin*; this was later given a Norman-French spin to re-emerge as 'Merlin'.

As for the lovely Creirwy or 'Heron', I have previously argued (in *The King Arthur Conspiracy*) that she was a priestess of the cauldron cult and a British princess of the North who was destined to become the mother of Arthur. Arthur himself was probably initiated at Llyn Tegid: at the southern end of the lake stood an old Roman auxiliary fortress, now known as *Caer Gai* –

'Cai's Fort' – after Arthur's steadfast servant.

The presence of Gwyddno Garanhir, or at least his horses, in the Taliesin story is also telling. Gwyddno – like Creirwy – was a royal youth of Strathclyde. His magical hamper became one of the Treasures of Britain.

The actual initiation required Gwion Bach to imbibe three drops of the cauldron's 'liquor of science and inspiration'. Any more than that might have been fatal. Gwion survived the ordeal, including the violent hallucinations, and gestated for nine months in the belly of the cauldron-goddess. He was then reborn. The initiatrix placed him inside a wicker coracle with a leather canopy and set him adrift.

Gwyddno Garanhir ('Tall-Crane') was residing on the Welsh coast. On the eve of May Day he sent his son, a 'most hapless' and 'needy' boy named Elffin, to fetch one hundred pounds worth of salmon from the weir on the River Dovey. Elffin found the coracle trapped in the weir. He drew back the leather canopy and saw a young man inside. The front of the young man's head had been shaved in the Druidic tonsure and possibly tattooed with salmon-like speckles.

Elffin exclaimed, 'Behold, a radiant brow!'

And so Gwion Bach received his new name: *tal iesin* ('beautiful brow').

With his own personal bard in tow, Elffin's fortunes improved immeasurably. He and Taliesin pitched up at the Deganwy court of Maelgwn, Lord of Gwynedd, who died in *circa* 547. There, Elffin underwent his own initiation. Taliesin outsmarted Maelgwn's 24 bards and released Elffin from his ritual imprisonment. Elffin son of Gwyddno was rewarded with a 'cauldron full of gold'.

Taliesin became one of the greatest poets of his age. He was recalled, three centuries later, as one of five British bards of renown, alongside Aneirin, who would nod to Taliesin in his elegiac *Y Gododdin* poem (*c* 600):

Of mead from the horn,
Of the men of Catraeth,
I not I, Aneirin,
As Taliesin
Of skilful song knows,
Sang 'The Gododdin'
Before the daybreak dawned brightly.

Aneirin's poem told of a catastrophic military campaign and ascribed the disaster to the 'yellow, sweet, ensnaring' mead which the warriors of Lothian had drunk and which turned to 'poison' in their bellies. Also mentioned in Aneirin's battle-poem are those princely northern heroes whose names are becoming familiar to us: Owain, Cynon, Elffin, Gwyddno, Peredur ...

And Arthur.

The Lion

From North Wales, Taliesin travelled to North Britain. He saw the Men of the North in action: 'From Glasgow [*penryn wleth*] to Loch Ryan [*lwch reon*],' he observed, 'The Cymry are battle-brave heroes'. And when he wasn't singing their praises, he was singing about the cauldron.

'Let the boiler simmer / the excellent cauldron of five-trees,' he declaimed in *The Seat of Taliesin*, '... and drunk-making mead-horns / to bring to the dragon [or 'leader'] the Druidic gift.'

In *The Seat of the Overlord* he sang in praise of the 'blessed Arthur': 'Exalted when wise from the cauldron / Gogyrwen of three inspirations'.

The meaning of *Gogyrwen* is obscure. In Welsh, a 'cuckoo' is *cog* or *y gog*. The equivalent in Scottish Gaelic is *cuach* – which is also the word for a drinking bowl or goblet, as in the Scots *quaich*, a two-handled cup of friendship. The compound *Gogyrwen* could therefore signify the 'Cup of inspiration': *Y Gog-yr-awen*. The later movement of medieval Welsh poets known as *Y Gogynfeirdd* would then have been 'The Cup of the bards'.

Thus, in his *Song of the Sons of Llyr,* Taliesin sang, 'Superior is the seat of the cauldron of Ceridwen, / From it comes my tongue's desire ever to praise Gogyrwen.' And another poet of the time could recite:

> Strong song, ode of Ceridwen, Gogyrwen of blended seeds,
> Mixed grain of riches, elevated speech, the skilful singer,
> Cuhelyn the Wise, pure Briton, exalted authority,
> Skilfully he sings, Áedán's clerical grandson,
> Cheerful cub of the Lion ...

Cuhelyn's reference to the 'Lion' (*llew*) recalls another story from *The Mabinogion*. The legend of *Math son of Mathonwy* is set in North Wales, where Taliesin underwent his initiation, and features the death of Pryderi in a war fought between the Britons, during which a princess falls pregnant. The child is raised by his uncle, who happens to be a wizard. When the time comes for the boy to be named, his mother is lured onboard a magic ship. She sees the boy take aim at a little wren and strike it 'between the sinew of its leg and the bone.' The princess laughs: 'Faith, with a deft hand has the fair one hit it.' The boy is duly named Lleu Llaw Gyffes ('Fair Skilful Hand'). The name is also rendered as Llew ('Lion').

The magician creates a wife for Llew out of flowers. She conspires with her lover to assassinate Llew. But Llew can only be murdered in the most unusual circumstances: he cannot be slain indoors or outside, on horseback or on foot, and the weapon which wounds him must be a whole year in the making.

The ambush is staged on a riverbank. A bath is set, with a thatched frame over it. Llew bathes and, as he rises, places one foot on the edge of the tub and the other on the back of a goat. He is therefore acutely vulnerable, and the poisoned spear finds its mark.

The word for a 'bath' or 'tub' in Welsh is *pair*. It is the same as the word for a 'cauldron'.

Given Taliesin's intimate knowledge of the cauldron and his connections with Arthur and his heroes, it is no surprise to find that the Primary Chief Bard appears in the *Mabinogion* stories. He is among the plethora of warriors cited in *Culhwch and Olwen*, while his son is named as one of Arthur's advisers in *Breuddwyd Rhonabwy* ('The Dream of Rhonabwy'), which presents a visionary account of Arthur's last battle. Afaon son of Taliesin is described therein as 'the most accomplished and wisest young man in the kingdom' and he is first seen with the 'cross-grained forward youth', Elffin son of Gwyddno – Taliesin's old playmate from Wales.

The blessed Raven

Taliesin is also named as one of the seven survivors of a terrible battle in the legend of *Branwen ferch Llyr*.

The story begins with Brân, the 'crowned king' of the Island of Britain, sitting on a rock overlooking the sea with his brother, Manawydan son of Llyr. They spy thirteen ships bringing Matholwch, king of Ireland, to seek the hand of Brân's sister in marriage.

Brân is the Welsh word for a 'raven' (the name Brân evolved into the 'Bron', 'Brons' and 'Bors' of the Grail tradition). He is called 'Brân the Blessed' – *Bendigeidfrân*. This chimes with the 'blessed Arthur' (*Arthur fendigan*) of Taliesin's *Seat of the Overlord* poem. As Taliesin boasted in his *Song of the Sons of Llyr*: 'I have been with Brân in Ireland.'

Brân's sister is Branwen – 'White-Raven'. The other child of Llyr ('Sea') in the tale is Manawydan who, elsewhere in *The Mabinogion*, is the stepfather of Pryderi.

The Irish counterpart of Manawydan was the Hebridean sea-god, Manannán mac Lir. The name denotes a 'dear one of Manau' and refers to the Manau Gododdin region around

Stirling on the River Forth, where the French poet Béroul located Arthur and his Round Table warriors.

The name of Matholwch, 'king of Ireland', derives from *math* ('sort', 'kind') and *golwch* ('worship' or 'prayer') – a most revealing designation.

Brân agrees to marry his sister to the Irish king. But one of his brothers takes umbrage and mutilates the horses of Matholwch. To make amends, Brân gives the Irish king a cauldron:

> ... and the virtue of the cauldron is this: a man of thine slain today, cast him into the cauldron, and by tomorrow he will be as well as he was at the best, save that he will not have power of speech.

The cauldron came originally from Ireland. Matholwch had seen it carried out of a lake by a pair of giants, but he found the cauldron's warriors 'hated and unwelcome' and tried to destroy them. Brân, by way of contrast, considered them 'the best that anyone has seen.'

Matholwch marries Branwen, but his followers mistreat her. When Brân hears of this he sets sail for Ireland, the masts of his numerous ships resembling a forest on the sea.

Brân could never be 'contained within a house' (like Llew, who could not be killed indoors). Nevertheless, the Irish build a hall, fill it with warriors hidden in sacks, and invite Brân and his men inside to parley.

A fight breaks out. The Irish kindle a fire under the cauldron of rebirth, so that every slain Irish warrior can be rejuvenated. Eventually, Brân's brother gets into the cauldron and breaks it.

The Irish are vanquished. Brân, however, has been wounded by a poisoned spear and only seven of his men remain alive. He instructs them to strike off his head and carry it away for burial.

Brân's disembodied head keeps the companions entertained for many years. It is possibly the same severed head on its blood-soaked platter which Peredur of York saw in the castle of his uncle, the Fisher King.

The cauldron of British tradition compares with the Grail of medieval romance – it provided nourishment of a mystical nature; it would serve only the brave, and it could restore the dead to life. But it was also a source of conflict.

Taliesin's *Treasures of Annwn* poem reveals that it was present at Arthur's burial, which was attended by the survivors of a catastrophic adventure:

> And when we went with Arthur, famous toil,
> Except for seven, no one rose from the Mound of Mead-Drunkenness.

And Aneirin put the shocking defeat of the army of Lothian down to the 'sweet, ensnaring' mead which turned to 'poison' in their bellies.

THE HORN

In *Culhwch and Olwen,* Arthur and his comrades seize the cauldron from Ireland. It is left in the care of a 'bishop', who uses it to trap Pryderi and his mother.

Another king or 'bishop' – Matholwch, of the 'Prayer-Sort' – tried to entrap a couple connected with the cauldron, although they escaped and took the cauldron to Britain. Brân the Blessed gives the cauldron to Matholwch, who deploys it when Brân goes to war with him over his abusive maltreatment of Branwen.

Pryderi and his stepfather Manawydan (whose name betrays his links with Manau Gododdin in the North) are both present when the cauldron becomes the focus of strife. They appear, with Taliesin, among the seven survivors of the devastation.

The cauldron seemingly had an Irish background. Amergin, an Irish Druid comparable with Taliesin, extolled it – 'I sing of the cauldron of wisdom, / Which bestows the gift of every art' –

and the heroic Cú Chullain captured it:

Much gold and silver was in it,
Excellent was the gain –
And I took away this cauldron,
Together with the daughter of the king.

It came to be thought of as the Cauldron of the Dagda, or Eochaid 'All-Father', a High King of the Druidic *Tuatha dé Danann* whose British counterparts, the Children of (the goddess) Dôn or Danu, populate the early stories of *The Mabinogion*, alongside the Children of Llyr. The Dagda's inexhaustible cauldron of plenty was one of four magical treasures brought from the Northern Isles, the others being a spear, a sword and a stone.

Notably, the Grail mysteries likewise involve a vessel of wisdom, abundance and rebirth; a spear which could wound and heal; a sword which could be broken and repaired; and a stone of power.

There are other Irish and Scottish sources which reveal the cauldron's impact on Arthur's family – and we should recall that the Grail-obsessed Nazis fashioned their own 'gold cauldron/celtic', presumably for use in arcane militaristic rituals.

For now, though, let us return to the Thirteen Treasures of Britain ('which were in the North').

One of these hallows was the Cauldron of Diwrnach the Irishman or Dyrnwch the Giant. Another was *Corn Brân Galed o'r Gogledd*: the 'Horn of Brân the Hard from the North'. The special property of this horn was that 'whatever drink might be wished for was found in it.'

In Chapter 1, we touched on Robert Biket's *Lai du cor*, an amusing 12th-century poem about a drinking horn which poured its contents over any man whose wife had been unfaithful (the only male who stayed dry was 'Garaduc' or Caradog: he surfaces in the legend of Brân the Blessed as 'Caradog son of Brân', the 'chief steward' of Britain). The Horn of Brân had similar Arthurian associations. Marginal notes scribbled on the Peniarth 147 manuscript indicate that it was the first treasure which Myrddin ('Merlin') had to acquire before he could collect the other twelve.

Guto'r Glyn, a Welsh poet of the 15th century, had this to say about the horn's owner:

> Brân the Hard they called him,
> Descended from the tribe of the Men of the North;
> Taliesin, that excellent magician,
> Made him better than the three Generous ones.

The ancient traditions preserved in the Welsh Triads or *Trioedd Ynys Prydein* confirm that 'Arthur himself was more generous' than the 'Three Generous Men of the Island of Britain'. This merely increases the suspicion that the 'blessed Arthur' was also known as the 'blessed Raven', *Bendigeidfrân*. Indeed, Arthur is said to have been reincarnated as a chough (a member of the Crow family). The Welsh name for the chough is *brân Arthur* – 'Arthur's crow'.

The significance of Arthur's alter egos – Brân ('Raven') and Llew ('Lion') – will become clear in a few chapters' time.

"Sir Rory's Horn, a medieval Scottish drinking horn made of an ox horn tipped with silver. Seen here with the Dunvegan Cup and Fairy Flag heirlooms of the Macleods of Dunvegan, Isle of Skye."

Sword and horn

If the original Grail was a mixing bowl like the two-handled *krater* of ancient Greece – and the early words for the Grail suggest that it was – then a delivery system would have been needed to transfer the liquor from the cauldron to the receiver.

In other words, the cauldron alone was not enough. A smaller receptacle was required to transport the three magical droplets to the mouth of the initiate: the *Gogyrwen*, perhaps, if that was indeed the Cup or 'quaich' of inspiration (*awen*).

A drinking horn would have fulfilled this function, especially if it was thought of as a 'horn of plenty', like the cornucopia of classical mythology. The Horn of Brân was indeed a form of cornucopia, providing 'whatever drink might be wished for'. In the 13th-century romance, *Sone de Nausay*, the Grail itself is depicted as an ivory horn 'carved with many stories' which had been brought out of Syria by Joseph of Arimathea.

The romances, meanwhile, refer to the Grail Castle as 'Corbenic': possibly from *cor benoît*, 'blessed horn', or the Old French *corbin*, a 'raven' or 'crow' (the Scots word for a hooded crow is *corbie – brân lwyd* in Welsh).

The horn had a dual purpose. One end could dispense liquor. The other end could be blown. And so the horn which served the 'yellow, sweet, ensnaring' mead to the warriors before battle then became an instrument of war, signalling the call to arms.

Two folktales are told of the horn in southern Scotland. One of these is set in the Eildon Hills, near Melrose in the Scottish Borders; the other at Rosslyn, 25 miles to the north, on the outskirts of Edinburgh.

A horse-trader called Canonbie Dick (see endnote) was crossing Bowden Moor, near Melrose Abbey, when he was accosted by an old man in ancient costume, who bought a couple of horses from him. Canonbie Dick returned with more horses and was led by the stranger through a secret entrance into a hill known as the Lucken Hare. Inside, Dick saw black horses stabled, each with a sleeping knight clad in black armour beside it. At the end of the cavern, a great sword and a golden horn lay on a table.

The old man told him that whoever drew the sword and blew the horn would be 'king of all Britain', but that everything depended on which of the items he picked up first.

The Rosslyn legend varies in its details. Beneath the ruins of Rosslyn Castle, an enchanted White Lady of the St Clair family slumbers in a secret chamber, a demonic creature watching over her. On a table beside her lie a magical sword and a golden horn.

As a newspaper article reported in the 1920s, whoever blows the horn 'shall awaken all the echoes in Roslin Glen'. He must then slay the demon 'with the charmed "Excalibur" in his hand'. The White Lady will awaken, and the two will share a treasure of 'untold wealth'.

A Highlander and his dog once ventured into the castle vault. His bagpipes were heard, fading away. Then silence – followed by a single blast of the horn.

And here the legend merges with that of Canonbie Dick, who snatched at the horn and blew it, rousing the sleeping knights, who advanced towards him. Terrified, he tried to raise the sword, but a great voice boomed:

> Woe to the coward, that ever he was born,
> Who did not draw the sword before he blew the horn!

Canonbie Dick found himself hurled back out onto the moor, where he had just enough time to tell his tale before he died.

At Rosslyn, the Highlander was never heard of again, though his dog, it is rumoured, still haunts the woods.

Son du cor

Melrose and Rosslyn were centres of Cistercian influence, flourishing at the time when the White Monks were repackaging the 'Holy Grail' as a Christian chalice. The legends of both places, however, recall an earlier form of the Grail: a horn (such as that which Fergus of Galloway, in *Le Roman de Fergus*, was challenged to take from the Black Knight) and a sword, like the one given to Perceval before he saw the *graal*, which could only be repaired at a lake beyond the River Forth.

A Cistercian monk named Jocelin served as abbot of Melrose before he became Bishop of Glasgow in 1174. During his 25-year tenure of the Scottish bishopric he commissioned his namesake, Jocelin of Furness, to write a hagiographical *Life of Kentigern*, Glasgow's first bishop and patron saint.

St Kentigern was a contemporary of those 6th-century northern princes – Rhydderch, Gwyddno, Clydno, Morgan, Gwenddolau – whose possessions were among the Treasures of Britain. A church dedicated to him at Stobo in the Scottish Borders has a window which shows him blessing Myrddin, the original 'Merlin', with whom he was associated.

The Glaswegian poet Edwin Morgan (1920-2010) based one of his *Sonnets from Scotland* on the supposed meeting of St Kentigern, a prince of North Britain, and St Columba, an Irish prince of the same period who had based his ecclesiastical mission on the Scottish island of Iona. Morgan's sonnet is entitled, *Colloquy in Glaschu* ['Glasgow']. It is written in four languages – English, French, Latin and Scots – and it begins:

> God but *le son du cor*, Columba sighed
> to Kentigern, *est triste au fond silvarum!*

St Columba found 'the sound of the horn ... sad at the far end of the woods'. Not so Kentigern, who saw no harm in it: '*J'aime le son du cor*, when day has died, / deep in the *bois*'.

'At the far horizon [*À l'horizon lointain*] is paradise,' said Kentigern, 'it disappears in silence [*abest silentium*], the horn sounds [*le cor éclate*] –

' – and dies [*et meurt*], Columba mused, but Kentigern /

replied, 'is reborn and lives on [*renaît et se prolonge*]. The cell / is filled with song.'

Outside, a young Highlander sings *Veni venator* – 'Come, hunter'.

The saints dip startled cups in Mungo's well.

(Mungo – 'dear friend' – was a familiar term for Kentigern.)

Edwin Morgan's *Colloquy in Glaschu* is undoubtedly an oddity, its medley of different languages doing much to obscure the sonnet's meaning. Why, we might ask, did the poet write in such a perplexing mix of tongues?

Was there something he wanted to say, but did not dare say it openly?

The dialogue between St Columba – a royal Irishman of the 'Prayer-Sort' – and St Kentigern, a friend of 'Merlin', concerns the 'sound of the horn' (*le son du cor*). Columba doesn't like it: it's 'sad' and it 'dies'. But Kentigern loves it; 'reborn', it 'lives on'. What are they on about?

The horn, as was noted above, appears as an ivory horn-of-plenty, which is also the Grail, in *Sone de Nausay*. 'Sone' is the name of the hero of that late-13th century romance. He visits the abbey where the horn is kept and sees it used in a service, along with a spear which drips blood. Sone also receives a sword with which he slays the King of Ireland.

If the Old French name *Sone* was associated with the sacred horn, we might look again at Morgan's multilingual sonnet, remembering that the disagreement between St Columba and St Kentigern was over *le son du cor* – 'the sound of the horn'.

In French, *son* also means 'bran'.

Could it be that what St Columba found so distasteful was not the 'sound' of the horn but the 'blessed Raven', Brân of the Horn?

4

The Rule of Three

Arthur's Three Great Queens:
Gwenhwyfar daughter of Cywryd Gwent,
and Gwenhwyfar daughter of Gwythyr son of Greidiol,
and Gwenhwyfar daughter of Gogfrân Gawr.
Triad 56

THE TWO groups most associated with the cauldron were warriors and poets. The latter received their liquor of 'science and inspiration' from it; the former were reborn from it. In the next few chapters, we shall try to understand what processes were involved in the initiation of heroes and seers.

At the same time, we need to keep track of the changes imposed on the Grail tradition from the outside.

The Church, as we have seen, showed considerable interest in the Grail in the early years of the 13th century. This was mostly the work of the Cistercians, whose order had been found in 1098 with the intent of reforming the monastic system. Their sudden interest in the Grail was unprecedented: there had been no such excitement beforehand.

Arthur, too, had been neglected. Five centuries had passed since his death before the Church paid him any attention – and then he became a convenient foil.

Starting in about 1100, a slew of legends advanced claims that certain religious establishments had been granted their lands by 'King Arthur'. Lifris of Llancarfan's *Vita Sancti Cadoci* featured Arthur as a would-be rapist and dupe of the saint. This 'Life of St Cadog' set much of its action in Scotland – St Cadog notably clashes with Rhydderch of Strathclyde, whose sword became one of the Treasures of Britain – and its portrayal of Arthur was clearly designed to exalt the churchman at the expense of 'the most illustrious King of Britannia'.

In *circa* 1130, Caradog of Llancarfan compiled his *Vita Gildae,* in which Arthur is again depicted as an aggressor. St Gildas was presented as one of many sons of a northern prince, several of whom rebelled against Arthur, and a mythical connection between Arthur and Glastonbury was forged to make out that Arthur had gratefully awarded lands around Glastonbury to the 6th-century saint. In the *Vita Sancti Paterni* (*c* 1120) Arthur tries to steal St Padarn's tunic, which we might recognise as the 'Coat of Padarn Red-Coat', another of the Thirteen Treasures.

Evidently, the medieval Church knew of Arthur's reputation but did not yet see him as the paragon of Christian virtues he would later become.

During this same period, the genuine legends were filtering out of the British heartlands. Bleddri, the 'well-known story-teller', took them to the French court of the Count of Poitou. His versions of the tales were undoubtedly more favourable to Arthur than those which were then being spun by the Church.

Parts of France already knew about Arthur. British refugees had fled to the coast of Armorica when Lothian was conquered by the Angles in the 7th century. Armorica duly became the 'Lesser Britain' – Brittany. When Lambert, Canon of St Omer, wrote in about 1120 of Arthur's palace 'in the land of the Picts' he was probably drawing on the race memory of those British émigrés who recalled their Lothian homelands as *Leonais* or 'Lyonesse'.

Shortly thereafter, Hugues de Payens, first Grand Master of the Knights Templar, visited Scotland. The Templars built the Preceptory of St Bernard of Clairvaux beside the River South-Esk near Edinburgh, on land granted to Hugues de Payens by King David I, and named their Scottish headquarters after the Cistercian figurehead who had drafted the Rule of their Order. Before long, the Cistercians had established abbeys of their own nearby at Melrose and Newbattle.

The Cistercians and their Templar protégés rapidly moved into various parts of Scotland, including Galloway, the Borders, Lothian and Aberdeenshire. These were the regions through which Fergus of Galloway passed in the Arthurian *Roman de Fergus* (*c* 1200). Though that romance is set in the age of Arthur its hero was partly modelled on a historical King Fergus who, along with David I of Scotland, founded the Cistercian abbey at Dundrennan in Galloway in 1142.

The battle for the Grail

The Cistercians were responsible for most of the Grail romances which appeared between 1200 and 1240. Under their influence, the Grail was transformed from the original *graal* of Chrétien de Troyes – which resembled the cauldron of British tradition – into the *Saint Graal* or Cup of the Last Supper.

The White Monks did not have everything their own way, though. Their persistent references to Scotland were brushed aside when their Benedictine rivals laid claim to the 'Holy Grail'.

Eleanor of Aquitaine, the granddaughter of the Count of Poitou to whom Bleddri the Welsh *latimer* had told his Arthurian tales, fell out with her first husband, King Louis of France, during the disastrous Second Crusade. She then married Henry II of England. When the church at Glastonbury burned down in 1184 it was King Henry who prompted the search there for Arthur's grave.

The actual dig was carried out under Eleanor's son, Richard the Lionheart, who would expropriate an Arthurian heritage by naming his sword 'Excalibur'. In no time at all the Black Monks were claiming to have unearthed the remains of King Arthur and his 'second wife'. The Grail inevitably followed, providing Glastonbury with a major source of income, even though the Grail – like Arthur – had never been there.

Ultimately, the Cistercians lost the propaganda war over the

Grail to the Benedictines of Glastonbury. Another of their campaigns was seemingly more successful. The papal army, led by the Cistercians, crushed the Albigensian heretics of southern France, massacring them by the thousand.

St Bernard of Clairvaux had admired the Cathars, declaring that 'No sermons are more Christian than theirs', and yet his order was at the forefront of the crusade against them. Ever since, rumours have abounded that the Cathars were the guardians of the Grail; this explains why Otto Rahn focussed his early Grail-hunting explorations on the Cathar region around Montségur.

The flurry of Grail romances produced by the Cistercians coincided with their crusade against the Cathar 'Pure Ones'. This was no accident. While the Cistercians were reinventing the Grail as the Cup of Christ, the Cathars appear to have represented a separate tradition, symbolised by the Grail. Their egalitarian, anti-materialistic faith relied on the experience of personal revelation or *gnosis*. They repudiated the Crucifixion (for reasons which will become apparent) and rejected the hierarchy of the Church in favour of a direct relationship with the Divine. The Cathars were destroyed, not because they were devil-worshippers, but because their Christianity was perhaps truer to the original than the version promoted by Rome.

Another body which came to be connected with the Grail was the Knights Templar. Their militaristic order had developed in tandem with the Cistercians, and if the White Monks were keen to revitalise the spiritual rigor of the monasteries – as their hijacking of the Grail tradition would suggest – the Templars were their favourite jihadists. Together, the White Monks and the Poor Fellow-Soldiers of Christ unleashed a holy war designed to purify medieval Christendom.

But something went wrong. Having failed to save Jerusalem, the Templars began to concentrate on growing rich and powerful. They became, in effect, Europe's first bankers. Their arrogance made them enemies. One of these was Philip IV of France, who owed them money. With Pope Clement V in his pocket, King Philip prepared his move against the Templars.

On Friday 13 October 1307, hundreds of Templar knights were arrested in a well-planned swoop. Many of their leaders were executed; some were roasted alive. Those who escaped, it has often been averred, found sanctuary in Scotland.

Baphomet

The charges levelled against the Templars were reminiscent of those which had previously been laid against the Cathars. They were accused of blasphemy, heresy, 'unnatural sexual practices'. Some, under duress, confessed that they had spat and urinated on the Cross. It was also alleged that the Templars required their initiates to prostrate themselves before a disembodied head or human skull, which they called 'Baphomet'.

Whoever this Baphomet was, the Templars arguably held him in the highest esteem. Rome insisted that:

> ... in their assemblies, and especially in their grand chapters, they worshipped the idol as a god, as their saviour, saying that this head could save them, that it bestowed on the order all its wealth, made the trees flower, and the plants upon the earth to sprout forth.

The Baphomet head was therefore Grail-like in its ability to confer abundance, fertility and victory in war.

The term 'Baphomet' had been recorded at the very start of the crusades. Anselm of Ribemont wrote in 1098: 'As the next day dawned, [the enemy] called loudly upon Baphometh while we prayed silently in our hearts to God.' The Occitan form of the name – *Bafometz* – appeared in a troubadour poem of about 1195, and a poem of *circa* 1250 referred to 'Bafomet' while bemoaning the failure of the Seventh Crusade. The standard assumption is that Baphomet was a corruption of 'Muhammad' and thus the

Templars were held to have been Muslim converts and idolators.

It ain't necessarily so. The word 'Baphomet' can be deconstructed to reveal a link between the sacred head of the Templar knights and the origins of the Grail tradition.

The final syllable – *met, meth* or *metz* – compares with the German word for 'mead': *Met* (genitive *Mets*). This derives from the same Proto-Indo-European root, **méd^{h}u,* which gave us the Proto-Germanic **meduz,* Welsh *medd,* Old Irish *mid,* Breton *mez,* Gaulish *medu,* and the Latin *medo* (Greek *methu,* 'wine'; *méthi,* 'drunkenness'). A 'mether' was an Irish communal cup for sharing mead.

If *met* signified 'mead' – the 'sweet, ensnaring' mead quaffed by warriors before battle – then the first syllable of Baphomet might recall the 'Battle Crow', Badb Catha.

In Irish mythology, Badb (pronounced 'bath-b') was one of three fatal sisters who presided over the battlefield. Badb took the form of a raven or hooded crow (*brân lwyd* in Welsh). The great epic poem of Ulster, *Táin Bó Cúailnge,* sees the goddess Badb terrorising the warriors of Queen Medb of Connacht; the name 'Medb' is cognate with the English 'mead'.

An alternative form of Badb was Bodb. Bodb Derg ('Red Crow'), the son of the Dagda, lord of the inexhaustible cauldron, was elected king of the Children of Lir – the Old Irish equivalent of the 'Children of Llyr' in the tales of the Britons.

Badb survives in Modern Irish as *Badhbh* (pronounced 'bav') and in Scottish Gaelic as *baobh* or *bàibh*: a terrifying vision, a mischievous spirit or fury.

When we recall that the head of Brân, the 'blessed Raven', entertained the survivors of his battle with Matholwch, 'king of Ireland', for many years after it was struck from his body; that Brân's cauldron and the Horn of Brân 'from the North' were precursors of the Grail; that Peredur of York saw a severed head on a platter in his uncle's castle – a vision which took the place of the *graal* in Chrétien's parallel romance of 'Perceval the

Welshman' – and that Arthur himself was reputedly reincarnated as a member of the Crow family, the chough or *brân Arthur*, we have to wonder whether the disembodied head worshipped by the Knights Templar was indeed a form of Arthur-and-the-Grail.

That would surely be the case if Baphomet derived from **Badb-O-Mid*, as in 'Raven son of Mead'.

THREE-IN-ONE

Like the Cathars before them, the Templars were destroyed by the prevailing orthodoxy. Both were associated with the reforming Cistercians – as victims of persecution or kindred spirits – and both practised initiation rituals, the content of which was almost certainly misrepresented by the Church. They were both, it could be said, followers of the 'hidden stream' of esoteric spirituality which rejected much in the way of mainstream Christian ideology.

Where the Church imposed doctrine, promoting Scripture as the cornerstone of religion, the adherents of the 'hidden stream' emphasised the *gnosis* of personal revelation, achieved through initiation. As such, the Cathars and the Templars were indeed the guardians of an authentic tradition at a time when the Cistercian Order was reclassifying the 'Holy Grail' as a Heroic age emblem of Christ's crucifixion.

This begs the questions: how did initiation grant an immediate and direct experience of revelation (*gnosis*) and to what extent were the Grail mysteries related to rites of initiation?

And why did those who followed the esoteric 'hidden stream' consider the Cross of the Crucifixion an irrelevance and even a symbol of evil?

The Celtic world had something of an obsession with the number 3. Goddesses appeared in triple form – e.g. the tripartite goddess of war and death, Macha, Mórrígan and Badb – or were believed to have three aspects. Gods and goddesses were often represented with three faces in stone carvings (so-called 'tricephalic' heads) and it is noteworthy that the Baphomet head allegedly venerated by the Knights Templar was reputed, in some cases, to have had three faces.

The legend of St Patrick using the three-leaf clover or 'shamrock' to explain the doctrine of the Trinity to the pagan Irish reflects this Celtic preoccupation with threes. The Celts were well-prepared for a God who exists simultaneously in three forms (Father, Son and Holy Spirit) because various Celtic deities already did. The shamrock legend is, in fact, of late invention: the 5th-century Irish to whom St Patrick preached would have had no difficulty at all in comprehending a three-in-one god.

The Celtic fascination with threes is exemplified by the Welsh Triads. Like the native tales of the *Mabinogion*, these are preserved in medieval transcriptions, including the Peniarth 16, 20 and 54 manuscripts, the White Book of Rhydderch and the Red Book of Hergest. A total of 86 triads were edited by Rachel Bromwich (1915-2010) and first published as *Trioedd Ynys Prydein* – 'Triads of the Island of Britain' – in 1963 (revised editions 1978 and 2006).

The triad system would appear to have been a mnemonic device used by Welsh bards. Let us suppose that a storyteller was required to recount three great fables from the past. These stories might be connected by a common theme, in the way that Greek tragedies were in the dramatic festivals of the 5th century BC, and so over the course of a weekend the bard could recite the legends of the 'Three Generous Men of the Island of Britain:

Nudd the Generous, son of Senyllt,
Mordaf the Generous, son of Serwan,
Rhydderch the Generous, son of Tudwal Tudglyd.

The moral in this instance being that 'Arthur himself was more generous than the three.'

On another occasion the bard might have been called upon to

describe 'Arthur's Three Great Queens' – 'Gwenhwyfar daughter of Cywryd Gwent, and Gwenhwyfar daughter of Gwythyr son of Greidiol, and Gwenhwyfar daughter of Gogfrân Gawr', the last appearing to have been a 'Cup of Brân/Raven the Champion/Giant' (see endnote) – and perhaps to contrast this tripartite figure with the 'Three Faithful Wives of the Island of Britain' or tell the complementary tales of the 'Three Faithless Wives':

> And one was more faithless than those three: Gwenhwyfar, Arthur's wife, since she shamed a better man than any.

The triple death

The grouping of these stories into sets of threes might have been a useful memory aid but it seems to have been carried to excess. Even the 'Twenty-Four Horsemen of Arthur's Court' (*Pedwar Marchog ar Hugain Llys Arthur*) were conveniently bundled into threes.

Thus, Peredur of York was one of the 'Three Virgin Knights', while Owain son of Urien (whose wife was one of the 'Three Faithless Wives of the Island of Britain') was one of the 'Three Battle Knights' and Cynon son of Clydno (who cast one of the 'Three Surpassing Bonds of Enduring Love' over Owain's sister) was one of Arthur's 'Three Counsellor Knights'.

So insistent was the urge to turn everything into threes that we might ask, was there something more to this?

Could there have been some cosmological or eschatological significance to the concept of triplicity?

The question takes on new urgency when we consider the Celtic motif of the three-fold death. The records abound with prominent figures who suffered a sacrificial triple death, and it is clear from the historical accounts that this practice was still observed in the time of Arthur.

Myrddin – the original 'Merlin' – reputedly died when he was struck by a stone, impaled on a stake and drowned in the River Tweed. Somewhat earlier, a Celtic prince, whose body was recovered from a peat-bog at Lindow Moss in Cheshire in 1984, was found to have been pole-axed, garrotted and bled to death in about AD 60.

These and other, similar, examples of ritual sacrifice would appear to have taken the Celtic rule-of-three a little too far. Unless of course there was a rationale – a belief which dictated that, in certain circumstances, key individuals had to be killed three times, using different methods. Whatever that belief might have been it was presumably the same reasoning that inspired the triple goddesses and the arranging of stories in threes, as evidenced by the Triads of the Island of Britain.

The creation of threes – or the subdivision of one thing into three things – was not the exclusive preserve of the Celtic imagination. Christianity, for example, developed the concept of the Holy Trinity. Likewise, the *Moirai* or 'Fates' of Greek mythology took the form of three sisters: Clotho the spinner, Lachesis the measurer, and Atropos the cutter. It may be that Kerberos, the Hound of Hell, had three heads for much the same reason, one representing birth (or the 'past'), one youth ('present') and one, old age ('future'). These three aspects were mirrored in the Celtic triple-goddess, reflecting three major stages in life: 'Maiden', 'Bride/Mother' and 'Crone'.

There is in fact something quite natural about such three-fold divisions. In 1973, the American neuroscientist Paul D. MacLean (1913-2007) published *The Triune Brain in Evolution*. MacLean's theory proposed that the human brain is, in reality, three brains in one.

The first of these is the oldest. It is the brain we share with reptiles and fish; MacLean called it the 'reptilian brain' or 'R-complex'. Comprising the spinal cord, brainstem and midbrain, the reptilian complex governs our most basic instinctual behaviour: reproduction and self-preservation.

The second brain, comprising the amygdala, hippocampus and septum, is the 'palaeomammalian complex', which governs much of our emotional and parenting behaviour. Another term coined by MacLean for this 'mammalian' brain is the 'limbic system'.

The last evolutionary development is the neo-cortex or 'neomammalian complex'. This part of the brain is the 'thinking' mind (the palaeomammalian complex being the 'feeling' mind and the reptilian complex the 'survival' mind). It holds the ability to plan, to conceptualise and to use language.

'It' and 'I'

The point about the triune brain theory is that it recapitulates the entire process of animal evolution and exists inside each and every one of us. At any moment, the logical processes of our 'thinking' mind can be subverted by a rush of emotion welling up from the mammalian brain or even the reflex 'fight-or-flight' impulses of the reptilian brain (which includes aggressive sexual urges). Another way of putting this – as Paul MacLean did – is to say that whenever a patient lies down on a psychiatrist's couch, a horse and a crocodile lie down beside him.

Fifty years before MacLean published his evolutionary theory of the triune brain, Sigmund Freud proposed his 'structural model' of the mind. In *Das Ich und das Es* ('The Ego and the Id'), Freud elaborated on a theory he had first put forward three years earlier in *Beyond the Pleasure Principle* (1920).

Freud posited a three-part structure of the mind. He called these parts *das Es*, *das Ich* and *das Über-Ich* – 'the It', 'the I' and 'the Over-I' – although it has become customary to refer to them in Latinate terms as the id, the ego and the super-ego.

The id compares with the primitive 'R-complex' of the brain, in that it is active from birth and contains the most fundamental drives. Freud remarked that 'the It' is the 'dark, inaccessible part of our personality ... we call it a chaos, a cauldron full of seething excitations'. The ego seeks to reconcile the id's desire for instant gratification with the realities of life and 'represents what may be called reason and common sense, in contrast to the id, which contains the passions'.

The third component of the mind is the super-ego, which acts as the 'conscience' and 'punishes misbehaviour with feelings of guilt.' According to Freud, the ego endeavours to steer a course through the external world while subject to conflicting internal pressures: the infantile needs of the id and the critical, moralistic attitudes of the super-ego.

MacLean implied that what we call the 'self' – a product of the advanced neo-cortex – sits atop two earlier developments, the reptilian and old-mammalian brains. Freud suggested that the 'self' strives to maintain the balance between the demanding id and the disapproving super-ego. Both men delineated a three-part structure to the personality: a basic, instinctual component, a more developed 'feeling' component and a higher 'thinking' component. These three aspects of the personality are constantly dragging us down and willing us upwards.

The theories put forward by Freud and MacLean belong to the Human age, as does the philosophy of G.W.F. Hegel (1770-1831), out of which grew the notion of the Hegelian dialectic. This again is a three-part model. An initial idea (*thesis*) is stated. This provokes a reaction (*antithesis*). The two battle it out, and a resolution (*synthesis*) is reached. Hegel's own terms were 'Abstract', 'Negative' and 'Concrete'.

Ideally, then, the logic of the Human age – when it works – follows a three-stage process:

1. Thesis, or proposition;
2. Antithesis, or opposition;
3. Synthesis, or solution.

For an example of three-fold division in Heroic age thinking we have the Blessed Trinity – in addition to which there were the 'Three Estates' of medieval society (clergy, nobility, commoners) and the three-tier model of the cosmos expounded in Dante's *Divine Comedy*. The spiritual journey undertaken by Dante through his epic poem leads him down into the depths of Hell (*Inferno*), then up the Mountain of Purgatory (*Purgatorio*) and finally through the celestial spheres of Heaven (*Paradiso*), where he receives a vision of the Triune God as:

> Three orbs of triple hue, clipt in one bound ...

Turning back to the magical mindset of the Divine age Celts we find the triplicities of the ritualistic three-fold death, the three aspects, forms or faces of the goddess (and Arthur's wife) and the multifarious threesomes of the Triads.

THE THREE SELVES

There is clearly something fundamental – universal and recurrent – about these three-fold divisions. Such tripartite patterns seem to be hardwired into our ways of thinking about human discourse, the personality and the cosmos. That is to say, they are *archetypal*, and what the essential archetype underpinning these various examples of triplicity might be is explained most elegantly, perhaps, by the 'Huna' philosophy of Polynesia.

The Hawaiian word *huna* means 'secret'. The mages who practised the spiritual disciplines of Huna were known as *kahuna*.

The religion of the *kahuna* had been outlawed by Christian missionaries before the schoolteacher Max Freedom Long arrived in Hawaii in 1917. Working alongside Dr William Tufts Brigham, curator of the Bishop Museum in Honolulu, Long strived to piece together what he could of the ancient secrets of the *kahuna*.

The revelation came to him in a dream in 1934 that the Hawaiian language must have retained some vestiges of the ideas and thought processes involved in Huna. He published the results of his investigations in *Recovering the Ancient Magic* (1936) and *The Secret Science Behind Miracles* (1948).

According to Max Freedom Long, the Huna practitioners believed that each of us has three distinct selves. He termed these the low, middle and High selves. The Hawaiian words given for the three selves are *unihipili, uhane* and *Aumakua*.

The 'lowest' of the three is *unihipili*, from a root word meaning 'sticky' (the Selk'nam tribes of Patagonia had a similar concept: their *yauategn* was able to leave the body but remained connected to it by a 'thread made of gum'). *Unihipili* is essentially a nature spirit, the 'child within', and is roughly analogous to the id or R-complex. Attached to the body via a subtle cord connected to the solar plexus, *unihipili* combines the functions of a life-support system, a database of personal memories and a kind of ever-willing servant eager to do the bidding of *uhane* or the 'middle' self.

Unihipili is, however, rather literal in its understanding. It also carries the memory of every bad feeling and negative thought which has ever occurred to the middle self. Consequently, it can struggle with the mixed messages it receives from *uhane* and, like the Sorcerer's Apprentice, inadvertently create chaotic and unwanted outcomes.

Uhane, the 'middle' self, is the thing we call 'I': the ego or 'self' as we perceive it; the conscious, reasoning mind which sets targets and goals. These instructions are passed down to the 'low' self, which seeks to carry them out faithfully but is frequently hampered by conflicts arising from past experiences and the contradictory nature of the ego's aspirations.

Each self thrives on a different type of life energy or vitality. *Unihipili* uses mana, which has the power to keep the body functioning and to realise and maintain physical forms. *Uhane* makes use of mana-mana, a kind of creative energy which powers thought, feeling and imagination.

The purest energy, Mana Loa, is the power of compassion. It is the life energy used by *Aumakua*, the 'High Self', which is connected to the body by way of a subtle cord attached either to the heart or the head.

Aumakua seems to correspond with Freud's super-ego, and yet it is never critical or disapproving. Whereas the super-ego is effectively an amalgamation of authority figures (parents, teachers, religious leaders, etc.), *Aumakua* belongs to a divine spiritual family – the 'Great Poe Aumakua' – which fulfils the noblest parental functions of guarding and guiding without judgement. These High Selves are all related, like the gods of Olympus, and they hold out the promise of supreme knowledge and wisdom as well as the ability to communicate telepathically and foresee future events.

If *unihipili* represents our elemental 'nature' intelligence, and *uhane* our rational 'human' intelligence, then *Aumakua* constitutes our 'divine' intelligence. Many people have a sense of the loving *Aumakua* presence in their lives and think of it as their 'guardian angel'.

Three souls

Each of the selves has its own subtle body or *kino-aka*. These overlapping auras are comparable with the 'Three orbs of triple hue, clipt in one bound' perceived by the poet Dante when he beheld the triune form of God the Father, God the Son and God the Holy Spirit.

The most compact subtle body belongs to *unihipili*. Known in some cultures as the 'etheric body', it is described as a fluid, sticky substance similar to the 'ectoplasm' of the Spiritualists. Less dense, and more expansive, is the subtle body of *uhane*, sometimes called the 'astral body'.

The least condensed of the *kino-aka* bodies is that of *Aumakua*, which is so expansive that its centre is believed to be above the head, like the 'crown' chakra or *Sahasrara* of Tantric yoga.

These *kino-aka* bodies interpenetrate each other: three ovals emanating from the physical body, with *unihipili*'s 'etheric' body inside *uhane*'s 'astral' body and both encompassed by the subtle aura of *Aumakua*'s unconditional love.

Max Long's reconstruction of the Huna way of thinking allowed him to comprehend how the Hawaiian *kahuna* achieved their reported miracles. They were said to have been accomplished healers, psychotherapists and visionaries, their skills seemingly drawn from their ability to harness the elemental energy of *unihipili* and access the divine wisdom of *Aumakua*.

Serge King, who was initiated by his father into the secrets of the *kahuna* at the age of 14, referred to their tradition as 'the Way of the Adventurer' (in contrast to the 'Way of the Warrior' followed by many Native American shamans), a path which 'emphasises ... the development of hyper-awareness and a goal-oriented self-discipline'. King described the *kahuna* as spiritual fishermen 'able to weave and cast [etheric] nets in order to capture ideas and events, symbolised by fish.' This insight provides us with our first glimpse of the true nature of the Fisher King of Grail lore, and we shall revisit the concept in due course.

The *kahuna* could have taught us much about the manipulation of subtle energies, and it is one of history's tragedies that their practices were stamped out by interloping missionaries – the Heroic age mentality refusing, as so often, to tolerate any knowledge but its own.

But the concept of the three selves was not peculiar to the Polynesian *kahuna*. Larry G. Peters studied the Tamang *bombo* of Nepal and discovered that they too believed in the existence of three souls.

The 'lowest' of these was known as *sem chang* and was located in the solar plexus. It provided the elemental energy used in *bombo* sorcery and was the first soul which the trainee shaman was required to master. That mastery was achieved through the *yidem bhla* or 'heart soul', the 'soul of compassion and speech'.

The third soul, *che wa,* was described as the 'light of consciousness', located between the eyes. Mastery of this soul empowered the shaman with the gift of magical flight. The final initiatory goal of the Tamang shaman was to release the *che wa* soul, which would leave the body via the 'heavenly doors' at the top of the head. By doing this, the *bombo* could reconnect his higher soul with the eternal family of High Selves and climb – like the poet Dante – to 'the highest heaven'.

It might be objected that we have strayed into the thickets of superstitious gobbledegook. Modern man struggles with the idea of a single soul – let alone three of them! – but the fact is that we cannot begin to grapple with the beliefs of the Divine age without an understanding of the three-selves/souls paradigm.

And, astonishingly, the Human age has found evidence to support the Huna theory.

OBEs

Robert Crookall (1909-1981) was a lecturer in Botany at the University of Aberdeen, a geologist for the National Coal Board and Principal Geologist for H.M. Geological Survey; he also held a BSc in Psychology. In the 1960s and 70s he published a number of books detailing his extensive research into 'out-of-the-body experiences' or OBEs.

Dr Crookall analysed numerous testimonies – 381 in one book alone – from people who claimed temporarily to have left their bodies or had witnessed the departure of an astral 'double' from someone else's body. He came to differentiate between two forms of this 'replica body': the 'semi-physical' vehicle of vitality, as he called it (which correlates with the 'vital body' of the Rosicrucians and the 'etheric double' of the Theosophists), and the 'super-physical' Soul Body, which Dr Crookall believed was an 'instrument of consciousness'.

Crookall noted a significant difference in the experiences of those who had died naturally – e.g. of old age – and those who had died suddenly (some of these reports were obtained via mediums). 'In many natural releases,' he wrote, 'the "double" consisted of the "super-physical" Soul Body only, while in enforced releases the Soul Body was accompanied by some of the enshrouding substance of the "semi-physical" vehicle of vitality.'

The differences between the two types of experience – natural 'releases' and sudden or 'enforced' ones – are extremely telling.

Many reports garnered from living people who claimed to have left their bodies referred to an initial impression of 'fog', 'smoke' or 'mist' ('everything seemed blurred and whitish') often accompanied by 'darkness', like 'a dark night'. Some testimonies described not only a 'thick grey mist' but also a 'rushing mighty wind' or 'cold air' with a 'spirit-of-the-wind' sensation.

(We are reminded of the storm unleashed by Cynon son of Clydno when he poured water from the silver bowl onto the marble slab in *Owain, or the Countess of the Fountain*, and the 'peal of thunder' and 'a fall of mist' which engulfed Pryderi and his mother when they became stuck to the golden cauldron and marble slab in the tale of *Manawydan son of Llyr*.)

The 'fog' reported by survivors of OBEs produced a 'stifled and cramped' feeling. This oppressive sensation was often associated with 'adverse powers' – blind and jealous 'hinderers' who obstructed the released double by surrounding and trying to 'possess' it. Commonly reported in cases of the sudden or enforced release of the 'semi-physical' double, this state was described by Robert Crookall as 'Hades'.

The attempts of the 'earthbound' hinderers to detain the 'semi-physical' double were not always successful. Sometimes the double would pass through a 'dark tunnel', a 'narrow, dimly lit passage' or a 'creek with high banks'. Professor J.H.M. Whiteman described in 1935 the experience of seeing 'some substance like granite on a sandy beach near the water's edge.' A lawyer named S.A. Wildman similarly 'dreamed' that he was 'on the shore of a sea or lake whose waves ... carried the fragment of something I was striving to capture and hold.' On the far side of this water was what Dr Crookall referred to as 'Paradise' (*'À l'horizon lointain* is paradise,' remarks St Kentigern in Edwin Morgan's *Colloquy in Glaschu*).

Witnesses reported seeing 'beautiful scenery', 'utter reality' – 'I [had] never been awake before'; 'the whole earth was aglow'; 'Everything looked so bright!'

Professor Whiteman observed that a 'new personal form' was 'condensed out of "the waters"' as the semi-physical vehicle of vitality was shed and the super-physical Soul Body made the transition from Hades to Paradise.

When the 'release' was natural, the double was more likely to proceed directly to the 'increasing light' of the '"Paradise" conditions' (Crookall's phrase), bypassing the sense of being mocked and choked by the disembodied 'hinderers' of Hades.

THE SPIRIT WORLD

At the start of our investigation, back at the beginning of Chapter 1, we considered Bérenger's memory (as relayed by Eugène Ionesco in *Tueur sans Gages*) of 'that dazzling radiance, that glowing feeling', when 'I felt I was there at the gates, at the very centre of the universe' and an 'indescribable bliss took hold of me!' This we compared with Wordsworth's recollection of a world 'Apparell'd in celestial light' in his *Intimations of Immortality*. Both instances seem reminiscent of the '"Paradise" conditions' described by Robert Crookall in his studies of OBEs.

The youthful experience of wonder – that moment of transcendence which, as Robert A. Johnson observed, 'usually happens around fifteen or sixteen years of age' – is perhaps a sort of presentiment of the 'Paradise' state which exists in the afterlife and can be apprehended if and when the individual is momentarily in touch with his or her High Self. This awakening of consciousness is seemingly consistent with the Grail experience, which starts with mist and confusion and ends with radiance and magical flight.

We have only begun to scratch the surface of astral projection and the adventures of the soul after death. Already, though, two things stand out from Dr Robert Crookall's research.

First, except when the release of the astral 'double' was natural, the journey of the Soul Body towards 'Paradise' was through a dark and windy environment ('Hades') populated by 'adverse powers'. Crookall thought of these earthbound 'hinderers' as 'weak and feckless discarnate souls'.

They could also be thought of as 'semi-physical' vehicles of vitality which, having left their bodies, never progressed to the Paradise state. Unable to accept that their physical bodies are dead, or simply too attached to the material plane, they seek to restrain those doubles which have been newly released. To proceed to Paradise, the double has to pass through Hades, shed its semi-physical form in the waters of the *second* death and then re-emerge as a 'super-physical' Soul Body.

The Huna philosophy teaches that the way to the High Self, *Aumakua,* is through the low self, *unihipili.* The middle self has 'no direct connection with the High Self' (although Bérenger's adolescent experience suggests that a connection can exist before the ego becomes fixated on material things) and so *uhane* must first learn to communicate with *unihipili,* which can then act as a channel to *Aumakua.*

Between the conscious ego and the super-conscious High Self or 'instrument of consciousness' lies the gloomy realm of *unihipili.* At death, the low self ('vehicle of vitality') is released from the body, hopefully to lose its 'semi-physical' nature in the water which separates Hades from Paradise. If it is held back for some reason – doesn't know it's dead, or clings hopelessly to the material realm – it cannot be reborn in the 'super-physical' state of pure consciousness and 'utter reality' which is *Aumakua,* the eternal Soul Body.

Dr Crookall also noted that the 'semi-physical' double (*unihipili*) is attached to the physical body by a '"silver-cord"-extension' extruding from the solar plexus.

Professor Whiteman, for example, described a sensation he had felt 'about one to two inches above the navel and perhaps two inches within the body' when his 'vehicle of vitality' was released from his body: 'I saw my own "silver cord" ... attached to the solar plexus.'

Many references to this 'silver thread of light' emanating from the subject's abdomen were recorded by Dr Crookall. Each one recalls the Huna tradition that *unihipili* is connected to the solar plexus by a subtle cord, the Tamang shamans of Nepal concurring that the 'lowest' soul is located in the solar plexus.

Lost souls

More rarely, a silver cord pulsating with vitality was reported to have emerged from the head.

Thus, a Dr R.B. Hout observed a 'silver-like substance that was streaming from the head of the physical body to the head of the spirit double' of his dying aunt.

Robert Crookall was moved to assert that the 'extension between the vehicle of vitality and the physical body is at the solar plexus, whereas that between the Soul Body and the physical body is at the head.'

This is precisely what we would expect if we accepted the beliefs of the Hawaiian *kahuna* and the Nepalese *bombo*: the 'low' self leaves the body from the solar plexus (to which it is attached by a 'thread made of gum') while the High Self exits via the 'third eye' or the 'heavenly doors' at the top of the head.

There is no record of a silver cord extruding from the heart, the seat of the 'middle' soul – *yidam bhla* – in the Tamang shamanic tradition.

In Ancient Egypt, the heart was the *Ib* part of the soul, where emotions, thoughts and intentions were based, and which was judged ('weighed') in the afterlife. The *Ka*, meanwhile, was the vital spark or essence. *Ka* required food and drink to sustain itself. Death occurred when the *ka* left the body (the word *ka* was formerly translated as 'double').

If the *ka* was the equivalent of *unihipili*, the Egyptian answer to *Aumakua* was the *Ba*, which lived on after death. Often depicted as a human-headed bird, the *Ba* represented the unique character or personality of an individual or a thing, as well as the aspect of a deity which could intervene in mortal affairs (this idea can be traced back some 17,000 years to a cave-painting at Lascaux, where a bird-headed man of the Upper Palaeolithic is shown lying recumbent, his soul having left his body in bird-form and alighted on a nearby pole; the man appears to be alive, though: his penis is erect). *Ka* and *Ba* were therefore similar but played different roles in the aggregate, tripartite soul, the one being a person's life-support mechanism or 'vehicle of vitality', the other their spiritual essence or Soul Body.

Larry Peters, writing of the Tamang shamans, remarked of the 'lowest' soul (*sem chang*) that, 'When an individual dies, this soul may stay on earth and cause trouble as an evil spirit.' This would account for the many tales of hobgoblins and elementals the world over, as well as those 'adverse powers' which hinder the passage of the soul through Hades.

At their most mindlessly repetitive, these earthbound spirits behave as ghosts, endlessly reliving moments of stress. The more childishly mischievous spirits become poltergeists, feeding on the vitality of a living person (usually a teenager) and utilising that energy to make noises and hurl things; as Dr Crookall noted: 'Some "doubles" (which contain very much of the vehicle of vitality) can move physical objects'. The *candomblé* cult of Brazil, which has its roots in African paganism, seeks to attract these restless entities with offerings of rich food, alcohol and tobacco, bribing them to plague the victim of a black magic 'job' or *trabalho*.

Closely related to the poltergeist are the phenomena of possession, in which a disembodied spirit invades a living body, and 'multiple personality disorder', in which one or more spirits take control of an individual. It could also be averred that hypnosis works by putting the 'middle' self (ego, *ib*, *uhane*) to sleep, leaving the 'low' self (id, *ka*, *unihipili*) to do the hypnotist's bidding.

Properly directed, *unihipili* can work wonders. At the command of a hypnotist, or a convincing physician, it can produce a miracle cure or present all the symptoms of illness. It does as it is told, and we should do well to be aware of this, for whatever thoughts it is programmed with, it will do its utmost to make them happen.

'Mr. Sludge'

Some of the most impressive demonstrations of supernatural powers ever witnessed were attributed by Daniel Dunglas Home to discarnate spirits.

Born near Edinburgh in 1833, Home (pronounced 'Hume') became something of a sensation after he moved to America at the age of nine and began to manifest mediumistic abilities.

He returned to Europe – and a mixed reception – in 1855. Staying at a London hotel, Home held séances in full daylight. Heavy objects moved, seemingly of their own accord; musical instruments played themselves, then disappeared; hands would materialise; spirit voices spoke.

Naturally, he had his detractors. Charles Dickens railed against him, though he declined to attend any of Home's séances, and Robert Browning slandered him in a long and vicious poem, *Mr. Sludge, 'The Medium'* (1864). Browning's spite was probably provoked by his wife's fascination with Home, but that does not excuse his unwarranted vitriol.

More recently, in his *Servants of the Supernatural* (2008),

Antonio Melechi presented an excessively cynical review of Home's career. In such ways does the Human age exhibit its intolerance. The true spirit of science would give exceptional individuals like Home a fair hearing, but this seldom happens. Rather, the inherent materialism of the scientific era produces an extreme reaction where the insubstantial is concerned, and then the Human age shows itself capable of an irrational dogmatism worthy of its Heroic age predecessors.

There were, however, scientists who remained open-minded and empirical. One of these was William Crookes, a pioneering physicist and chemist who chose to investigate Home's performances. Much to the alarm of his peers, Crookes's report – published in the July 1871 issue of the *Quarterly Journal of Science* – found no fault with Home's methods.

Crookes had observed the medium levitating, elongating himself, handling red-hot coals and rubbing them into his face without a trace of injury, as well as the more familiar spirit-related activities – grand pianos floating in mid-air, accordions played by invisible hands, flowers falling from the ceiling, etcetera, etcetera. He professed that his rational mind knew that the things he had seen were impossible. But he had studied them and discovered no evidence of trickery. As far as Crookes could determine, Home was genuine.

It was Viscount Adare, later the 4th Earl of Dunraven and Mount-Earl, who was present – along with Captain Wynne and Lord Lindsay (elected president of the Royal Astronomical Society in 1878) – when Home drifted out of a third-storey window, which was open about a foot wide, and then back into the room *through another window*.

The sheer range of Home's repertoire, the huge number of witnesses (many of them utterly reputable) and the fact that he was never exposed as a fraudulent charlatan argue in favour of Home's authenticity. And yet he often seemed at a loss to account for his gifts. It was, he would say, all down to the 'spirits'.

For a whole year, from 10 February 1856 until midnight on 10 February 1857, the spirits withdrew their services because they were unhappy with Home's snobbish affectations. Some years later, a publisher named Vizetelly met Home in a café. Home was fasting and explained that 'the spirits will not move me unless I do this. To bring them to me, I have to contend with the material part of my nature.'

When Home allowed himself to become too materialistic he lost the support of his 'spirit' helpers. Just as we, who are so preoccupied with material concerns these days, have little or no awareness of the spiritual dimension.

Unlike our Divine age forefathers, who saw the universe in three parts: a lower, middle and upper realm, reflecting the three selves or souls present in every living person.

"Daniel Dunglas Home (1833-1886). Seen here levitating at Ward Cheney's house in Connecticut in August 1852. Illustration by Louis Figuier, Les Mystères de la science, *1887."*

5

The Topography of Avalon

Seven years before the Judgement,
The sea shall come over Ireland in one tide,
And over blue-green Islay,
But float will the Isle of Columba the cleric.
Gaelic Proverb

THE ISLAND in which Arthur was buried – popularly known as Avalon – was no ordinary isle. It was the burial place of kings, where the veil separating this world from the next was preternaturally 'thin'.

Moreover, it was the site of sacred rituals involving the object we know as the Grail.

The 'Holy Grail' did not take on its familiar form (a cup or chalice) until the Middle Ages. Before that, various items were associated with the Grail mysteries.

These items, of which there appear to have been four – a mixing bowl or cauldron, a bleeding spear, a sword which could be broken and repaired, and a 'block of dark stone' or marble slab – hint at the provenance of the tradition.

They appear in several Middle Irish manuscripts. The latest of these, the 14th-century *Leabhar Buidhe Leacáin* (Trinity College Dublin MS 1318), contains a poem concerning four treasures of the *Tuatha dé Danann* (known in Britain as the 'Children of Dôn').

The poem asserts that the Children of Dôn/Danu 'came upon perfect wisdom / In Druidism, in devilry':

Four gifts were brought hither [to Ireland]
By the nobles of the Tuatha dé Danann:
A sword, a stone, a cauldron of worth,

A spear for the death of great champions.

These four treasures can be seen as the inspiration for the four suits of the Tarot and the standard deck of cards:

Treasures:	Sword	Spear	Cauldron	Stone
Tarot:	Swords	Wands	Cups	Coins
Cards:	Spades	Clubs	Hearts	Diamonds

The *Leabhar Buidhe Leacáin* ('Yellow Book of Lecan') states that the four treasures of the Children of Danu were associated with 'Druidism' and 'devilry'. It is hardly surprising, then, that when the medieval Church began to appropriate the Grail legends for its own use these tainted treasures should have been converted into Christian artefacts. The 'cauldron of the Dagda of lofty deeds' therefore evolved into the Eucharistic cup of the Last Supper, while the 'deadly spear of Nuada' became the lance which pierced Christ's side on the Cross.

But even as the Cistercian monks were transforming the Grail legends into Christian parables a separate tradition was flourishing, manifested in various folktales involving a horn.

Robert Biket composed his *Lai du cor* ('Lay of the Horn') – in which Arthur gets drenched with liquid from a magical drinking horn – in about 1170, before the 'grail' made its first appearance in Chrétien's *Perceval, le Conte du Graal*.

At the same time, an Anglo-Norman romance told of an orphan named Horn who sailed to Brittany with twelve companions and fell in love with the daughter of the king. Accused of seeking to usurp the throne, Horn was banished to Ireland, where he proved his worth and was offered the Irish king's daughter in marriage. Horn turned her down, however, and returned to Brittany to marry his true love.

The *Romance of Horn* (*c* 1170) inspired the later romance of *King Horn* (*c* 1225). In this, Horn is the son of King Murry (**muir-rí* – 'sea-king'; compare the name of Brân's father Llyr, 'Sea') whose realm lies by the ocean. Horn's father is slain by Saracen invaders. Horn himself is set adrift in a boat with two companions.

They travel to 'Westernesse', where Horn falls in love with the king's daughter. She gives him a ring as a token of their betrothal but then Horn is betrayed and banished to Ireland. After seven years, Sir Horn returns to claim his betrothed, who is about to be forced into marriage with another.

In these stories, the magical drinking horn has become merged with the identity of the hero.

Sir Uallabh

A Hebridean folktale – *Sgeulachd air Sir Uallabh O'Còrn* – was recited by Donald Campbell of Tiree in the 19th century and translated into English by Rev. M.E. Campbell for the Gaelic Society of Inverness. The story begins:

> There was a King in Ireland called Chief Arthur son of Iuthar, and Sir Uallabh son of Horn, his sister's son, went to see him.

The King takes his nephew, Sir Uallabh (Gaelic *ullamh*: 'wise man' or 'bard'), to the 'hunting-hill'. A dark mist descends. Having failed to provide shelter for Arthur and his men, Sir Uallabh sails across the wild sea to Ireland. He defeats a champion in single combat and discovers that the king has just buried his queen and is morosely 'playing chess on a board of gold'.

A coracle comes to the shore. Sir Uallabh son of Horn finds inside it 'the loveliest drop of blood, the fairest he ever saw on earth, of womankind.' Proudly, Sir Uallabh takes this woman to the king to be his new queen.

But the king grows jealous of his bride, whom he suspects has a lover. He does battle with 'the Big Lad', son of the 'King of

Innean' (Gaelic *innean* – a smith's anvil), and is defeated. The queen laughs at this. Sir Uallabh then challenges the Big Lad and strikes off his head.

Sir Uallabh brings the head to the king and queen while they are at supper:

> The Queen clasped it in her arms, shed three tears of blood from her eyes, then sprang away, taking the head with her, and none knew where she went. It was the head of her brother...

The queen then compacts with her father to deprive Sir Uallabh of his armour, which they do with the aid of the queen's younger sister. Sir Uallabh is surrounded and overwhelmed. Arrangements are made for him to be burned between two fires and pulled apart by horses. But the queen's younger sister has fallen in love with Sir Uallabh and helps him escape.

Sir Uallabh takes a boat to 'the remote island', where he hides in a dark cave. A great giant places a cauldron over Uallabh's head, promising to kill him when daylight comes. Sir Uallabh stabs the giant with his sword; the giant rushes out of the cave, pushing aside the stone which blocks the entrance, and plunges into the sea, where he drowns.

The hero remains on the remote island for a while and then returns to Ireland. He learns that the younger daughter of the king has been promised to the King of the Iron Throne in punishment for her having freed Sir Uallabh. Inevitably, Sir Uallabh challenges the King of the Iron Throne, overcomes him, and marries the princess, becoming the King of Ireland in his turn.

This *Saga of Sir Wiseman son of Horn* was not recorded until 1863. It would be a mistake, though, to dismiss it as a late development. The tale undoubtedly has more in common with native Arthurian lore than it does with the Christianised medieval romances.

One striking feature of the Hebridean folktale is the confusion of identities. Sir Uallabh is the 'son of Horn' and his uncle is 'Chief Arthur son of Iuthar', who is a 'King in Ireland'. Does this mean that Arthur is also the King of Ireland who has buried his first wife and whose second washes up in a coracle (and whose brother is then beheaded by Sir Uallabh)?

That Uallabh's father was named Còrn (Gaelic *còrn*, a drinking or musical horn) suggests that the various 'Horn' romances of the Middle Ages grew out of an early Arthurian tradition which – like *Sgeulachd air Sir Uallabh O'Còrn* – had Irish connections.

Scéla Cano

The *Leabhar Buidhe Leacáin* contains another legend that is germane to our Grail quest.

Scéla Cano meic Gartnáin dates, at least in part, from the 9th century and tells of the adventures of Cano son of Gartnait mac Áedáin.

Áedán mac Gabráin was a historical king of the Scots in the late-6th century. His eldest son, Gartnait, became king of the Picts of the Scottish Highlands in about 584.

The *Scéla Cano* relates that Gartnait had been living happily on a royal island, drinking mead and maintaining his fifty fishing nets, until his son Cano ('Song') was born. Gartnait sent his son away to be raised by foster-parents and had a vat of gold and silver buried in the sand at low-tide. He killed the four men who hid the vat so that only he, his wife and Cano would know of its whereabouts.

Áedán mac Gabráin invaded the royal isle and slaughtered its inhabitants. Cano sought sanctuary with his kinsmen in Ireland. King Áedán, meanwhile, discovered the hiding place of the precious vat:

> Now they say that Satan came to Áedán and told him where the vat was, so that it was taken by him to his own store-room, and there was not a penny of it lacking.

The Scottish king resolved to use some of this wealth to procure the death of Cano. Men were sent to Ireland with a bag of silver, which was then counted (there is a parallel here with the 30 pieces of silver offered to Judas in return for betraying Jesus), but Cano was forewarned by a young woman who had fallen in love with him. He sent the Scotsmen home, declaring: 'If it is destined for me, I shall be the one to use this silver.'

Cano won the absolute devotion of a married woman who had loved him before he ever came to Ireland (her name – Créd – appears to derive from *credo* or 'creed'). He presented Créd with his 'stone of life', which contained his soul, vowing that he would come back for her when he became king. Cano returned to Scotland to claim the kingship, but his every attempt to meet up with Créd again was thwarted. Créd finally killed herself, breaking Cano's life-stone in the process. Cano allegedly died nine days later in Scotland.

This legend has much to tell us. Its main interest for the present is the 'vat of gold and silver' which Gartnait buried on the seashore when his son was born, and which was later seized by his father Áedán, the historical King of the Scots.

We should be familiar by now with cauldrons of gold and/or silver and priceless vats which provoke bloodshed. So it should not have gone unnoticed that Sir Uallabh son of Horn spent a night under a cauldron inside a cave on 'the remote island' before he slew a 'great giant'.

Similarly, the story of Cano son of Gartnait tells of an island on which a 'vat of gold and silver' is buried. This isle is called *Inis Moccu Chéin* – 'Island of the Son of Cian' (the Old Irish *cían* or *cén* – 'long time' – compares with *cenn*, the Old Irish word for a 'head' or a 'chief'; a by-form of *cían* being *céin*: 'remote', 'foreign').

Evidently, a tradition shared between Ireland and the Western Isles of Scotland linked a hidden cauldron or vat of gold and silver with a 'remote island' which was also a royal residence.

The Anglo-Norman romances of 'Horn' and 'King Horn' also involved Ireland, as did the French *Sone de Nausay* romance, with its sacred horn.

And both Arthur (in *Culhwch and Olwen*) and Brân the Blessed (in *Manawydan son of Llyr*) went on cauldron-related expeditions to Ireland.

THE BLESSED ISLE

The Welsh Triads inform us that Arthur was 'wounded to death' at the Battle of Camlann:

> And from that he died, and was buried in a hall on the Island of Afallach.

Another triad recalls that the first of the 'Three Perpetual Harmonies of the Island of Britain' was 'at the Island of Afallach', which had apparently become a prominent Christian centre.

The root of 'Afallach' is the Welsh word *afal*, an 'apple' (Old Irish *aball*, Gaulish *avallo*). The Gaelic *abhall* – pronounced 'av-ull' – can signify an 'orchard', an 'apple-tree' or a 'chieftain', while *ubhalach* means 'apple-bearing' and is cognate with Afallach. The Welsh *afallen* also denotes an 'apple-tree' and is probably the etymological origin of 'Avalon', as well as being the title of a poem attributed to Myrddin Wyllt ('Merlin').

That the Island of Afallach was an 'apple-bearing' isle was seemingly confirmed by the 12th-century churchman, Geoffrey of Monmouth. In his *Vita Merlini* (*c* 1150) Geoffrey staged a summit meeting involving Taliesin, the 6th-century Chief Bard of Britain, and Myrddin, the prophet who 'went mad' at a battle in North Britain in about 573.

It is Taliesin who, in Geoffrey's *Life of Merlin*, provides a description of the Island of Apples (*Insula Pomorum*), which was also known as 'Fortunate' because:

> It produces crops in abundance and grapes without help; and apple trees spring up from the short grass in its woods ...
>
> That is the place where nine sisters exercise a kindly rule over those who come to them from our land. The one who is first among them has greater skill in learning, as her beauty surpasses that of her sisters. Her name is Morgen ...

Taliesin reports that 'It was there we took Arthur after the battle of Camlan, where he had been wounded.'

The leader of the 'nine sisters', incidentally, reappears in the Triads as a 'daughter of Afallach' who was also the mother ('Modron') of the Arthurian hero, Owain son of Urien.

Geoffrey's word-portrait of the Island of Apples, which he put into Taliesin's mouth, was drawn from an earlier account. St Isidore of Seville, who lived from about 560 to 636, commented in his encyclopaedic *Etymologiae* on the 'Isles of the Fortunate' which were 'happy and blessed in the abundance of their fruits':

> Pagan error and the songs of the secular poets have held these islands to be Paradise because of the fecundity of the soil.

These islands were situated in the Atlantic Ocean, 'very near the west'.

The traditions surrounding the Fortunate isles went back a long way indeed. Plutarch (*c* 46-120) referred to the 'Isles of the Blessed' which abounded in 'fruit and birds of every kind' – 'The islands are said to be two in number, separated by a very narrow strait, and lie 10,000 furlongs [roughly 1,250 miles] from Africa.' So delightful were these islands that 'a firm belief has made its way, even to the barbarians, that here are the Elysian Fields and the abode of the Blessed of which Homer sang.'

Plutarch also described the islands off the coast of Britain:

> The natives have a story that in one of these, Kronos has been confined by Zeus, but that he, having a son for a jailer, is left sovereign lord of these Islands, and of the sea, which is called the Gulf of Kronos.

Kronos, a god of fertility and the harvest, had been overthrown and castrated by his son Zeus, the chief god of Ancient Greece.

The lyric poet Pindar (*c* 522-443 BC) had previously indicated that those individuals who kept their souls clean and pure were

> ... led by Zeus at the end –
> To the palace of Kronos,
> Where soothing breezes off the Ocean
> Breathe over the Isle of the Blessed.

Emain Ablach

Irish tradition also spoke of the wondrous islands which lay to the north of Ireland. Principal among these was Emain Ablach (Middle Irish *Emhain Abhlach*), which preserved the sense of 'apple-bearing'.

The word 'Emain' can be derived from the Old Irish *main*, 'goods' or 'hoarded wealth', which came to signify 'cultivated land' (Scots *Mains*, a 'farm'; Gaelic *mànas*) and a 'place' (Welsh *man*, Gaelic *ionad*). Emain Ablach would therefore have been 'The Apple-Bearing Place' or 'The Garden of Apples'.

It was said to have been the abode of Manannán mac Lir, the Hebridean sea-god whose British equivalent, Manawydan, was the brother of Brân the Blessed and one of the few survivors of Brân's battle with the Irish king Matholwch ('Prayer-sort').

The 8th-century *Voyage of Bran* recounted the marvels of Emain Ablach at great length. The hero, Bran, was walking in Ireland one day when he was lulled to sleep by enchanting music. He awoke to find a silver branch lying by his side. Bran took this silver branch back to his stronghold, where a beautiful woman sang to him of the 'distant isle / Around which sea-horses glisten ...

> An ancient tree there is with blossoms,
> On which birds call the canonical Hours ...

Bran set out to find this magical island, receiving directions from Manannán mac Lir. The isle was inhabited by women. Their chief threw out a ball of sticky thread to draw the mariners ashore. Bran and his companions were royally entertained on Emain Ablach for many years and lost all track of time.

The *Voyage of Bran* was later rewritten as the *Voyage of St Brendan*, a Christianised account of a legendary seven-year quest for *Tír Tairngire*, the 'Land of Promise'.

The historical St Brendan was a contemporary and former schoolfellow of Columba, the saint who founded his church on the tiny Scottish island of Iona; the likelihood that Iona was *Tír Tairngire* is entertained in an old Irish poem which describes a meeting of St Columba with the son of Manannán and reveals that Columba came 'from the flock-rich Land of Promise'.

Yet another retelling of the *Voyage of Bran* appears in the form of the *Voyage of Máel Dúin*. Again, the travellers sail north from Ireland and are welcomed on an Island of Women – but when the time comes for Máel Dúin and his companions to leave, they are held back by a clew of sticky thread cast by the 'noble mother' of the island's maidens.

We have encountered something like this 'sticky thread' before. The Selk'nam shamans of Patagonia believed that their lower souls could leave their bodies while remaining attached by a 'thread made of gum'. The *kahuna* of Polynesia likewise thought of their low selves as *unihipili*, from a root word meaning 'sticky'.

The ball or 'clew' of sticky thread which was thrown out by

the leader of the Island of Women to attract voyagers to her isle and keep them there was surely similar to the 'sticky' substance of the low self. In other words, the 'noble mother' – named Morgen in Geoffrey of Monmouth's account – was able to project her 'semi-physical' vehicle of vitality out towards the men who approached her apple-isle, luring their souls into her net of subtle energy.

Which brings us back to the *Scéla Cano meic Gartnáin*. There we find that the eldest son of Áedán mac Gabráin, a 6th-century king of the Scots, lived comfortably on an island – 'on his flock-bed, drinking mead' – until the birth of his son upset the applecart. According to the story of Cano, Gartnait son of Áedán had fifty fishing nets, each attached to a rope, with a bell on each rope, so that whenever a fish was caught a bell would ring.

Lugh Long-Hand

It seems reasonable to suppose that Gartnait's fifty fishing nets were comparable with the 'etheric "web"' or 'etheric "net"' described by Serge King in his account of the *kahuna* of Hawaii (Nicolson: *Shamanism*, page 193).

'In the web concept,' wrote King, 'the shaman sees himself as a spider at the centre of a three-dimensional web stretching out in all directions to every part of the universe. Like a spider, he can be aware of vibrations of activity anywhere along the web ...

'In the net concept, the shaman sees himself as a weaver and a fisherman, able to weave and cast nets in order to capture ideas and events, symbolised by fish.'

Irish tradition recalled both an Island of Women, where a sticky thread was extruded by the 'noble mother' to bring men to the isle, and a royal island on which the eldest son of the Scottish king wove and cast his fishing nets. These islands compare with 'the remote island' upon which Arthur's nephew, Sir Uallabh son of Horn, slept under a cauldron in a cavern and slew a great giant.

Geoffrey of Monmouth thought of it as the 'Island of Apples', taking his description of its fecundity from St Isidore's 'Isles of the Fortunate', which in turn borrowed from the accounts of the Blessed Isles given by Plutarch and Pindar.

The Welsh Triads called it the 'Island of Afallach' – which was none other than Emain Ablach, the mystical 'apple-bearing' isle where Manannán mac Lir lived and to which Bran sailed:

Without grief, without sorrow, without death,
Without any sickness, without debility,
That is the sign of Emain ...

In *Scéla Cano*, the isle is called Inis Moccu Chéin, the 'Island of the Son of Cian'. Another Irish legend tells of Lugh Long-Hand's determination to avenge the destruction which had been wreaked on the land of Bodb Derg, the son of the cauldron-owning Dagda. Three men promised to assist Lugh, including his own father, Cian. But Cian was soon cornered by his enemies. Cian disguised himself as a pig, but the ruse was spotted and he was slain by the Sons of Tuirenn (Irish *tuireann* – 'spark from an anvil').

Lugh demanded that the killers pay a fine. He required them to undertake a series of challenges akin to those faced by Arthur and his heroes in *Culhwch and Olwen*. The first of these tasks was to fetch 'three apples from the Garden in the East of the World' (see endnote).

These apples 'are the colour of burned gold, and they are the size of the head of a child a month old, and there is the taste of honey on them, and they do not leave the pain of wounds or the vexation of sickness on anyone that eats them.'

The only help that Lugh would allow his father's killers was the loan of Manannán's boat.

Their task was made harder by the fact that 'the king's champions and the fighting men of the country are always guarding it [the garden of apple-trees], and the king himself is chief over them.'

The Sons of Tuirenn succeeded in stealing three golden apples by turning themselves into hawks, although they were scorched by flashes of lightning directed at them by the king's 'wise, crafty daughters'.

If Lugh Long-Hand was the son of Cian – as the *Fate of the Children of Tuirenn* discloses – then the 'Island of the Son of Cian', on which Gartnait son of Áedán buried his vat of gold and silver, was actually Lugh's island.

Lugh's associations with Manannán mac Lir (he rides Manannán's horse and lends Manannán's coracle to Cian's murderers) suggest that the island was in fact Emain Ablach – the 'Apple-Bearing Place' – which was also the Island of Afallach, where Arthur was buried.

AXIS MUNDI

There is a further connection between Lugh and Emain Ablach.

Raghnall son of Somerled was a Norse king of the Western Isles who died in 1229, at the height of the European Grail craze. A Gaelic poem written in praise of Raghnall included the lines:

> Emhain Abhlach of the yews,
> Glossy the appearance of its tree-tops –
> Fresh place of the dark blackthorn,
> Where Lugh the poet's son was raised.

The poem exalted the 'fruitful place, the *sídh* [burial mound] of Emhain' as a 'fort finer than all dwellings, where bright apple-trees abound ...'

> Fair the place of the man of the mound
> Who has drunk the honey's liquor:
> To go to the burial cairn, the fair *sídh*,

Is to go to the fine mead-fort.

Better 'for honey and mirth', sang the poet, 'was Lir mac Midhir's Emhain.' Even as late as the 13th century, Emain Ablach was associated with a hero named Lir (Welsh *Llyr* – 'Sea') and with Lugh, the gifted son of Cian.

Raghnall son of Somerled built a Benedictine monastery on the Isle of Iona in 1203, although the clergy of Northern Ireland tore it down. He also founded a nunnery on Iona, installing his sister as its first prioress. It was this, perhaps, that upset the churchmen of Ulster.

Traditionally, women had been banished from the Isle of Iona to the adjacent islet of *Eilean nam Ban* ('Island of the Women'). By establishing a nunnery, the pink granite ruins of which still stand above the main village on Iona, Raghnall was reawakening the memory of a time when Iona was *Í nam ban bòidheach* – 'Iona of the beautiful women'.

Raghnall's maritime kingdom was centred on the Isle of Man. The poet who sang his praises noted that Emain Ablach was 'without lie Man's Tara' and therefore the sacred centre of Raghnall's realm. It would be wrong, though, to assume that Emain Ablach was the Isle of Man: the poem indicates that Emain lay closer to 'Mull's harbour' and 'Mull's ploughed field'.

The 'noble brood of Sadhbh,' sang Raghnall's poet, 'are Emhain's green-branched apples.' In Irish mythology, Sadb was the daughter of Bodb Derg ('Red Crow'), the son of the Dagda of the marvellous cauldron.

A 14th-century Irish poem also referred to Emain Ablach as 'the comparable capital' (*an chinnlitir chomhardnach*) of Tara, the seat of the High Kings of Ireland.

Emain was the insular equivalent of the Irish Hill of Tara, which would imply that it was a coronation site and a seat of kingship. Further evidence for this was provided by the Scottish historian Hector Boece, who made reference in 1527 to *Evonium* –

a Latinised version of 'Emhain' – which he described as the seat of 40 kings of the Scots.

The 'lost' city of *Evonium* was surely Emain Ablach, the 'apple-bearing' place. The Britons thought of it as the Island of Afallach, where Arthur was buried.

Today, we know it as Iona (see endnote), the burial place of no fewer than '48 crowned Scots Kings', 'four Ireland Kings', eight 'Kings of Norway' and 'the most part of the Lords of the Isles, with their lineages', as Donald Munro, Archdeacon of the Isles, reported in 1549.

The Hebridean island of Iona is just three-and-a-half miles long and a mile or so wide. It is separated from Mull, its larger neighbour, by a narrow sea channel. To the north-west lies Tiree, the island where, in 1863, Rev. Campbell transcribed the 'Saga of Sir Wiseman son of Horn'.

Kings and champions were ferried from the Scottish coast to the Isle of Iona for burial because, in Donald Munro's words, 'it was the most honourable and ancient place that was in Scotland in their days.'

Ioua insula

One historical king who was crowned on Iona was Áedán mac Gabráin, the father of Gartnait and grandfather of Cano. Áedán's reign began in AD 574, when he was ceremonially 'ordained' by St Columba.

Columba had arrived on Iona in 563, having been banished from his native Ireland for raising an army against the (pagan) High King. Two years after he established his mission on Iona, Columba visited Áedán's brother-in-law, Bruide, King of the Picts. The saint took with him a young man named Drostán who, according to some accounts, was related to Áedán mac Gabráin.

The name Drostán was originally Pictish – 'Drust' – but the Scots added their familiar suffix *–án* ('little'). To British ears, this sounded like 'Drystan'. Continental romancers later rendered it

'Tristan'.

St Columba's choice of Iona for his ecclesiastical base was no random act. Like many a pagan site, the island was adopted by the Church and its history completely rewritten. It became *I Chaluim-chille,* the 'Isle of Columba of the church'. But something of its remarkable past can still be divined.

An account of the ordination of King Áedán was given in the *Life of Columba,* written by Adomnán, ninth abbot of Iona, in about 697.

Adomnán referred to Iona as the 'Iouan' island, *Ioua insula,* the root of which would appear to have been *Ivo* – the 'yew'. Iona was the 'Yewy' isle. This squares with the early names for Iona (*Eo, Io*) and Columba's insistence that the island be called *Í,* the Gaelic letter styled after *iubhar* ('yew-tree') – *í* also being the genitive form of the Irish *eo,* 'yew'.

But as N.J.A. Williams of the Department of Modern Irish, University College, Dublin, has observed: '*Eo* in Irish seems to have meant "large (sacred?) tree" as much as "yew".' Iona, then, was the 'Isle of the Sacred Tree(s)'.

Irish tradition speaks of five 'magical' trees, recalling Taliesin's remark about the 'cauldron of five-trees' (*peir pumwyd*) and the 'drunk-making mead-horns' which brought the 'Druidic gift' to the 'dragon' or 'leader'. These five trees were said to have been a yew, an oak, and three ash trees.

The yew is implicit in the early names for Iona. The oak, meanwhile, was the Druidic tree *par excellence*. The word 'Druid' appears to derive from 'oak' (Proto-Indo-European **deru-*) and to have meant something like 'oak-knower' or 'oak-seer'.

The oak hosts two fascinating parasites: the mistletoe, a Druidic 'cure-all', and the oak-apple or gall from which iron-gall ink was made. These 'golden' apples (the oak gall is *afal* – 'apple' – in Welsh), and especially their ink, facilitated the transition from the Divine age – in which writing was a secret/sacred art – to the Heroic age of Scripture.

St Columba held the oak to be sacred, routinely founding his monasteries in oak groves and praising the little gall wasps whose eggs formed the precious ink-yielding 'apples'. He established his Christian settlement on Iona between the Hill of the Oak (*Cnoc Daraich*) and Cian's Well (*Tobar Cheathain*) – Cian being the father of the Lugh Long-Hand who was associated with Emain 'of the apples'.

On the opposite, west-facing coast of Iona stands the rocky Hill-Fort of Manannán (*Dùn Mhanannáin*), south of which lies the Gully of Little-Bran's Man-Servant, *Sloc 'ille Bhranáin*. The 'palace' of Manannán was in Emain Ablach, which is why he was able to give Bran the Voyager directions to the island.

The Britons remembered that Brân the Blessed had been sitting on a rock overlooking the sea with his brother Manawydan (Manannán's Welsh counterpart) when they saw the ships of Matholwch, king of Ireland, approaching.

And it was Manannán's boat which Lugh loaned to the killers of his father, Cian, so that they might steal three golden apples from the 'garden' guarded by the king and his champions.

The World-Tree

The third 'magical' tree was the ash, which seemingly accounted for three of the 'five-trees' of Taliesin's cauldron.

To the Ancient Greeks, the ash was *melías*. It secretes a sugary substance which the Greeks thought of as 'honey' (*melí*). They believed that when Zeus castrated his father Kronos, the nymphs known as Meliai were born. These nymphs were said to have fed the infant Zeus with the 'honey' or 'manna' of the ash tree.

The Norsemen, who ruled the Western Isles in the Middle Ages, fermented this sugary extract and called it the 'Mead of Inspiration'.

The Gaelic and Welsh words for the 'ash' (*uinnse* and *onnen*) derive from the Old Celtic *onnâ*, which raises the possibility that Iona was *I-onnâ*, the 'Ash-isle'. Certainly, the letter 'n' in the

Gaelic alphabet was styled after *nuin* – 'ash' – which, in its Irish form, *nion* (Old Irish *nin*), signified the alphabet as a whole. It was the tree of letters.

In his poem *Preiddeu Annwn*, Taliesin referred to the 'cauldron of five-trees' as the 'cauldron of the Lord of Annwn'. The term *annwn* appears to have been Taliesin's version of the Gaelic *a' nuin* – 'the ash'. So often misinterpreted as an Otherworld of Celtic fantasy, Annwn is more likely to have been the place of the sacred Ash tree, which Taliesin described elsewhere as the 'honey isle'.

Norse tradition held that the World-Tree was an ash; they called it Yggdrasil (F.R. Schröder suggested that Yggdrasil might have meant 'yew-tree pillar', reminding us that any large sacred tree could be thought of as a 'yew'). The World-Tree was a universal concept, however. It was the *axis mundi*, the pillar or pole which stood at the symbolic centre or birthplace of the Earth and formed an umbilicus connecting the three worlds.

To the Divine age mentality, 'similar' was as good as 'same'. Just as every person had three selves or souls, so the World-Tree existed simultaneously on three different planes.

The roots of the World-Tree reached down into the Underworld. The trunk was manifested in the terrestrial realm, while the branches stretched up towards the Heavens (the Irish word *nion* – 'ash' – also means 'wave' or 'branching', in the sense of having boughs, and anticipates *Nionon*, 'Heaven').

The World-Tree therefore functioned as a symbolic ladder, granting access to the lower realms, occupied by the low souls of the dead, and the celestial realm, inhabited by the higher Souls.

Consequently, the *axis mundi* was a kind of metaphor for the human body – specifically, the spinal column. The Ancient Greeks believed that the first men were made from the ash, and at the base of the spine we find the *os sacrum* or 'sacred bone', **os-* also being the Proto-Indo-European root word for the 'ash'.

The lower part of the World-Tree existed in the netherworld of the 'semi-physical' vehicle of vitality and the jealous 'hinderers' of Hades, signified by the five *lumbar* bones (from the Latin for 'loins'); the trunk was comparable with the heart, the seat of the ego-self, and the 12 *thoracic* vertebrae (from the Greek for a 'breastplate'), while the branches extended up towards the Paradise of the 'super-physical' Soul Body, represented by the seven *cervical* bones (from the Latin for 'neck').

It was the task of the shaman to venture up and down the World-Tree in order to visit the dead (below) and the gods (above). The Renaissance philosopher Giovanni Pico della Mirandola considered this to be the essential role of the magician – to 'wed earth to heaven' and join 'lower things to the endowments and powers of higher things'.

The best place for such a connection to be made would be the site of the World-Tree, where the shaman's spine met its match in the *axis mundi*.

THE SERPENT

The World-Tree can be thought of as a metaphor for Man as the physical bridge between the three worlds (lower, middle, upper) and an image of the spinal column as a 'ladder' connecting the low self (or lumbar region) with the High Self (or cervical region) by way of the middle self (thorax).

As such, it is a perfect example of Divine age thinking: the Tree which grows from the Underworld up to the Heavens is like unto/the same as the Man whose spine stretches between the 'low' realm of *unihipili* and the 'High' plane of *Aumakua*.

The speciality of the shaman in all cultures was to ascend or descend the World-Tree/spinal column, and the practice survives in modern yoga, where the subtle energy of *Kundalini* ('coiled') is envisioned as a serpent sleeping at the base of the spine.

The 'serpent power' of Kundalini can be awakened by meditation, rhythmic chanting, breath control and other exercises. With sufficient training the Yogi can unblock the seven chakra centres of the body, allowing this vital energy to rise up the spine. When the Kundalini energy reaches the 'crown' chakra at the top of the head the Yogi experiences the 'awakening of inner knowledge' and a profound sense of 'pure joy, pure knowledge and pure love', which is represented as the union of the goddess Shakti with the Supreme Being, Shiva.

In Human age (i.e. 'scientific') terms, this transcendent state is achieved by controlling the amplitude and frequency of brain waves.

The fastest brain waves oscillate at frequencies in the 30-42 Hertz range. These 'gamma' waves produce alertness and ecstasy and are associated with the frontal lobes of the brain. Thus, the skilled shaman or Yogi learns to direct the serpentine energy of his 'low' self up the spinal column in order to stimulate the frontal lobes, quickening his brain waves until a state of intense consciousness is attained.

It was presumably through such a process that the Buddha achieved enlightenment whilst seated under the Bodhi Tree. Likewise, the Norse god Odin hung for nine days and nights on the World Ash, sacrificing himself to himself in exchange for a higher state, including the gifts of literacy and inspiration.

Just as the spine has the 'serpent power' of Kundalini coiled around its base – the so-called 'root' chakra, *Muladhara* – so the World-Tree comes with its own serpent.

The World Ash of Norse mythology had a 'dragon', Nidhogg Nadar, chewing at its roots. And while Gautama Buddha was meditating under the Bodhi Tree a storm blew up and the serpent king, Mucalinda, rose up from the depths of the earth and enveloped the Buddha in seven coils for seven days.

Apollo slew the monstrous Python at the famous *omphalos* – the 'navel' or World-Centre – at Delphi. In the *Book of Genesis* we read that the Tree of the knowledge of all things ('good and evil'), which grew in the midst of the Garden of Eden, had its resident serpent. There is nothing in the Bible to indicate what the forbidden fruit of this World-Tree was, but it is generally assumed to have been an apple.

The Greek hero Herakles was tasked with stealing three 'golden apples' from the 'Western Maidens' who tended the garden of Hera in the Atlantic Ocean (Hera, the daughter of Kronos, was known to the Romans as *Iuno*, which derives from *iuuen-*, 'youth', 'vitality'; compare Eve, from the Semitic *hyw*, meaning 'to live'). To safeguard her precious golden apples, Hera wound a sleepless, hundred-headed dragon around the tree.

The most familiar of all World-Trees is, of course, the 'Holy Rood' to which Christ was nailed at the 'place of the skull' – although the serpent in this instance is less easy to spot.

The kingship ceremony

The fabled golden apples were as much a source of conflict as the cauldron of rebirth. Women prized the 'golden' oak-apples as a beauty product – they contain a powerful astringent – while the ink they yielded was vital for the reproduction of the Book.

The most coveted galls grew in the 'Garden in the East of the World' or on the 'Fortunate Isle' (Gaelic *I-shona*, the 's' being silent), 'very near the west', which was associated with the goddess Hera (*Iuno*) and her Golden Age father, Kronos.

This 'apple-bearing' garden was known to the Irish as Emain Ablach (Old Irish *main* = Welsh *man* = Gaelic *ionad*), from whence came the 'Island of Afallach', where the wounded Arthur was taken. It lay to the north of Ireland and was the home of Manannán mac Lir, whose *Dùn Mhanannáin* fortress stood on the west coast of Iona.

The island was defended by the king and his champions (Gaelic *drèagan*, 'dragon' or 'champion'). It was the 'Yewy isle' – *Ioua insula* – or the island of 'five-trees', where the World Ash secreted the honey of the Mead of Inspiration, the 'Druidic gift', and where kings and heroes were buried – the Gaelic word for a 'tomb' (*uaigh*, pronounced 'u-ah'; plural *uaighean*) suggesting another possible derivation for *Ioua* as the 'Island of the Grave'.

Kings were also inaugurated on Iona. The account given by Adomnán of Iona of St Columba's ordination of Áedán mac Gabráin as King of the Scots in 574 is unintentionally revealing.

Adomnán was writing from a Christian point-of-view. His subject was Columba – not the ordination of kings. He therefore neglected to mention the cauldron.

Many years later, Gerald of Wales described a kingship ceremony which he claimed to have witnessed in 13th-century Ulster.

First, the new king copulated in public with a white mare. The mare was then sacrificed and its flesh boiled in a cauldron. The king bathed and washed his face in the broth, after which the meat was shared out among the celebrants.

Gerald of Wales is not the most reliable of commentators. He invented a false etymology for Glastonbury in England in order to promote the lie that it was once known as *Inis Avallon*, thereby helping to cement the pernicious myth that 'King Arthur' was buried there with his 'second wife'. His Heroic age ideology tended to refract everything through the prism of its dogmatically religious-aristocratic worldview. But Gerald's account of the ceremony in Ulster must provide some hint of how the Divine age celebrated kingship, and since the Scots were of Irish extraction it offers a glimpse of what might have happened when Áedán was ordained on Iona.

The white mare in Gerald's account would have been a totem animal representing the goddess of the land and its people. The sacred marriage of the king to the land was celebrated – maybe in an act of public copulation – and then the goddess, in her animal form, was sacrificed and consumed.

The result was a sort of pagan Eucharist, a 'Last Supper' which also marked the start of a new reign.

In that regard, the plentiful cauldron of the Dagda or

'All-Father' compares with the communion chalice, and so the medieval monks who converted the original *krater* or *graal* into the cup of Christ's blood were not wholly wrong.

We should recall that it was Áedán's son Gartnait who reputedly buried a precious 'vat of gold and silver' on the 'Island of the Son of Cian' – possibly in the Meadow of the Hidden Treasure (*Liana na h-uilidh*), beside the Haven of the Fishing-Basket (*Port nam Murlach*), immediately adjacent to St Columba's monastic enclosure or 'garden'.

Another omission from Adomnán's account of Áedán's ordination was the sacred stone of kingship.

Stone of Destiny

The site of the World-Tree was the *omphalos* or 'navel' of the world. The Omphalos itself often took the form of a sacred stone (Greek *baetylus*, from which came the Hebrew *Beth-El* or 'House of God').

The Omphalos stone at Delphi in Greece, for example, had a hollow interior. Its outer surface was carved to represent a knotted fishing net. This net 'caught' the visions wafting up from the carcase of the Python which had been slain by Apollo, and so the wisdom of the Underworld was made known through the Oracle.

On Iona, the Omphalos stone was known as the Stone of Destiny or *clach-na-cinneamhain* – 'Stone of the Chief-of-Emain'. It supposedly housed Scota, the ancestral goddess of the Scots, and emitted a raven-like shriek when the true king set foot on it.

"The Omphalos stone, Delphi."

According to Hector Boece, writing in 1527, this 'marble chair, or fatal stone like unto a chair' had accompanied the Scots on their migration from the ancient world: 'wherever it was found would be the kingdom of the Scots.'

John of Fordun, writing in the 14th century, stated that it had been dredged up from the sea off the Irish coast. Andrew of Wyntoun (early 15th century) indicated that it had been brought to Iona ('Icolmkyll') by King Áedán's great-grandfather, Fergus Mór mac Eirc, and Hector Boece seems to have concurred:

> Fergus, son of Ferchard the first king of the Scots in Scotland, moved the chair from Ireland to Argyll, and was crowned in it ... Forty Scottish kings were descended from Fergus. The twelfth king, Evenus, founded the town of *Evonium* ['Emain'] ... The Stone was moved to *Evonium*, where the rest of the forty kings were crowned, reigned, and were buried.

The Scots were expelled to Ireland during the reign of the last of those forty kings, but returned to Scotland under Fergus mac Erc, who was crowned in the marble chair. Fergus founded a church on Iona, and this became the burial place of the Scottish kings.

The Stone was later transferred to Scone when the centre of the Scottish kingdom shifted eastwards. It was stolen by King Edward I in 1296, and for the next 700 years every English monarch was crowned on it in Westminster Abbey.

However, the Stone that was eventually returned to Scotland in 1996 is a crude bloc of red sandstone. It is conceivable that King Edward was fobbed off with a worthless substitute. The original Stone, by all accounts, was marble.

A band of Lewisian marble extends out into the sea from the south-east end of the Isle of Iona; the quarry where it was mined in bygone years can still be visited. Iona marble is distinctive for its green mottling caused by the presence of a mineral known, appropriately, as serpentine.

Although Scottish mythology traces the Stone back to the biblical Bethel, where Jacob dreamt of a Stairway to Heaven, it is more likely that the 'marble chair' was taken from the coast of Iona, becoming the oracular Omphalos and coronation stone of the early Scottish kings.

Áedán mac Gabráin was almost certainly ordained on the Stone of Destiny. But the Stone's associations with Druidic 'devilry' (it was one of the 'treasures' of the Children of Danu, along with the Dagda's Cauldron, the Sword of Nuada and the Spear of Lugh) ensured that it was left out of Adomnán's *Life of Columba*.

One ancient tradition was retained in Adomnán's account. During the ceremony, St Columba prophesied the future.

When asked which of Áedán's sons would succeed him – would it be Artúr, Eochaid Find or Domangart? – Columba replied:

> None of these three shall be king, for they shall fall in battle, slain by enemies.

This is the earliest dateable reference to any individual named Arthur.

6

Into the Cave

My heart aches, and a drowsy numbness pains
My sense, as though of hemlock I had drunk ...
John Keats

THE PREVIOUS chapter opened with a Gaelic proverb, predicting that the 'Isle of Columba the cleric' will still 'float' when its neighbours have vanished beneath the waves, and the disclosure that Iona has long been considered a 'thin' place, where the veil between worlds is unusually permeable.

In this chapter, we shall consider Iona's status as a sacred centre and the role of initiation in the ancient Mystery tradition.

It is unclear why Iona was expected to survive a catastrophic rise in sea-level. But what is beyond doubt is that the isle was one of the first outcrops of land to appear on the planet's surface. Its bedrock is largely composed of Lewisian Gneiss, which solidified more than 2.5 billion years ago. Iona was – to all intents and purposes – the birthplace of the world.

Like his Human age counterpart, the tourist, the Heroic age pilgrim generally saw only what he had come to see. For reasons of survival, though, the Divine age seeker tended to see more; her eyes were trained to read the natural environment in ways ours are not. The notable absence of fossils in the rocks of Iona might have assured her that the island was special. It was primeval, antediluvian – in a word, *Ogygian*.

'Ogygian' (meaning 'primal', 'from the dawn of time') comes from Ogyges, a mythical king of Greece. He survived the 'Ogygian Flood', which Plato dated to around 10,000 years BC, and either he or his sons founded the ancient cities of Eleusis and Thebes.

Ogyges also gave his name to an island: Homer referred to it in his *Odyssey* as 'the island of Ogygia, where is the Navel of the sea'.

Homer's phrase, *Omphalos thallasses*, indicates a World-Navel – a sacred centre on a par with Delphi, except that this one was situated in *Okeanos*, the great river which encircled the world. In other words, the 'Navel of the sea' lay in the Atlantic Ocean.

Plutarch determined that the 'isle Ogygian' was located to the west of Britain, in the 'Gulf of Kronos'. It was therefore equated with the Isle of the Blessed on which Zeus had imprisoned his father, the god of fertility and abundance.

According to legend, Kronos had been forewarned that he would be overthrown by one of his sons, and so he devoured each of them at birth. The mother of Zeus wrapped a stone in swaddling clothes and tricked Kronos into swallowing it in place of her newborn son. This stone was the Omphalos Stone which was later installed at the cult centre of Delphi, in the shadow of Mount Parnassus.

There was a connection, then, between the Greek *omphalos* or 'World-Navel' at Delphi and the Atlantic 'Navel' off the coast of Britain. The one comprised the stone which Kronos had swallowed, believing it to be his son Zeus; the other was the western isle on which Zeus interred his father, setting the hundred-headed Briareos to stand guard over him, the tradition being (in Plutarch's words) that 'sleep is the bond forged for Kronos'.

It was to this 'palace of Kronos,

Where soothing breezes off the Ocean
Breathe over the Isle of the Blessed

that those who had scrupulously honoured their oaths were taken by Zeus 'at the end' – as the poet Pindar wrote in the 5th century BC.

Kronos evidently combined the functions of an agricultural deity and a god of the dead – as did the Egyptian Osiris, amongst others. It was in the latter capacity that Kronos was depicted with a raven, his name – as Robert Graves argued – possibly deriving from *korone*, the Greek word for a 'crow'.

Kalypso

The hero of Homer's *Odyssey* was washed up on the 'island of Ogygia' after he was shipwrecked.

As he made his way home from the Trojan War, Odysseus lost his ship and its crew in a series of misadventures. A beautiful nymph then held him captive on 'the remote island', intending to make Odysseus her immortal consort. Her name, Kalypso, derived from a word meaning to cover or conceal.

Previously, Odysseus had crossed the 'River of Ocean' to the mysterious Grove of Persephone, where he had raised the dead:

> ... unmarried youths, old men who had suffered greatly, once-happy girls with grief fresh in their hearts, and a great throng of warriors killed in battle, their spear-wounds gaping and all their armour stained with blood.

Odysseus had spoken with several unhappy shades, including that of Achilles, who demanded to know how Odysseus dared to 'come below to Hades' realm, where the dead live on as mindless disembodied ghosts?'

This is clearly the underworld of those 'weak and feckless discarnate souls' which we encountered in Chapter 4. It is the Hades described by Dr Robert Crookall in his study of Out-of-the-Body Experiences, where jealous 'hinderers' remain trapped in a dark place, held back by emotional attachments.

Homer's account of the 'Halls of Hades' contrasts sharply with his description of the Ogygian isle, where Odysseus is later held prisoner.

Zeus sends his messenger Hermes to instruct Kalypso, the 'Nymph of the plaited tresses', to release Odysseus. Hermes flies across the sea to 'the remote island' and the 'great cavern where the Nymph of the lovely locks was living.'

Her cave was 'sheltered by a copse of alders and fragrant cypresses', the haunt of 'wide-winged birds ... birds of the coast'. Around the mouth of the cave trailed a 'thriving garden vine'. Four springs poured forth 'crystal rivulets', and 'in soft meadows on either side iris and wild celery flourished'.

Even an 'immortal visitor' must 'pause to gaze in wonder and delight' at such a setting.

Odysseus was spending his nights in the 'vaulted cavern', sleeping with Kalypso. His days, though, were passed 'sitting disconsolately on the shore' and looking out 'with streaming eyes across the watery wilderness.'

Having raised the earthbound spirits from Hades, Odysseus had now graduated to becoming the lover of the queen of the dead (Kalypso) and to sitting on the shore of 'the remote island' which – like the 'remote island' of the Hebridean *Saga of Sir Uallabh son of Horn* – had a 'great cave' on it.

The position of Odysseus, gazing out across the 'Sea of Shadows', as the Atlantic was known, recalls Professor Whitehead's description of 'some substance like granite on a sandy beach near the water's edge'. That is to say, Odysseus was poised between the '"Hades" conditions' of the earthbound spirits and the '"Paradise" conditions' which lay beyond the oceanic 'river'. And there, in his 'accustomed place', he wept for the 'mindless disembodied ghosts' of his comrades and yearned for the Paradise across the waves.

There is a 'vaulted cavern' on the Isle of Iona. It is a large Neolithic chambered cairn known as *Sithean Mór*. This was the '*sídh* of Emain' – the 'fruitful place' of 'bright apple-trees'.

Recent speculation has suggested that certain Norse names for Iona signified an 'Island of the Cave' – in Gaelic, *I-uamha* (pronounced 'ee-oo-va'), which might have been what Adomnán had in mind when he wrote of the *Ioua insula*.

"The great grave or Spirit-Mound of Sithean Mór, *also known as the Hill of Angels, on the west side of the Isle of Iona. The island's only metalled road ends nearby, facing the Atlantic Ocean."*

The *Sithean Mór* burial mound stands on the west side of Iona, between the Hill-Fort of Manannán and the Gully of Little-Bran's Man-Servant. Granite spurs poke out into the Atlantic Ocean from the sandy beach nearby.

One of them, immediately to the west of the 'vaulted cavern', is called *Sgeir na Caoneig* – 'Rock of the Weeper'.

Eo Feasa

Ogyges was an 'aboriginal' who made it through the cataclysmic deluge, thereby preserving the primeval wisdom which would inform the Mystery cult of Eleusis in Greece.

In Irish mythology, the Flood-survivor was called Fintan. His legend, as told in the 11th-century *Lebor Gabála Érenn* ('Book of the Taking of Ireland'), relates that Noah's granddaughter was advised by an idol to escape the deluge in a ship.

She sailed for seven years with three men and 49 women,

finally reaching Ireland. Fintan became responsible for all the women, but he abandoned them. They all perished in the Flood – apart from Fintan, who transformed himself into a salmon and hid in a cave known as Fintan's Grave.

Fintan lived on for many years, acquiring the epithet 'Wise'. He was the original 'Salmon of Knowledge', *Bradan an Eòlais* or *Eo Feasa*. Later Druids thought of themselves as 'salmon' (Old Irish *eó*, Welsh *eog*) and were often described as 'speckled' (Gaelic *breac*, Welsh *brych*), implying that they were tattooed with salmon-like spots.

The legendary Hebridean hero, Fionn mac Cumhail, received the gift of knowledge directly from a salmon – although another legend has him acquiring youthfulness and wisdom by drinking from a golden cup which was kept in a burial mound. Taliesin's initiatory ordeal (see Chapter 3) ended with him being fished out of a salmon-weir.

The Arthurian tale of *Culhwch and Olwen* features the search for an imprisoned youth, during which the heroes consult a series of ancient animals until they come to the eldest and wisest, the Salmon of Llyn Llyw. This Salmon had fifty fishing spears sticking out of its back, recalling the fifty fishing nets tended by Gartnait mac Áedáin, the elder brother of the first 'Arthur' on record, on the royal burial isle of the Scots.

Eo – a name used for Iona until the 9th century – could mean either 'yew' or 'salmon'. Being comfortable with correspondences, the Divine age mind would have recognised the similarities between the oldest of trees and the most ancient of creatures. The common theme is antiquity, that *Ogygian* quality, and given that Iona (*Eo*) is made up of the world's oldest rocks it was reasonable to think of its 'World-Tree' (*eo*) as the home of a Druidic 'Salmon' (*eó*). In fact, a Hill of the Salmon stands in the very centre of the island, its Gaelic name – *Cnoc nam Bradhan Beag* – also suggesting a 'Little Hill of Knowledge' or 'Hillock of Judgement'.

Fintan survived the Flood (by becoming a salmon). So too did Ogyges, whose name was applied to an island off the British coast. Both preserved beliefs from before the 'Ogygian deluge'. That Flood was dated by Plato to the end of the last ice age (around 10,000 years BC) when sea levels rose by as much as 130 metres and Britain was cut off from the Continent.

Julius Caesar remarked that Druidism was 'supposed to have been devised in Britain'. Perhaps the primordial wisdom of Fintan, the first Salmon of Knowledge, had indeed survived the flooding caused by melting glaciers in the now-isolated British Isles.

Alexander of Miletus reported in the 1st century BC that the Druids believed in the 'Pythagorean doctrine ... that the souls of men are immortal'. Caesar likewise noted the Druidic belief that 'the soul does not die and that after death it passes from one body into another'.

The antiquity of this belief might be indicated by the cave-painting at Lascaux which shows a bird-headed shaman lying supine, still alive (penis erect) even though his soul has left his body in the form of a bird.

Predating the 'Ogygian deluge' by at least 5,000 years, the Lascaux image hints at the ancient understanding that the soul can live on outside the body.

OANNES

In Chapter 3 we encountered the Sword of Strange Hangings – the sword which Sir Galahad sailed to a 'lonely' isle to find.

Another adventurer before him had carried the sword to 'a western island, far removed', where he was attacked by a giant. The sword had snapped, although it was later repaired by magical means. It was, then, essentially the same as the sword, designed to break at a critical moment, which was given to Perceval the Welshman in the 'hidden retreat' of the Fisher King and the sword which Peredur of York practised breaking and repairing in *Peredur fab Efrog*.

The sword is described in the *Queste del Saint Graal* (*c* 1230) as having a hilt made of two ribs, 'and each of these was taken from a most unusual beast ...'

> The first belonged to a species of serpent more often found in Caledonia [Scotland] than elsewhere ... The second came from a fish, which is not unduly big and which lives in the river Euphrates and no other.

The first rib renders a man impervious to heat. The second deprives him of his memories of joy and sorrow, allowing him to focus on the task in hand.

There is no obvious connection between an apocryphal Scottish 'serpent' and a mythical Mesopotamian 'fish'. But we know that the 'serpent power' of Kundalini, which is thought to lie coiled at the base of the spine, has its equivalent in the mighty serpent which sleeps among the roots of the World-Tree.

The Yogi or shaman raises the 'serpent power' up through his spine to achieve enlightenment. This discipline, or something like it, might explain why British Druids were described as 'snakes' (Welsh *naddred,* singular *neidr* – 'adder'; *neidrwydd,* 'serpent-presence', being an old Welsh word for a temple). Christian writers certainly referred to pagan priests as 'vipers' with 'three-forked tongues' and claimed that St Patrick banished them all from Ireland, much as St Columba was said to have rid the Isle of Iona of 'serpents'.

If the Scottish 'serpent' was really a Druidic Salmon of Knowledge, then there is an intriguing parallel in Mesopotamian mythology.

Fragmentary tablets dating from the 14th century BC tell of seven sages who passed their antediluvian wisdom on to mankind after the Flood. The first of these was known in Sumer as Adapa, U-An or Uannes – a name rendered in Greek by

Berossus, a Babylonian historian of the 3rd century BC, as 'Oannes'.

Early Mesopotamian literature described the wise men who brought to the people between the Tigris and Euphrates rivers 'all the knowledge that they would ever receive' as 'pure *paradu*-fish'. Their bones were associated with holy shrines.

Oannes himself was depicted as having the head of a fish resting on top of his head, his human body 'covered by the scales and tail of a fish'. He came up from the Persian Gulf every day to teach people the secrets of writing, mathematics and geometry, the arts of city-building and the proper way to conduct rituals, but returned to the ocean at the end of each day 'because he was amphibious'.

The remembrance of some kind of primordial Fish-Man permeated Proto-Indo-European culture. The earliest stone sculptures in Europe were found at Lepenski Vir in Serbia; dating from around 7,000 BC, many of these sandstone figurines are humanoid in form but piscine in nature: they are people with fish-like features.

"Sculpted sandstone heads or 'out-of-place artefacts' from Lepenski Vir, Serbia. (Source: world-archaeology.com)"

Migrating outwards from their East European homelands, the

Indo-European peoples transported their memories of these sea-based pioneers far and wide. Thus, in the ancient Indian *Agnipurana* text, for example, a Divine Fish saves Manu and the seven Richis from the apocalyptic Flood, after which he blesses the survivors with the redeeming and purifying *Matsyapurana* or 'Fish-Legend'.

Ioannes

Writing – one of the arts taught by Oannes – flourished in Sumer, beside the Euphrates. The *Epic of Gilgamesh* (3rd millennium BC) tells of the Sumerian city-building king who tracked down a 'Faraway' survivor of the Flood in an attempt to discover the secret of immortality (the secret lay in a plant which grew under-water; Gilgamesh found the plant but then lost it to a serpent).

Long thought of as the original Garden of Eden, Mesopotamia had something in common with the Isle of Iona. Both featured World-Trees with resident serpents: the one caused the Fall of mankind by introducing the art of writing, for which the golden oak-apples provided ink; the other became the site of a busy *scriptorium*. And the Druidic 'serpents' of Scotland and the Fish-Men of the Euphrates were both associated with the antediluvian wisdom embodied by the Salmon of Knowledge.

The claim has yet to be made that the 'Iouan' isle was named after U-An, or Oannes, the semi-aquatic Mesopotamian sage. A comparable suggestion was put forward in the 18th century, however, when *Ioua* became 'Iona'.

Based in part on the presence of two granite outcrops and a sliver of sand known as John's Island (*Eilean Eoin*), immediately to the east of Iona, and John's Graveyard (*Cladh Iain*) on the east side of Iona itself, the theory went that Iona was *I-Eóin*, the 'Isle of John' – St John, that is, who predicted the coming of a greater prophet than himself and initiated Jesus into his ministry by baptising him at Bethabara, the 'House of the Ford' on the River Jordan, after which Jesus began to recruit his disciples, promising to make them 'fishers of men'.

The Greek name for John – *Ioannes* (Armenian *Hovhannes*) – compares with that of the Mesopotamian Fish-Man, Oannes (Armenian *Hovhannes*), raising the possibility that we are looking at the same tradition.

The folklorist Joseph Campbell noticed the comparison and argued that the baptism ritual practised by John went back as far as the 'God of the House of Water' in the Sumerian city of Eridu.

Oannes brought his wisdom up from the Euphrates; John baptised people in the Jordan. The latter ritual involved a passage through the river from east to west. It took place at the House of the Ford, suggesting that the aim was not so much immersion as transition – replicating the journey of the released 'double' as it makes its way from the '"Hades" conditions' to Paradise through the waters of the *second* death (which is also a rebirth).

This practice had probably originated in a Proto-Indo-European 'Fish' cult, and so the early Church adopted the *Ichthys* symbol of the fish as its secret sign.

The *croix pattée* or Cross of St John, as worn by the Knights Templar, is distinguished by the splayed ends of its arms, *pattée* coming from the French word for an animal's paw. It effectively has eight arms – like the compass rose which indicates the eight cardinal and intermediate directions – and was therefore a symbol of totality; it was also known as the Fishtail or Regeneration Cross, its eight points being related to the symbol for infinity – ∞ – which is also the *Ouroboros* or snake-biting-its-own-tail image of the eternal cycle of death-and-rebirth.

Being 'very near the west', the Isle of Iona stood at the edge of the Sea of Shadows, that oceanic river which the souls of the fortunate dead must cross. Baptism was a preparation for that final journey. But the association with St John does not end there.

The head of John the Baptist was placed on a bloody platter – like the gory head seen by Peredur of York in his uncle's castle, or the head of Brân the Blessed at the 'fair and regal spot overlooking the ocean'.

Blood and water

There was an element of play-acting in the baptism ritual. It signified that the initiate had shed his 'semi-physical' vehicle of vitality in the waters to re-emerge as a 'super-physical' Soul Body, represented in the Bible by the descent of the Spirit in the form of a 'dove' (Hebrew *Yonah*, Latin *Columba*).

But to make contact with the higher realm of the eternal Souls, something more was needed.

The World-Tree was the natural site for the more advanced level of initiation. The biblical location is Mount Calvary (*Calvariae locus* in Latin, *Kraniou topos* in Greek), otherwise Golgotha, the 'place of the skull', where the skull of Adam, the original man and the first farmer, was buried.

Another appropriate place would have been the *Omphalos thallasses* or 'Navel of the sea', that 'remote island' where Kronos, the god of the harvest, was buried.

It was essential that there was an enclosed space nearby in which the initiate could be rested, the chances of surviving a cardiac arrest being greatly increased if the body is kept cool. In the Bible, this was a 'sepulchre, which had been hewn out of a rock'. On Iona, it was *Sithean Mór*, the 'vaulted cavern' or chambered burial mound which the monks of Columba dubbed *Colliculus angelorum* – 'Hill of the Angels'.

Jesus was crucified at Golgotha. A relatively common form of punishment, crucifixion caused an agonisingly long-drawn-out death. But Jesus spent very little time on the Cross. He was crucified in the morning and was dead by mid-afternoon. This amazed Pontius Pilate, who 'marvelled if he were already dead'.

It was possible to survive such a brief crucifixion. Titus Flavius Josephus, a 1st-century historian born in Jerusalem, recalled that three men of his acquaintance had been crucified but, at his request, were 'taken down' to receive care – 'yet two of them died under the physician's hands, while the third recovered.'

Two men were crucified alongside Jesus. The *Gospel of John* states that soldiers broke the legs of the others to hasten their demise but that Jesus' legs were not broken because he was already dead.

The cause of his death is hinted at in *John* 19:

> Now there was set a vessel full of vinegar: and they filled a sponge with the vinegar, and put it upon hyssop, and put it to his mouth.
>
> When Jesus therefore had received the vinegar, he said, It is finished: and he bowed his head, and gave up the ghost.

Luke also mentions the vinegar. The *Gospel of Mark* indicates that Jesus was offered 'wine mingled with myrrh, but he received it not'; he later drank vinegar from a sponge and 'gave up the ghost'.

Matthew explains – 'They gave him vinegar to drink, mingled with gall: and when he had tasted thereof he would not drink', although Jesus did eventually drink the vinegar from a sponge.

Vinegar is a stimulant. And yet it seems to have had the opposite effect on Jesus: he drank it and 'gave up the ghost'.

Then something very odd happened. According to *John*, 'one of the soldiers with a spear pierced his side, and forthwith came thereout blood and water.'

The other Gospels only mention a Centurion in the vicinity. The wound to Christ's side, however, became the standard medieval explanation for the blood-dripping spear of the Grail tradition.

The issue of blood and water was taken as proof that Jesus had died.

But corpses do not spout water.

It was not just vinegar that Jesus was offered. *John* refers to 'hyssop'. *Mark* has 'wine mingled with myrrh'. *Matthew* suggests a concoction of vinegar 'mingled with gall'. The Hebrew word used in the latter instance is *rosh*.

Elsewhere in the Bible, *rosh* is usually translated as 'hemlock'.

THE SPEAR

Hemlock – *Conium maculatum* – contains a number of pyridine alkaloids, including a nicotine-like neurotoxin, coniine, which disrupts the workings of the nervous system. It was used in Ancient Greece to poison condemned prisoners.

The philosopher Socrates was given an infusion of hemlock after he was sentenced to death in 399 BC. Plato described the death of Socrates in *Phaedro,* his treatise on the immortality of the soul.

Socrates lay down when his legs began to grow heavy. His jailer pinched his feet, asking him if he could feel that. Socrates said 'No'. The paralysis moved up his thighs towards the groin. The jailer told him that when the 'chill' reached his heart, 'he would be gone'.

The coniine in hemlock blocks the neuromuscular junction. As few as five seeds mixed with alcohol are enough to prove fatal. The respiratory muscles become paralysed. Only artificial respiration can keep the victim alive long enough for the effects of the coniine to wear off, 48-72 hours later.

The Gospels reveal that Jesus drank vinegar (soured wine) mingled with a bitter substance – 'gall' or hemlock – and then 'gave up the ghost'.

Christ's side was then pierced by a spear. A similar fate befell Llew Skilful Hand in the Welsh tale of *Math son of Mathonwy*. Llew was struck by a poisoned spear 'which smote him in the side'. He 'flew up in the form of an eagle' and was later found perched among the upper branches of an oak or World-Tree.

Llew received his name when his mother saw him striking a

wren 'between the sinew of its leg and the bone'. The Welsh word for a 'wren' – *dryw* – was also the word for a 'seer', and so the leg-wound dealt by Llew Skilful Hand was possibly part of the ritual initiation of a prophetic bard.

Brân the Blessed was fatally wounded – in the foot – by a poisoned spear. His nickname, *Morddwyd Tyllion* ('Pierced Thighs'), suggests however that he too had previously been 'pierced' as part of some initiatory ritual.

Arthur likewise sustained an initiatory leg-wound, as we shall soon discover.

The wound which Llew Skilful Hand inflicted on the little 'wren' or seer was surgically precise: 'between the sinew of its leg and the bone'. It would appear that the spear-point had entered the flesh beside the tendon of the popliteus muscle, puncturing one of the five or six oval-shaped lymph nodes embedded in the fatty tissue at the back of the knee.

The word 'lymph' comes from Lympha, a Roman goddess of fresh water who was associated with Fons ('Source'), the god of springs and fountains, and with healing, inspiration and divine frenzy (Latin *lympho, lymphare* – to become crazy). To see a vision of a water-goddess was to become 'Nymph-possessed' (Greek *numpholêptoi*), which was rendered in Latin as *lymphatici*.

Lymph is, of course, the watery substance which flows through the lymphatic system. It is related to blood, in that it carries recycled blood plasma back to the heart, and it contains white blood cells ('lymphocytes'). These cells attack pathogens which have entered the body. The increase of immune system cells fighting the infection from the intruding pathogens causes the body's lymph nodes to expand and become swollen.

A puncture wound to a swollen lymph node would release both blood and 'water' (lymph). Jesus was reputedly pierced 'in the side', which implies a wound to the inguinal lymph nodes at the top of the thigh and in the groin area. The piercing of the leg by Llew Skilful Hand, meanwhile, suggests a wound to the popliteal lymph nodes behind the knee-joint.

Either way, rupturing the lower lymph nodes would drain some of the poisonous pathogens which had been ingested in the sour-wine-and-hemlock infusion out of the bloodstream.

The healing wound

If the chthonic serpent coils around the World-Tree, where was the snake at the Crucifixion?

The answer must be: *in the body of Jesus himself.*

It was the 'serpent power' which was raised up his spine to achieve transcendence.

Poison hemlock works from the feet upwards, paralysing the muscles and eventually depriving the victim of the power of speech (the cauldron, we remember, paralysed its initiates and prevented them from speaking). Piercing the lymph nodes in the knee or upper thigh would partially arrest the progress of the neurotoxins before they reached the heart. Blood and water would flow from the wound, indicating that the initiate had 'died'.

Indeed, a kind of death had taken place. The coniine in the bloodstream produced a nicotine-like 'head rush' akin to the surge of vital energy up the spine towards the 'heavenly doors' at the top of the head. The initiate lost consciousness ('gave up the ghost').

The effects of the coniine would last for 2 to 3 days. It was during this period that Jesus descended into 'Hades' ('And the graves were opened; and many bodies of the saints which slept, arose' – *Matthew* 27), the ultimate aim being for the released 'double' to attain the 'Paradise' state of the Soul Body ('And it came to pass, while he blessed them, he was parted from them, and carried up into heaven' – *Luke* 24).

As we have seen, several groups – Muslims, Cathars, Templars, etc. – repudiated the Crucifixion, some even holding the Cross in contempt. They might have considered the crucifix irrelevant: it was not the cross that killed Christ, but the 'vinegar ... mingled with gall'.

The early Church was rather embarrassed by this. Origen, writing in AD 248, referred to an officiating priest of Athens who took hemlock to 'restrain his passions within the limits prescribed by himself' and to 'check them at their seat' – 'and thus he was accounted pure'. But Christians, Origen insisted, had 'no need of hemlock to fit them for the pure service of God', their faith being quite sufficient for the task (*Contra Celsum* 48).

John Chrysostom (late 4th century) wrote in one of his *Homilies* that the Crucifixion trumped every alternative form of knowledge. Others had preached the soul's immortality, but none of them mattered:

> But among them also, it will be said, many have been found contemners of death. Tell me who? Was it he who drank the hemlock?

Chrysostom declined to name Socrates. He did, however, insist that the Greek philosopher had no choice in the matter: 'he drank when he was not at liberty to drink or not to drink'. Only Christian martyrs *elected* to suffer. Everyone else took the easy way out, whether they meant to or not.

The reasoning was disingenuous, but it had its purpose, which was to proclaim that only one individual had ever hung on the World-Tree. Only one person had died and been resurrected, and only His followers chose torment and death of their own free will.

By taking the hemlock, Jesus had ensured that nobody else had to. Such, at least, was the position of the Church, which would not tolerate any repetition of the ritual.

That it was a ritual is implicit in the Bible. There was 'a vessel full of vinegar' close by. A substance – probably hemlock – was mixed with the wine and administered to Jesus.

In other words, the ritual involved a mixing bowl or *krater* which, like the Grail, dispensed a 'liquor of science and inspiration' infused from 'blended seeds'.

As this potion took effect, the swollen lymph nodes of the leg were carefully pierced. Blood and water flowed. And after three days of intensive care in a rocky 'sepulchre' or 'vaulted cavern', the initiate was 'reborn'.

Bron Trogain

In the town of Ruthin, North Wales stands a boulder known as Maen Huail. The local legend goes that Arthur and Huail were rivals (Huail son of Caw being one of the three 'Royal Knights' of Arthur's Court). The two men fought when Huail tried to seduce one of Arthur's mistresses. Arthur was wounded in the knee. He later took his revenge by beheading Huail on the stone which bears his name.

Garbled though it is, this folktale recalls an initiatory rite. Arthur drank from the poisoned chalice – the Horn of Brân or 'Cup-of-inspiration' – and his lymph nodes were pierced. Three days of seclusion followed (the Triads indicate that Arthur underwent three such 'imprisonments') while his body recovered. Meanwhile, his soul was exploring the lower and upper worlds of 'Hades' and 'Paradise'.

There is further evidence that Arthur belonged to a Mystery cult predicated on the soul's journey after death.

Let us remind ourselves that Brân the Blessed and Llew Skilful Hand were both wounded by poisoned spears. Brân lived on in Arthurian romance, his name evolving through 'Brons' to become the Grail knight known as 'Bors'. He also appears in Irish legend as the traveller who found the 'apple-bearing' island of Manannán mac Lir (who, in British legend, was the brother of Brân). One form of his name – 'Bron' – derives from the Gaelic *bròn*, meaning 'sorrow' or 'grief'.

The *Acallam na Senórach* ('Colloquy of the Ancients') is a

Middle Irish poem which dates from the latter part of the 12th century, when the Grail romances were beginning to proliferate. During the course of the poem we learn that a major festival was called *Bron Trogain – trogan* being an Irish word for a 'raven'.

The festival fell on 1 August, 'the first day of the Trogan-month'. The same verse in the *Acallam na Senórach* states that the festival had a new title: *Lughnasadh*. The 'Sorrow of the Raven' was also the 'Gathering of Lugh', an occasion which involved sporting competitions and the sacrifice of a bull.

Lugh is often portrayed as an Apollo-type figure. Apollo the Sun-god sent a raven to bring a cup (*krater*) of water to a banquet held by Jupiter (Zeus); he was also said to have delivered his prophecies via the raven and to have appeared in raven-form. Both Lugh and Apollo therefore compare with Brân, the 'blessed Raven' whose magical drinking horn became one of the Treasures of Britain.

It is surely significant that when St Columba was banished from Ireland for having rebelled against his High-King he griped about sailing to 'Alba [Scotland] of the ravens'.

Lugh was also associated with a spear known as 'Slaughterer' or the 'famous yew of the wood'. It was rumoured to have belonged to Pisear, 'King of Persia', and its point had to be kept in water or else it would burst into flames. Lugh's spear was in fact one of the 'treasures' of the *Tuatha dé Danann*; it resurfaced in the Grail legends as the blood-letting spear which wounds and heals.

The name 'Lugh' relates to the Old Irish *luige*, an 'oath' (Welsh *llw*). The Britons rendered the name as Lleu ('Light'), Llyw ('Leader', 'Governor') and Llew ('Lion'). The latter converts back into Early Irish as *Léu* or *Léo* (Gaelic *leóghann* or *leómhann*, pronounced 'li-oh-vun').

We might also note that the Gaelic *leòn* – a 'wound' or 'grief' – compares with *bròn* ('sorrow') and anticipates the 'Pierced Thighs' nickname for Brân in Welsh: *Morddwyd Tyllion*. *Lion* –

'lee-un' – in Gaelic can signify a 'fishing-net'; *llion* – 'lyunn' – means 'liquor'.

Lugh Long-Hand and Llew Skilful Hand were, respectively, the Irish and British names for the same person. Equally, Brân and Bron were two designations for the selfsame individual.

One was 'Lion', the other 'Raven'.

MITHRAS

Raven and Lion were two of the initiatory grades in the Mysteries of Mithras.

These Mysteries had originated in Persia, around the headwaters of the Euphrates, several millennia BC, with a god known as Mithra. The Persian Mithra compares with Mitra, a god praised in the Sanskrit *Rig Veda* ('Mitra ... makes men organise themselves ... Mitra observes ... human establishments') whose name meant 'Friend' or 'Friendship'.

In fact, the Indo-Iranian word *mitra* appears to have signified a 'contract' or 'agreement'. Mithra was indeed a god of oaths and covenants. His initiates were known as *syndexioi*: 'united by the handshake'.

The cult of Mithra spread through Mesopotamia into Anatolia (modern Turkey) and thence throughout the Mediterranean, the Ancient Greeks altering his name to Mithras. By the 2nd century AD, his Mysteries were celebrated across the Roman Empire. Inscriptions in many parts of the Roman world honoured *deo Soli invicti Mithrae* – 'god of the unconquered Sun, Mithras' – and in some places he was revered as 'Apollo-Mithras-Helios', a sort of composite solar super-deity.

He was said to have been born from a rock, from which he later drew water, and so depictions of his birth often showed a two-handled water vessel on standby. In remembrance of his rock-birth, Mithraists met in natural or artificial caves. Each of these caverns or cellars was thought of as a microcosm representing the universe in miniature.

Porphyry, writing his *De antro nympharum* ('Cave of the Nymphs') in the 3rd century AD, described the Mithraic cave:

> Similarly, the Persians [Mithraists] call the place a cave where they introduce an initiate to the mysteries, revealing to him the path by which souls descend and go back again. For Eubulus tells us that Zoroaster was the first to dedicate a natural cave in honour of Mithras, the creator and father of all. This cave bore for him the image of the cosmos which Mithras had created, and the things which the cave contained, by their proportionate arrangement, provided him with the symbols of the elements and climates of the cosmos.

"Marble statue of Mithras slaying the Bull (British Museum)."

A distinguishing feature of the Mithraic temple or *Mithraeum* was the carved relief which stood at the inner end of the cave and depicted Mithras killing a huge bull, an image known as the *tauroctony*. Typically, Mithras – nude or wearing Anatolian dress – knelt on the bull's back, pulling its head up by its nostrils and plunging a blade into its neck. A two-handled vessel (*krater*) collected the bull's blood; a dog and/or a snake were usually seen heading towards the wound, while a scorpion seized the bull's genitals. A raven flew above the bull or perched on its back and an ear of wheat grew from the bull's tail.

On either side of this image stood the twins Cautes and Cautopates, holding flaming torches – one pointed upwards, the other downwards – along with representations of Luna ('Moon') and Sol ('Sun').

A banqueting scene, showing Mithras and Sol feasting on the bull's hide, was frequently depicted on the reverse of the *tauroctony*. By slaying the bull, Mithras had conferred abundance on the world – as Franz Cumont commented:

> From the dying body of the victim were born all the herbs and beneficial plants. From his spinal cord grew the wheat which would become bread and from his blood came the vine which produced the sacred beverage of the mysteries.

The *tauroctony* displayed the constellations from the spring to the autumn equinoxes, taking in Taurus the Bull, the twins (Gemini), the dog (Canis Major/Minor), the snake (Hydra), the lion (Leo), the vessel (Crater), the wheat-ear (Spica in Virgo), the raven (Corvus) and Scorpio.

The bull-slaying scene therefore revealed a cosmic drama at the centre of which was Mithras, 'Father and source of all life'.

All-Father

The Mithraic initiate was required to face as many as 80 increasingly demanding challenges in order to demonstrate mastery of fire and hunger, water and thirst (the Sword of Strange Hangings might have proved helpful here). There was also a baptismal element: the Pseudo-Augustine manuscripts describe a ritual in which the initiates had their hands bound with chicken intestines and were 'thrown across pits filled with water'; they were then liberated by a Saviour who cut through their bonds with a sword.

Once they had proven their worth, the initiates were able to work their way up through the seven grades of Mithraism.

Each grade represented a rung on the cosmic ladder, allowing the initiate to follow the course taken by Mithras when, after his triumphant banquet with Sol, he ascended through the planetary spheres to the heights of immortality.

Like alchemy, the 'royal art' in which the purification of the soul was thought of as an ascent through seven levels, from gross matter to perfect 'gold', Mithraism re-enacted a seven-stage spiritual journey.

The seven grades were associated with the known planets, ranked roughly in accordance with their relative sizes and perceived attributes:

Corax	'Raven'	(Mercury)
Nymphus	'Male Nymph/Bride'	(Venus)
Miles	'Soldier'	(Mars)
Leo	'Lion'	(Sun)
Perses	'Persian'	(Moon)
Heliodromus	'Sun-courser'	(Saturn)
Pater	'Father'	(Jupiter)

On those occasions when a Mithraic cult had more than one Father an extra grade – *Pater Patrum* or 'Father of Fathers' – was instituted.

One of the symbols or accoutrements of the Father grade was the *patera*, a Grail-like libation bowl. In Irish tradition, the inexhaustible cauldron of plenty belonged to the Dagda, otherwise known as Eochaid Ollathair ('Yew-of-Battle All-Father'), whose son was the 'Red Raven', Bodb Derg. The Old Irish *athir* – 'father' – was conjoined with *eo* ('yew'/'salmon'/ 'Iona'), or the Greek prefix *eu-* ('good'), to form the familiar pseudonym for Arthur's father: Uthyr or Iuthar.

The cultic objects associated with the Raven grade, at the other end of the initiatory scale, were the drinking cup and the *caduceus*, a staff entwined with two serpents, which represented healing.

The Lion grade appears to have been pivotal. It marked the mid-point of the soul's progress through the celestial spheres and was equated with the Sun. Like Lugh Long-Hand, the 'Lion' – *Llew* in Welsh – had the attributes of Apollo.

Mithras himself was often portrayed as a winged and naked human figure with the head of a lion and a serpent coiled around his body. These depictions identify Mithras as the archetypal god or shaman whose 'serpent power' is raised up through his spine: the serpent's head rests on top of the head of the solar lion on the shoulders of the man.

This *leontocephaline* or 'lion-headed' Mithras stood between the mercurial Raven, with his 'Horn of Brân' beaker and *caduceus*, and the magisterial Father, with his libation bowl or cauldron, as a symbol of the initiate and the ascent of the spirit from the 'root' of the spine to the 'crown' of the head. It was a transitional image of Mithras straddling the three worlds – rather like Jesus, the 'Lion of Judah', when he was pierced by a lance-wielding 'Soldier' and committed his spirit into the hands of the 'Father'.

The *Lughnasadh* festival of Lugh-of-the-spear was celebrated in Ireland on 1 August. Also known as the 'Raven's Sorrow', *Bron Trogain,* it took place just as the Sun entered Leo.

This was no doubt a crucial moment in the Mysteries of Mithras – a sacrifice, at the start of the harvest season, when the blood of the Taurean bull flowed into the cosmic libation bowl (Crater) between the lion (Leo) and the snake (Hydra).

Inveresk

By the 4th century AD, Mithraism was Christianity's main competitor. Arguably, the two systems had a common source in the Mystery tradition which had emerged from Mesopotamia, the origins of which seemingly predated the Flood.

Constantine the Great proclaimed tolerance of all religions throughout the Roman Empire in 313, thereby placing Christians and Mithraists on an equal footing. Eight years later, he determined that everyone should observe the 'venerable day of the Sun'.

This is often held up as proof that the Emperor Constantine had converted to Christianity. But Sunday had been kept holy in honour of Mithras. The *Shabbat* of Jewish observance lasted from sundown on Friday till Saturday night. The Church moved its Sabbath to Sunday, the holy day of Mithraism, in response to Constantine's decree.

The feast of *natalis Solis invicti* – the 'birth of the unconquerable Sun' – was celebrated by Mithraists on 25 December. There is no hint in the Bible as to the time of year when Jesus was born. The Christmas festival was appropriated from the worship of Mithras.

Other traditions flowed from Mithraism to Christianity, including elements of the Last Supper and Holy Communion. The virginal mother of the celibate Mithras was known as the 'Mother of God'; shepherds and Persian magi honoured Mithras at his midwinter birth.

The Church also made a habit of building its places of worship on pre-existing shrines. The Vatican stands on the site of a Roman necropolis which appears to have been dedicated to the 'rock-born' Mithras and to have honoured *Sol Invicti*, the invincible solar hero. St Peter's Basilica in Rome was similarly constructed over a Mithraic temple. The Pope himself is a 'Father of Fathers'; his ceremonial Mitre – another Mithraic 'Father' symbol – represents the head of a fish (evoking memories of

Oannes).

In the 360s, the Emperor Julian – dubbed 'Apostate' and 'Transgressor' by the Christians – described Mithras as 'the guide of souls'. This could be considered the last gasp of Mithraism before its light was extinguished by the Church.

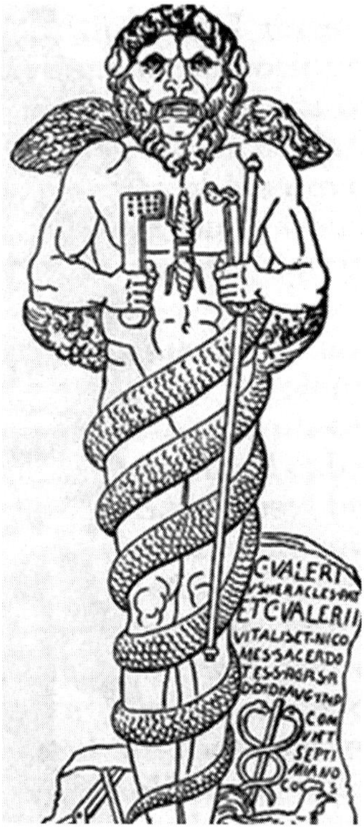

"Leontocephaline Kronos-Mithras, from the mithraeum of Caius Valerius Heracles and sons at Ostia Antica, Italy, late-2nd century AD."

But in the farthest flung reaches of the Empire, the Mysteries took a little longer to die out.

At least three *Mithraea* were built along Hadrian's Wall, that 2nd-century barrier between the Roman-occupied southern parts of Britain and the barbarian tribes of the North. The remains of one of these temples can be visited at Carrawburgh in Northumberland. Rome's influence did not terminate at Hadrian's Wall, however, and traces of Mithraism have been found even further to the north.

Rosslyn Chapel stands above the River North-Esk in Midlothian, near Edinburgh. Mithraic iconography has been detected among the profusion of carvings which adorn the chapel's walls and ceiling, leading to the suggestion that this quirky 'Grail Chapel' was built over an ancient *Mithraeum*.

Realistically, Rosslyn forms a link in the chain between Mithraism and Scottish Freemasonry, which drew on Mithraic tradition. Another link was the Knights Templar, who possibly revived the Mysteries of Mithras. The Templars established their foothold in Scotland at the Warrior's

Town (Balantradoch, now Temple) on the east bank of the River South-Esk, six miles from Rosslyn Chapel.

The River North-Esk joins the South-Esk near Lugton (Welsh *llug* – 'light') and then proceeds north to meet the Firth of Forth at Fisherrow. Just before it reaches the Forth estuary, the river passes an old Roman fortress at Inveresk ('Mouth-of-the-Water') where, in 2010, two altar stones were unearthed – one dedicated to Sol Invictus, the other to Mithras.

This is a mere five miles east of Arthur's Seat in Edinburgh.

The Inveresk altar stones are the first dedications to Mithras to be found in Scotland. Their engravings of a jug and bowl seem reminiscent of those key Grail objects: the horn of the 'Raven' and the cauldron of the 'Father'.

Evidently, the death-and-rebirth Mysteries of Mithras were celebrated, once upon a time, in the heart of what the Grail-hunter Otto Rahn called 'Arthur's bosom'.

"Rosslyn Chapel, near Edinburgh; interior, showing the Apprentice Pillar and other carvings. Illustration published in Heath's Picturesque Annual, 1835."

7

Arthur and Merlin

Still, a man hears what he wants to hear
And disregards the rest
Paul Simon

HEROES TEND to appear when they are most needed. Such was the case with Arthur, who led the Britons against a host of enemies. In subsequent years, however, the emphasis shifted away from his historical role to his mythical status. He became the 'Once and Future King', destined to return in Britain's hour of need.

This began as wishful thing. The alleged discovery of his grave by the Benedictines in 1189 might have turned Glastonbury into a tourist trap but the motives behind the deception were also political: it discomfited the rebellious Welsh, who had long anticipated the reappearance of their national hero.

Today's Welsh are the descendants of those native Britons who looked up to Arthur as their 'duke of battles'. They considered him a champion – the Early Irish *caur*, a 'hero' (also *coraid*; Gaelic *curaidh*), is cognate with the Welsh *cawr*, a 'giant', and so Arthur frequently appears as a gigantic figure in British lore. But the subtle move away from him being the leader of the Britons against all comers to him becoming *rex quondam rexque futurus*, a paragon of Christian chivalry, was no less political than the exhumation of his purported remains. In both instances, the deed was done by his enemies, who rewrote his legend to suit their ends.

Much the same could be said of the Grail, the traditions of which were cynically manipulated by medieval monks who had little or no interest in its original form and function.

An understanding of the Grail is not possible without an understanding of who Arthur really was. Just as a fantasy Grail accompanies the fictional Arthur, so the actual Grail and the genuine Arthur are of a piece.

It is not enough merely to establish who Arthur was and what the Grail was for, though, because both continue to be the subjects of reactionary and revisionist scholarship. It behoves us to recognise the nature of this blight, and that requires us to grapple with the psychobiology of Heroic age thinking.

Arthur Koestler, in *The Sleepwalkers* (1959), sought to explain how our perceptions of the cosmos have changed over time. In a section entitled 'Dark Interlude' he quoted Professor Whitehead:

> In the year 1500 Europe knew less than Archimedes who died in the year 212 BC.

Archimedes is on record as having observed that Aristarchus of Samos (born in 310 BC) 'supposed that the fixed stars and the sun are immoveable, but that the earth is carried round the sun in a circle'.

The place of the Sun at the centre of our solar system was no secret. Julian – the so-called 'Apostate' – wrote of the Sun in the 4th century AD:

> He leads the dance of the stars; his foresight guides all generation in nature. Around him, their King, the planets dance their rounds; they revolve around him in the perfect harmony of their distances which are exactly circumscribed, as the sages affirm, who contemplate the events in the skies ...

The science was basically sound, even if the lyricism smacked of Sun-worship. But all that was about to be forgotten.

The Church opposed the pursuit of knowledge – as St

Augustine made clear at the end of the 4th century:

> ... there can also be in the mind itself ... a certain vain desire and curiosity, not only of taking delights in the body, but of making experiments with the body's aid, and cloaked under the name of learning and knowledge ... Thus men proceed to investigate the phenomena of nature – the part of nature external to us – though the knowledge is of no value to them ...

So what had gone wrong?

Left vs right

Looked at from above, the human brain resembles a large walnut. It consists of two halves connected by a tough bundle of nerve fibres known as the corpus callosum.

The twin cerebral hemispheres carry out somewhat different functions. Generally, the left hemisphere controls the right side of the body and is usually the logical, analytical half of the brain: both the major areas involved in language skills are located in the left hemisphere.

The right hemisphere controls the left side of the body and leads in the fields of intuition and imagination. It also excels at interpreting non-verbal forms of communication (e.g. intonation, accentuation, overall meaning).

To be born is to enter a world of apparent dualities: male/female; mind/body; day/night; us/them, etc. The brain appears to have evolved to reflect and encompass duality, so that – up to a point – the left brain 'thinks' and understands words while the right brain 'feels' and comprehends tone of voice.

These functional differences have taken on a cultural complexion. The right brain controls the left (Latin *sinister*) hand, whereas the left brain controls the right; the dominance of right-handedness evolved in tandem with tool-making and language abilities, both of which require a measure of dexterity – from the Latin *dexter*, meaning 'right'. If the left-brain is effectively objective and 'masculine' (abstract thought; 'light'; 'spirit'), the right-brain is correspondingly subjective and 'feminine' (body-image; 'dark'; 'matter').

One of the principal aims of magic is the *union of opposites*. This is often represented as a 'sacred marriage' (*hieros gamos*) in which the male/female elements combine to form a new wholeness. In such a state there is no inner and outer, no subject and object, no self or other. All things become one.

The union of opposites can be thought of as a process which, under the right conditions, takes place in the brain itself. It is the perfect marriage of the cerebral hemispheres and the formation of an 'androgynous' unit, like the hermaphroditic child that is born of the combination of (male) Sun and (female) Moon in the spiritual practice of alchemy.

The harmonious functioning of both hemispheres allows for an equal balance of the *Logos* (from the Greek *lego*, 'I say') principle of the left-brain and the *Eros* (a Greek word meaning 'intimate love') principle of the right. In other words, the logical, discriminatory, 'masculine' side of the brain is married to the imagistic, connection-seeking, 'feminine' side, allowing us to see both the minute details and the bigger picture.

When the shaman awakens the 'serpent power' of Kundalini – the vital energy of his 'low' self or *unihipili* – and coaxes it up the length of his spine, that energy spreads first into the right hemisphere, which has more extensive connections with the limbic system or 'palaeomammalian' brain than the left.

If the left hemisphere can be lulled into co-operating – say, through repetitive drumming, which relaxes the left-brain, or the use of psychoactive drugs, which reward the left-brain by releasing the neurotransmitter dopamine – the 'serpent power' can be used by both hemispheres to energise the frontal lobes, quickening and intensifying the brain waves until a higher state of consciousness is reached.

Breaking down the imaginary divisions between 'male' and 'female' is a necessary precursor to enlightenment (the goal of initiation). The trainee shaman is therefore presented with peculiar sights – people wearing animal heads; men dressed as women – in order to dissolve the boundaries of cultural conditioning.

The coniine in hemlock, meanwhile, binds to the acetylcholine receptors in the brain, triggering the release of dopamine and creating a sense of euphoria. This is one way of pleasuring the left-brain hemisphere (there are heavier concentrations of dopamine in the left amygdala) into opening itself up to the 'erotic' embrace of its feminine counterpart.

The Fall

As expressions of *Eros* go, the Venus of Willendorf statuette (roughly 23,000 BC) is surely as good as any. Primitive cultures rejoiced in the nurturing feminine and the intuitive, image-forming, pattern-recognising abilities of the right-brain hemisphere. They also heard the gods speaking to them directly *through their right brains* – just as Mozart claimed that tunes wandered spontaneously into his head from the right side.

The Biblical 'Fall' from innocence – or primal connectedness – occurred in the Fertile Crescent, between the Persian Gulf and the Valley of the Nile, perhaps 10,000 years ago. Oannes the Fish-Man came up from the sea to teach the people of Sumer mathematics, writing and city-building:

"The Venus of Willendorf. Discovered in Austria in 1908 and dated to roughly 28,000 – 25,000 BC."

all left-brain activities.

In the Bible this is associated with the birth of agriculture. Adam disobeyed God ('YHWH' or 'IHOH') by eating the fruit of the World-Tree, 'a tree to be desired to make one wise', and as a result of his disobedience he was compelled to work the land.

But it was Eve who took the blame. She had been advised by the 'serpent' to try the fruit. Adam and Eve thus became 'as gods, knowing good and evil': 'And the eyes of them both were opened'.

The fruit was the original 'golden apple' or oak-gall, from which we acquired iron-gall ink. In short, we learnt how to read and write. The antediluvian wisdom handed down by Oannes gave rise to the Neolithic Revolution, setting mankind on the road to modernity.

Something, however, was lost. The formation of letters (initially, symbolic hieroglyphs) is a function of the right-brain hemisphere. Grammar, spelling, syntax and verbal comprehension, though, are left-brain specialities. The cost of literacy was that we became locked in the left – logical, analytical – sides of our heads. We learnt how to discriminate and forgot how to assimilate.

The Divine age was alert to the dangers of left-brain dominance. The switch from right-brain *Eros* to left-brain *Logos* creates an obsession with order and bookkeeping, with codified laws and divide-and-rule. This is why the Celtic Druids, like the Mithraists, memorised their knowledge, transmitting it orally. The Druids ensured that only the most highly-trained sages were entrusted with the art of writing. They knew that, in the wrong hands, literacy led to bickering and nit-picking.

The most important secret passed on by Oannes to the people of Mesopotamia might have been the means by which such a lapse into left-brain imbalance could be averted. The *Gospel of John* would later insist that the foundation of all things was the Word – even though the only 'sign' that Jesus offered to his 'evil generation' had been 'the sign of the prophet Jonas'. This must have been the symbol of the Oannes-like Fish-Man, Jonah (Hebrew *Yona*, Greek *Ionas* – 'dove'), who spent three days in the belly of the 'Whale', anticipating the three days Jesus would spend in the rock-tomb.

It would appear that, far from seeking to establish a new religion of The Word (*Logos* incarnate), Jesus himself followed an ancient path which required the 'sacred marriage' of the cerebral hemispheres, the 'death' of the divided self and the 'rebirth' of the unified – i.e. 'individuated' – initiate.

By his own actions, Jesus dissolved the apparent dualities which arise whenever the left-brain becomes too dominant. But his followers were trapped in the world of The Word and began rigorously to reinforce those very divisions which Jesus had sought to abolish.

Denying the initiatory experience which breaks down the barriers erected by the left-brain in order to assert its dominance over the right, the Church became schizoid. Increasingly suspicious of the right-brain realm (femininity, physicality, sensuality) the Heroic age descended into paranoia, haunted by phantoms – imagos of its own making – and confirming its identity ('us') by dehumanising and demonising its enemies ('them').

ARTHUR – THE EVIDENCE

The Bible, as we know it, came into existence at the end of the 4th century AD, when the final selection of texts to be included was ratified by a Church council (although the Bible still takes different forms, from the 66 books of the Protestant Bible to the 81 books of the Ethiopian Orthodox Church). The Church now had a powerful weapon – a book of rules which theoretically stipulated the proper responses to all of life's eventualities.

The Church then proceeded to alter perceptions of reality to fit the blueprint outlined in its scriptures. The Greeks in the 6th century BC had known that the Earth is spherical. By the 6th century AD, it had become a 'disc' and was placed firmly back at the centre of the cosmos, with the Sun obliged to circle around it.

Most medieval maps bore no relation to the arrangement of the heavenly bodies or the layout of the continents. Astonishingly, the Church knew that its atlases did not reflect the world-as-it-was. Mariners in fact had accurate maps which faithfully replicated the actual world. But the Church would only authorise maps which presented an idealised, 'theological' view of things. To do otherwise would have required an engagement with reality which the Church – like a 'split-brain' patient – was incapable of accommodating.

The Church was also conscious of the similarities between its Christian religion and the Mysteries of Mithras, which had preceded it. To account for this, a number of early Christian writers (Augustine, Julian Martyr, Tertullian and Julius Firmicus Maternus) devised a bizarre explanation.

The Devil – they said – had knowingly pre-empted the advent of Christ by inventing a religion, hundreds of years beforehand, which almost exactly mirrored Christianity, in order to confuse and corrupt the pagans.

"The rock-born Mithras."

At once, we see the flaw in Heroic age thinking. The reasoning centres of the left-brain had been set a task: to dismiss Mithraism as an inferior copy of Christianity. The reality principle of the right-brain would have told them that Christianity had quite obviously helped itself to whatever it fancied from the earlier religion. But the left-brain refused to consult the right. Having predetermined the outcome it wanted (it was 'only obeying orders') it set about torturing logic and common sense to make the pieces fit, regardless of the evidence.

Any mindset capable of convincing itself that what came first must have been modelled on what came much later is unlikely to produce honest witnesses. Then as now, the Heroic age mentality decides what it prefers to believe and then seeks out the evidence to confirm its position, burying that which contradicts it. Being mentally divided against itself, it cannot accept that it is doing this and angrily accuses its opponents of the same intellectual dishonesty. Metaphorically and – to some extent – literally, its left hand doesn't know what its right hand is doing. Like a psychopath, it neither knows nor cares when it is telling lies.

With that in mind, let us now look at what many commentators claim is the historical evidence for the existence of Arthur. This typically takes the form of just four sources:

> *De excidio et conquestu Britanniae* ('Of the Ruin and Conquest of Britain'), written by Gildas the Wise in about 545;
> *Historia ecclesiastica gentis Anglorum* ('Ecclesiastical History of the English People'), by the Venerable Bede, *circa* 731;
> *Historia Brittonum* ('History of the Britons'), attributed to a monk named Nennius and composed in about 829;
> *Annales Cambriae* ('Annals of Wales'), compiled in the 12th century.

Two of these sources (Gildas and Bede) do not mention Arthur at all. They are counted as evidence simply because – unlike those historical sources that *do* mention Arthur – they make possible the persistent misrepresentation of who Arthur really was.

Annales Cambriae

The Annals of Wales were collated from notes jotted in the margins of Easter Tables.

Easter is a moveable feast, its dating dependent on the phases of the Moon. Early monasteries kept records to track the 84-year cycle which was used to calculate the dates of Easter up until the

Synod of Whitby in AD 664. Significant occurrences were sometimes noted down alongside the annual entries for Easter. These marginalia were later transcribed into separate 'annals', which therefore provide a basic historical chronicle.

Two entries in the *Annales Cambriae* refer to Arthur:

(Year 72) The Battle of Badon, in which Arthur carried the cross of Our Lord Jesus Christ on his shoulders for three days and three nights and the Britons were victors ...

(Year 93) The Strife of Camlann in which Arthur and Medrod perished.

The entry for 'Year 9' states that 'Easter [was] altered on the Lord's Day by Pope Leo.' This happened in AD 455, and so it would appear that 'Year 1' in the annals was 447 in the Anno Domini dating system. Consequently, the 'Battle of Badon' (*Bellum badonis*) can be dated to AD 518 and the 'Strife of Camlann' (*Gueith cam lann*) to AD 539.

Both entries, however, were added in later – probably hundreds of years after the events concerned. They may not be entirely accurate.

The Heroic age mindset is still prevalent among historians, though, and some point to the *Annales Cambriae* as 'proof' that Arthur flourished in the late-5th and/or early-6th centuries. This is a triumph of faith over reason.

It also explains the inclusion of the *De excidio et conquestu Britanniae* as one of the 'admissible' sources for Arthur, for, in describing the aftermath of the Roman occupation of southern Britain, St Gildas referred to a 'siege of Badon Hill' (*obsessionis Badonici montis*) at which the native Britons fought the invading Saxons to a standstill.

Gildas, as we have noted, said nothing at all about Arthur. Even so, the assumption that the 'siege of Badon Hill' mentioned by Gildas was the same as the 'Battle of Badon', which the Welsh

Annals apparently ascribe to *circa* 518, justifies the belief that Arthur was essentially a man of the south.

Nennius, compiling his *Historia Brittonum* in about 829, observed that Arthur was a soldier (*miles*) and the commander-in-chief (*dux bellorum* – 'duke of battles') who led the Britons to a series of 12 remarkable victories against the Saxons. The last of these was on 'Mount Badon' (*Mons Badonis*). Again, this is generally assumed to have been the 'Badon Hill' siege to which St Gildas had previously referred.

Such assumptions are dangerous. But here we find Heroic age thinking in all its duplicitous glory: the *assumption* that the three separate 'Badon' references all concerned the same battle is presented as *fact* by commentators who want Arthur to have been something he wasn't. They won't admit that – as we shall discover – there is evidence which strongly suggests that they were not the same battle at all.

Evidence contrary to established beliefs is usually discounted. For example, the Canon of St Omer in Brittany used a Gaelic version of Arthur's name in his *Liber Floridus* (*c* 1120). Like Nennius before him, Lambert of St Omer considered Arthur to have been primarily a soldier, but while Nennius only left clues as to where Arthur had been active, Lambert was more specific:

> There is in Britain – in the land of the Picts – a palace of the warrior Arthur, built with marvellous art and variety, in which the history of all his exploits and wars is to be seen in sculpture.

Lambert had given the game away: Arthur the warrior (*Artuir militis*) was based in the North. And so Lambert's testimony is routinely ignored.

'No Arthur'

St Gildas was born in North Britain in about the year 500. His celebrated open letter, *De excidio et conquestu Britanniae,* contains a blistering verbal assault on five contemporary princes. The last to feel the lash of the saint's tongue was Maelgwn, the 'dragon of the island'.

Maelgwn the Tall was the ruler of Gwynedd. His death is dated in the Welsh Annals to 547 or 549.

The story of Taliesin (see Chapter 3) also involves Maelgwn. After his cauldron initiation at Llyn Tegid in Gwynedd, the Chief Bard pitched up at Maelgwn's court on the coast of North Wales. This offers a start date of sometime in the 540s for Taliesin's career, just as it dates the vituperative open letter penned by St Gildas to roughly the same decade.

Much of Taliesin's life was spent in North Britain during the latter half of the 6th century. He repeatedly mentioned Arthur in his poetry, beginning with his *Cad Goddau* ...

> Druids versed in letters
> Prophesy that Arthur
> Is the longed-for one of the tribe ...

...and culminating with *Preiddeu Annwn*:

> And when we went with Arthur, famous toil,
> Except for seven, no one rose from the Mound of Mead-Drunkenness.

The clear implication is that Arthur was a late-6th century northerner. This contradicts the orthodox view of Arthur – active many years earlier in the South – and so Taliesin's reportage is not accepted as valid evidence.

Neither is one of the greatest poems of ancient Britain. Aneirin, a princely bard of the North, composed his *Y Gododdin* towards the very end of the 6th century. The poem laments the deaths of many warriors of Lothian, the oldest surviving version including these lines:

Gochore brein du ar uur
caer ceni bei ef Arthur
rug ciuin uerthi ig disur ...

This was translated by Professor Skene in the 19th century:

Black ravens croaked on the wall
Of the beautiful Caer. He was an Arthur
In the midst of the exhausting conflict ...

It has since become customary to translate the lines thus:

He fed black ravens on the rampart
Of the fortress, though he was no Arthur
He did mighty deeds in battle ...

The difference is telling. Scholars now claim that the poem referred to someone who was 'no Arthur' – even though *there is no negative in the original.*

The lines composed by Aneirin actually meant something like this:

Black ravens sang in praise of the hero
of Circenn. He blamed Arthur;
the dogs cursed in return for our wailing ...

The black ravens were warriors: we also encounter them in the *Mabinogion* tale of the *Dream of Rhonabwy* when, during a lull before the battle of Badon, Arthur's troops and Owain's ravens attack each other. The hero (*arwr*) of Circenn – pronounced 'keer-ken', crudely transliterated into Welsh as *caer cen*(*i*) – would have been Arthur himself, who died fighting there shortly before

Aneirin's poem was composed. The confrontation with the 'dogs' recalls the account of Arthur's burial given in the *Preiddeu Annwn* poem of Aneirin's contemporary, Taliesin:

> Thrice twenty missionaries watched on the wall;
> A miserable tryst, the speech of their overseer.

The point is that by mistranslating *Y Gododdin* scholars have ruled Aneirin's poem inadmissible as evidence in the quest for Arthur. The notion that Arthur must have been a southerner who warred with the Saxons in about AD 500 requires any contemporary source which places him in North Britain in about AD 600 to be misconstrued. And so a rogue negative has been sneaked into *Y Gododdin* – 'he was no Arthur' – simply to distance Arthur from the North.

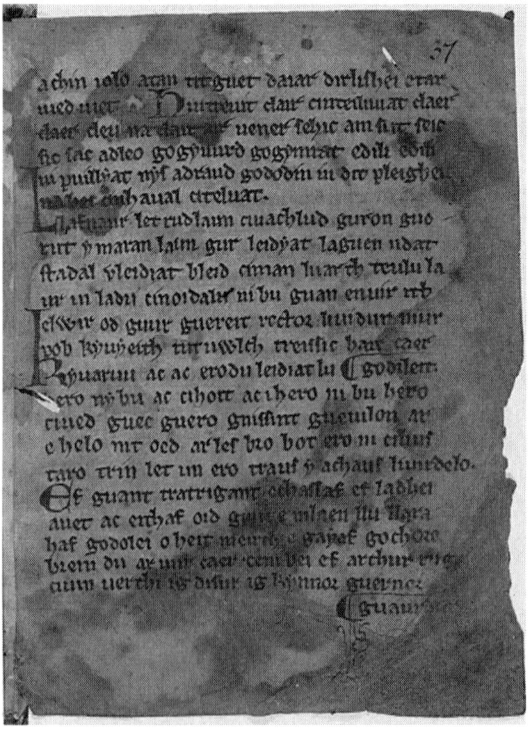

"Section of Aneirin's Y Gododdin *poem, c. AD 600, including reference to Arthur (bottom-right of page)."*

It seems that any evidence which challenges the consensus can be distorted or discarded, because the myth of the southern Arthur must be preserved at all costs.

THE FIRST ARTHUR

The earliest dateable reference to anyone by the name of Arthur occurs in the *Life of Columba,* written by Adomnán of Iona.

A copy of Adomnán's *Vita Columbae* was discovered at Reichenau in Germany in 1621; it had been transcribed by a monk of Iona who died in AD 713. The likelihood is that Adomnán wrote his hagiography for the centenary of Columba's death (St Columba died in 597) and so it predates the first 'acceptable' document to mention Arthur – the *Historia Brittonum* of Nennius – by more than 100 years.

Adomnán disclosed that Columba had prophesied the fates of the sons of Áedán mac Gabráin, a Scottish king ordained by Columba in 574. Artúr or Artuir was one of three sons of Áedán who were destined to 'fall in battle, slain by enemies.'

According to Adomnán, St Columba's prediction came true: Artúr and Eochaid Find were killed in a 'battle of the Miathi'. Domangart was also 'defeated and slain in battle in Saxonia [England]'.

The Miathi – otherwise *Maeatae* – were one of 'the two most important tribes of the Britons (in the North)'. They were the Picts who inhabited the low-lying lands of central Scotland, in contrast to the 'Caledonian' tribes of the Highlands. Johannes Xiphilinus, in his abridgement of Cassius Dio's writings, indicated that they dwelt 'close to the wall which divides the island [of Britain] into two parts' – this rampart being the Antonine Wall, constructed by Roman troops in the 2nd century AD between the estuaries of the Forth and Clyde rivers. The tribal name of the Miathi is recalled at Dumyat, the 'Hill-Fort-of-the-Miathi', north-east of Stirling, and at Myot Hill, near Falkirk.

A date for the 'battle of the Miathi' in which Artúr mac

Áedáin fell is provided by the 14th-century Annals of Tigernach, from the Irish monastery of Clonmacnoise. The entry for the year 594 in the Tigernach annals records:

> ... The slaying of the sons of Áedán i.e. Bran & Domangart & Eochaid Find & Artúr, in the battle of Circhenn, in which Áedán was the victor ...

The 'battle of Circhenn' (*cath Chirchind*) would have been fought in the Pictish province of Circenn – that is, Angus and the Mearns, immediately north of the Tay estuary in eastern Scotland. This was the territory of the Miathi.

Arthur son of Áedán apparently fell in a battle of about 594, fought against those perennial enemies of the Romanised Britons, the fearsome spearmen of the Lowland Picts.

Bran son of Áedán – who also fell in the battle of the Miathi – is named in the 15th-century Annals of Ulster, which date the battle to 595 or 596 and list only 'Bran and Domangart' as casualties.

The presence of Bran ('Raven') in these Irish chronicles reminds us that the 'Horn of Brân ... from the North' was one of the Thirteen Treasures of Britain, and that Bran son of Llyr was associated with the magical 'apple-isle' of Emain.

We have seen that Brân seems to have been linked to an individual known as Lugh or Llew ('Lion'). Lugh is identified in Irish literature as a son of Cian, and he appears as such in Aneirin's late-6th century *Y Gododdin* elegy:

> The one son of Cian from beyond Bannog,
> In the trampling of the Gododdin, on the raining of wounds,
> Fie! when not Lliw Sea-Born*, no one.
> (**Llyrnach* – 'Llyr's man')

It was on the 'Island of the Son of Cian' that Áedán mac Gabráin,

King of the Scots, recovered the 'vat of gold and silver' which had been buried by his eldest son, Gartnait.

The same Gartnait mac Áedáin was the king of the Highland Picts at the time of the 'battle of Circhenn' in which Arthur son of Áedán was 'slain by enemies.'

Geoffrey of Monmouth

The first Arthur on record fell in a battle against the Miathi or Lowland Picts in Circenn (Angus) in about 594.

Lambert of St Omer remarked that the 'palace of the warrior Arthur' was located 'in the land of the Picts', where 'the history of all his wars and exploits is to be seen in sculpture' (Lambert was presumably referring to the battle scenes depicted on Pictish symbol stones).

Up until 1120, then, Arthur seems to have been recognised as a figure of the North who fought and died in Scotland. So how did the conviction arise that he was born and buried at the opposite end of Britain?

The fault lies with a 12th-century churchman called Geoffrey of Monmouth.

Born around the year 1100, Geoffrey's background was probably Breton. His forebears had followed William, Duke of Normandy, across the English Channel and perhaps even took part in William's defeat of the Saxons in 1066.

Unlike the Anglo-Saxons, who did their best to forget about Arthur, the Normans were fascinated by the legends of the British hero. Indeed, the so-called 'Grail Chapel' of Rosslyn, near Edinburgh, was built by one of the original Norman families, the Sinclairs or St Clairs from Saint-Clair-sur-Epte in northern France. The Norman obsession with all things Arthurian meant that Geoffrey of Monmouth was writing for an eager audience when he authored his *Historia Regum Britanniae* in about 1137.

Geoffrey's main sources for his *History of the Kings of Britain* were those which we have already come across: *Of the Ruin and*

Conquest of Britain (Gildas), the *Ecclesiastical History of the English People* (Bede) and the *History of the Britons* ('Nennius'). Out of these, Geoffrey wove a fabulous narrative history of the British Isles, beginning with Brutus – 'the leader of those who survived the fall of Troy' – and ending with the death of Cadwaladr, King of Gwynedd, in the late-7th century.

About one-fifth of Geoffrey's *Historia Regum Britanniae* was devoted to 'King Arthur'. In fact, there never was – there never has been – a king named Arthur. The Britons referred to their original Arthur as *ymerawdwr*, from the Latin *imperator*, meaning 'emperor'.

Geoffrey singlehandedly concocted the muddled legend of King Arthur. He took what he could find about the historical Arthur, processed that information through the religious-aristocratic belief system of his time, and came up with a lot of nonsense. Sadly, his pseudo-historical gibberish appeals to scholars of a similar Heroic age persuasion, with the result that Arthur – the 'King' who never was – became decidedly English, and a Christian to boot.

It was Geoffrey who set the scene of Arthur's conception in the far south-west of Britain. The error might have been an innocent one (Geoffrey probably did not speak Welsh); alternatively, he might have been swayed by a cynical desire to flatter his patron, Robert, Earl of Gloucester, whose brother was the Earl of Cornwall. Either way, Geoffrey took a Welsh place-name – *Cernyw* – and mistranslated it as 'Cornwall'.

One of the Thirteen Treasures of the Island of Britain was *Llen Arthur yng Ngernyw*, the 'Mantle of Arthur in Cernyw'. The lack of any hard evidence for a historical Arthur in, or even near, southern Britain makes it unlikely that Arthur would have worn his cloak in Cornwall.

A better derivation of *Cernyw* would be from the Welsh *carn*, a burial cairn, or the Early Irish *cern* – 'corner', 'region' – and *yw*, 'yews'. This would suggest that the *Cernyw* where Arthur wore his mantle of invisibility was the chambered burial cairn on Iona: the 'fair fort' of the 'Yewy' isle or 'Island of the Sacred Trees'.

By misinterpreting *Cernyw*, Geoffrey dragged Arthur and his comrades southwards, where – thanks to the obstinacy of Heroic age thinkers – they have remained ever since.

Myrddin Wyllt

Arthur was not the only victim of Geoffrey's meddling. The character he named 'Merlin' plays a minor role in the *History of the Kings of Britain* – he improbably transports the Giant's Ring (Stonehenge) from Ireland to Britain and colludes in the seduction of Arthur's mother by 'Utherpendragon'.

Geoffrey took a fable from the *Historia Brittonum* about a boy called 'Ambros' and retold it as the story of 'Merlin'. The original tale had actually concerned the young Ambrosius Aurelianus, a Romano-British commander who rallied the Britons against the Saxons in the late-5th century. There was no connection between Ambrosius and Arthur, who flourished 100 years later. Geoffrey had got the wrong 'Merlin'.

He returned to the subject of Merlin several years after completing his *Historia Regum Britanniae*. Geoffrey's *Vita Merlini* (*c* 1150) features a very different Merlin from the one he had previously presented to the world.

Geoffrey's two Merlins – the sorcerer of the *History of the Kings of Britain* and the prophet of the *Life of Merlin* – are poles apart. The former, drawn from a folktale concerning a 5th-century leader of the Britons, is a figure of fantasy. The latter sprang whole from the traditions surrounding a *myrddin* or 'crazy man' of the late-6th century. Though Geoffrey struggled to merge the two characters, they were in reality two different historical persons.

The *Vita Merlini* recounts the adventures which befell Myrddin Wyllt – also known as Merlinus Caledonensis (the 'Caledonian' Merlin) or Merlinus Silvestris ('Merlin of the

Forest') – after the traumatic incident which sent him insane (Welsh *gwyllt* – 'wild', 'mad'). Various poems attributed to this Myrddin were collected in the ancient books of Wales, and Geoffrey must have borrowed from these to create his *Life of Merlin*; notably, the *Dialogue of Myrddin and Gwenddydd his Sister*, from the Red Book of Hergest, and the *Dialogue of Myrddin and Taliesin* from the Black Book of Carmarthen.

A large part of the *Vita Merlini* is taken up with Taliesin's meeting with Myrddin Wyllt. This includes the Chief Bard's description of the 'Island of Apples' – 'It was there we took Arthur after the battle of Camlann, where he had been wounded.'

Evidently, a tradition of some antiquity recognised Taliesin and Myrddin Wyllt as acquaintances. What is more, both 6th-century poets were associated with the Old North. Taliesin spent many years following the struggles of the *cymry* or 'compatriots' of North Britain:

From Glasgow to Loch Ryan,
The Cymry are battle-brave heroes ...

The poems of Myrddin, meanwhile, indicate that his twin sister Gwenddydd was married to Rhydderch, a historical prince who ruled Strathclyde from his chief seat at Dumbarton in the late-6th and early-7th centuries. Rhydderch also crops up in Adomnán's *Life of Columba* – he secretly consulted the saint about his life expectancy – and his white-hilted sword, Dyrnwyn, became one of the Thirteen Treasures of Britain.

Scottish tradition remembered Myrddin in the context of Rhydderch's court. The *Life of Kentigern*, written by Jocelin of Furness in the late-12th century (see Chapter 3), refers to 'a certain foolish man, who was called Laleocen'. This afflicted soul mourned the death of St Kentigern, first bishop of Glasgow, and prophesied the imminent demise of Rhydderch (both men died in *circa* 614).

The name Laleocen – or 'Lailoken' in John of Fordun's 14th-century *Life of St Kentigern* – is a Scottish approximation of the Welsh *Llallogan* ('Little Honoured One'), which was how Myrddin was addressed by his sister in the poem of their dialogue. Thus, the Laleocen or Lailoken of southern Scotland was in fact the wild and hairy 'Merlinus Caledonensis', Myrddin Wyllt. He is even identified as 'Myrddin' in a stained glass window, which shows him being blessed by St Kentigern, in a church dedicated to Kentigern at Stobo in the Scottish Borders.

THE ACTION OF ARDERYDD

The Welsh Triads tell us that there were three 'Skilful Bards' at Arthur's court:

> Myrddin son of Morfryn,
> Myrddin Emrys,
> and Taliesin.

This reflects the damage done by Geoffrey of Monmouth. Myrddin Emrys – the 'Ambros' or Ambrosius of the *Historia Brittonum* – did not belong there. But the other two, Taliesin and Myrddin son of Morfryn ('Sea-Hill') or Morfrân ('Sea-Crow'), were contemporaries of Artúr mac Áedáin.

The Triads also recall the 'Three Futile Battles of the Island of Britain'. These were the 'Battle of Goddau', the 'Action of Arderydd', and the third and worst – 'Camlan'.

The first of these inspired one of Taliesin's masterpieces, *Cad Goddau* ('Battle of Goddau'), in which the Chief Bard announced that the literate Druids were prophesying that Arthur was 'the longed-for one of the tribe.' In another of his poems, Taliesin referred to the armies of Rheged and Goddau doing battle with a common enemy by the River Leven, north of Dumbarton. Goddau was therefore Taliesin's name for a particular region – most likely, the thickly-forested domain of the Gododdin warriors of Lothian.

The 'Battle of Goddau' apparently took place in the mighty Caledonian forest. The *Historia Brittonum* listed one of Arthur's 12 victories as *Cat Coit Celidon*, the 'Battle of Celidon Wood', and Celidon features repeatedly in the native Arthurian tradition and the romances of the Cistercians: the lead character of *Culhwch and Olwen* was the grandson of Celyddon Wledig ('Ruler of Celidon'), while an early version of the Tristan legend has 'Trystan' and his lover absconding into the Forest of Celidon.

The 'Action of Arderydd' was fought in much the same region of southern Scotland. Professor W.F. Skene set out to identify the site of Arderydd, presenting his findings to the Society of Antiquaries of Scotland in February 1865. Skene established that the focus of the battle was the Moat of Liddel, or Liddel Strength, a fortified hill-top in the Cumbrian parish of Arthuret, on what is now the English-Scottish border.

The Welsh Annals reveal that the Action of Arderydd was fought in *circa* 573. A copy of the *Annales Cambriae* now kept in the National Archives adds the information that the battle was:

> ... between the sons of Eliffer and Gwenddolau son of Ceidio; in which battle Gwenddolau fell; and Merlin went mad.

Robert Vaughn's 18th-century edition of the Triads also disclosed that the Arderydd conflict had flared up from a dispute between the 'shepherds' of Rhydderch of Strathclyde and Áedán mac Gabráin, soon-to-be King of the Scots.

The Welsh Annals identify the main combatants as the 'sons of Eliffer' and 'Gwenddolau son of Ceidio'. Eliffer had governed the former Roman *civitas* of York, which was known to the Britons as *Caer Efrog*. He had perished in 559, defending York against an assault by the Germanic Angles from the east, after which the lordship of York passed to his sons. The Triads name the two sons of Eliffer as Gwrgi and Peredur.

Peredur [son] of York was, of course, the model for Chrétien de Troyes's 'Perceval the Welshman', the native Briton who saw the *graal* and the blood-dripping spear in the hidden retreat of the Fisher King.

Gwenddolau son of Ceidio was another northern prince. Like Peredur, he was descended from Coel Hen, the 'duke' who had commanded the forces of the North at the time of the Roman withdrawal from Britain.

Sometime around 559, Gwenddolau took control of the wild lands of the Selgovae ('Hunters'), a sub-branch of the Gododdin federation of Lothian. Their tribal centre was among the Eildon Hills, above the site of Melrose Abbey and the massive Roman fortress of Trimontium. But in about 573, Gwenddolau moved his war-band into the hill-fort above the Liddel Water to defend his western border.

Peiryan faban

The Triads describe Gwenddolau as one of the three 'Bull-Protectors' of Britain – a Mithraic designation, perhaps. He was also the owner of a magical chessboard, *Gwyddbwyll Gwenddolau ap Ceidio*, of which we are told that 'if the pieces were set, they would play by themselves. The board was of gold and the men of silver.'

The golden *gwyddbwyll* of Gwenddolau became one of the Thirteen Treasures of Britain '(that were in the North)'. We caught a glimpse of it in Chapter 5 when, in the *Saga of Sir Uallabh son of Horn*, the Irish king was seen sadly 'playing chess on a board of gold' after burying his wife.

The Action of Arderydd might have involved Peredur and Gwenddolau, but the trouble began with two other princes of the North: Rhydderch and Áedán.

Rhydderch was a confidante of both Myrddin Wyllt and St Columba. His religious affiliations are hard to determine, but the Christians certainly thought of him as a 'defender of the faith'.

The challenge he presented to Gwenddolau was partly sectarian: his 'shepherds' or pastors were gathering on Gwenddolau's western flank. Áedán seems to have opposed this. The outcome of the squabble between Christians and pagans was the 'futile' battle of Arderydd, which Rhydderch won 'after great slaughter' and 'Áedán fled the country'.

Myrddin had been on Gwenddolau's side. He had attempted to raise a tactical smokescreen, but the ruse backfired. Under cover of the 'battle-fog', Gwenddolau's enemies stormed the ramparts. Gwenddolau was killed, as were Myrddin's brothers, the 'sons of Morfryn'.

Myrddin escaped into the forest, where he hid from the men of his brother-in-law, Rhydderch the Generous, in an 'apple-tree'. He had lost his mind. In poem after poem, he bemoaned the tribulations he had suffered since the deaths of his lord and kinsmen.

He was not entirely alone. His sister visited him, as did Taliesin; both were treated to self-pitying laments. A commanding youth also tracked him down to his mountain lair. This young man seems to have been even more upset about the outcome at Arderydd than Myrddin was. So Myrddin sang to him, assuring the 'son of the cauldron' (*peiryan faban*) that Áedán would have his revenge:

Peiryan faban, cease your weeping.
Áedán will come across the wide sea ...
On the islands on the way to the hill of the Irish,
A series of bloody encounters, like a race.

'*Peiryan faban,*' Myrddin chanted – 'The encounter of Rhydderch and Áedán by the bright Clyde will resound from the northern border to the south.'

The 'son of the cauldron' is not named. At the same time, though, Taliesin was claiming in his *Cad Goddau* poem that

'Druids versed in letters' were declaring Arthur to be 'the longed-for one of the tribe'. And only a year after the Action of Arderydd, St Columba would predict that Arthur son of Áedán would never be king, but would 'fall in battle, slain by enemies.'

Just four miles from the Moat of Liddel in Cumbria sits the hamlet of Catlowdy. The Celtic place-name expert, W.J. Watson, interpreted Catlowdy to mean 'Battle of Lothian'. A mile or two east of Catlowdy is a spot called Arthur Seat, and south of Arthurseat House we find an incline known as Kays Bank, close to the settlement of Cays House. The name 'Kay' or 'Cay' echoes that of Arthur's faithful servant, Cai.

To find places named after Arthur and Cai in the immediate vicinity of Catlowdy, and so close to the place where 'Merlin went mad', is surely to identify the locations of the first two 'Futile Battles of the Island of Britain'. The Battle of Lothian (*Cad Goddau*) and the Action of Arderydd were both 'futile' internecine conflicts – and the youthful Arthur was there.

Revising the dates

The Action of Arderydd – which involved Peredur ('Perceval'), Myrddin ('Merlin') and Áedán mac Gabráin, the father of the first Arthur on record – took place in AD 573, according to the Annals of Wales.

The 'battle of the Miathi' or 'battle of Circhenn', in which Artúr mac Áedáin was killed, was fought in AD 594, according to the Annals of Tigernach.

These are not the same as the dates given for Arthur's battles of 'Badon' (518) and 'Camlann' (539) in the *Annales Cambriae*. But one thing should strike us straightaway.

The gap between the historical battle of Arderydd – which was probably contemporaneous with Taliesin's 'Battle of Goddau' – and the battle with the Miathi of Circenn was 21 years. Likewise, the battles of 'Badon' and 'Camlann' were 21 years apart:

'Battle of Badon'	518	Action of Arderydd	573
'Strife of Camlann'	539	Battle of Circenn	594
	———		———
Interval:	21 years		21 years

It would be quite a coincidence if the first and last battles of Arthur son of Áedán and the most famous battles of an entirely separate and thus far undiscovered Arthur were, in both instances, exactly 21 years apart. Could it be, then, that the dates given for Arthur's battles in the *Annales Cambriae* are essentially correct but have somehow been wrongly ascribed?

As we saw earlier, the Welsh Annals do not follow the Anno Domini dating system. Their Year 1 corresponds to AD 447, so that Year 72 ('Battle of Badon') works out as AD 518 and Year 93 ('Strife of Camlann') as 539.

The Anno Domini method of dating was pioneered by Dionysius Exiguus in 525 and was introduced into Britain by the Venerable Bede, whose *Ecclesiastical History of the English People* is cited by some as a historical source for Arthur – even though Bede never mentioned Arthur. Bede in fact used two dating systems side-by-side: one dated events from the founding of Rome in 753 BC, the other being the system devised by Dionysius Exiguus, which dated events from 'the incarnation of our Lord Jesus Christ'.

The dates of Arthur's battles were inserted into the *Annales Cambriae* many years later. The monk who interpolated those entries into the Welsh Annals faced the problem of having to juggle two or more different systems for calculating dates. He knew that Arthur's first and last battles had been 21 years apart. What he had to do was to figure out the dates according to the Anno Domini system and then transpose them into the system used in the Welsh Annals.

He ended up being out to the tune of 55 years. Both of the

dates he hit upon (518 and 539) were 55 years earlier than the dates of Arthur's battles (573 and 594). This margin of error can be explained by referring back to Bede.

The first historical event recorded by Bede in his *Historia ecclesiastica gentis Anglorum* was Julius Caesar's short-lived incursion into Britain, which occurred in 55 BC.

Knowing that Bede had introduced the Anno Domini dating system to Britain, the unknown monkish scribe perhaps tried to determine when Bede's system began and mistook 55 BC as the first date in British history – which is, after all, the impression given by Bede in his second chapter. When the scribe then adjusted the dates of Arthur's battles to fit them into the scheme adhered to in the *Annales Cambriae,* he was 55 years out. By misunderstanding the Anno Domini system, or at least Bede's trailblazing use of it in Britain, the monk succeeded in putting Arthur's first and last battles back 55 years: to 518 and 539, instead of 573 and 594.

That anonymous scribe set a hare running. He gave scholars an excuse to deny the real Arthur.

8

Men of the North

Men, it has been well said, think in herds;
it will be seen that they go mad in herds,
while they only recover their senses slowly,
and one by one.
Charles Mackay

IN HIS *Vita Merlini*, Geoffrey of Monmouth recounted a strange incident. Merlin and Taliesin were deep in conversation in the Caledonian forest when a madman appeared, filling the woodland with his terrible cries and 'foaming at the mouth like a savage boar when it threatens to attack.' Merlin looked closely at the man and recognised him.

The madman had once been brave and handsome, a 'noble descendant from the line of kings' who – back in the days when Merlin was 'rich', before the horrors of Arderydd – had been part of his retinue. They had been out hunting one day when they came to 'an oak-tree whose branches spread high into the air.' Lying on the soft grass around the oak were 'fragrant apples'. Merlin's companions greedily fell upon these apples:

> Instantly a dreadful madness seized them all, including this man; they lost their wits and tore at themselves, biting each other like dogs.

The men hissed, frothing and rolling on the ground, before fleeing into the forest, where they howled like wolves. Merlin later realised that the 'poisoned' apples had been left there for him by a jealous lover.

Geoffrey of Monmouth seems to have had little idea what this bizarre episode was all about. It is unlikely that he invented the story – it adds little to the narrative – and so what we are looking at here is probably a fragment of authentic tradition (later variants have 'Queen Gaynor' or 'Guenever' inadvertently killing a Scottish knight with an apple which had been poisoned, and intended for Arthur's nephew, 'Sir Gawain', by a murderous Irishman).

One of the poems attributed to Myrddin Wyllt is known as *Afallen* ('Apple-tree'):

> ... Sweet apple-tree, flourishing fruitfully,
> Growing in the earth at the heart of the wood,
> The prophetess predicts increasing death.
> The huge one with the aspect of a battle-spear
> Before excellent Dragon-lords croaks a warning;
> Ardently the heathen lay waste at the edge of the wood.
> From the longed-for youth a signal is raised.
> The Saxons uprooted by the first swarm of the bards.

Nothing in Myrddin's poem suggests that the fruits of the 'apple-tree' were poisonous. And yet the 'fragrant apples' which lay scattered beneath the oak – a World-Tree 'whose branches spread high into the air' – induced a raging madness in those who tasted them: they foamed at the mouth, biting each other like dogs and howling like wolves.

Their behaviour calls to mind one of Taliesin's poems. *Preiddeu Annwn* ('Treasures of Annwn') concerns the burial of Arthur in the 'Mound of Mead-Drunkenness' or 'Fort of Spirits', the treasures of the title being those grave-goods – the Thirteen Treasures of Britain – which were deposited in the chambered cairn with Arthur's remains.

The funeral ceremony was interrupted by 'Thrice twenty missionaries' and their 'overseer'. The Chief Bard of Britain displayed his contempt for these people:

> Monks howl like a choir of dogs
> Meeting with lords of wisdom ...

And again:

> Monks howl like wolves
> After meeting with lords of science ...

These were no random insults. Taliesin's Divine age way of thinking naturally interpreted the behaviour of the monks as little more than canine – lupine, even – when they confronted the initiates of the cauldron of the Lord of Annwn (which, as we shall discover, was buried with Arthur). Like those unfortunates whose contact with the poisoned apples sent them mad, the monks had become howling wolves, a 'choir' of howling dogs.

Before we proceed, we should analyse the 'poisoned' apples of the oak-tree and the madness they caused – for that madness brought about the death of Arthur, and it is still with us today.

Golden apples

In many mythologies, apples are the cause of trouble.

Eve, prompted by a serpent, ate the fruit of the tree of knowledge (long rumoured to have been an apple) with epoch-making consequences. Adam and Eve had their eyes opened: they became 'as gods, knowing good and evil'. But this was also the beginning of mankind's troubles. We were evicted from the paradise of innocence, another word for which might be 'un-(self)consciousness'.

The goddess of Discord started the Trojan War by rolling a golden apple into the banqueting hall of the gods. Herakles was tasked with stealing three golden apples from the garden of the Hesperides and the maidens who sang to the sunset on their western isle. In similar fashion, Lugh son of Cian commanded his father's murderers to fetch three golden apples from the

'Garden in the East of the World', which was defended by the king and his champions.

These golden apples were associated with a World-Tree – like the 'gleaming tree, with golden leaves, and golden twinkling branches' which grew 'in the best part of the island of Cyprus', and from which Aphrodite plucked three golden apples to help Hippomenes, the 'great-grandson of the king of the ocean', win the hand of Atalanta (the couple married but then defiled a holy sanctuary and were turned into lions). The apples were the gift of the goddess – Gaia gave them to Hera on the day of her wedding to Zeus – and whenever men came into contact with them, blasphemy and bloodshed ensued.

No ordinary apples could wreak such havoc. But then, the 'golden apples' of the World-Tree were surely those oak-apples which carried the key ingredient of iron-gall ink. They were not in themselves poisonous (indeed, the tannins of the oak-apple, mixed with charcoal and magnesium oxide, produced a 'universal antidote' to poisoning) but the effects of the golden galls could be nothing short of calamitous.

The ability to read and write took us out of the timelessness of prehistory and set us on the timeline of history. Previously, time had been cyclical, a never-ending interplay of 'then' and 'now'. Literacy established time as a linear concept, the arrow of 'now' moving ever further away from 'then'.

From a world in which past and present were constantly mingling in a state of flux – death and decay, birth and renewal – we entered a world in which time is of the essence. Time itself became an enemy.

This new awareness of time grew out of the imbalance of the cerebral hemispheres. Right-brain time is a mutable 'dream-time'; left-brain time is a relentlessly ticking clock. Time duly became one of our obsessions, wedded inevitably to a consciousness of ageing and the fear of death. And the more we became locked in the logical processes of the left-brain, the more we lost sight of our place in the natural world.

The right hemisphere, influenced (perhaps) by our internal 'low' spirit, *unihipili,* apprehends the patterns in nature and recognises the fundamental unity of all things, as summed up by William Blake in his remark that 'every thing that lives is Holy'. The left hemisphere, however, thrives on division. It sees nature as an adversary to be feared, mastered and exploited – as Francis Bacon argued in the 17th century, nature should be 'put on the rack and tortured for her secrets.' Obviously, these two perceptions of nature could scarcely be more incompatible.

The left-brain's attitude towards nature as something to be conquered and controlled has brought us to a pretty pass. It is no coincidence that the strident voices attacking the scientific consensus on climate change and ecological crisis are those of the religious-aristocratic mindset whose dysfunctional left-brain dominance caused the problems in the first place.

Entropy

Consider this case, outlined by the biologist Lyall Watson in *Beyond Supernature* (1978).

Watson was staying in a remote village in the Philippines when a ten-year-old boy was brought to the tribe's female shaman. The boy's mother had been run down by a truck three years earlier. She was holding her son's right hand when she was killed.

The left side of the boy's body was perfectly normal. The entire right side, though, was utterly disfigured. He shuffled uncomfortably, and when he spoke he snarled in an unfamiliar language (Watson recognised some of the boy's words and phrases as Zulu).

The fact that only one half of the boy – the right side – was so badly affected points to a collapse in left-brain function. This would appear to be confirmed by the strange behaviour of the left-brain language centre. The right hemisphere, which controls the left side of the body, remained functional; the left hemisphere had gone haywire.

A cure was eventually achieved by the shaman shouting angrily at the boy, overriding the twisted commands of his left-brain and ordering it to get a grip. But the important thing here is that, in his divided, dissociated state, he snarled when he spoke, howling and foaming at the mouth like Taliesin's monks or Merlin's madmen.

Armed with its biblical book of rules, the Heroic age sought to impose a new form of 'order' ('God's will') on the universe, often with horrific results. There were so many contradictions in its rulebook that any atrocity could be justified by a selective quotation. A balanced mind would find such inconsistencies as those thrown up by *Exodus* ('Thou shalt not kill'), *Leviticus* ('thou shalt love thy neighbour as thyself') and *Joshua,* who 'destroyed all that breathed, as the Lord God of Israel commanded', baffling. But the 'rational' left-brain, determined to go it alone without heeding its right-brain sister, is capable of picking and choosing its moral injunctions, depending on whatever it wants at that moment in time.

Living in balance, the Native American or African Bushman had no real defence against a fair-skinned double-talker who listened to one half of his mind, whose 'logical' brain could only prepare legalistic booby traps and whose morality was expedient, to say the least. Time and again, tribesmen found themselves face-to-face with a kind of madness they had never seen before – and it crushed them.

This madness can be explained by the laws of entropy.

Left to themselves, all systems tend towards disorder. It is a law of physics that, action and reaction being equal and opposite, any attempt to create order in one place will result in an increase in disorder somewhere else.

There is some evidence that the two brain hemispheres oscillate in activity roughly every 90 minutes. Every now and then, the right-brain becomes more dominant than the left, like a piston rising only to fall again.

For an individual trapped in the left-brain world of The Word, this hemispherical oscillation produced nightmares. Daemons and sexual fantasies overwhelmed the reasoning apparatus. The left-brain fought back, mortifying its body and cursing the products of its own imagination, which it externalised or 'projected' in an attempt to destroy them. Many 'witches' – women, mostly – died as a result of this insanity.

The madness was not literacy *per se*. Rather, it was the schizoid state of the divided self (the ego seeking to impose artificial 'order', only to unleash compensatory disorder) and the paranoid siege-mentality which arose from it.

It was the madness of those who, instructed by the Book, were forced to suppress their humanity and twist reality out of shape.

Their heirs are still among us, leading us all to hell for the sake of power and money.

THE ROUND TABLE

Assuming that Geoffrey of Monmouth's account of the madman and the apples preserved a snippet of traditional lore – the distant memory of a time when exposure to the ink-yielding oak-apples and their products led to a form of psychosis – and remembering Taliesin's remarks about the howling, irascible monks, we might begin to suspect that not all of Arthur's enemies were 'Saxons'.

The Church would later lay claim to Arthur. This was sheer opportunism, of the kind which encouraged the Benedictines of Glastonbury to pretend that they had found Arthur's grave. In fact, the Church did not really mention Arthur until 500 years after his death – and then it was to portray him as a 'rebel king'. Arthur's conversion to Christianity came late indeed!

Christianity had been introduced into Britain during the latter years of the Roman occupation. It had flourished in the cities, but probably made little impact in the more widespread rural areas. Judging by what St Gildas had to say about his contemporaries, the Church had failed to put down strong roots: when the last Roman legion departed in 409, and the Britons faced attack from all directions, Christianity faltered. A later wave of missionaries was required to re-establish the faith, and that wave came from Ireland, initially, in the time of Arthur.

The claim that Arthur was a Christian can be taken with as ample a pinch of salt as the insistence that he was a man of southern Britain. Just as it would be dishonourable to assert that Geronimo was a church-going president of the United States, so it is dishonest to aver that Arthur was a God-fearing 5th-century Southerner.

'King Arthur' was a Heroic age invention – a myth perpetuated by the same propagandist attitude which perverted the legends in the Middle Ages. But the 'emperor' Arthur was real, and we can know him by the company he kept.

A checklist of qualities we might expect of the historical Arthur should include the following:-

- He was known, in his own time, as Arthur
- He was of royal blood
- He was wholly or partly British
- He was associated with other heroes, some of whom are remembered in the early literature and subsequent romances
- He can be linked to the objects which we have come to think of as the 'Holy Grail'
- Some of his battles, at least, are a matter of historical record
- His enemies included the 'Saxons' (a catch-all term which took in other Germanic settlers, such as Angles and Franks)
- He died in battle
- His last resting place can be identified as the 'Island of Afallach' or 'Avalon'

- He was not immediately forgotten, but rather his memory lived on in place-names, personal names and local lore

Various candidates have been put forward as the 'original' Arthur, mainly by enthusiasts who, hooked on the medieval fables, can only conceive of Arthur as a 5th-century southerner (and, of course, a Christian). None of these candidates meets the above criteria; most fall at the first hurdle.

Artúr mac Áedáin fares better. For a start, he was called Arthur (the first of that name to appear in the written records) and his father was a king. But was he named after an earlier Arthur, the true hero?

No – for the simple reason that Artúr mac Áedáin was contemporary with the other heroes of the romances. Even if evidence for an earlier Arthur were to appear, that so-far unidentified Arthur would not have been connected, temporally and geographically, to the individuals who accompanied Arthur into the legends.

The 24 horsemen

A number of Welsh manuscripts name the *Pedwar Marchog ar Hugain Llys Arthur* ('Four-and-Twenty Horsemen of Arthur's Court'):

Gwalchmai son of Llew
Drudwas son of Tryffin
Eliwlod son of Madog son of Uther
Bors son of Brons
Peredur son of Earl Efrog
Gwalhafed son of Lanslod Lak
Cadwr 'Earl of Cornwall'
Lanslod Lak
Owain son of Urien Rheged
Menw son of Teirgwaedd

Drystan son of Tallwch
Eiddilig the Dwarf
Nascien son of Evelake
Medrod son of Llew
Hoel/Huail son of Caw
Blaes
Cadog son of Gwynlliw
Pedrog Splintered-Spear
Morfrân son of Tegid
Sandde 'Angel-Face'
Glewlwyd 'Great-Grasp'
Cynon son of Clydno Eidyn
Arawn son of Cynfarch
Llywarch the Old

Some of these names may be unfamiliar because the later storytellers moulded them into something more medieval. Thus, Drostán – who accompanied St Columba on his mission to King Bruide of the Picts in about 565 – started out with a Pictish name, Drust, which the Scots parsed as 'Drostán'. This sounded like 'Drystan' to the Welsh-speaking Britons. The continental romancers altered it to 'Tristan'.

The **Drystan** legend was later assigned to Cornwall. The earlier accounts, however, told a different story. The Cardiff 43 manuscript, for example, has 'Trystan' eloping with his lover, 'Esyllt', into Scotland's Caledonian forest. Béroul's verse romance of *Tristan*, composed in about 1200, explicitly states that Arthur's Round Table was to be found at Stirling, on the River Forth.

Owain and his father, Urien (died *c* 590), were rulers of the Cumbrian territory of North Rheged. Taliesin, the Chief Bard of Britain, was attached to Urien's court for a while – he wrote poems in praise of Urien and Owain – and Owain also received recognition in Aneirin's *Y Gododdin* poem of the final disaster.

As well as having his own Welsh romance, Owain appears

elsewhere in the *Mabinogion*: in the hallucinatory *Dream of Rhonabwy* and the legend of ***Peredur** son of* [*Earl*] *Efrog*. Chrétien de Troyes called him 'Yvain'. Sir Thomas Malory renamed him 'Uwaine'.

In Malory's *Le Morte d'Arthur* (1485), 'King Uriens' is Arthur's brother-in-law, married to 'Morgan le Fay'. The Triads state that Owain was a product of Urien's marriage to Modron ['Mother'], 'daughter of Afallach'. Arthur, according to the Triads, was buried 'in a hall on the Island of Afallach'; Geoffrey of Monmouth, meanwhile, indicated that the leader of the nine sisters who inhabited the sacred 'Isle of Apples' was called 'Morgen'.

The Irish *Félire Óengusso* ('Martyrology of Óengus') – which dates from about 830 and is therefore contemporary with Nennius's *Historia Brittonum* – refers to an individual called Muirgein ('Sea-Birth'). In addition to having a son called Artúr, Áedáin mac Gabráin, King of the Scots, had a daughter named Muirgein – later, 'Morgen' or 'Morgana' – who was almost certainly the superior of a sacred sisterhood and the mother ('Modron') of Owain son of Urien.

The Peniarth 47 manuscript describes the meeting of Urien and Muirgein, at which she identifies herself as a 'daughter to the King of Annwn'. This would make her father (Áedán) the king who owned the cauldron of the Lord of Annwn and the other 'Treasures of Annwn'.

Owain appears alongside Arthur, Cai and Cynon son of Clydno in the Grail-related romance of *Owain, or the Countess of the Fountain*. Cai – later 'Sir Kay' – was invariably cast as Arthur's trusty man-servant and can therefore be identified as **Drudwas** ('Brave-Servant'), the 'son of Tryffin' in the list of Arthur's knights. Cai's background was Irish (Tryffin the Bearded was an Irish chieftain of Dyfed in south-west Wales), and his natural father, Conchrad, was also father-in-law to Diarmait mac Cerbaill, the pagan High-King of Ireland against whom St

Columba rebelled in AD 561.

The Irish form of Cai's name – Ceathan – resolved into Cian (compare *ceathairn*, a 'foot-soldier', which evolved into the Scots word *kern*), suggesting that Cai was the foster-father of Lugh Long-Hand, whom the Britons knew as Llew ('Lion').

Seers and saints

Clydno Eidyn, the father of **Cynon**, ruled Edinburgh in the mid-6th century and owned one of the Treasures of Britain. Cynon himself was one of the few survivors of Arthur's last battle and is honoured in Aneirin's *Y Gododdin* (*c* 600). The Latin form of his name, *Cunomorus* ('Great Hound'), identifies him as the father of *Drustanus* – Drystan – and compares with the name of Glasgow's patron saint (Kentigern: 'Hound-Lord').

A 12th-century *Life of Kentigern* states that the saint was chased from the North by 'a certain tyrant' called 'King Morken'. In the *Tristan* romance of Gottfried von Strassburg, Tristan's father is persecuted by 'Duke Morgan' (a slightly earlier account paired 'duke' Morgan with 'duke' **Hoel**, another of Arthur's 24 knights). The tyrannical 'Morken' was properly known as Morgan the Wealthy or Morcant Bulc; he seized the throne of Lothian from Cynon's father in about 559.

Morgan evolved, via the Welsh *medrod* ('skilful'), into the 'Mordred' of lasting memory. He appears on the list of the 24 horsemen as the Royal Knight, **Medrod** son of Llew.

Cadog was a 6th-century saint, born in Wales. An 11th-century *Life of St Cadog* was one of the earliest hagiographies to feature Arthur (as a would-be rapist); it also recounts Cadog's meeting with Rhydderch of Dumbarton and his arrival at 'a certain fort, which is on this side of mount Bannog' (Bannockburn Hill, south of Stirling). There, Cadog dug up the bones of the father of Hoel or Huail and transferred them to his new monastery near Doune.

Bláán, the nephew of St Cadog, is commemorated at Dunblane, near Doune, and was rumoured to be the illegitimate son of Arthur's father, Áedán. His name was later conflated with that of the medieval storyteller, Bleddri, whom the French poets thought of as 'Blaise', which is why 'triumphant Bláán of the Britons' appears as **Blaes** on the list of Arthur's knights.

St **Pedrog** 'of the Splintered Spear' is the patron saint of Cornwall, his death ascribed to the year 594 (the year of Artúr mac Áedáin's last battle). His name is related to that of Pedr ('Peter'), a 6th-century King of Dyfed. Arthur was seemingly raised in Dyfed by his foster-father, Cai son of Conchrad, and Pedr appears to have named his own son 'Arthwyr' in honour of Áedán's son. To avoid confusion, Arthwyr ap Pedr became known as the 'Birch-Man', Bedwyr: he duly appears in the *Mabinogion* as 'Bedwyr son of Pedrod'.

Morfrân son of Tegid was another survivor of Arthur's last battle – 'all thought he was a devil helping'. The story of Taliesin's initiation indicates that the cauldron's bounty was originally intended for Morfrân Frych, whose 'Speckled' epithet suggests that he eventually became an initiated Salmon-of-Wisdom.

As 'Morfryn', Morfrân was the father of the poet Myrddin Wyllt, who appears among Arthur's cavaliers as **Menw** ('Little'), the Triads identifying him as Menwaedd ('Little-Shout') son of Teirgwaedd ('Triple-Shout'). In the Scottish sources, Myrddin's sister is named Languueth (from the Welsh *glân gwaedd*, 'clear shout'). These designations recall those *awenyddion* – 'inspired ones', 'poets' – who, as Gerald of Wales reported in the 12th century, entered an ecstatic trance by shouting.

Menw was a shape-shifter as well as a 'Battle-Horseman'. One of the 'Three Great Enchantments of the Island of Britain', we are told, was the 'Enchantment of Uthyr Pendragon (which he taught to Menw son of Teirgwaedd)'. Conceivably, this was the Irish art of raising a Druidic *airbhe* or 'mist'. Myrddin went mad after his 'battle-fog' ruse backfired at Arderydd in 573, and it may be that Arderydd actually derives from **airbhe-derwydd* –

'druid-mist'.

The last name on the list of Arthur's cohorts is that of **Llywarch** the Old. A cousin of Urien of North Rheged, Llywarch governed the adjoining territory of South Rheged (Cheshire/Lancashire) until North Britain fell to the Angles after Arthur's demise. He fled to Llyn Tegid in Wales, where he died in about 634.

ARTHUR'S BATTLES

Already we have identified half of the names on the list of Arthur's knights as historical figures of the late-6th century, predominantly associated with North Britain. So why do scholars maintain that Arthur was a 5th-century warlord of the South?

It makes no sense – unless the unspoken aim is to foster a false impression of Arthur. The reasons for doing so are very simple. Heroic age commentators implicitly demand that any outstanding individual must conform to their religious-aristocratic ideals. Only 'civilised' Christian noblemen can be heroes, and if evidence has to be fabricated or concealed to promote that paradigm, so be it. The end justifies the means.

This is hardly unusual. The Church in the Middle Ages held up the so-called 'Donation of Constantine' as proof that the Emperor Constantine had willed the entire Western Roman Empire, including Rome itself, to Pope Sylvester I. It was not until 1440 that the 'Donation of Constantine' was proven to have been an inept forgery.

Glastonbury Abbey, supposedly the site of Arthur's grave, was described as a 'laboratory of forgeries', a 'factory of fraud', by the French historian, Ferdinand Lot. The surprise is not that the medieval Church manufactured so many falsehoods, but that modern scholars continue to parrot Heroic age misinformation.

Further evidence of Arthur's activities in northern Britain is to be found in a 9th-century list of his battles.

Chapter 56 of the *Historia Brittonum* notes that Arthur fought

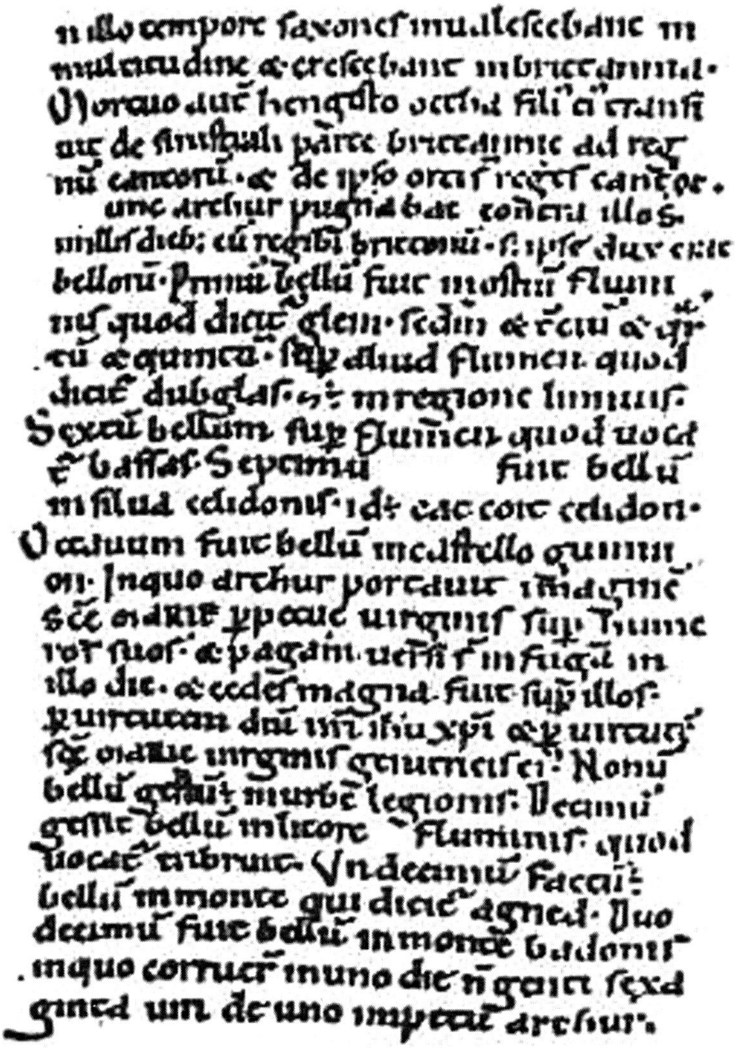

"*Section of* Historia Brittonum, c. *AD 829, listing the twelve battles of Arthur.*"

alongside 'the kings of the Britons' against the Germanic invaders, and that 'he was a commander in the battles.' The first of these battles 'was at the mouth of the river called *Glein*'.

The river is now known as the Lyne. It appears on a map produced in 1654 as a stream called 'Leuin', an earlier form of which is likely to have been *Lleuyn* (pronounced '*g*ley-in'), meaning 'Lleu-related'.

Two waters, the Black Lyne and the White Lyne, rise in the vicinity of Arthur Seat, east of the Arderydd battlefield near Arthuret in Cumbria, and come together at the foot of Kay's Bank, just south of Catlowdy, between the positions apparently occupied by Arthur and his man-servant-cum-foster-father, Cai. The lie of the land suggests that Arthur and Cai had prepared an ambush to prevent the warriors of York from reaching the Moat of Liddel, where Gwenddolau and Menw – soon to be known as Myrddin – were besieged.

Arthur's first battle, fought at the junction or 'mouth' of the river called Lyne, was therefore contemporaneous with the battle of Arderydd (*c* 573).

Myrddin stressed in his poems that Áedán mac Gabráin would seek revenge for the civil strife of Arderydd. The Triads relate that one of the 'Three Unrestrained Ravagings of the Island of Britain' occurred when:

> Áedán the Wily came to the court of Rhydderch the Generous at Alclud [Dumbarton]; he left neither food nor drink nor beast alive.

Though it suited the Christians to present Áedán as the aggressor (hence his nickname, *bradog* – 'treacherous') it was Rhydderch who had sparked the 'futile' conflicts of Arderydd and Catlowdy by giving the Christians too much rein. But if the Men of the North were to unite against their common enemies they could not be undermined by sectarian troublemakers. Rhydderch had to be punished. Fearing for his life, Rhydderch, the 'defender of the faith', sent a messenger to St Columba.

Only a year after Arderydd, Áedán became King of the Scots.

St Columba had preferred another candidate. The antipathy between Arthur's father and Columba in 574 is apparent in the accounts of Áedán's ordination provided by Adomnán of Iona and his predecessor, Cumméne the White.

Linnuis

The 'second, third, fourth, and fifth' battles of Arthur were 'on another river, which is called *Dubglas* and is in the region of *Linnuis*'.

A 2nd-century Roman geographer identified two places in Britain as *Lindum* ('Lake-fort'?). One was at Lincoln, the other near Loch Lomond, in the region of Lennox.

Lennox is dominated by a huge lake – Loch Lomond – and a triple-peaked mountain, Ben Arthur. The region was governed by the 'Learned' or 'Literate' Lleënog (**Lanslod Lak** or 'Lancelot of the Lake') who, along with his 'Defective' son Gwallog, otherwise 'Summer-Madness' (**Gwalhafed**, later 'Sir Galahad'), was the subject of eulogies sung by Taliesin.

The term *Linnuis* preserved the Welsh word for a 'lake' in conjunction with *gwys*, a 'summons'. W.J. Watson traced the root of 'Lomond' to *llumon*, a 'beacon', and quoted the Arthurian tale of *Culhwch and Olwen*: 'Cai and Bedwyr sat on a beacon cairn on the summit of Pumlumon'. Thus, Loch Lomond was the 'Lake of the Signal-Beacon' or 'Lake of the Summons' – *Llynwys* in Welsh; *Linnuis* in the *Historia Brittonum*.

There are four Douglas waters (*dubglas* – 'dark-grey') in the Lennox region, commensurate with the four *Linnuis* battles fought by Arthur. The first of these took place, according to Taliesin, 'at the ford of Alclud', beneath the fortified Rock of Dumbarton.

Myrddin had predicted this encounter of 'Rhydderch and Áedán by the bright Clyde'. The Triads confirm Áedán's 'Unrestrained Ravaging' of Rhydderch's court. Arthur's presence is attested in the landscape: there is an Arthur's Seat (*Suidhe*

Artair) on the twin-crested Rock of Dumbarton, while across the River Leven, which empties into the Clyde nearby, stands Castle Hill – known, at least as far back as the 11th century, as *Castellum Artorius*.

The next battle was recorded in the Irish Annals.

The Annals of Ulster note the death, in 574, of Conall mac Comgaill who 'granted the island of Ia [Iona]' to St Columba. That same year, according to the Annals of Tigernach, Conall's son fell in the 'Battle of Delgu in Kintyre', along with 'many of the followers of the sons of Gabrán'. Those sons of Gabrán included Arthur's father, Áedán mac Gabráin, who had battled his way to the Scottish throne.

Two more battles were fought in the same region against the Angles. Taliesin wrote of the Battle of Argoed Llwyfain ['Fore-wood of the Leven'] at which the combined forces of Rheged and Goddau opposed 'four armies' led by Theodoric the Flame-Bearer. Another conflict took place at 'Clyde Moor'. Known as the Battle of Ardunion, it saw the defeat of Hussa by the North Britons. Arthur is said to have directed the allied forces from a natural rock formation, the Cat ['Battle'] Craig. An Arthur's Stone (*Clach Artair*) stands close to where the Angles made their last stand at Dunglass.

Subsequent battles were fought 'on the river called *Bassas*' (the Tweed, near Bass Hill, or perhaps the Carron, near Dunipace):

- in the Caledonian forest (*Cat Coit Celidon*);
- at the 'Castle of Guinnion' (probably Abernethy, at the end of Strathearn, where several of Arthur's followers are commemorated);
- at the 'City of the Legion' (to which we shall return);
- on 'the shore of the river called *Tribruit*' (the Fords of Frew on the River Forth, near Stirling);
- and 'on the mountain called *Agned*'.

Geoffrey of Monmouth and John of Fordun both indicated that 'Agned' was an old name for Edinburgh. The ancient *Pa gwr* poem – essentially, the death-song of Arthur and Cai – referred to the bloodshed at Mynydd Eidyn ('Mountain of Edinburgh', now known as Arthur's Seat or, locally, the Lion's Head). The presence of a large boulder, the Caiy Stone or 'General Kay's Monument', in the Edinburgh suburb of Fairmilehead bears witness to the defence of Lothian by Arthur and his comrades.

Badon

Arthur's twelfth battle was 'on *Mons Badonis*, where in one day 960 men were killed by one attack of Arthur, and no one save himself laid them low.'

The Welsh Annals indicate that there was more than one 'Battle of Badon':

> (Year 222) *Primum pasca apud Saxones celebrator. Bellum badonis secundo. morcant moritur.*
>
> ['First celebration of Easter among the Saxons. Second Battle of Badon. Morcant dies.']

Going by the dating system used in the *Annales Cambriae*, this would appear to relate to the year 668. But Morgan the Wealthy ('Morcant Bulc') did not die in that year. Once again, the Welsh annalists got the date wrong.

The early monasteries used an 84-year cycle to track the movements of the Easter festival. This system was abandoned at the Synod of Whitby in 664, the substitution of a new method for dating Easter being hinted at in the Welsh Annals – 'First celebration of Easter among the Saxons' – which would have occurred in about 668.

However, the recurring nature of the 84-year cycle previously in use meant that events recorded in the original Easter tables could easily be assigned to the wrong cycle when those entries were later transcribed. An example of this kind of mistake can be found in the Irish annals, which drew their information from the monastery of St Columba on Iona.

The Annals of Ulster record the 'Death of Bruide son of Maelchú, king of the Picts' for AD 584, as do the Annals of Inisfallen. The corresponding entry in the Annals of Tigernach – 'Battle of Asreth in the land of Circin between the Picts, in which Bruidhi son of Maelchú fell' – is ascribed to the year 752.

Bruide, a younger son of Maelgwn of Gwynedd, became king of the Highland Picts in the 550s. He was visited by St Columba and Drostán, or 'Tristan', in 565 and was succeeded, after his death in 584, by Gartnait, the son of Áedán mac Gabráin, who reputedly buried a gold-and-silver cauldron on the royal Scottish 'Island of the Son of Cian'.

The date given for Bruide's death in the Tigernach annals – 752 – is manifestly wrong. The difference between that date and the date given in the Annals of Ulster – 584 – is 168 years: that is, *two full Easter cycles* of 84 years. The Tigernach annalist had simply assigned the 'Battle of Asreth in the land of Circin' to the wrong 84-year cycle.

A similar discrepancy accounts for the apparent dating of the 'Second Battle of Badon' and the death of Morcant Bulc to AD 668. By taking the *Secundo bellum badonis* back one full Easter cycle, to the actual lifetime of Morgan the Wealthy, we arrive at the year 584 – the very year in which Bruide of the Picts died in a battle fought 'in the land of Circin'.

'Circin' – or, properly, Circenn – was the Pictish province immediately north of the Tay estuary. It is perfectly feasible that Bruide should have died there, fighting against the Lowland or 'Miathi' Picts. The selfsame region would witness the death in battle of Arthur son of Áedán ten years later.

Morgan the Wealthy, as we shall see, can be identified as the 'Medrod' who appears on the list of Arthur's cavaliers. He is alleged to have died at a 'Second Battle of Badon', fought in the same year – 584 – as the 'Battle of Asreth' in Angus, in which King Bruide of the Picts also perished. These battles were fought during the lifetime of Artúr mac Áedáin, whose brother Gartnait was Bruide's nephew and immediate successor.

Unfortunately, most scholars ignore the 'Second Battle of Badon' because it does not support their claim that Arthur was active in southern Britain.

'LITTLE-BOAR'

Locating the battle 'on *Mons Badonis*' is crucial if we are to rescue Arthur from the deadweight of outdated propaganda and gain a fuller understanding of the Grail, for there is physical evidence of the Grail's existence in close proximity to the site of Arthur's greatest victory and his tragic betrayal. That evidence has gone unnoticed, though, because scholars insist on misplacing and misdating Arthur.

They have been encouraged in this by St Gildas, who wrote in his *De Excidio et Conquestu Britanniae* of a 'siege of Badon Hill' and indicated that this success for the Britons occurred around the close of the 5th century. The location of this 'siege of Badon Hill' was probably near Bath, many miles from the site of Arthur's battle.

By focussing, irrationally, on the *obsessionis Badonici montis* of St Gildas, and quietly overlooking the *Secundo bellum badonis* of the Welsh Annals, scholars have convinced themselves that an unknown Arthur was somehow involved in the southern siege. But Gildas did not mention Arthur, who hadn't been born when the saint penned his vitriolic open letter, and his 'siege of Badon Hill' was unrelated to Arthur and his exploits.

To find the location of *Mons Badonis* we must first grapple with the meaning of 'Badon'.

The early Arthurian tale of *Culhwch and Olwen* features a character named Maelwys son of Baeddan. A similar-sounding individual appears in the 12th-century *Life of Gildas*, written by Caradoc of Llancarfan. There, we read that Melwas, a king of the 'Summer Country', abducted Arthur's queen and imprisoned her in an 'Isle of Glass'. By means of false etymology, this 'Isle of Glass' is usually interpreted as Glastonbury in Somerset.

Chrétien de Troyes – in his Lancelot romance, *Le Chevalier de la Charette* – altered Melwas to Meleagant and made him the son of Bagdemagus, King of Gorre. This Meleagant also abducts Arthur's wife and holds her captive in his 'Isle de Voirre', the capital of which is 'Bade'.

We can assume that these three characters – Maelwys, Melwas and Meleagant – were essentially the same. Moreover, the composite character performs the same role as that which Geoffrey of Monmouth assigned to 'Mordred', the trusted nephew who rebelled against Arthur and lived 'adulterously and out of wedlock with Queen Guinevere'. In the Triads, this same individual is named Medrod ('Skilful'), and he appears on the list of Arthur's knights as 'Medrod son of Llew'. His alternative designations suggest a subservient nobleman or royal underling (*mael*, 'prince' + *gwas*, 'man-servant'), while his given name in *Culhwch and Olwen* – Maelwys son of Baeddan – signifies a 'Prince-Pig son of Little-Boar'.

The *Culhwch and Olwen* story incorporates two boar-hunts. The last, and the most devastating, is the hunt for a king who, 'for his wickedness', was turned into a swine. Before that, however, another boar is hunted to extinction: his name is Ysgithrywyn Penbaedd – 'White-Tusk Chief-Boar'.

Both boar-hunts take place 'in the North'. The obvious setting for these risky ventures would have been the Pictish province of Circenn, the name of which derives from the Old Irish *cír*, a 'comb', and *cenn*, 'head' (Gaelic *ceann*, genitive and plural *cinn*). Circenn was the realm of the 'Comb-Heads' or 'Tufted' ones (Gaelic *bad*, a 'tuft'; genitive *baid*, plural *badan*).

Like their compatriots, the *Orcoi* of Orkney, the 'Miathi' Picts of Circenn modelled their appearance on the boar, shaving their heads to represent the tufted 'crest' or 'comb' of that fierce animal.

The names of the two monstrous boar-kings in *Culhwch and Olwen* preserve two Welsh words for a 'boar': *twrch* and *baedd*. The diminutive form of the latter, *baeddan*, is also the name given for the father of the 'Prince-Pig', Maelwys son of Baeddan, who elsewhere stands accused of kidnapping Arthur's queen and holding her captive in his 'Isle of Glass'.

Cennaleth

Bruide, king of the Highland Picts, died in a 'Battle of Asreth in the land of Circin'. This occurred just a few years after the death of his Lowland rival.

The Annals of Ulster record the death of 'Cennaleth, king of the Picts' in 580, the Tigernach annals offering the date of 578 for the fall of 'Cennfhaeladh king of the Picts'.

The *Cennaleth* epithet points to the power centre of Galam, king of the Miathi. It translates as 'Chief of Alyth'. The Hill of Alyth looms over the valley of the River Isla in Angus (Circenn). The alternative epithet – *Cennfhaeladh* – suggests a shaved or 'tonsured' head or the chief of a high, rounded hill, and was eventually shortened, phonetically, to 'Isla', the name of the river which flows past the Hill of Alyth.

The Annals of Ulster also note that Áedán mac Gabráin undertook an expedition to the Orkneys in 580-81. Áedán's son, Gartnait, stood to inherit the throne of King Bruide (Gartnait's mother was Bruide's sister) and so the best explanation for Áedán's naval campaign in the isles of the *Orcoi* (Old Irish *orc*, a 'young boar') is that he was defending Bruide's Highland kingdom for his eldest son's benefit. Geoffrey of Monmouth – who remembered that Arthur had fought battles around Dumbarton and Loch Lomond – would also remark that the King of the Orkneys promised to 'do homage' to Arthur.

The 'Miathi' Picts were allied with the *Orcoi*, the boar being their mutual totem, and if Bruide was facing a challenge from his northern neighbours in the Orkneys it is probable that the Picts of Circenn would simultaneously threaten Bruide's Highland domain from the south. Áedán therefore set sail to crush the *Orcoi* rebellion, leaving his distinguished son, Artúr, to tackle the Miathi and their 'Chief-Boar', Galam Cennaleth. Hence the reference in the *Historia Brittonum* to Arthur singlehandedly slaying 960 men in one charge: with his father busy in the Orkneys, Artúr was effectively operating on his own.

Bruide survived the conflict of 580, only to die four years later in a 'Battle of Asreth'. This appears to have been concurrent with the 'Second Battle of Badon' and was fought in the same Circenn region where Artúr mac Áedáin would fall in battle in 594. It is probable that the 'Battle of Asreth' was indeed the 'Second Battle of Badon' – the battle, that is, of the 'Little-Boar' (Welsh *Baeddan*) or the 'Tufted Ones' (Gaelic *Badan*) – the Welsh Annals incorrectly associating the death of Morgan the Wealthy with this battle, when in fact Morgan died at Arthur's last battle *which was fought in the same place.*

The 'Asreth' battle was fought in a valley (Old Irish *israth*) in 'the land of Circin'. The largest valley in Angus is Strathmore ('Great Vale'), where we find the Hill of Alyth, formerly the headquarters of Galam Cennaleth. Galam's death is recreated in *Culhwch and Olwen* as the first boar-hunt, which culminated with the slaying of 'White-Tusk Chief-Boar'.

In tandem with the 'Young Boars' of the Orkneys, Galam launched an assault on Bruide's Highland kingdom in 580. Leaving his stronghold in Strathmore, Galam led his tattooed spearmen along the River Isla, heading up through Glen Isla where the river cuts through the southern rim of the Highland massif. This brought Galam and his warriors into a narrow defile below Badandun Hill.

It was the perfect spot for an ambush – much like the ambush at the 'mouth' of the River Lyne, with which Arthur had attempted to prevent enemy warriors from attacking his allies at the start of his military career.

Mons Badonis

Badandun Hill rises to a height of 740 metres on the edge of the Highlands. Its name means 'Hill of the Tufted Ones' or 'Mount of the Little-Boar' (compare the district of Badenoch – Gaelic *Bàideanach* – immediately to the north, and the stream known as Baden Burn in the Forest of Clunie, a few miles south-west of Badandun Hill). The unfamiliar term 'Badandun' could easily pass into English as 'Mount Badon', or *Mons Badonis* in the Medieval Latin of the *Historia Brittonum*.

The natural route for an incursion into the Highlands by Lowland Picts emanating from Strathmore was along the western flank of Badandun Hill. This drew them into the Glen Isla bottle-neck. The horn sounded. Arthur's cavalry swept round from their position behind the hill and hacked into Galam's thinned out warriors beneath the Duke's Lairs.

One of Arthur's horsemen died there. **Eliwlod** ('The Lord who Seeks a Boar') son of Madog (M'Aedóc – 'My Cadog') was later the subject of a poem in which Arthur speaks with his nephew, 'Eliwlod', in eagle form. Before he sought the Boar, though, Eliwlod was probably known as Fergus. A frequent companion of Drystan, Fergus fell at the Fergus Burn on Badandun Hill. His body was taken by Kentigern – otherwise Cynon, the father of Drystan – to a 'green hollow' near the River Clyde, where Glasgow Cathedral now stands.

The *Culhwch and Olwen* legend recalls that one of Arthur's heroes was injured when the 'Chief-Boar' was killed. The story goes that once Arthur and his men had 'boldly and gallantly set upon the boar and split his head in two', Menw the enchanter was sent to check up on that other Boar-King, Twrch Trwyth. Menw transformed himself into a bird to snatch one of the 'treasures' which were between Twrch's ears, but managed only to seize one of his bristles. The boar rose up angrily and shook himself, 'so that some of his venom fell on Menw' – and the enchanter was never the same again.

Menw was, of course, traumatised at the Action of Arderydd in 573, becoming the 'crazy man' – *myrddin* – several years before Galam Cennaleth was ambushed in Glen Isla. His insanity should not be confused with that of the men who tasted the 'poisonous' apples of the oak-tree, for that was the madness of left-brain dominance, brought about by exposure to the products of the oak-apple: dogmatic laws and 'sacred' texts. But what makes Menw's infirmity so interesting is that a parallel tale is told of the neighbouring valley to Glen Isla.

King Fingal – the Scottish Fionn mac Cumhail, whose elite war-band so closely resembles Arthur's Round Table – sent one of his followers, Diarmaid, to exterminate a dangerous boar. Diarmaid cornered the boar below Ben Gulabin in Glenshee. As he slew the boar, Diarmaid was poisoned by one of its bristles. He was buried, according to local legend, in a grave marked by four stones, just east of the Spittal of Glenshee.

The Clan Campbell, a cadet branch of the Clan Arthur, took the boar's head as its emblem, along with the motto *Ne Obliviscaris* – 'Forget Not' (see endnote). The slaying of the 'Chief-Boar' in Glen Isla, or the adjacent 'Valley of the Spirits', it seems, was a game-changing moment in Scottish history. The fact that near-identical legends are told of Glenshee and Arthur's first boar-hunt 'in the North' – which can be dated to 580 – also points to the ambush at Badandun Hill, where '960 men were killed by one attack of Arthur'.

This was Arthur's twelfth battle, the battle on 'Mount Badon' which resulted in the death of Galam Cennaleth, king of the Miathi.

A second 'Battle of Badon' took place in 584, and then it was Bruide who fell, yielding his Highland throne to Arthur's brother,

Gartnait.

And ten years later, in the same valley of the River Isla, Arthur son of Áedán fell in a 'battle of the Miathi'.

9

The Terrible Desire

... I could foretell the future and understand the mysteries of nature, the flight of birds, the paths of the planets, and the swimming of fishes.
Geoffrey of Monmouth

THE HILL of Alyth looms over the town of Alyth in the vale of Strathmore. The Gaelic name for the town is *Àilt* or *Allaid – àilt,* signifying something 'noble', 'high' and 'stately', being comparable with the Old Irish *allud,* 'fame'. Other interpretations include 'The Strength' and a 'steep bank' or 'rugged place'.

Until his death in 580, Galam, the king of the 'Miathi', bore the epithet *Cennaleth* ('Chief-of-Alyth') or *Cennfhaeladh* – 'Shaved-Head' or 'Chief of the High Rounded Hill'. The latter resolved into the name of the river which flows past Alyth. Now known as the Isla (from *Cennfhaeladh* – pronounced 'ken-eye-la') it appears in Welsh literature as the Cynfael river, where Llew Skilful Hand was treacherously slain.

Galam's stronghold was not on the Hill of Alyth, but on a neighbouring hill to the east. This is Barry Hill, from the Scots word for a 'barrow' or mound (the Gaelic name, *Dum Bhairraidhe,* suggests a 'Hill of the Overlord' or feudal 'Baron-Baillie' – *barraidh;* Irish *barraidhe,* a 'tall, proud, ambitious person'). Barry Hill is crowned with an Iron Age hill-fort, roughly oval in shape, with an inner wall – over 10 metres thick – enclosing an area of 61m x 36m, and an outer wall, 15m thick and 3.5m high. These walls had been heated by fire until the stones fused into a glassy mass. A deep trench protected the hill-fort from the south and east, two additional ramparts protecting it from the north and west.

This was once Arthur's territory.

In about AD 525, Gabrán mac Domangairt – the father of Áedán mac Gabráin – invaded Perthshire. His name is remembered in the district of Gowrie (Taliesin called it *Gafran*) and such places as Blairgowrie, five miles south-west of Alyth. Gabrán became King of the Scots in 538. The substantial territories which he had annexed in the 520s were lost in about 559, when the Pictish king Bruide swept the Scots out of Perthshire and Gabrán was killed.

With the annihilation of the Pictish chieftain, Galam Cennaleth, at Badandun Hill, Arthur reclaimed the Gowrie lands which were named after his kingly grandfather.

The 9th-century *Martyrology of Óengus* records the 27 January birth of Muirgein daughter of Áedán. Whitley Stokes, editing and translating the *Martyrology* in 1905, identified her place of birth as 'in Bealach Gabráin'.

Bealach – 'pass' or 'gorge' – usually appears on the map these days as 'Balloch'. The Alyth Burn runs through one such Balloch along the foot of Barry Hill. In *Forfarshire Illustrated* (published in 1843), G.G. Cumming described a connection between the vitrified Barry Hill fort and the ruined Castle of Inverquiech in the Balloch below:

> Beneath the fragment of the Castle there is a vault, which is popularly believed to be the entrance of a subterranean passage, which communicates with the old British hill-fort, on the summit of Barry Hill, in the adjoining parish of Alyth.

The existence of a secret tunnel linking the sheltered settlement in the *bealach* with the 'glassy' fort on the hill above might be fanciful – and yet, we shall see that the Arthurian legends recall a very similar underground passage! Moreover, it lends weight to the likelihood that Arthur's sister Muirgein, later immortalised as 'Morgan le Fay', was born in the *bealach* between Barry Hill and a tributary of the River Isla, in the very Gowrie lands which had been conquered by her grandfather, Gabrán.

Vanora's Mound

The ruined Castle of Inverquiech stood near the meeting of the Alyth Burn with the River Isla. The Alyth Burn is known as the Water of Quiech as it flows through the Balloch, with Quiech probably deriving from the Gaelic *cuach*, a 'cup' (as in the Scots *quaich*). Muirgein, the mistress of the cauldron, was therefore born in the 'Pass of Gowrie', beside the stream of the two-handled drinking cup.

This is not the only reference to the cauldron in the Alyth area. Just north of Barry Hill the River Isla forms a stunning waterfall known as the Reekie Linn (i.e. 'Smoky Pool'). Writing in 1915, J.H. Ramsay recounted the local legend of 'Sir James' who, banished into exile, studied under a magician in Spain. Sir James was sent back home to 'catch by night a wonderful white serpent that haunted a rocky cavern' at the Reekie Linn. He was then required to brew 'a deadly broth from the poisonous flesh of the serpent' in a cauldron, but was 'charged at his peril not to taste of the broth, or allow it to boil over.' A drop of the broth splashed onto his finger. He licked it and was 'endowed with preter-natural powers of vision'.

This legend of 'Sir James' so clearly echoes those of Taliesin (scalded by the brew from a magical cauldron) and Fionn mac Cumhail (fingers burnt by a roasting salmon) that we are surely dealing with an ancient tradition, concerning poetic initiation and the acquisition of supernatural abilities, recalled at the 'smoky' waterfall behind the Hill of Alyth.

In other words, both north and south of the vitrified hill-fort above the town of Alyth we find memories of the wisdom-granting cauldron.

The most famous allusion to Arthur in the immediate area was recorded by the Scottish historian, Hector Boece, in 1527, when he wrote of Vanora's Mound in the churchyard at Meigle, four miles south of Alyth, and the Pictish symbol stone – known as Vanora's Stone or Meigle 2 – which is now in the Meigle Museum. Boece stated that 'Guanora', Queen of Britain and wife of King Arthur, was buried in the mound outside Meigle church, and that any female who walked on her grave became barren, so that 'every woman, except nuns, abhors to stamp on that sepulchre'. Vanora's Stone supposedly depicts the gruesome execution of Arthur's queen.

Boece was drawing on local tradition, which recalled the kidnapping of Gwenhwyfar and her being held hostage in the Grampian Mountains, north of Alyth. Arthur finally did battle with Gwenhwyfar's lover. Gwenhwyfar was then imprisoned in the 'glassy' fortress on Barry Hill while her fate was decided.

It is common for scholars to dismiss the tale of Vanora's Mound. We shall discover, though, that evidence of a particularly durable kind does indeed connect the cauldron, and the death of Arthur's queen, with the Alyth and Meigle settlements in Strathmore. Those connections will prove invaluable in helping us to understand Arthur's last battle and the role of the cauldron in the catastrophe.

British tradition remembers Gwenhwyfar (the original form of 'Guinevere') and her sister Gwenhwyfach as the 'golden-chained daughters of this island', of which Gwenhwyfar was the 'chief lady'. The sisters' names might recall Venus – *Gwener* in Welsh – perhaps in conjunction with *chwyf*, a 'stir' or 'motion'; alternatively, the names possibly suggested a 'Sacred Way' (*gwen* + *hwyl*, Gaelic *uidh*, pronounced 'oo-y'), a 'blessed' female salmon (*hwyfell*) or 'White-Face' (Welsh *wyneb*, Gaelic *aghaibh*; compare *aoibh*, a 'cheerful countenance'). But the word which seems most apposite is the Welsh *gwenwy(n)* – 'poison' (Gaelic *guineach*, 'venomous'). Arthur's wife might therefore have been the 'Great Poison' and her sister the 'Little Poison'.

Little Anna

The Triads reveal that one of the 'Three Harmful Blows' was that which 'Gwenhwyfach struck upon Gwenhwyfar: and for that cause there took place afterwards the Action of the Battle of Camlan.'

Arthur's sister, we now know, was almost certainly born in the Balloch of Gowrie (*Bealach Gabráin*) at the foot of Barry Hill, while Arthur's wife – Muirgein's sister-in-law – is traditionally associated with the 'glassy' fort on Barry Hill and the nearby village of Meigle. We also know that two battles were fought beside the River Isla: one at Badandun Hill, resulting in the death of Galam Cennaleth in 580, and the 'Battle of Asreth' in which Bruide of the Picts perished four years later. These were the first two battles of Badon, where 'Badon' relates to the Pictish Miathi and their tufted 'Chief-Boar' (*Penbaedd*), who was also the 'Chief-of-Alyth'. We know, too, that Arthur son of Áedán fell in battle in the same region in 594.

The cause of Arthur's climactic battle was a 'blow' which Gwenhwyfach struck upon her sister. Whatever happened between these two redoubtable women presumably took place in the valley of the Isla, where Muirgein was born, Artúr mac Áedáin was killed and Gwenhwyfar was executed.

The apocryphal 'Sir James' was sent to catch a 'wonderful white serpent' at the Reekie Linn and to boil up a poisonous broth from its flesh. The Gaelic words for 'serpent' (*righann*) and 'princess' (*rìghinn*) are similar, while the Welsh words for 'white' (*gwên*) and 'poison' – *gwenwy*(*n*); *gwenwynbar*, a 'poisoned spear' – are suggested in the names of Gwenhwyfar and Gwenhwyfach.

Poison is also mentioned in Aneirin's epic poem of the last battle, which name checks the Hill of Alyth:

Eil with gwelydeint amallet
Y gat veirch ae seirch greulet
Bit en anysgoget bit get ...

['Again they came into view around the Allaid,
The battle-horses and the bloody armour,
Still steadfast, still united ...']

Aneirin blamed the disaster on the contents of the cauldron: 'Pale mead was served to them – it was poison.' The cauldron had let them down.

This 'poison' was associated with Arthur's sister, the leader of the sacred sisterhood on the Isle of Iona. Her entry in the *Martyrology of Óengus* – 'My Lord loved Muirgein, a wondrous birth with victories!' – is paired with another: 'Agna with ten virgins won a pure victory before kings.'

If Agna (also 'Agnetis') bears us in mind of the 'Mount Agned' designation for Edinburgh, we might note that Geoffrey of Monmouth named Arthur's sister, the Queen of Lothian, 'Anna'. The name was possibly Irish – Eithne, pronounced 'enya', meaning 'Fire' – but it was also related to the goddess Ana or Danu, patroness of bards and artists.

A peculiar story told by William Sharpe, who wrote in the 19th century under the pen-name Fiona Macleod, has Mary Magdalene buried in a cave on the Isle of Iona. The legend was relayed to Sharpe by a fisherman of Tiree, where the Arthurian saga of Sir Uallabh son of Horn was recorded at about the same time.

The tale of the Magdalene's burial on Iona might be a distant memory of Muirgein or 'Anna'. A short distance to the north of the *Sithean Mór* burial mound, a rock bursts through the greensward. There is a horizontal hollow at the base of the rock, large enough to accommodate the body of a small person.

The hollow is known to this day as the 'Cave of Little Anna of the Poison'.

LIFE AND DEATH

The cauldron produced a poison which, in the right

circumstances, bestowed the 'Druidic gift' – those 'preternatural powers of vision' which the legendary Sir James acquired at the Reekie Linn.

As an instrument of initiation, the vessel was associated with death and rebirth. Its paradoxical death-dealing, life-enhancing properties are evident in the cauldron's earliest appearance in Western literature.

Apollonius wrote his *Argonautica* in the Egyptian city of Alexandria in the 3rd century BC. It was greeted with ridicule. He then retired to the island of Rhodes, where he reissued his poem to widespread adulation.

The story of the *Argo* and its heroes, its captain – Jason – and the quest for the Golden Fleece was considered old even in Homer's day (8th century BC). The fleece had been taken from a winged ram sired by the sea-god Poseidon on a nymph who was also the granddaughter of Helios, the Sun. Phrixus escaped from his jealous stepmother by flying away on the ram. He arrived on a remote island, where the ram was sacrificed. Its fleece was hung on an oak-tree, guarded by a dragon, in a sacred grove. This implies that the Golden Fleece was related to the 'golden apples' or ink-yielding oak-galls of immortality; it was, perhaps, the original sheepskin manuscript.

The Argonauts set out to retrieve the fleece. Their adventures brought them to Aea. Later tradition held this to have been the island home of Circe, where Odysseus spent a year on his return from the Trojan War, which they believed was near Colchis on the Black Sea. The *Orphic Argonautica,* however, describes the heroes sighting Ireland as they made their way back from Aea by way of the Atlantic. The location of Aea is open to doubt, but the pronunciation – 'ee-a' or 'ee-*ee*-a' – bears comparison with certain early names for Iona (e.g. Ea, Ia, Hii), so that the 'Isle of the Sacred Trees' or 'Island of Apples' must be a candidate for the sanctuary of the golden oak-apples and the Golden Fleece (see endnote).

Circe's niece, Medea, fell in love with Jason. She prepared a magical salve to help him brave the challenges set by her father Aeëtes, King of Aea.

To win the fleece, Jason had to yoke two fire-breathing bulls and plough a four-acre field, sowing the teeth of a monstrous serpent from which sprang full-armed warriors, whom he destroyed. With Medea's aid, Jason then lulled the 'giant snake' which guarded the sacred oak to sleep, using a soporific 'mead' brewed in Medea's cauldron. The heroes returned to Greece, taking with them the Golden Fleece and the love-struck Medea, whom Jason had promised to marry.

The Roman poet Ovid would later describe how Jason begged Medea to extend the life of his father. Medea duly prepared a 'potent liquid of mysterious power' in her cauldron. She slit the old man's throat and skilfully replaced the blood in his veins with her potion:

> Aeson absorbed it, both by mouth and through the wound she had made. Quickly his beard and his hair lost their whiteness ... New flesh filled out his sagging wrinkles, and his limbs grew young and strong.

The old king was thus rejuvenated, thanks to this primitive form of blood transfusion. But Medea's witchcraft had its darker side. She offered to revitalise Aeson's brother – Jason's uncle, Pelias, who had seized the throne – using the selfsame method. When he consented, she persuaded the usurper's daughters to cut his throat and allowed King Pelias to bleed to death.

The cauldron gave new life, and it took life away.

There can be little doubt that the ancient legend of Medea informed the subsequent literary treatment of Arthur's sister. As 'Morgan le Fay', Muirgein nic Áedáin was described in the 13th-century *Lancelot* as 'the hottest, most lustful woman in all Great Britain', while Gerald of Wales referred to her as 'a certain fantastical goddess' (but then, Gerald was dismissive of the native traditions, preferring to promote the Heroic age fabrications of the Glastonbury monks).

This is not to say that 'Morgan le Fay' was merely a revamped portrait of Medea, but rather that both priestesses/princesses represented different stages in the story of the cauldron and its magical uses.

The silver bowl

We are now in a position to piece together a composite image of what the Grail cauldron actually looked like.

Chrétien de Troyes, in his 12th-century *Perceval*, described the *graal* as being of 'fine, pure gold' set with precious stones. The parallel Welsh tale of *Peredur* – based on one of Arthur's 24 horsemen – instead featured a 'large salver' in which lay a man's head 'surrounded by a profusion of blood'.

Wolfram von Eschenbach referred to the 'Gral' as a shining Stone – a Venusian emerald – which sustained the 'formidable fighting-men' of the Grail's 'warlike company'. It had the power to make mortal men young again, like Medea's cauldron, or the golden cup, kept inside a burial mound, from which the Hebridean hero Fionn mac Cumhail drank and which restored his youth and vigour.

The Welsh tale of *Owain* has its eponymous hero, another of Arthur's elite band, setting out to find a fountain at the foot of a tree. Beside the spring is a marble slab, and on the slab a silver bowl. By splashing water from the bowl onto the slab, Owain causes a tremendous storm and is challenged by a black knight (in somewhat similar fashion, the tale told on Tiree has Arthur's nephew, Sir Uallabh, sleeping under a cauldron in a cavern on a 'remote island' and then killing a giant). Another of the Welsh legends involves a 'golden bowl' on a marble slab beside a fountain inside a shining fortress. Pryderi was impressed by the 'great beauty of the gold and the exceeding good workmanship of the bowl', but he became paralysed and mute the moment he touched it.

In *Culhwch and Olwen*, Arthur and his men travel to Ireland to fetch the cauldron of Diwrnach, which is needed to boil the meat for Culhwch's marriage to Olwen ('wheel' – *olwyn* – or *Ôlwen*, 'Sacred-Path'). The heroes take the cauldron by force and return with it 'filled with the treasures of Ireland'. As the cauldron of Dyrnwch the Giant, it became one of the Thirteen Treasures of Britain '(that were in the North)'. It would only boil meat for a brave man, and so it compares with the 'cauldron of the Lord of Annwn' as described by Taliesin:

> By the breath of nine maidens it is warmed ...
> A band about the rim, around the edge,
> It will not boil the meat of coward, it will not avail him.

The Chief Bard also sang of the 'excellent cauldron of five-trees' and the 'drunk-making mead-horns' which dispensed the 'Druidic gift'. Taliesin had received the gift of lofty utterance from the cauldron in circumstances which precisely matched the means whereby 'Sir James' acquired his 'preternatural powers of vision' at the Reekie Linn, behind the Hill of Alyth.

Another of the Thirteen Treasures was the Horn of Brân 'from the North'. Brân has his own Welsh legend: he gave the Irish king Matholwch ('Prayer-Sort') a cauldron which could bring dead warriors back to life, though they would lose the power of speech. Matholwch was already familiar with the cauldron, the provenance of which can be traced back to Ireland.

It was the inexhaustible cauldron of the Dagda or 'All-Father' and one of the four 'treasures' of the Children of Danu, whose Druids were said to have resurrected the fallen warriors of Athens during their years spent in exile at Thebes.

The golden cup

Some sources describe the cauldron as silver, others as golden.

One, at least, has both. In the *Scéla Cano meic Gartnáin* it is a vat of gold *and* silver that is buried by Gartnait, the brother of Artúr and Muirgein, on the royal 'Island of the Son of Cian'. This island was clearly associated with the family of Áedán mac Gabráin, who was himself the 'All-Father' and 'Lord of Annwn'.

According to Taliesin, the cauldron had a 'band about the rim, around the edge'. This helped to hold the vessel together: the cauldron had a tendency to fall apart.

It emitted a shriek and broke into pieces after Taliesin tasted the three vital droplets of the 'liquor of science and inspiration'. Brân's brother 'on his mother's side' climbed inside the cauldron and shattered it when the Britons were being overwhelmed by Matholwch's resuscitated warriors. The cauldron therefore had something in common with Manannán's golden cup of truth.

Manannán mac Lir can be identified as Fiachna mac Báetáin, an Irish chieftain who became an ally of Áedán mac Gabráin. Consequently, in his British guise of Manawydan son of Llyr, he is the brother of Brân, the 'blessed Raven' who was, of course, Arthur by another name. Based on Iona – 'Emain Ablach', the 'Island of Afallach' – Manannán vouchsafed his magical sword to Lugh Long-Hand (known to the Britons as Llew Skilful Hand, the 'Lion' who was pierced by a spear whilst balancing on the rim of a cauldron beside the Cynfael river). His golden cup would break into pieces if three falsehoods were spoken over it, but if three truths were uttered it would reassemble itself.

A legend recorded in St Columba's native Donegal in 1870 has Columba breaking the golden cup. Manannán repaired the cup of truth and was then upbraided by the saint for using witchcraft. Offended, Manannán mac Lir turned his back on the Church.

Our best clue for identifying the cauldron, though, was touched upon in the coda to Chapter 2. The superstitious Nazis invested much in the way of time, effort and resources in the pursuit of various objects of supernatural power. One of these was the 'Holy Grail'. Otto Rahn, the foremost Grail-hunter of his day, was tasked with finding it.

Rahn's supposed suicide in 1939 has long been a source of rumour: it was suggested that he fetched up in a U-Boat in the Clyde estuary, near Glasgow, in 1940. There are certainly indications that Rahn had begun to recognise the Grail's links with Scotland; he might have got the idea when visiting Rennes-le-Château, where Bérenger Saunière had commissioned an image of a tartan-clad child for his Stations of the Cross. The same Scottish connections had previously struck the medieval Cistercian monks, before English opportunists transposed the legends to another place.

Even if Otto Rahn did perish in Austria in March 1939, his researches might already have garnered enough information on the Grail for his superiors to order their own copy of the original. This ersatz replica was discovered in Bavaria's largest lake in 2001.

It was a 'golden cauldron weighing more than 10 kilograms' which had been manufactured in Munich 'by means of the paddle and anvil technique', apparently at the behest of Heinrich Himmler.

In Himmler's papers it was described – innocuously enough – as a 'gold cauldron/celtic', although it had most likely been intended for use at the 'Elite NSDAP school' near Lake Chiemsee where, like the original Grail, it would have served to initiate the highest grade of SS warrior.

The Chiemsee cauldron is decorated with relief work depicting Celtic gods and military figures. The images are instantly recognisable as crude reproductions inspired by a more ancient artefact: an Iron Age cauldron made up of silver plates, highlighted with gold, which were held together by a tubular 'band about the rim'.

THE GUNDESTRUP CAULDRON

On 28 May 1891, three Danish peat cutters made an extraordinary find in a peat bog near Gundestrup, on the Himmerland peninsula of Jutland.

Neatly stacked inside a curved base section were twelve silver plates, a decorative disc and two fragments of metal tubing. There were five long, rectangular plates and seven (originally eight) shorter ones. These formed, respectively, the inner and outer sides of the reconstructed cauldron.

With a diameter of 69cm and a height of 42cm, the Gundestrup cauldron is the largest example of Iron Age silverwork in Europe, the golden Chiemsee replica being just 70% of its size.

The curved base plate had been fitted with a decorative horse brass or *phalera*. It depicts a large bull, with a sword-wielding figure above its back and two dogs, one over the bull's head, another under its hooves. This striking image instantly recalls the cosmic *tauroctony* of the Mithraic mysteries, the twin dogs possibly representing Canis Major and Canis Minor.

The outer plates of the reconstructed cauldron present a sequence of male and female figures accompanied by various animals. The five longer interior plates depict curious vignettes, including a bull-slaying scene, a cross-legged and antlered male gripping the head of a horned serpent, and a tableau showing a file of soldiers lining up before a large plated vat: a giant dips a warrior headfirst in the vat and a phalanx of horsemen ride away from the cauldron, above the heads of the infantrymen, from which they are separated by a horizontal 'tree of life'. The story appears to be one of initiation, in which foot-soldiers are elevated to horsemen.

The silver which formed the panels was pre-Roman. Gold layers had been applied at different times, and with differing levels of skill. Coloured glass inlays had provided the 'eyes' of the godlike figures. The panels had been soldered together when the cauldron was assembled. Puncture marks passing through the inner and outer plates suggest that, at one time, the cauldron had been roughly dismantled.

The Gundestrup cauldron was made of both silver and gold, its glass inlays creating the impression of 'precious stones'. It was of 'rich workmanship' and had a tubular band 'about the rim, around the edge'. When necessary, it could be disassembled – made to fall apart.

The late addition of the Mithraic horse brass connects the cauldron to the world of Arthur. One of the poems of Myrddin Wyllt, composed after the Arderydd debacle of 573, refers to a disconsolate youth as *peiryan faban* ('son of the cauldron'). A few years later, Aneirin sang of a son of 'Hero-Horse':

> And at the ford of the grey/holy mount, foremost his horses,
> Far-reaching his fame, perforated his armour,
> And before Gwair the Tall was buried under turf
> He earned mead-horns, the prime son of Hero-Horse.

We shall encounter Gwair the Tall again shortly.

Another burial is referred to in Aneirin's *Y Gododdin*:

> *A chynn e olo dan eleirch*
> *Vre ytoed wryt ene arch ...*
> ['And before he was buried under the Hill
> Of Swans, the wise earth of his coffin ...']

An Irish tradition has the four Children of Lir (Welsh *Llyr*, 'Sea') transformed into swans by a wicked stepmother; they were eventually restored to human form on the remote 'Glory Isle' by a sympathetic saint.

Swans were the focus of some fascination in the Western Isles. Vows were even sworn upon them. But there may be some misunderstanding here. The Gaelic word for a 'swan' is *eala* (genitive *ealaidh*). The same word – *eala*, properly *ealadh* – is used of a stone sanctuary or tomb. A funerary mound on the Isle of Iona is known as the *Ealadh*. The 'Swans Hill' (*eleirch fre*) of Aneirin's epic might be better translated, then, as the 'Mound of the Tomb'.

The wounded man

The largest chambered burial cairn on Iona, the *Sithean Mór* or 'Hill of the Angels', had a historic association with horses. It was reported in the 18th century that the islanders brought their horses to the mound on the eve of St Michael's Day (29 September) and led them thrice round the knoll in a sun-wise direction.

Arthur was laid to rest in a 'hall on the Island of Afallach'. Taliesin would imply, in his *Treasures of Annwn* poem, that the 'cauldron of the Lord of Annwn' was present when Arthur was buried, along with the remaining Treasures of the Island of Britain, which were his grave-goods. Like the burial mound, the cauldron was associated with horses: it was decorated with an ornamental *phalera* from a horse's bridle and it depicted the initiation of foot-soldiers, by way of the cauldron, into the elite ranks of the cavalry. Conceivably, the 'son of the cauldron' was also the prime son of 'Hero-Horse' (*ffêrfarch*) – the latter describing both the equine vessel and its patron, the Lord of Annwn.

(In the first of the *Mabinogion* stories, a prince swaps places with the 'King of Annwn' for a year and a day and then sits on a mound called Gorsedd Arberth – *gorsedd aberth*: 'seat of sacrifice' – where he sees his future wife riding by on a 'big fine pale white horse'; this same woman, along with her son, later gets stuck to the golden bowl in a deserted fort, the trap sprung by a 'bishop' who was also Arthur's 'chief huntsman' and the guardian of the cauldron.)

Like the shaman's drum, which was often referred to as a 'horse', the cauldron facilitated magical flight and the ascent/descent of the spirit. Its liquor was poisonous. A few drops of the 'sweet mead' could produce a crisis which no coward would face.

Hemlock – which grows on Iona – provided the coniine which created the 'head rush', like the 'storm' caused by Owain when he spilled the bowl's contents onto the marble slab. Paralysis set in; speech became impossible. The 'serpent power' was chased up the spine and out through the 'heavenly doors' at the top of the head. But the initiate was dying. Only a surgical wound could preserve his life. This wound was made by the lightning spear of Lugh, the 'famous yew of the wood', the point of which had to be kept in water to stop it bursting into flames.

A hint of the antiquity of this practice might be seen in the Palaeolithic cave art of Lascaux. The cave painting of the Wounded Man, referred to in earlier chapters, comprises three elements:

- a bird-headed shaman lies prone (penis erect);
- a bird perches on an adjacent staff or pole;
- a bison stands nearby, apparently unaffected by the fishing-spear which has pierced her bowels, entering through her sexual organs.

These three elements – bison, man, bird – compare with the three selves of the Huna philosophy. The bison, representing the animal nature of the 'low' self, has been wounded by a spear which penetrates the abdomen: it is, therefore, the *ka* or *unihipili* which suffers the wound.

The shaman's ego or 'middle' self lies inert, unconscious but very much alive. The operation has been successful.

The animal spirit has been wounded *but is unharmed*. The mortal spirit lives. The eternal spirit, symbolised by the bird atop the staff, has been freed from the body.

"The Wounded Man cave painting, Lascaux."

If this interpretation of the Wounded Man scene at Lascaux is correct, then the practice of piercing the low self in order to release the High Self is ancient indeed – at least 17,000 years old!

A tradition dating from Arthur's time links this archaic ritual with the Scottish island of Iona.

Gwair

Adomnán told the tale in his *Life of Columba*.

Gúaire mac Áedáin was the 'most powerful' layman of his tribe in those days. He asked Columba 'how death would overtake him'.

Columba replied: 'Neither in battle nor at sea will you die. But a companion of your journey whom you do not suspect will be the cause of your death.'

Gúaire wondered whether one of his retinue was thinking of killing him, or maybe his wife was planning to destroy him 'through sorcery' for the love of another man. But Columba would say no more.

Several years later, Gúaire was sitting under an upturned boat, scraping away at the barbed point of a fishing-spear, when he heard some men arguing nearby. As he rose to his feet, 'he struck against the knife he had carelessly dropped on the ground and his knee was grievously wounded.' Straightaway, Gúare realised that the knife was the 'companion' he had been warned about. He died 'some months later, overcome by this injury.'

No other source mentions a son of Áedán named Gúaire – which seems odd, if Gúaire was indeed the most powerful layman in the kingdom of the Scots.

The Welsh sources, however, repeatedly mention a person with a remarkably similar name.

'Gweir of Great Valour' was one of the 'Enemy-Subduers of the Island of Britain'. Gweir 'son of Strange-Speech' was one of the 'Three Exalted Prisoners'. 'Gwair of Great Valour' was also one of the 'Stubborn Men' (the adjective *caled* – 'hard', 'severe' – was similarly applied to Brân of the marvellous horn). From Aneirin, we learn that 'Gwair the Tall' was the 'prime son of Hero-Horse'.

Most famously, Gwyar was the father of **Gwalchmai** (later known as Gawain, although he was remembered in the Hebrides as 'Sir Uallabh son of Horn'). Usually described as Arthur's nephew, when he wasn't designated 'son of Gwyar' he was 'Gwalchmai son of Llew'.

The Irish *gúaire* meant 'hair of the head'. The phonetic equivalent in Welsh – *gwair* – means 'hay'; *gwyar* can signify 'blood' or 'battle'; *gwaywr* meant 'spearman'. Gúaire was the nominal forefather of the MacQuarrie clansmen of Iona's neighbouring islands, some of those descendants calling themselves MacKcurra or MacKwra (from the Gaelic *cùra* – 'protector', 'guardian'; *curraidh*, 'champion', 'hero').

The wound which Gúaire inflicted on himself cut his knee (a Gaelic word for 'knee' being *lùgh*; Old Irish *lue*, a 'heel'). Arthur reputedly received a similar wound from his companion, Huail son of Caw. Gúaire was whittling away at a fishing-spear when he maimed himself. The imagery recalls the Wounded Man of Lascaux, the Maimed King or Rich Fisher who presided over the Grail mysteries and the wound which Llew Skilful Hand made to the knee of a Druidic 'wren' or seer, the weapon presumably having been the spear of Pisear, King of Persia, which came down to Lugh Long-Hand, the 'son of Cian'.

Adomnán, who recounted the 'strange death of Gúaire son of Áedán', was a churchman, and so he was unlikely to offer a sympathetic account of such pagan activities as the initiatory ritual of the cauldron, the liquor and the healing wound. That very wound became the cause of Gúaire's death, 'some months later', simply because such practices were wildly at odds with the teachings of St Columba.

To put it another way: the most valiant non-churchman of his time had to die (as Columba predicted) because he was a pagan. The wound was proof of this – even though it was much the same as the wound made in Christ's side when he drank the hemlock and 'gave up the ghost'.

The Church had seemingly forgotten that.

THE SACRED JOURNEY

The Grail ritual involved a graduation – e.g. from infantryman to equestrian – which was also a transmutation, metaphorically speaking, from raven to dove (or 'swan'). Brân was the 'blessed Raven'; Owain's warriors were known as 'ravens' and Columba grumbled about sailing to Scotland 'of the ravens'. 'Raven' was also the lowest initiatory grade in the Mysteries of Mithras.

The yang to the raven's yin was the dove (Latin *Columba*, Hebrew *Yonah*), a perennial symbol of spiritual grace.

The theory that the Grail dispensed a poison which could work this transformation is founded on the Divine age concept of the three selves or souls. And we do not have to go very far back in time to find evidence in support of this concept.

Charles Lindbergh took off from New York in a monoplane called *Spirit of St. Louis* on 27 May 1927. He landed in Paris thirty-three hours later, having flown solo across the Atlantic.

Lindbergh was tired when his adventure began. Nine hours into the journey, he was struggling to stay awake. His mind seemed to detach itself from his body. He entered what he described as an 'unearthly age of time' – 'I'm on the borderline of life and a greater world beyond' – and began to feel that he was not one person but three: an exhausted body, a semi-conscious mind and something he could only think of as a 'spirit', which continually reassured him.

'Death no longer seemed the final end it used to be,' he wrote, 'but rather the entrance to a new and free existence which included all space, all time.'

His skull had become 'one great eye', allowing him to perceive ghostly presences passing in and out of the fuselage behind him. Lindbergh felt that he was 'almost one with these vapour-like forms', which were 'less tangible than air, universal as ether' and which spoke to him, conveying 'messages of importance unattainable in ordinary life'. With their help, he was able to complete his pioneering transatlantic flight.

Charles Lindbergh had put his life at risk, pushing himself beyond his physical and mental limits. Like Schrödinger's cat, he was both dead and alive. His semi-detached 'spirit' intervened to guard and guide him (which is supposedly the function of the High Self) and he became aware of a host of presences. These insubstantial entities told him things of great importance as he glimpsed a 'new and free existence' beyond the regular bounds of time and space.

A 'scientific' explanation might be that his brain had flooded itself with endorphins as a survival mechanism; this was almost certainly a side-effect of the Grail's liquor, too. But the simple fact is that Lindbergh had discovered what shamans already knew: at the limits of mental and physical endurance, direct contact with the spirit realm becomes possible.

The trick which Arthur and his cohorts would have learnt – by way of the Mithraic mysteries, say – was what to do when the veil between worlds had been rent. They had prepared themselves through dozens of ordeals before admission to the cult was granted. They were then instructed by the Father in 'the path by which souls descend and go back again', so that they could retrace the journey taken by Mithras, the Persian solar hero, when he ascended to the celestial sphere after slaying the horned Moon bull (a variant of the bison in the Wounded Man scene at Lascaux).

Many survivors of near-death experiences have reported the release of the 'semi-physical' double, the 'Hades' conditions of the earthbound hinderers and the 'Paradise' which lies beyond the waters of the second death, without really knowing where they were going or what to expect. The Mithraists, though, had a route-map to guide them through the afterlife.

Rose and cross

The actual composition of the cauldron anticipated this 'release' from the earthly to the cosmic plane. Five long plates, portraying stages in the initiatory ritual, form the inside of the Gundestrup cauldron. Eight shorter plates originally constituted the outer wall, each one depicting a deity.

The inner plates were arranged as a pentagram – like the five-pointed star which, in occult lore, represents the Earth, or the pentacle presented by Leonardo da Vinci's *Vitruvian Man*.

Five orbits of the Earth around the Sun are the equivalent of eight solar orbits of the planet Venus.

Wolfram von Eschenbach identified a connection between Venus and the 'Gral', which he claimed was a green Stone that had fallen to Earth from the brow of Lucifer (i.e. Venus, the Morning Star). The emerald was the sacred gemstone of Venus, while the Star of Ishtar – the Babylonian Venus – had eight points.

The cauldron's outer plates therefore replicated the eight-point 'compass rose' of the *croix pattée,* otherwise known as the Fishtail, Regeneration or St John's Cross, as worn by the Knights Templar. It also compares with the *Ouroboros* or 'figure-of-eight' symbol of death-and-rebirth.

If the interior of the cauldron represented the Earth, and the exterior Venus, then the cauldron itself straddled the boundary between the mortal-terrestrial and the eternal-celestial.

"The Gundestrup Cauldron."

"Base plate of Gundestrup Cauldron – an ornamental horse brass or phalera.*"*

"Detail of cauldron initiation scene from interior of Gundestrup Cauldron."

The ratio of the five inner plates to the eight outer plates was 1:1.6. This is pretty close to the Golden Ratio, an irrational mathematical constant roughly equal to 1:1.618.

Look at any point of a pentacle, and what you see is an isosceles triangle, the height of which, relative to its base, is equivalent to the Golden Ratio. The same goes for each diagonal line of the pentagram, the ratio of the length of the shorter section to the longer section being approximately 1:1.6. Da Vinci's *Vitruvian Man* is consequently an illustration of the Golden Ratio (also known as the Divine Proportion) which occurs throughout nature – the pine cone, for instance, which formed the head of the phallic *thyrsus*, often paired with a uterine two-handled cup in the Mystery cult of Dionysus, consists of alternating spirals numbering five and eight.

The plated walls of the cauldron juxtaposed two numbers – representing man and spirit, Earth and Venus – which, in proportion to each other, posed a mathematical enigma: the universal significance of the Golden Ratio. The solution to this puzzle was perhaps best expressed by the Rosicrucian brotherhood.

The mysterious Order of the Rose-Croix emerged in Europe in the late-16th century, their most famous manifesto – the *Chymical Wedding of Christian Rosenkreutz*, published in 1616 – being an alchemical treatise on the magical metaphor of the Sacred Marriage. Their symbol, a rose crucified on a cross, reflected the belief that the soul (a wild rose) was attached to the body (the Cross) by three nails. If these 'nails' were drawn out, the roseate soul would be freed from its corporeal husk.

These 'three nails of the Passion' match up with the three selves of Divine age tradition. The first 'nail' was symbolic of the 'low' self, the process of extracting it being much the same as the ritual piercing which drew both blood and water and released the 'semi-physical' double from the abdomen.

The second 'nail' was the 'middle' self or heart-based ego; its removal signified the death of the physical body.

Extracting the third and final 'nail' allowed the High Self to exit the body through the 'heavenly doors' in the crown of the head.

By such a method, which involved the awakening of the 'serpent power' and the Sacred Marriage of the cerebral hemispheres, the black raven of the Underworld was transformed into the celestial white dove of Venus and the eternal spirit freed to seek its home among the stars.

Sant grathail

None but the brave would risk it. The potential rewards were considerable: secret knowledge ('messages of importance unattainable in ordinary life'), preternatural powers of vision ('entrance to a new and free existence which included all space, all time') and the eradication of the fear of death ('no longer ... the final end it used to be'). But it was a fearsome prospect, a longing to experience death and rebirth – symbolised by the breaking of a sword which then magically repairs itself – that was profoundly unnerving.

The sense of 'desire' could be expressed by the Gaelic *sannt* (Early Irish *sant*, Welsh *chwant*). The desire itself was 'fearful', 'terrible' – in Gaelic, *grathail*, pronounced 'gra-hal'.

What we think of as an object, the *Saint Graal* or 'Holy Grail', was in fact an ordeal which was both appealing and appalling. It was a 'dreadful longing' – *sant grathail*: the 'terrible desire' to drink the mead.

One component of the 'poison' was surely hemlock (Welsh *pumbys*, 'five-finger'; Gaelic *minmhear*, 'insane-meal') which brought light-headedness and paralysis. Another likely ingredient was Sweet Gale or bog myrtle, a hallucinogenic herb which was probably the substance imbibed by the Norse Berserkers. Like other kinds of myrtle, it was sacred to Venus – or her Christianised form, as in the Welsh name for the bog myrtle, *helyg Mair*: 'Mary's willow' – and it enjoyed a long association with Artúr mac Áedáin's descendants, who wore sprigs of bog myrtle in their bonnets. Significantly, bog myrtle also provides a safe refuge for juvenile salmon in river estuaries.

Naturally, the cauldron would 'not boil the meat of a coward'. Among the Welsh words for 'brave' we find *dewr* (the cauldron belonged to an 'Irishman' named Diwrnach), *eofn* (suggested in the variant form of 'Annwn' – *Annwfn*) and *hy* (an early name for Iona). And while the cauldron separated the men from the boys, the horn which dispensed the liquor tested the faithfulness of the initiate's partner.

The Sacred Marriage of left-brain and right-brain, mortal and eternal, Earth and Venus, was celebrated as a male-female union. Thus, Arthur had 'Three Great Queens' and 'Three Mistresses', commensurate with his three initiatory spells as an exalted prisoner.

Early in the romance of *Perceval*, the hero takes a ring 'set with a shining emerald' from the finger of a woman he finds sleeping in a tent. Peredur likewise takes a 'thick gold ring' from a solitary damsel. Owain, whose own adventure starts with a silver bowl on a marble slab, receives a ring set with a stone from a spirited maiden. According to some sources, this ring-and-stone, which allowed the wearer to become invisible, was one of the Thirteen Treasures of Britain.

A legend concerning Artúr mac Áedáin's contemporary, St Kentigern, also features a ring. The story was related by Jocelin of Furness in his 12th-century *Life of Kentigern*.

Queen Languueth, the sister of Myrddin and wife of Rhydderch of Dumbarton, fell in love with 'a certain young soldier'. She gave him a 'royal ring of gold that enclosed a precious gem'. Rhydderch discovered his wife's treachery. Finding her lover asleep, he carefully removed the ring from the soldier's finger and threw it into the River Clyde. He then demanded that his wife produce the ring which had once been his gift to her.

In desperation, Queen Languueth turned to Kentigern, who despatched a messenger to the river with a fishhook. The messenger caught a salmon. Miraculously, the ring was found inside the fish.

The story was first told by Herodotus in the 5th century BC. It predates St Kentigern by more than 1,000 years. Undoubtedly, though, the archaic legend of the ring discovered in the belly of a fish relates to the initiatory ordeal which transformed a young soldier into a Salmon of Wisdom.

A noblewoman agrees to become the soul-partner, Venus substitute or Mary Magdalene equivalent, to a warrior who must face the 'terrible desire'. She gives her protégé a ring, set with an emerald, as a symbol of their sacred marriage. Like the bog myrtle in a tidal estuary, the ring will help the young 'salmon' to remain invisible to earthbound spirits during his Otherworldly journey.

The foot-soldier then receives the Druidic gift, becoming a 'knight' and a 'Wise Salmon' reborn from the baptismal waters of the second death.

10

Camlann

I predict a battle in Pictland ...
For the many who come, by the means of the white-headed one,
Except for seven, death brings them misery afterwards.
Myrddin Wyllt

ROME FAILED to conquer the whole of Britain. Huge fortifications were built right up to the edge of the Highland line but, even so, the indigenous peoples of the far north remained free from Roman rule.

Those independent tribesmen were dubbed *Picti* by the Roman soldiers – or *Pecti,* as Ammianus Marcellinus once spelled it. The term is usually taken to mean 'painted' or 'tattooed', as in 'picture'. The variant *Pecti,* however, compares with the Old Scots *Pecht* – 'Pict' (Welsh *Peithwyr,* 'Pict-men') – and probably derived from the Latin *pecten,* a 'comb'.

Two walls were constructed across Britain. The more formidable of these 2nd-century barriers was the great wall of Hadrian, which straddled the shoulders of Britain from the Tyne in the east to the Solway in the west. Soon afterwards, the more northerly rampart of Antoninus Pius was created between the estuaries of the Forth and Clyde rivers. Begun in AD 142, the Antonine Wall was vacated by the legionaries just twenty years later.

By the 3rd century, Britain was divided. Everything to the south of Hadrian's Wall was governed, taxed and policed by Rome. Everything to the north of the Antonine Wall was barbarian; this region was described as a veritable hell on earth by Procopius of Caesaraea, immediately before the time of Arthur. Between the Roman walls stretched miles of upland country which was home to two major tribes: the Damnonii of Strathclyde and the Votadini (later the Gododdin) of Lothian. The Roman authorities bribed these Britons to keep the peace along the edge of the empire. They became *foederati* – frontier mercenaries in the pay of Rome.

These political divisions forged a lasting legacy. The Romanised south eventually resolved into England, the wild Highlands becoming decidedly Gaelic. The intervening buffer zone, which we now think of as the Scottish Lowlands, became the land of the Sassenach, the 'Little Englander' who spoke a language that, like English, had evolved from the old Germanic tongue; this was the dialect known as Lowland Scots.

Even when Scotland became a country in its own right it remained a land divided, the southern Scots sharing a language, more or less, with their English neighbours and abhorring the Highlanders whose culture remained fiercely tribal. This antipathy had taken root when Rome occupied the southern half of Britain. The western Damnonii and the eastern Votadini tribes of North Britain came to see themselves as Rome's allies (hence the early spread of Christianity through Strathclyde) and the boar-like, barbarian Picts as their mutual foe.

Two Pictish tribes – the 'Caledonians' and the 'Maeatae' – were identified by Cassius Dio in the 3rd century. In the late-4th century, these tribes were described as 'Dicalydones' and 'Verturiones', the latter occupying the low-lying lands to the south and east of the Highlands. Their name corresponded with the Pictish province of *Fortriu* and probably meant 'People of the Forts' – a reference to the massive fortifications built in Strathearn and Mentieth before the Romans abandoned Scotland.

The southern Britons habitually saw the 'Picti' and the 'Hiberni' (Irish) as their enemies, according to Eumenius, writing in AD 297. Before long, the Picts had allied themselves with those Irish settlers who had crossed the sea from Antrim to Argyll and became known as the *Scoti*. In 367, these northern tribes, in conjunction with the Saxons and the Attacotti – a 'warlike race of men' – formed a 'barbarian conspiracy' against Roman Britain.

Like the Jacobite army which invaded England in 1745 under the Bonnie Prince, Charles Edward Stuart, the Picts and their Scottish allies had become the terror of the 'civilised' South.

The Old North

St Gildas – himself a child of North Britain – described the Picts and the Scots as 'differing from one another in manners but inspired with the same avidity for blood, and all the more eager to shroud their villainous faces in bushy hair than to cover with decent clothing those parts of their body which required it.' Those southern prejudices which would later insist that Arthur must have been a man of the South were already entrenched by the mid-6th century.

When the last Roman legion was withdrawn from Britain in AD 409, the southerners hired Germanic mercenaries to deal with the northern tribes. In return, the forerunners of the English demanded land on the east coast, next to Hadrian's Wall. Having gained their foothold in what would become the Anglian kingdom of Northumbria, the 'Saxons' took to ravaging post-Roman Britain.

The Scots, meanwhile, had enjoyed good relations with the Pictish *Epidii* ('Horse-People') since they first established their Irish colony in Argyll. Driven back from the Old North by the Germanic mercenaries, the Scots retrenched. Fergus Mór mac Eirc travelled over from Antrim to become their first king in *circa* 498. He was buried on Iona where, according to Hector Boece, he had founded a church which became 'the burial place of the Scottish kings'.

It was the grandson of Fergus Mór – Gabrán, the grandfather of Arthur – who redrew the political map of the North. In about 525, Gabrán joined forces with the Britons, overturning the longstanding alliance of Scots and Picts, and invaded Pictish territory, stamping his name on the map in the form of 'Gowrie'. His son, Áedán mac Gabráin, married the sister of Bruide, who became king of the Highland ('Caledonian') Picts in 552.

By then, the Scots and their allies controlled most of what we would now recognise as Scotland. But internecine rivalry soon put paid to any hopes of peace. Bruide unleashed his Pictish spearmen against the Scottish settlers in Perthshire, slaying Gabrán, King of the Scots, in about 559.

St Columba negotiated a truce between Bruide's Picts and the chastened Scots in 565. Trouble flared up again, though, in 573, when a dispute between Áedán's pagan priests and the Christian pastors protected by Rhydderch of Strathclyde escalated into the Action of Arderydd. Gwenddolau – a pagan prince – was killed; 'Merlin' went mad; but a new hero had appeared on the scene. Taliesin sang:

> Druids versed in letters
> Prophesy that Arthur
> Is the longed-for one of the tribe.

The next year, Áedán led a punitive raid on Rhydderch's stronghold at Dumbarton and then secured the Scottish throne, before the combined forces of the North checked the advance of the land-hungry Angles into the Lennox (Loch Lomond) region.

The ensuing years witnessed battle after battle. The Angles were forced back into their east coast enclaves. The Irishmen of Ulster launched attacks on Manau Gododdin (Stirling, on the River Forth) and were repulsed. The 'Miathi' Picts were vanquished, first in Strathearn and then, in 580, in Angus, when Arthur retook the Gowrie lands, named after his grandfather Gabrán.

The success of the princely alliance which had constellated around the figure of Arthur – the 'Round Table' of 24 horsemen based, according to the French poet Béroul, writing in about 1200, at Stirling – meant that the North was pacified by 584. Bruide died in a Pictish civil war, fought in Angus, and Áedán's son Gartnait inherited the Highland throne. That same year, Áedán's Irish ally, Fiachna mac Báetáin, was awarded the guardianship of Manau Gododdin, becoming *Manannán*, the 'Dear One of Manau'.

After years of fighting, the Men of the North were at last free to focus on driving the 'Saxons' back into the sea which had brought them over from Germany.

Mordred

Lindisfarne is a tidal islet on the Northumbrian coast. A short distance to the south stands Bamburgh, once the principal bastion of the Northumbrian Angles.

In 590, the combined British forces of the North had the Angles pinned down at Lindisfarne – or *Ynys Medcaut*, as the Britons called it.

Many scholars presume that Arthur played some unrecorded role in delaying the Saxon advance through southern Britain. His real achievement was much greater. Thanks to his commanding genius, the Men of the North had been brought to the brink of a historic triumph: the eradication of the incipient English.

Arthur had turned the tables on the Angles. Britain – or at least the northern half of the island – stood poised on the threshold of freedom.

Fiachna mac Báetáin, the land-holder of Manau, collaborated with Áedán mac Gabráin, King of the Scots, in besieging Bamburgh, one source claiming that Fiachna stormed the Anglian fortress and established a garrison. Another Irish tale states that while Fiachna was fighting with Áedán in 'Saxon-land', Mannanán mac Lir sired a son in his stead. The boy was named Mongán ('Little Long-haired One'), the 'son of Fiachna' and the 'son of Manannán'; he was probably the boyish hero known to the Britons as Gwalchmai ('Gawain'), the nephew and foster-son of Arthur.

But as Áedán and his allies achieved victory at Bamburgh, disaster struck further up the coast. Urien, the father of Owain, was murdered by a paid assassin. It was left to Llywarch – one of Arthur's 'Counsellor Knights' – to retrieve his cousin's head from Aber Lleu ('Mouth of the Lleu').

The traitor was Morgan the Wealthy; one text lays the blame on the princes of Edinburgh, but since Morgan was the 'Prince-Servant' of Lothian it amounts to the same thing. The motive, wrote Nennius in 829, was 'jealousy'.

Arthur's queen, we should recall, was forcibly abducted by a subordinate nobleman named 'Mordred' or 'Medrod' ('Medrod son of Llew' in the list of Arthur's horsemen). The Triads insist that this happened while Arthur was away from home, doing battle against 'Rome':

> When Medrod heard that Arthur's host was dispersed, he turned against Arthur, and the Saxons and the Picts and the Scots united with him to hold this Island against Arthur.

Geoffrey of Monmouth said much the same in 1137. Arthur went to war with 'Rome', leaving his 'nephew' and his queen in charge of the kingdom. Mordred then 'placed the crown upon his own head ...'

> What is more, this treacherous tyrant was living adulterously and out of wedlock with Queen Guinevere, who had broken the vows of her earlier marriage.

Mordred reputedly struck a deal with the Saxons, offering them 'that part of the island that stretched from the River Humber to Scotland' in return for their support. The traitor also 'brought the Scots, Picts and Irish into his alliance, with anyone else he knew to be filled with hatred for his uncle.'

The Triads tell us that the first of the three 'Unrestrained Ravagings' occurred when Medrod came to Arthur's court: 'And he dragged Gwenhwyfar from her royal chair, and then he struck a blow upon her.'

And so Gwenhwyfar was abducted. Morgan the Wealthy – otherwise the 'Skilful' (Welsh *medrod*) – undermined the British alliance at Lindisfarne, probably in collusion with the embattled Angles of Northumbria, and then he kidnapped Arthur's queen.

The same 'Morken' was – according to the *Life of Kentigern* – the 'certain tyrant' and 'vile slave of Mammon' who had previously persecuted St Kentigern or Cynon son of Clydno of Edinburgh, forcing him to flee from the North to the distant settlement of St David's in south-west Wales.

Morgan had eventually been brought back into the fold, becoming an honoured member of Arthur's circle.

But he betrayed them all.

THE GODODDIN

As we have seen, the Scots of Angus maintained the tradition that Gwenhwyfar and her abductor sought refuge in the Grampian Mountains. Their most likely destination was the fortified Hill of Tillymorgan, the seat of the *Clann Morgainn*, in Strathbogie. There were two old Roman camps nearby.

The medieval *Book of Deer* from Aberdeenshire described the chief of the Morgan clan as a *tóisech* – not a king so much as a feudal rent-collector or 'baron-baillie'. Morgan had become a subservient prince, the adoptive 'son' of the Pictish 'Little-Boar' (Welsh *Baeddan*).

Morgan the Wealthy surrounded himself with the comb-headed spearmen of the 'Miathi', who had not forgotten Arthur's destruction of their Chief-Boar, Galam Cennaleth, at Badandun Hill ten years earlier. The 'Miathi' Picts embraced Morgan as their new leader. He became their 'boar-king', the prince who – as we read in the legend of *Culhwch and Olwen* – was transformed into a swine.

What is remarkable is that the realm of the 'Caledonian' Picts, which lay just west of the Hill of Tillymorgan, had been governed for six years by Gartnait mac Áedáin. The fact that Morgan's retreat neighboured the Highland territory then ruled by Arthur's half-brother should have made Morgan's position extremely precarious. And yet Gartnait did nothing to bring the treacherous 'boar-king' to book.

Morgan had destroyed the Britons' chance of ridding their lands of the Anglian intruders. He had commissioned the assassination of the much-loved Urien and had stolen Arthur's queen. Why, then, did Gartnait mac Áedáin not move against him?

One clue can be found in the Annals of Ulster, which record the 'conversion of Constantine to the Lord' in 588 (the Annals of Tigernach date this event to 586, the *Annales Cambriae* to 589).

For his Christian conversion to have warranted mention in the annals, this Constantine must have been a significant person. Geoffrey of Monmouth would later claim that, with his last breath, Arthur 'handed the crown of Britain over to his cousin Constantine'. Constantine – Welsh *Cystennin* – similarly appears as Arthur's cousin in *Culhwch and Olwen*, while his son Goreu ('Gilded') makes several appearances of his own: he was said to have liberated Arthur from each of his three spells of ritual entombment. The medieval *Life of Pedrog* also features a wealthy man named Constantine who was given an ivory horn when he was converted by one of Arthur's celebrated horsemen.

Jocelin's *Life of Kentigern* states that Constantine became king of Strathclyde after the death of Rhydderch in about 614. Better known as St Constantine, he seemingly resigned the throne soon afterwards and was buried in his own church at Govan, the 'Town of the Smith', which is now part of Glasgow.

Constantine was a baptismal name. His original name was surely Cano ('Song'), the son of Gartnait whose birth or baptism drove a wedge between the Pictish king and his father Áedán.

According to the *Scéla Cano*, much of the family strife revolved around a gilded cauldron, or vat of gold and silver, which Gartnait buried on a royal island after sending his son to Ireland.

The *Aberdeen Breviary* confirms that Constantine lived incognito as a monk in Ireland before he carelessly revealed his true identity. Like Cano, he eventually returned from Ireland to claim his throne.

Constantine was supposedly the son of Rhydderch and Languueth (Myrddin's sister), although this was almost certainly a fosterage arrangement. He was the natural son of Gartnait mac Áedáin, and his baptism preceded Morgan's treachery and the rape of Arthur's queen.

The conversion of Constantine reopened old wounds, reviving bitter memories of Arderydd and the discord fomented by religious extremism. This renewal of sectarian hostilities meant that when Arthur needed his half-brother Gartnait's support in tackling the renegade Morgan, it was pointedly withheld.

Camelot

Another plan was needed. If Arthur could not approach Morgan by land – because Gartnait had closed the Highlands to him – he would have to attack from the sea.

A special fleet capable of transporting men and horses had to be assembled. Geraint son of Erbin, one of the 'Three Seafarers of the Island of Britain', travelled up from faraway Cornwall to assist the expedition; he would be rewarded with his own *Mabinogion* romance and tributes from the leading poets of the day.

Warriors gathered in Lothian:

Men came to Gododdin, laughing, persistent,
Bitter in battle, blades marshalled,
A brief year of peace they observed.

Thus sang Aneirin –

Mead they drank, yellow, sweet, ensnaring;
For a year there was many a joyous singer ...
Wine and golden mead was their liquor
For a year; against the noble duo,
Three men and three score and three hundred gold-collared ones.

The 'noble duo' was, of course, the treacherous Morgan and the adulterous Gwenhwyfar.

The year-long delay can be explained by the need to induct the new arrivals into the cauldron cult. They had to be 'knighted' and to swear the battle-oath – Mithras, we recall, was the god of oaths, while the root of the name Lugh would appear to have been *luige*, an 'oath' (Welsh *llw*, Old Celtic *lugio-n*).

The correct time for such initiations was Beltane, the great fire festival of early May which ushered in the summer and the battle season (see endnote). Later versions of the legends glossed over the pagan festivities by referring to the Christian festival of Whitsun, or Pentecost, which took place at around the same time. Thus, in Malory's *Le Morte d'Arthur*, the Round Table knights behold a vision of the 'Holy Grail' on Whitsunday.

Aneirin's *Y Gododdin* states that the drinking-horn was carried to the warriors at the 'court of Eidyn'. This would seemingly indicate Edinburgh – *Din Eidyn* to the Britons. But the territory of Lothian extended westwards into Manau Gododdin, along the River Forth, and it is there that we might start our search for Arthur's headquarters.

A massive Roman base had been established a little to the north of the Antonine Wall. The original fort was constructed by a detachment of the Twentieth Legion around a Pictish round-house overlooking the River Carron. A short distance away stood a Romano-British temple, 'built without lime or mortar', which was recorded in 1293 as *Furnus Arthuri* – 'Arthur's Oven'.

The remains of the Roman fortifications near Falkirk were discussed by Edward Gibson, Bishop of London, in 1695:

> There is yet a confused appearance of a little ancient city, where the common people believe there was formerly a road for ships. They call it Camelot.

Similarly, William Stukeley reported in December 1720: 'We may still discern the track of the streets, foundations of buildings and subterranean vaults. The country people call it Camelon or Camelot.'

The Gaelic name for Camelon is *Camlan* (Scots *Kemlin*). The more familiar name, 'Camelot', probably derives from *Camulodunum*, a Roman citadel dedicated to a Celtic war-god. Robert Sibbald argued in 1707 that Camelon, near Falkirk, was once known as *Camulodunum Brigantium* – the 'Camelot' of North Britain.

The name 'Camelot' first occurs in Chrétien de Troyes's Lancelot tale, *Le Chevalier de la Charette*, where it seems to have been used synonymously with 'Caerleon', another name for Arthur's court. Properly, this was *Caerllion* – from *Caer Legionis*, the 'City of the Legion', which was also the location given by Nennius in the *Historia Brittonum* for Arthur's ninth battle. Camelon's legendary associations, its size, strategic importance and close proximity to the 'Round Table' at Stirling, make the old Roman fort a strong candidate for the original 'Camelot'.

Geraint

At the eastern end of the Antonine Wall stood another Roman fortress, formerly known as *Kair Eden*. The headland of Bo'ness, adjacent to this 'Fort of Eidyn', was known to the Angles as *Berwardeston* – 'Town of the Bear-Guardian' – recalling the 'bear' element (*arth*) in the name of Arthur.

However, the common assumption that Arthur's court was at Caerleon-on-Usk in South Wales should give us pause. For one of the most easterly of the Roman fortifications in North Britain was on the bank of the River Esk, east of Edinburgh. Like 'Usk', 'Esk' comes from a Celtic root word meaning 'water'.

The fort at Inveresk covered 6.6 acres and had probably been a major cavalry station. A substantial civilian settlement, incorporating what appears to have been an amphitheatre, grew up alongside the Roman fort. Evidence of Mithraic worship was unearthed there in 2010 (see Chapter 6).

In his *Inveresk Parish Lore from Pagan Times* (1894), R. M'D. Stirling suggested that Aneirin had meant Inveresk when he sang of the 'court of Eidyn': 'Here were a municipium and colonia, and the remains of a Roman villa prove a banqueting hall there also.'

A study of the *Geraint and Enid* romance points to the Grail cult having been active in this region.

The area was colonised by the Knights Templar and their Cistercian counterparts in the 12th century. The Templars were granted the lands of the 'Warrior's Town' – Balantrodach – a little further up the Esk by King David I in 1127, the Cistercian monks receiving the nearby site of Newbattle Abbey from the same Scottish king in 1140.

According to legend, King David was hunting near Edinburgh in 1128 when, close by Arthur's Seat, he was startled by a huge white stag. The miraculous vision of a shining crucifix between the stag's antlers inspired the king to found Edinburgh's Holyrood Abbey.

Another white deer was hunted along the banks of the River Esk by Robert the Bruce. Sir William St Clair of nearby Rosslyn wagered his own head that the white hart would be caught before it crossed the March Burn. Sir William won his bet, and the chief huntsman that day was knighted, thereafter displaying the hunting horn on his family crest.

The romance of *Geraint and Enid* opens with the Whitsuntide hunt for a white hart across the River Usk (or Esk) from the 'City of the Legion'. In Chrétien de Troyes's version of the legend, Arthur and his barons then participate in a grand tournament 'in the plain below Edinburgh'.

The story ends with Geraint son of Erbin entering the Enchanted Games. Passing through a hedge of mist surrounded by heads impaled on stakes, he comes to a clearing. A large apple-tree stands at the entrance to a tent. A hunting horn hangs from a branch of the tree, and inside the tent sits a maiden in a golden chair.

Geraint sits in a chair facing the maiden and is instantly challenged by a knight, whom he overcomes. As his prize, Geraint demands that the lethal game should no longer be played. The defeated knight tells him to blow the hunting horn, 'and when thou soundest it, the mist will vanish.'

Geraint son of Erbin was one of the last to be inducted into the cult, his encounter with death romanticised in his legend, which also features such luminaries as Arthur and Gwenhwyfar, Gwair Great Valour, Cai, Gwalchmai, Owain, Peredur, Goreu son of Constantine and Gwallog son of Lleënog. The 'game' ceased following Geraint's initiation because no one faced the 'terrible desire' after him.

But the memories remained, revived in the days of David I and the Bruce, and retold by the monks of Newbattle and Melrose – who perhaps glimpsed the significance of the horn, a blast of which signalled the initiate's 'rebirth' after three days of enchanted imprisonment.

THE ROAD TO CAMLANN

The sources agree that Arthur's final campaign began with an amphibious assault.

The Triads state that after 'Medrod' had united with the 'Saxons and the Picts and the Scots' in rebellion, Arthur 'turned back with all that survived of his army, and succeeded by violence in landing on this Island in opposition to Medrod.' Geoffrey of Monmouth remarked that 'Mordred inflicted great slaughter on those who were trying to land', but in the end, and 'only with enormous difficulty, Arthur's men occupied the sea-shore.'

Myrddin foresaw a 'battle in Pictland' and the arrival of seven warships from across the sea, with only seven Britons surviving the catastrophe. Taliesin observed that three times the capacity of Arthur's ship went on the sea, but only seven men returned – just as seven men survived Brân's battle against a devious Irish king over the cauldron.

The fleet sailed in the summer of 594, probably from the mouth of the River Esk at Musselburgh (which the Romans, as R. M'D. Stirling noted, 'compared not unfavourably with the Bay of Naples'). The flotilla turned northwards, heading for what Taliesin called the 'coast of Mordei' – from *mordai*, 'large houses' or 'courts', the 'Miathi' Picts also being known as the Verturiones or 'People of the Forts'.

Arthur's companion, Drystan ('Drostán'), had spent several years in Aberdeenshire, where he helped to establish a monastery at Old Deer after St Columba's conference with Bruide in 565. With Drystan as navigator and Geraint as admiral of the fleet, the armada sailed towards the great headland of Peterhead, 95 sea-miles from the mouth of the Firth of Forth.

They beached on a wide, curving stretch of sand due east of Morgan's refuge in Strathbogie. The Irish annals recorded the battle of 'The Headland' (*Áird Sendoim*), although Taliesin knew it by another name:

In Llongborth I saw Arthur,
Right bold, hewing with steel,
Emperor, leader and champion.

Llongborth (literally, 'Ship-port') appears on the map today as

Long Haven, the name of an inlet at the north end of the beach where Arthur's warriors came ashore. The name is repeated in the Hill of Longhaven and Longhaven House, nearby. Arthur himself is commemorated at Cave Arthur, south of the beach, and the Steps and Busks of Arthur Fowlie (*foghlais*, a 'little stream') to the north.

The beach is the Bay of Cruden – that is, the Bay of Steel or 'Severe Affliction'. Taliesin described the grain-fed horses charging ashore, 'white with foam', to become 'jaded and gory from battle'. There were 'biers beyond number', 'men in terror, bloody heads'. Morgan's Pictish spearmen were braced for Arthur's assault, and 'before they were overpowered, they committed slaughter'.

'In Llongborth,' sang Taliesin, 'Geraint was slain'.

The seafarer had travelled up from south-west Britain to join Arthur's enterprise. He brought the Gododdin warriors to the Bay of Cruden. Then he passed through a hedge of mist lined with human heads – a Druidic 'ghost fence' at the head of the dunes, now marked on the map as Ardendraught or 'rising ground of the enchantment' (*àrden* + *draoidheachd;* also Scots *draucht*, an 'artful scheme') – and there his journey ended.

Geoffrey of Monmouth would later confuse Geraint with Gawain, believing that it was the latter who fell when 'Mordred inflicted great slaughter on those who were trying to land'. But Aneirin, who witnessed the campaign, paid Geraint a proper tribute in his *Y Gododdin* epic:

Geraint from the south gave a shout,
Lightning-white the gleam on his shield.
Lord of the spear, liberal lord,
Sound of the sea, praise of the sea,
The way of the sea was the way of Geraint:
A generous lord you were.

With the beachhead secured, Arthur and his men advanced inland to attack the Hill of Tillymorgan.

The boar-hunt

The Annals of Tigernach list four battles for the year 594:

> The battle of Ratha in Druadh & the battle of Áird Sendoim. The slaying of the sons of Áedán i.e. Bran & Domangart & Eochaid Find & Artúr, in the battle of Circhenn, in which Áedán was the victor, & the battle of Corann.

The first two battles were closely linked, the battle of *Áird Sendoim* ('The Headland', near Peterhead, on the 'coast of Mordei') being immediately followed by Arthur's 'Unrestrained Ravaging' of Morgan's Tillymorgan hill-fort. The Annals of Ulster described this as the 'battle of Ràth in druaid' (Early Irish *ràth,* a 'residence surrounded by an earthen rampart'). It took place in the 'Sorcerer's land' (Early Irish *drui* – a 'Druid'; genitive *druad*). Morgan was considered 'skilful' (*medrod*) by the Britons, which would imply some level of Druidic knowhow – including, no doubt, the art of raising a 'ghost fence', such as that which Geraint fatally crossed above the sands of Cruden Bay.

The Arthurian legend of *Culhwch and Olwen* recalls that 'when Arthur had landed in the country' in pursuit of the fearsome king-turned-boar, Twrch Trwyth, 'there came unto him the saints of Ireland and besought his protection.' There were Irish monks at Old Deer, just west of Peterhead. Arthur then went 'as far as Esgeir Oerfel' – the 'Cold Ridge' of the Grampians – 'where the Boar Trwyth was with his seven young pigs.'

There followed three days of fighting, after which Arthur sent in his interpreter to parley. Morgan's spokesman vowed that he would yield nothing to Arthur: '"And tomorrow morning we will rise up hence, and we will go into Arthur's country, and there we will do all the mischief that we can."'

Morgan escaped with Gwenhwyfar, quite possibly in the Chariot of Morgan the Wealthy (*Car Morgan Mwynfawr*), which became one of the Thirteen Treasures of Britain: 'if a man went in it, he might wish to be wherever he would, and he would be there quickly.' Arthur, meanwhile, sought to block the arrival of any hostile reinforcements from his half-brother's Highland kingdom.

The evidence for this move on Arthur's part is the presence of an Arthur's Seat (*Suiarthour* in 1638; now it is just *Suie*) at the head of Glen Livet. This was the channel, on the eastern edge of the Highlands, through which Gartnait's warriors might have hastened to Morgan's defence.

What happened next was hinted at by Myrddin:

I predict a summer of fury,
Contention of brothers,
Treachery out of Gwynedd:
The lofty exile and the good-pledge [i.e. 'hostage'],
The tall one [Gwenhwyfar] from the land of Gwynedd.
Seven hundred-ships from Saxon-land,
Blown north by the wind;
And in Aberdeen they confer.

Morgan's 'Saxon' allies – the Angles of Northumbria – sent seven ships, each carrying 100 men, to supplement his Miathi spears (Geoffrey of Monmouth later bumped this up to 'eight hundred ships'). Arthur almost certainly spied these reinforcements from the hill of Bennachie in Aberdeenshire (an Arthur's Cairn – *Arthouriscairne* – was recorded there in 1595), having paused at Percylieu (*perc-y-llew*, the 'Lion's Perch'; rendered as 'Preseleu' in the *Culhwch and Olwen* legend) en route to the coast.

The Gododdin were with Arthur, meaning that Lothian was barely defended. Morgan and his supporters saw their opportunity to race south and seize Manau (Stirling) and the

Edinburgh capital of Lothian.

The tale of *Culhwch and Olwen* recounts the bloody pursuit of the Boar-King from the 'Cold Ridge' towards the 'Vale of Manau' (*Dyffryn Amanw*). Morgan's spokesman had sworn that they would 'go into Arthur's country' and there do 'all the mischief that we can.' And so Morgan, with his Saxons and his Picts, made for the crucial bulwark of Manau Gododdin.

Arthur and his battered war-band followed them into Angus.

Catraeth

Aneirin's *Y Gododdin* has been misinterpreted for many years. 'Men went to Gododdin', stated the poet; 'Men went to Catraeth'.

It has long been assumed that *Catraeth* was the Roman fort of *Cataractonium* – now Catterick – and that the poem laments the annihilation of a Lothian war-band at an unknown battle in North Yorkshire. But there is no evidence that such a battle took place.

The poem mentions landmarks that are many miles from Catterick – the *Allaid* or Hill of Alyth being one – and nobody has yet explained the presence of 'Irishmen and Picts' at the battle. Furthermore, part of the poem refers to the death of Domnall the Speckled at the Battle of Strathcarron in AD 642. Evidently, that section is a later interpolation, but it is telling that a verse was added to *Y Gododdin* which dealt with a historical battle in Scotland and the killing of a Scottish king who was actually a nephew of Artúr mac Áedáin!

Taliesin, in one of his poems, cited the 'men of Catraeth' and their 'victorious battle-lord', Urien – the implication being that the 'men of Catraeth' were a sort of standing army, analogous with the fabled Round Table and sworn to defend a 'battle-shore' (*cad* + *traeth*). Their 'soldier-oath' (*cadwr* + *rhaith*) bound them together, as it bound Arthur's equestrian band and the warriors who worshipped Mithras, the patron of soldiers and oaths. The 'battle-shore' these warriors protected (*cadwriaeth* –

'guardianship') would have been the Lothian shore of the Firth of Forth, repeatedly targeted by Germanic raiders, and the strife-torn plain of the River Forth (Manau Gododdin).

Aneirin's elegy does not relate to a long-forgotten British disaster at Catterick. It tells of Arthur's last campaign, the roll call including such heroes as Owain and Cynon, Taliesin, Elffin, Peredur, Llywarch, Gwyddno, Geraint, Áedán and 'Gwair the Tall'.

Catraeth was not the scene of the last battle. The familiar name – 'Camlann' – reveals where it took place.

The earliest mention of '*cam lann*' is found in the Welsh Annals. These date from the 12th century, although they were probably copied from a 10th-century original. Subsequently, the Triads of the Island of Britain referred to a 'Battle of Camlan' as having taken place after Arthur 'succeeded by violence' in landing on the coast. Geoffrey of Monmouth also wrote of a bloody landing, a cross-country pursuit and a climactic battle by the 'River Camblam'.

The mistake made by many commentators is to presume that *Camlan* is a Welsh place-name. We have already seen that *Camlan* is the Gaelic name for Camelon, where a 'little ancient city' had been founded by the Twentieth Legion in central Scotland, and so the insistence that *Camlan* can only be Welsh is irrational.

Within a year of the death of Arthur son of Áedán in the 'battle of the Miathi' in 594, the Northumbrian Angles had overrun much of the Old North. By the following century their language, known as Northumbrian Old English, was established throughout southern Scotland; the Scots dialect evolved from this primitive form of English.

In Lowland Scots, the terms *came, kem* and *camb* all meant 'comb' (a *kame* could be a heap of stones or a mound formed by silt and gravel beside a river). *Lan', laan* and *lann* all signified 'land'. Thus, in Anglo-Saxon, as well as its Scots derivative, *Camlann* meant 'Comb-land'.

Artúr mac Áedáin was killed in a battle of Circenn (*cír* meaning 'comb' or 'crest'; *cenn*, 'heads'). He died in Angus, the land of the 'Comb-heads'. As we have seen, the very word 'Pict' might be a corruption of *Pect*, from the Latin for 'comb'.

The Strife of Camlann – '*Gueith cam lann*' – therefore took place in the 'Comb-land' of the 'Comb-heads': the Pictish province of Circenn.

THE FINAL CONFLICT

The Heroic age, with all its prejudices, altered the stories of Arthur and the Grail. But the people of Angus honoured his memory. An Arthur's Seat can be found at Dumbarrow, close to Dunnichen, near the town of Forfar. Writing in 1845, the Reverend James Headrick remarked:

> A confused tradition prevails of a great battle having been fought on the East Mains of Dunnichen, between Lothus, King of the Picts, or his son Mordred, and Arthur, King of the Britons, in which that hero of romance was slain.

This tradition was not as confused as Headrick imagined. If propagandists hadn't invested so much energy in spreading falsehoods about Arthur we might all know where his last battle was fought – *and we would have recognised the Grail in the carved Pictish stones of the area.* The rival armies did indeed pass this way, standoffs and skirmishes punctuating their progress, until the battle lines were finally drawn up a few miles west of Dunnichen.

The *Culhwch and Olwen* legend tells us that Morgan was making for Llwch Tawy (Loch Tay). Arthur and his men chased him into Cwm Cerwyn. Geoffrey of Monmouth probably misread this as *Caerwyn* – 'White-Castle' – and invented a battle at Winchester, but Cwm Cerwyn really means 'Vale of the Vat' and points to the Balloch through which the Alyth Burn flows at the foot of Barry Hill. This was almost certainly the birthplace of

Arthur's sister, Muirgein, the Alyth Burn being known here as the Water of Quiech – as in *cuach* or *quaich*, a two-handled drinking cup.

The Gododdin had tailed Morgan's army into the great valley of Strathmore. Morgan finally 'went between Tawy and Ewyas', and there he was driven into a river 'between Llyn Lliwan and Aber Gwy'.

The precise spot can be pinpointed. Arthur, in one of his legendary guises, was ambushed when he rose from a cauldron or vat beside the River Cynfael. This was a corruption of *Cennfhaeladh* – 'Shaved-Head'. The river is now known as the Isla.

The River Isla flows through Strathmore to its meeting with the River Tay ('Tawy'). Between that confluence and a place identified as 'Ewyas' (probably Eassie, with its farmstead of Ewnie, six miles south of the Hill of Alyth) the epic boar-hunt came to a bloody end.

Midway between Eassie and the Tay, a T-junction is formed where the River Ericht (*Areicht* in 1570, from *airecht* – a 'gathering') joins the River Isla. Aneirin's *Y Gododdin* confirms that the final conflict took place at an *aber* or 'river-mouth'. Overlooking this confluence is a natural ridge or 'kame' known as Arthurbank.

The Bankhead of Kinloch, adjacent to Arthurbank, suggests that the south bank of the Isla here was a watery meadow or marshy 'lake'; the farmstead known as Glenluie or Glenlouie, due east of the Kings of Kinloch, calls to mind the Welsh *Llyn Lliwan* (see next chapter). This had once been the realm of Arthur's grandfather: the town of Blairgowrie, four miles up the Ericht from the Arthurbank ridge, reminds us that this was *Blàr Ghobhraidh*, the 'plain' or 'battlefield' of Gabrán's land.

Llew Skilful Hand was attacked on the bank of the Cynfael river as he stood with one foot on the rim of a cauldron and the other on the back of a goat. Curiously, a mosaic dating from 1165 in the Italian cathedral of Otranto features 'Rex Arturus' riding what appears to be a goat.

In Welsh, a 'goat' is *gafr* (Gaelic *gobhar*, which is also a 'branching river'). The 'goat' was Arthur's grandfather, Gabrán.

With one foot in his grandfather's land, Arthur met his destiny at the mouth of the Ericht. As Aneirin remarked, rather ominously:

> No one living will relate what befell
> Lliw, what came about on Monday at the Lliwan lake.

The ford

This was border territory. The junction of the Ericht with the Isla is marked on the map as 'Aberbothrie', in which the Celtic place-name expert W.J. Watson detected the Roman name for the River Forth – *Boderia*.

The Forth (*Gwerid* in Welsh) marked the original boundary between the Britons and the Picts. Arthur had effectively pushed the Forth northwards when he killed Galam 'Chief-of-Alyth' and reclaimed his grandfather's land of Gowrie (*Gouerin* in the Middle Ages). The Isla then became the 'new' Forth.

The new border was marked by a 'red cross' or pillar-stone which was recorded in 1534 as standing between the Hill of Alyth and Bamff (*Banbha* – 'Ireland'), approximately five miles north of Aberbothrie. One side of this stone depicted a man with a sword pointing at his head; the other showed 'ane picture of ane schier with the manner of ane ball within the plaits and schering of the schiers' (Ramsay, *Bamff Charters A.D. 1232-1703*).

The Bamff pillar-stone clearly marked where the land of Arthur (the man with the sword pointing to his head) met the land of the Pictish 'Comb-heads' (the picture of the shears cutting the hair in Mohawk fashion). The deadly mission undertaken by Arthur and his men in *Culhwch and Olwen* was to seize 'the comb, razor and shears' which were 'between the two ears' of the

Boar-King, Twrch. Morgan had adopted the boar's-crest tonsure of the 'Miathi' Picts. Arthur was after his scalp.

The pursuit of the king-turned-boar had brought both armies into Strathmore. Arthur confronted his nemesis at the 'mouth' of the Ericht. The place where last ditch talks were held is described in the *Mabinogion* tale of the *Dream of Rhonabwy*.

In his hallucinatory dream, Rhonabwy crosses a great plain with a river running through it. He meets a man who identifies himself as Iddog son of Mynyo, also known as the 'Churn of Britain', for it was he who provoked the 'battle of Camlan'.

Together, Rhonabwy and Iddog approach the Ford of the Cross (*Rhyd-y-Groes*). An army is encamped on either side of the road, and Arthur is seated with his counsellors on a little flat islet beside the ford. Iddog draws Rhonabwy's attention to the ring, set with a stone, which the Emperor Arthur wears, since the gemstone will 'enable thee to remember that thou seest here tonight'.

The ford was also mentioned by Aneirin as the ford of the 'grey' or 'holy mount' (*rhyd benclwyd*).

A ford did indeed cross the Isla at its junction with the Ericht. In his *Agriculture of Perthshire,* published in 1799, Rev. Dr Robertson noted that a 'large Druidical temple' had been discovered at Coupar Grange, adjacent to this ford. The temple consisted of two concentric walls, with a paved way leading from east to west and a 'large free stone, standing erect between the circles', rising several feet above the pavement. In Christian times, this stone might have been rebranded as a cross – hence the 'Ford of the Cross' in Rhonabwy's *Dream* and Aneirin's ford of the 'holy mount' (or 'Greymount', as it appears on the map near Aberbothrie).

The ford passed immediately to the west of an oval-shaped islet, measuring 100m x 40m, which lies close to the south bank of the Isla, below the Arthurbank ridge. The *Dream of Rhonabwy* has Arthur seated on a flat islet beside the Ford of the Cross on a boundary river, his troops spread out along the riverbank. Aneirin, meanwhile, had 'Gwair the Tall' in position 'at the ford of the holy/grey mount' ('foremost his horses, / Far-reaching his fame, perforated his armour') before he was 'buried under turf'.

This was at the *aber* or 'mouth' of the *Boderia* – the boundary of the Gododdin's border.

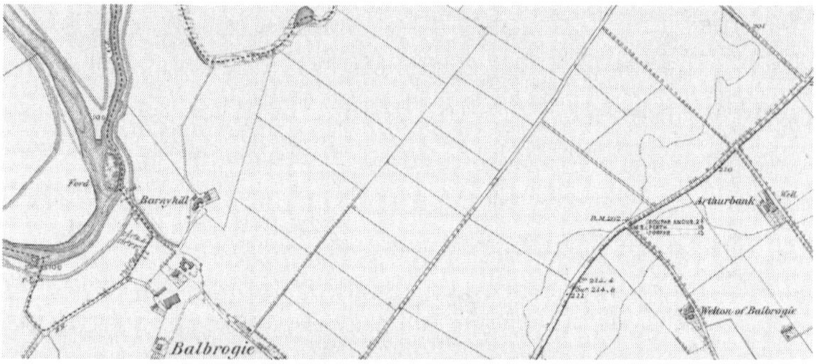

"The flat, oval-shaped islet beside the ford at the junction of the Ericht and Isla rivers (left), a short distance to the west of Arthurbank (right).
Detail from Ordnance Survey map of Perthshire, Six-inch 1st Edition (survey date 1863), National Libraries of Scotland."

Churn of Britain

Morgan and his warriors – 'some of them pagans and some Christians', wrote Geoffrey of Monmouth – occupied the north side of the Isla and the timber-laced fortress on Barry Hill: this vitrified hill-fort, *Dum Bhairraidhe* (pronounced 'doom varri'), was later romanticised as the Island of Glass or *Isle de Voirre,* where Gwenhwyfar was held prisoner.

Arthur's horsemen were ranged along the south bank of the Isla, from the Roman fort at Cardean to the ridge of Arthurbank. Arthur then moved onto neutral ground – the islet in the river – in order to parley. But the talks failed. Iddog explained why to Rhonabwy:

> I was one of the messengers between Arthur and Medrod his nephew, at the battle of Camlan ... and through my desire for battle, I kindled strife between them, and stirred up wrath, when I was sent by Arthur the Emperor to reason with Medrod ... and to seek for peace, lest the sons of the Kings of Britain, and of the nobles, should be slain.

In his *Y Gododdin* poem, Aneirin also indicated that the peace talks got nowhere:

> The little men scorned the sanctity of the temple:
> The wrath of the fire, strong that protection.
> Tuesday, they put on their black gear.
> Wednesday, they made ready their armour.
> Thursday, it was inevitable, they said.
> Friday, the struggle ensued.
> Saturday, it was clear they were acting in concert.
> Sunday, their blades red with action.
> Monday, as far as the Peak of the Pasture,
> there was slaughter to see.

The 'Peak of the Pasture' (*benn clun*) points westward from Barry Hill, and the Hill of Alyth, to the Forest of Clunie (*Cluainidh* – 'Meadowy'; Early Irish *clúain*, Welsh *clun*) on the west bank of the Ericht. The Baden Burn runs along the flank of Benachally hill, above the Glasclune ('Green-Meadow') Burn. The latter flows into the Morganston Burn, through Morgie Den, at the edge of the Clunie forest, passing the field of the Morganstone before it joins the River Ericht north of Blairgowrie.

Arthur's pleas for peace had been twisted into provocations. There was now no avoiding the battle.

The *Dream of Rhonabwy* states that Arthur then moved his men into position 'below Caer Faddon'. This was the fort of the 'Little-Boar' (*Baeddan*), atop Barry Hill.

From the raised ground of Belmont, above Balmacron (*Balmachreon* in 1661, possibly from *baile ma chridhean*, 'place of the gallant favourite'), Arthur stared across the River Isla at the *Allaid* (the Hill of Alyth) and Morgan's rebel army. He had been lured into a trap – like the blessed 'Raven', Brân, who was invited to peace talks by a religious Irish prince only to find himself surrounded by hidden enemies.

St Columba, meanwhile, summoned his monks and told them, 'Let us now pray fervently to the Lord for this people and for King Áedán, for even now they are going into battle.'

A little later, he announced: 'Now the barbarians are turned in flight and victory is granted to Áedán, though it is not a happy one.'

We know that Áedán won the fight but lost his sons, including Artúr, in the 'battle of the Miathi', just as St Columba had predicted.

The Triads indicate that Arthur divided his force into three, probably to attack both flanks of Morgan's army. Peredur died at the 'Pigsty Castle' or 'Bloody Fort'. Lleënog perhaps found the secret passage which led into the fortress on Barry Hill from the Balloch below: a later tradition has 'Lancelot' going to war with the Northumbrian Angles at Guinevere's request and gaining access to their stronghold by way of an underground cavern.

But while Arthur waited at Belmont for Morgan's panicked spearmen to come streaming towards him, his real enemies were approaching from the rear.

11

Saints and Stones

Le corbeau dit:- Oiseaux chantez!
Vous n'avez rien à regrettez:
Vous mourûtes en ces campagnes,
Mais nous, si loin de la Bretagne.
Breton Folksong

THE CRISIS came at the confluence of a river. The future of Britain hung in the balance, teetering on the shoulders of a battered band of famous warriors and their leader, the 'emperor' Arthur. There was treachery and betrayal in the air.

Much of southern Britain was already under Saxon control. The battle for North Britain, however, was still raging.

Artúr mac Áedáin, the first 'Arthur' on record, was around when the Britons finally joined forces to counter the threat posed by the Angles of Northumbria. Taliesin the bard had promoted the young Arthur as 'the longed-for one of the tribe', and so successful were his military campaigns in the North that by AD 590, the Angles were clinging by their fingertips to their coastal redoubts of Lindisfarne and Bamburgh.

Just four years later, the first Arthur on record was killed in a battle of Circenn, fighting the 'Miathi' Picts. Within a year of that battle much of the Old North had been overrun by the resurgent Angles.

What happened to Arthur in the vale of Strathmore had irreversible consequences. His death removed a vital obstacle to the Germanic invaders – those Angles who went on to found *Engla land*. The native Britons were soon confined to such regions as Wales and their shrinking territories in the North: Lothian, which fell to the Angles in 638, and Strathclyde, which was eventually subsumed into the kingdom of Scotland.

The death of Arthur meant nothing less than the end of Britain.

On the face of it, much of the internal strife which culminated in Arthur's last battle was focussed on the cauldron of rebirth.

We remember – for example – that Artúr's half-brother, Gartnait, buried a vat of silver and gold on the 'Island of the Son of Cian' (Cian being the Irish form of Cai, Arthur's bodyguard and foster-father) when his own son, Cano, went to Ireland. Artúr's father subsequently invaded the island, massacred its inhabitants and took the precious cauldron 'to his own store-room'.

Arthur and his heroes wrest the cauldron of Diwrnach from Ireland by violence in *Culhwch and Olwen*. In the *Mabinogion* legend of the 'blessed Raven', Brân, the Irish king Matholwch ('Prayer-Sort') explains that he is familiar with the cauldron. He dismisses the warriors it has produced as 'hated and unwelcome', whereas Brân, the 'crowned king' of Britain, regards those same warriors as 'the best that anyone has seen.'

Matholwch accepts the cauldron as a peace offering. The Irish king and his followers then mistreat Brân's sister. When Brân discovers this, he launches a fleet of warships against Ireland. The Britons are lured into a purpose-built hall on the promise of talks, but they soon discover that the Irish king has surrounded them with warriors hidden in sacks.

The Irish have the advantage of the cauldron, until Brân's brother destroys it. Only seven Britons survive to carry Brân's head to its burial mound at a 'fair royal place overlooking the sea'.

Le Chevalier Bran

When Lothian finally fell to the Angles, British refugees fled across the sea to Armorica – now Brittany, the 'Lesser Britain' – taking their memories of Arthur with them. They thought of their

Lothian homeland as the 'Lion's Land', *Leonais*, which became the 'Lyonesse' of later romance.

A Breton folksong was published in 1842 under the title, *Le Chevalier Bran ou le Prisonnier de Guerre* – 'The Horseman Bran, or the Prisoner of War'. It begins:

À la bataille de Kerlouan
Fut blessé le chevalier Bran!
À Kerlouan, sur l'océan,
Le petit fils de Bran le Grand.
Prisonnier, bien que victorieux,
Il dont franchir l'océan bleu.
['At the battle of Kerlouan, the Horseman Bran was wounded! At Kerlouan, by the sea, the grandson of Bran the Great. Captured, even though he was victorious, he was taken across the sea.']

The song describes how the wounded Bran was incarcerated in a tower beyond the sea. He begged a messenger to take his gold ring to his mother with the request that she should come to set him free. If she agreed, her ship was to fly a white flag; if she refused, the flag should be black (this motif, borrowed from Greek myth, was also woven into the French romances of Drystan or 'Tristan', whose native land was 'Lyonesse').

The Breton song reveals that an oak-tree stood over the battlefield at Kerlouan:

C'est là que les Saxons ont pris
La fuite quand Even surgit.
['It was there that the Saxons were put
To flight when Even suddenly appeared.']

Birds gather every night at this oak, singing hauntingly – all except for a white female crow and a young male raven. The raven tells the birds to sing: 'You have nothing to regret; You died in this country – But we, so far from Britain.'

The Arthurian elements in the folksong are unmistakable. A horseman named Bran was wounded and taken hostage, even though the victory was his. He was the grandson of 'Bran le Grand', just as Artúr was the grandson of King Gabrán. The 'Saxons' were put to flight by the sudden appearance of 'Even' (Owain son of Urien – or 'Yvain', as Chrétien de Troyes called him). Owain's presence at the climactic battle is attested in *Y Gododdin*, while the *Dream of Rhonabwy* portrays Arthur and Owain as being at loggerheads before the conflict of 'Camlan'.

Like Arthur, the wounded Bran was borne away across the sea and his death mourned by a 'white crow' (the literal meaning of 'Brânwen', who was the sister of the 'blessed Raven', Brân).

We know from the *Life of Columba* that Áedán was the victor in the 'battle of the Miathi', although two of his sons ('Artúr and Eochaid Find') died there. The Irish annals similarly report that Áedán won the battle but lost his sons ('Bran & Domangart & Eochaid Find & Artúr', according to the Annals of Tigernach; the Annals of Ulster have only 'Bran and Domangart' dying in the 'battle of Circenn').

The Horseman Bran – later romanticised as 'Bron' or 'Brons' – was obviously Arthur, spirited away as a 'prisoner of war' from his last battle, which was fought at 'Kerlouan' or *Kêr Leon*, the 'Lion's Fort', as W.J. Watson rendered it in his *Celtic Place-names of Scotland*.

Kerlouan is a commune in the Finistèrre department of Brittany. The place-name had followed the British refugees from Lothian to their exile in northern France. It derives from *kêr* (Welsh *caer*) and the name of St Elouan, otherwise known as Luan or Llywan.

Luan

St Elouan is an elusive figure. He was known in Scotland and

Ireland as Lughaidh – also Moluag – and is thought to have been an Irish 'Pict' of the 6th century. Variations on his name include: Lua, Molua, Mo-Luóc, Moloch and Murlach (meaning 'fishing-basket' or 'kingfisher' in Gaelic). He is most famously associated with the island of Lismore, which he supposedly won by beating St Columba to it in a desperate race, and he is credited with bringing Christianity to the northern Picts, just as Columba spread the Gospel among the southern 'Miathi'. His death is ascribed to 592 – two years before Arthur fell in the 'battle of the Miathi'.

A charter of 1544 suggests that 'Saint Moloc' was the patron saint of Argyll, the original kingdom of the Scots. He was also commemorated at Clatt, near Percylieu in Aberdeenshire (see previous chapter), and his 'Simmalogue Fair' was held at Alyth in Angus.

Indeed, the only place where Elouan/Molua was venerated as 'Luan' was at Alyth, where the Church of St Luan now stands in Alexander Street. The Alyth Arches are all that remain of an earlier church, dedicated to Luan, which was built on the site of a chapel believed to date back to the time of Arthur.

Kerlouan, where the horseman Bran was wounded, compares with *Caerleon*, the legendary court of Arthur, and indicates a fortified enclosure named after 'Luan'. One such 'Fort of Luan' evidently existed at Alyth, where the last battle of Artúr mac Áedáin was fought. The name also occurs in the *Culhwch and Olwen* legend, where Arthur and his men corner the monstrous boar at a river 'between Llyn Lliwan and Aber Gwy' (*Lliwan* or *Llywan* being the Welsh form of 'Luan').

A Scottish tradition recalls that Arthur's queen was held in the 'glassy' fort on Barry Hill and then buried at Meigle, adjacent to the 'Glenluie' position held by Arthur before he was wounded. The floodplain of the River Isla was marshy here – hence the 'Luan Lake' (*Llyn Lliwan*), now indicated on the map by the Bankhead and Kings of Kinloch, between Meigle and

Arthurbank.

Aneirin's *Y Gododdin* implies that the battle came to an end on a Monday. In Gaelic, *luan* means 'Monday' (or 'moon'). It is also the Gaelic word for 'Doomsday'.

The name that hovers behind all of these *Luan* references is *Llew* – 'Lion' (Gaelic *leóghann*, pronounced 'li-oh-unn'). Like 'Raven', 'Lion' was one of the initiatory grades in the cult of Mithras, and it is therefore telling to note that St Columba absent-mindedly blessed a knife belonging to Molua (a 'grandson of Brian') which was to be used to slaughter bulls. Columba then hurriedly prayed that the blade would 'never wound men or cattle', so that Molua was unable even to puncture the bull's hide. The smiths of Columba's monastery melted down the knife and applied a thin coating of its metal to all their iron tools.

What this story suggests is that the weapons with which Arthur ('Molua' = 'My Luan') was attacked were partly composed of the same material which had been used in re-enactments of the Mithraic bull-slaying ritual. Arthur's magic had been turned against him: he was slain by his own sacrificial blade.

Notably, the cauldron was also present when the adulterous wife of Llew Skilful Hand tricked him into demonstrating his vulnerability. Llew rose from the cauldron on the bank of a river and was pierced by a poisoned spear. The spear had been a year and a day in the making because it could only be worked on during Sunday services.

LE MORTE D'ARTHUR

The Angles were not the sole beneficiaries of Arthur's death. There were also 'Scots, Picts and Irish' ranged against him – 'some of them pagans and some Christians'.

The Church would conveniently forget that Christians had helped to bring down Arthur. But the Triads remind us that three battles – 'Goddau' (Catlowdy), Arderydd and 'Camlan' – were 'futile': that is, they were civil conflicts caused by fanaticism and the determination of one religion to stamp out another.

The battle of Camlann was fought, not just over the body of Britain, but over its soul. Though Heroic age propagandists would later insist that Arthur and his knights received a vision of the 'Holy Grail' and sought it as a symbol of Christian grace, the reality was very different. Before the 'terrible desire' (*sant grathail*) could be transmuted into a Christian chalice, it first had to be neutralised – destroyed – along with the warrior-poets it had initiated. St Columba, an Irish prince of the 'Prayer-Sort', considered these cauldron-born warriors 'hated and unwelcome', even though they were all that stood between Britain and oblivion.

Columba had taken possession of the Isle of Iona at Beltane in the year 563, having been exiled to the Scottish colony for raising a rebellion against the Irish High-King, Diarmait mac Cerbaill, who was closely related to Arthur's foster-father, Cai or 'Cian'. On the 30th anniversary of his arrival on Iona, Columba watched as his pagan rivals celebrated their Beltane rites on 'a rock across our island Sound' (this would have been the Island of the Women, *Eilean nam Ban*). Displaying the paranoia which is symptomatic of the Heroic age mentality, Columba declared that the pagans were out to get him. Even after thirty years he had failed to rid the Scottish kingdom of its ancient traditions and the warrior-cult of the cauldron.

A little over a year later, Arthur was dead – ambushed by the 'hidden warriors' of the Irish prince.

The records state that Columba had predicted this: Arthur son of Áedán would 'fall in battle, slain by enemies', while the mysterious Gúaire son of Áedán would be killed by a companion – his own knife! – whom he did not suspect.

That other prophet, Myrddin Wyllt, foresaw the costly treachery of the 'white-headed one' (Columba was in his seventies) whose scheming would result in the deaths of all bar seven of Arthur's men. Taliesin would soon denounce the 'chief of baptism' who had broken 'our shield' against the Miathi, leaving Britain defenceless.

Two of the followers of Columba who conspired against Arthur were themselves described as saints. They appear, suitably disguised, in *Culhwch and Olwen,* where they side with the rebellious Morgan.

One is named Llwydog Gofynniad – the 'Holy One of Govan' or the 'Smith'. When Arthur's men chase the Boar-King south into Angus, this 'Holy One' escapes to Ystrad Yw, the 'Vale of Yews' (probably Iona, the 'Yewy' isle or 'plain of yews').

The other is designated Grugyn Gwallt Ereint – 'Ant Silver Hair'. In *Culhwch and Olwen,* he flees to 'Din Tywi'.

Grugyn

Aneirin's poem of Arthur's last battle also mentions Grugyn:

> Season of storm, storm season,
> The spears ranked before the royal champion.
> From Din Dywydd they came,
> Passionate in their piety,
> Grave in their godliness,
> Keen as bees.
> A complete hundred-man army,
> Grugyn's shield.
> Before the bull of battle
> The vanguard gave way.

This compares with a parallel stanza in the older version of *Y Gododdin*:

> A standing stone on open ground
> In the manner of Lleu's land,
> The boundary of the Gododdin border.
> To battle, to battle, blow the horn, blow the horn!

A tempest of pilgrims*, a righteous pilgrim army,
Swarming blades measured in a broad line.
From Din Dyrwyrt they attacked,
Grugyn's fellowship – before the battle-crisis,
The front line broke.
[**tramerya* – could mean 'foreigner', as in 'across the sea', or a 'wayfarer' who travels to and fro.]

Grugyn appears in *Culhwch and Olwen* as the Boar-King's mouthpiece who separates from Morgan's army and makes his way to 'Din Tywi'. According to Aneirin's *Y Gododdin*, meanwhile, Grugyn's 'fellowship', his human 'shield', attacked from 'Din Dywydd'.

Both *Din Tywi* and *Din Dywydd* suggest a 'Fort of David' (Welsh *Dewi*, formerly *Dewydd*). This should remind us that Iddog, the 'Churn of Britain' who, in the *Dream of Rhonabwy*, admits that he caused the Battle of Camlann by twisting Arthur's conciliatory words, was styled 'son of Mynyo'. The Welsh name for the site of St David's community in south-west Wales was *Mynyw* (Latin *Menevia*).

Some of Arthur's closest companions were associated with *Tyddewi*, the 'House of David' in Dyfed. Pedr ('Pedrog') and his son Bedwyr ('Bedivere') were its overlords. St Kentigern (otherwise Cynon, whom Aneirin praised as a 'foe-searing serpent') sought sanctuary at St David's when he was hounded from Lothian by 'Duke Morgan'. It is probable that Arthur himself was raised by his foster-father Cai at the 'Red Fort' – *Caer Goch* – close to St David's little city at *Mynyw*.

Another of Arthur's heroes came from South Wales. St Cadog almost certainly spent time at St David's: a medieval *Life of Cadog* reveals that Cadog reacted angrily when David was elected Archbishop of Wales. The same *Life* describes Cadog's wanderings in North Britain, his founding of a monastery in central Scotland and the duplicitous trick he played on Arthur,

Cai and Bedwyr when the 'most illustrious king of Britannia' demanded compensation for the killing of three of his soldiers.

Cadog was originally known as Cadfael ('Battle-Prince'). After he underwent his own cauldron initiation in North Wales he was given the Druidic-sounding name, Collen ('Hazels'). He appears to have acted as foster-father to Arthur's queen: *Croes Gwenhwyfar* ('Gwenhwyfar's Cross') stands in Collen's parish of Llangollen. In Scotland, he became known as the 'Little-Cat', Catán or Cathan – a name which compares with the 'Cathen' who conspired to drive Kentigern out of Lothian when Morgan the Wealthy seized the throne from Cynon's father, Clydno of Edinburgh, in about 559.

He was also known by a shortened form of his name as 'Docus the Briton'. This found its way into Gaelic as M'Aedóc – 'Madóc the pilgrim' in the Irish *Leabhar Breac* – and it was as 'My Aedóc' that Cadog was honoured at St Madoes in Gowrie and at Kilmadock, the 'Hermitage of My Docus', near Doune, north of Stirling. The 9th-century *Martyrology of Óengus* referred to him as *Mo Maedóc mind nAlban* – 'My Maedóc, Scotland's diadem'.

Traditionally, St Cadog was one of the three knights who became 'keepers of the Grail'.

The Fort

The Gaelic *Aedóc* became *Iddog* in medieval Welsh. It was 'Iddog son of Mynyo' who provoked the battle in Circenn. He was Arthur's trusted companion, Cadog, but he was under orders to thwart any peace talks and thus he became, in a sense, Morgan's spokesman – the ant-like 'Grugyn' who vowed to do as much mischief as he could.

In the *Dream of Rhonabwy* he explains:

> ... three nights before the end of the battle of Camlan I left them, and went to the Llech Las ['Grey Stone'] in North Britain to do penance. And there I remained doing penance

seven years, and after that I gained pardon.

The Grey Stone still exists. It is a landmark boulder which lies on the bank of the River Teith, a mile from the old Roman fort at Doune.

The name of the Teith possibly derives from the Welsh *taith* (a 'message' or 'pilgrimage'). The river is formed by two waters, one of which emerges from Loch Venachar as *Eas Gobhain* – 'Cascade of the Smith' – and runs past Kilmadock and the promontory of Doune before its meeting with the River Forth near Stirling.

The *Life of Cadog* states that the saint was ordered to spend seven years at 'a certain fort ... which is said to be situated in the middle of Scotland'. This 'certain fort' was almost certainly at Doune (Gaelic *An Dùn*: 'The Fort'). The time Cadog spent there is commensurate with the seven years penance which Iddog did at the Grey Stone nearby, and according to tradition St Cadog passed seven years at the 'Hermit's Croft', where he built his own church beside the River Teith. The site of his ruined chapel is by the mouth of the Annet Burn (*annaid* – an abandoned 'mother-church'), below a waterfall known as the Cauldron Linn. It was perhaps a northern offshoot of St David's community at *Mynyw*, its alternative name (*Din Dyrwyrt*) suggesting a 'Fort of Penance' (cf. *dirwyol*, 'pertaining to a fine').

Iddog confesses to Rhonabwy that he quit the field 'three nights before the end of the battle of Camlan' – presumably on the Friday, after the negotiations had failed and, as Aneirin remarked, 'the struggle ensued'. He had made sure that the conflict was not averted; he then slipped away to his settlement near Doune, approximately forty miles from Alyth. It is conceivable that he took the cauldron with him for 'safe keeping'.

Warrior-monks had travelled up from *Mynyw* in distant Dyfed. On the Sunday, they celebrated Mass and the poisoned spear that would take Arthur's life was prepared. They then set out on their mission to attack Arthur whilst two-thirds of his force was assaulting Morgan's stronghold: the vitrified fortress on Barry Hill.

The anguish still sounds in Aneirin's voice –

> To battle, to battle, blow the horn, blow the horn!

Just as the battle was being won across the River Isla, Arthur – the Mithraic 'bull of battle' – was attacked by Cadog's 'fellowship'.

Aneirin indicated where the attack took place:

> A standing stone on open ground ...
> The boundary of the Gododdin border.

A large cup-marked megalith stands just south of Arthur's position at Belmont. It is misleadingly known as 'Macbeth's Stone', although it was Arthur who was attacked here, on the border of the Britons' territory.

The front rank of his guard scattered. Fighting for his life, Arthur battled his way across the level ground of Camno to Arthurbank, a mile to the west. Numerous cropmarks discovered near the farmhouse of East Camno hint at a host of burials in this fertile plain.

A monolith stood at the east end of the Arthurbank ridge, until it was taken down in the 1790s and used in the building of Arthurstone House.

Known as the Arthurstone, it marked the spot where Arthur fell.

GWAIR'S PRISON

The Irish sources associate Cadog ('Maedóc') with the monastery of Fid Dúin in Kilkenny. However, we learn from the *Life of Columba* that the monastic establishment on Iona had a daughter-house on the Scottish mainland. This was known in Latin as *cella Diuni* – the 'hermitage of Doune' – and the name of its prior was given as Cailtan, the Gaelic equivalent of Collen.

An Arthurian connection is evident in the *Life of Cadog*, wherein the saint has a bizarre encounter with one Caradog Pendiuin, a 'malicious' guard and kinsman of Cadog's, whose epithet meant 'Chief-of-Doune'. He also appears in Welsh legend as the 'Caradog son of Brân' who was left in charge of Britain when Brân the Blessed went to war with the treacherous Irish prince. Caradog's heart broke when he and his fellows were attacked by a sword which hacked at them from a veil of mist (Welsh *caddug* – 'darkness', 'fog').

St Columba, we are told, had foreknowledge of the imminent death of his prior on the mainland. The *Life of Cadog* confirms this. St Cadog had been miraculously 'translated' to the 'Beneventan' monastery (the Latin name points to a town or market on the 'horn' of land, which aptly describes the Fort at Doune). Cadog was then allowed to choose martyrdom.

He was told that 'a certain cruel king' would ravage his monastery, and a 'certain soldier, leaving his confederates, will enter the monastery, and piercing thee with the point of a spear will cruelly slay thee over the altar.'

Returning to the Irish annals, we remember that after the battles of 'The Headland' (Cruden Bay), the 'Fort in Druid-land' (Tillymorgan) and 'Circenn' (Angus), in which Arthur was killed, there was a 'battle of Corann'. The term *corran* indicates a tapering promontory, like the 'horn' of land upon which Doune stands. The last of the battles of 594 was therefore an overspill of the conflict in Strathmore: it was a revenge attack on St Cadog's monastery in retaliation for the assassination of Arthur.

Corroboration of this can be found in the poem *Pa gwr* ('What Man is the Porter?'), which is essentially the death-song of Arthur and Cai. The two warriors apply for entry to the Otherworldly hall of heroes and cite their many battles. The poem ends abruptly, with Cai heading off to tackle a ferocious cat:

His wonderful shield went
Against *cath palug*.
When the people inquire
Who killed *cath palug*?
Nine score wild
And angry ones were its meat.
Nine score princes ...

This monstrous creature, which killed 140 of Arthur's men, was properly the 'cat priest' (*cath + balog*), otherwise Cadog or Cathan.

The hagiography of Cadog, who had now acquired the epithet 'Wise', states that 'the aforesaid tyrant, having collected his army, wasted the suburbs contiguous to the town' and then 'one of the horsemen ... with impetuous speed and fuming wrath pierced him [Cadog] with a lance as he stood by the altar'. Cadog was buried nearby. A 'great basilica' was built over his tomb, 'into which no Briton is permitted to enter.'

Cai did not long survive this act of retribution. He appears in the list of Arthur's 24 horsemen as the 'Brave-Servant', Drudwas. An ancient legend claims that 'Drudwas' was mistakenly slain by his own 'griffin' warriors.

Aneirin's *Y Gododdin*, meanwhile, refers to Cadog's hermitage as Maedóc's tent or 'tabernacle', and remarks:

The Gododdin spoke truly after their exertions:
When they returned from Madog's tabernacle,
But one man in a hundred would come back.

St Cadog was just one of the two treacherous individuals named in *Culhwch and Olwen*, where he masquerades as 'Grugyn Silver Hair' – the same Grugyn ('Ant') whose fellowship attacked

Arthur on the last day of the Camlann conflict.

What, then, of that other figure, the 'Holy One of Govan', Llwydog Gofynniad, who escaped to the 'Vale of Yews'?

The Smith

The betrayal of Arthur began with the 'conversion of Constantine', which turned Gartnait mac Áedáin against the rest of his family. Constantine sought refuge in an Irish monastery, remaining there until he blew his own cover. He then returned to claim the throne of Strathclyde in about 614.

St Constantine was principally associated with Govan (*Baile a' Ghobhainn*, the 'Town of the Smith') near Glasgow; a 'Chapel of my Smith' (*Cill mo Ghobhannan*) also adjoined St Columba's monastery on Iona. The early sources hint at the involvement of a 'Smith' in the death of Arthur (see endnote).

Both Brân and Llew were slain by poisoned spears. So, too, was Arthur. The anonymous *Vera historia de morte Arthuri* (*circa* 1200) depicts the emperor leaving the battlefield with a heavy heart, 'although he had gained the victory'. Leaning on his shield, he sat down and told his companions to remove his armour.

A tall, pleasant-looking youth then approached on horseback. In his right hand he held a shaft of elm:

> ... which was firm, and neither twisted or knotty but smooth, with a sharp point like a lance, since at some time in the past it had been hardened with fire by a smith and made harder by being tempered in water. It had been dipped in adder's venom, so that it wounded less by the force of the thrust than by the poison ...

This 'high-spirited' youth rode up to Arthur and 'cast the weapon just described at the king, adding to his already serious wounds a yet more grievous one.' Arthur's death was assured:

'And he gave the realm of Britain to Constantine.'

But while Arthur and his alter egos – Brân and Llew – were pierced by a poisoned spear, Llew's aquatic twin, Dylan Eil Ton ('Ocean Son of Wave'), was the victim of a fatal blow which was dealt by his uncle Gofannon ('Smith'). Taliesin sang of this:

> A rebellious groom, poison-inspired, worked up by fury,
> Piercing Dylan, a malignant church, violence visited upon us.

The identity of this avuncular figure who slew his own nephew – the obscure 'twin' of Llew – is alluded to in the *Life of Cadog*. There, we read that 'a certain very brave leader of the British' named Ligessoc son of Eliman had killed three of Arthur's soldiers. He was given sanctuary for seven years at Cadog's monastery.

Arthur finally brought his army to a 'very large river', where Cadog volunteered to arbitrate (as he did in Strathmore). There was a tense standoff, with bitter words and a lengthy battle, after which Arthur was offered compensation in the form of marvellous cattle. These were driven to 'the middle of the ford', where Arthur, Cai and Bedwyr received them.

But the cattle were an illusion: they turned into 'bunches of fern' when Arthur brought them to the riverbank. The 'most illustrious king of Britannia' then saw the error of his ways and begged St Cadog's forgiveness.

The Christian legend shows Cadog playing his 'Iddog' role of the forked-tongued go-between, tricking the 'bull of battle' into receiving monkish warriors posing as Mithraists at a showdown by a river. But it is Ligessoc son of Eliman who killed Arthur's men.

The name 'Ligessoc' contains the element *cess* – a 'spear' – which relates him to the St Kessog or Cessóc who was once considered the patron saint of Scotland. As Cessán ('Little-Spear') he was the son of a king of Alba (Scotland). His fair was held at Callander on the River Teith, close to the Cascade of the Smith, and he was primarily associated with the Lennox region, hence the designation 'son of Eliman', where *Eliman* stands for 'The Liman' or Loch Lomond (Gaelic *Loch Laomainn*).

One son of a Scottish king was Cano, whose father Gartnait was the king of the northern Picts and the half-brother of Artúr mac Áedáin. The legends assure us that Arthur did battle with his nephew at Camlann, and that he chose Constantine as his successor. Cano apparently took the baptismal name Constantine on his conversion to Christianity, and Constantine did briefly hold the throne of Strathclyde before surrendering it to Neithon or Nechtán – who was also present, as 'Nwython' the 'son of Gwyddno', at Arthur's last battle.

Constantine was buried at Govan. In December 1855, a workman unearthed a sandstone sarcophagus in the graveyard of St Constantine's old church. The sarcophagus is believed to have been made to house the remains of Arthur's nephew, Constantine. Among the ancient carvings on its side panels is the image of a long-haired warrior on horseback, clearly identified by the letter 'A' (see endnote).

Caer Sidi

The means chosen for Arthur's death – a poisoned spear thrust into his groin or 'side' – was a perversion of the Grail ritual. Instead of the 'knee' or 'thigh' being pierced to drain the toxins from the initiate's body, the fatal spear, which could only be worked on during the Mass on Sundays, injected its poison into Arthur's bloodstream. Like Brân (wounded in the foot), Llew (wounded in the side) and Gúaire (wounded in the knee), Arthur was destined to die from his poisoned wound.

He was whisked away from Arthurbank by boat, down the River Isla to the River Tay and so westward to his final resting place in a 'hall on the Island of Afallach'. *Le chevalier Bran* was locked up in a tower 'beyond the sea'. The legend of Brân the

Blessed describes it as a 'fair royal place overlooking the sea, and a great hall it was.' Llew, meanwhile, flew away in eagle-form to a mighty oak, the 'sanctuary of a fair lord'.

Aneirin declaimed that the 'hero of Circenn' was buried in the Swans' Hill (*eleirch fre* – from the Gaelic *ealadh,* a 'tomb', here interpreted by the British poet as *eala,* a 'swan'; Welsh *alarch*). Like the cursed Children of Lir, Arthur and his heroes enjoyed a post-mortem existence as 'swans', the dead of the battlefield similarly living on as 'birds' which gathered every night at an oak-tree. We might also note that Brân's brother, Manannán son of Lir, kept his booty – including the 'shears' of a Pictish king and the girdle and crook of the 'Smith' – in a 'crane-skin bag', visible only at high tide, in which sacrificial victims were restored to life.

St Columba reputedly cared for an exhausted heron or crane which arrived on Iona and departed again three days later. The crane was traditionally associated with the sacred art of writing (and therefore with the ink-yielding 'golden apples' of the oak-tree) and so it is instructive to find that a wounded 'crane' was thought to have recuperated on the west side of Iona, at the Great Spirit-Mound or *Sithean Mór* where the Grail initiates spent their three days of ritual imprisonment. The same 'Mound of the Tomb' was also the 'Hill of Fires' – although Columba's monks preferred to think of it as the 'Hill of the Angels'. According to an Irish bishop who visited Iona in 1760, it had once boasted a 'Druidic temple of twelve stones, each with a human body buried beneath it.'

This burial mound was the '*sìdh* of Emhain', the 'fort finer than all dwellings, where bright apple-trees abound', as the 13th-century praise poem for Raghnall, the Lord of the Isles, described it.

Taliesin called it *caer sidi* – 'Fort of Spirits' – and noted that the 'prison of Gwair' was prepared in it (like Aneirin's 'Gwair the Tall', this refers to Arthur in the guise of Gúaire mac Áedáin, the 'most valiant' layman in the kingdom of the Scots). The 'prison of

Gwair' was Arthur's tomb, and into the chambered cairn with him went his 'faithful servant' (Cai/Cian) and 'the man of the Leven' (Llëenog, otherwise 'Lancelot'), along with Rhydderch's 'sword of lightning slaughter' and such other Treasures of the Island of Britain as the horn of Brân and the cauldron of the Lord of Annwn.

And so Arthur and his comrades were buried on the island of the sacred trees where the precious oak-apples grew: the Island of Apples, or Isle of the Blest, where those who had kept their oaths were transported to the Neolithic 'palace of Kronos', the god of abundance who was himself a prisoner in the western isle.

This was the 'Island of the Son of Cian', where 'Lugh the poet's son was raised'. It was the Otherworldly Land of Promise, *Hy-Brasil* or the Island of the Mighty, where the native equivalent of Kronos – the agricultural deity known to the Britons as Hu Gadarn, 'The Mighty' – had given his name to the island of *Hii*.

In the late-8th century, Iona was indeed *Hí Bresail* – for the abbot who proclaimed the Law of St Columba in Ireland in 778 was named Bresal mac Ségéni.

'BLACK-CRANE'

Arthur's burial on the Isle of Iona formed the substance of a strange legend attached to St Columba.

Columba's attempts to establish his church had not been entirely successful. He resolved to sacrifice one of his retinue – 'Someone among you should go down into the soil of the island to consecrate it' – promising the victim that 'no one who makes a request at my tomb or resting-place will be granted it unless he first seek it of you.'

St Oran was chosen. Other forms of his name include Odhrán and Dòbhran. According to some, he was Columba's brother.

Oran was buried alive. Three days later, St Columba opened the tomb 'to see what might be the fate of his friend'. To Columba's dismay, Oran 'opened his swimming eyes' and said:

Heaven is not special,
Nor is hell all darkness;
The good are not transformed,
And the bad are not punished.

Columba demanded that Oran's tomb be closed again, 'lest he blab any more'.

Realistically, Oran is the patron saint of Iona – dozens of kings and lords were buried in his graveyard – although his identity is obscure. His name, *Òran*, means 'Song' in Gaelic (like *ealadh*, which can mean a 'stone tomb' or a 'skilful song'), although the proper word is *amhran* – Middle Irish *ambrán* – which sounds like 'The Raven', as in Brân the Blessed, *le chevalier Bran* and the Brân 'from the North' whose marvellous horn was buried with Arthur.

Only the head of Arthur was buried in the 'hill of the Sidhe of Emhain'. It was the part of him in which the 'High Self' resided, and it continued to display its prophetic powers long after Arthur's death. The rest of him was buried in a mound or *sithean* beside the Stream of the Sons of Arthur, above Pennyghael ('Head-of-the-Gael') on the adjacent Isle of Mull. His ghost still haunts this area.

The 'best-known and most dreadful spectre in the West Highlands' takes the form of a headless horseman, reportedly last seen in 1958 and known as *Eoghann a' Chinn Bhig* ('Ewen of the Little Head'). Supposedly a member of the Maclaine (*Mac'ill-Eathain* – 'Son of Áedán's Lad') family of Mull, Ewen is said to have married a difficult woman called *Corr-dhu*, 'Black-Crane'. She insisted that her husband demand more land from his uncle. The dispute intensified. Battle loomed.

On the eve of the battle, Ewen encountered a *bean-nighe* or Washer at the Ford – a role played elsewhere by Arthur's sister Muirgein – who told him that if his wife offered him butter with his breakfast, he would prevail; but if no butter was proffered, he would be slain. There was no butter on the breakfast table, and

Ewen's head was struck from his body in the battle with his uncle.

Of course, it was not the absence of butter which proved fatal to Arthur on the morning of his last battle but the disappearance of his trusted companion, Iddog or Aedóc, known as *Cordd Prydain* ('Churn of Britain'), who had slipped away to unleash his warrior-monks against Arthur. It was not 'butter' that was missing, but the 'churn'.

The remains of 'Ewen' (*Eóghan* – 'yew-born', 'noble') were eventually transported to Iona for burial. Visitors to Iona in the 19th century were shown a carved stone which reputedly honoured the headless warrior. This was almost certainly Maclean's Cross, a remarkable 15th-century stone slab which has the image of an armed and mounted horseman on its base. The cross stands beside the medieval Street of the Dead on the approach to St Oran's Chapel and its graveyard of kings.

On Mull, meanwhile, Ewen's phantom pony is said to leave round indentations in the earth, 'as if it had wooden legs'. Evidently, this small black horse belonged to an age before the invention of the horseshoe, when war-ponies were shod with iron plates or oval-shaped cups. Known as 'hipposandals', these had been introduced to Britain by the Romans. They would have been used by Arthur and his horsemen.

Orddu

If the Mull legend remembers Arthur's wife as *Corr-dhu* ('Black-Crane'), in the *Culhwch and Olwen* story she appears as a witch called *Orddu* ('Very-Black').

Morgan, the king-turned-boar, had been hunted down. Only one task remained for Arthur and his heroes: to take the blood of the witch Orddu, whose cave was located 'on the confines of Hell'. Arthur 'set out for the North' and the uplands of the hellish territory of the Picts. He found the hag's cave at Penn Nant Gofid, the 'Head of the Brook of Grief' (there is a pun here –

another Welsh word for 'grief' is *alaeth*; Gwenhwyfar was held at the 'Head of the Water of Alyth').

Nennius, the 9th-century monk who compiled a list of Arthur's battles, up to and including his victory at Badandun Hill – *Mons Badonis,* the first Battle of Badon – also recorded a 'wonder' of Scotland. This was a 'valley in Angus, in which shouting is heard every Monday night; Glend Ailbe is its name, and it is not known who makes this noise.'

W.J. Watson tentatively identified the *Glen Ailbhe* of Nennius as the valley of the River Isla in Strathmore. Arthur's last battle ended on a Monday – and, as the song of *Le Chevalier Bran* implied, the ghosts of the slain gathered nightly in bird-form on the battlefield to mourn their fate. Perhaps the area around the *Allaid* of Alyth was once known as 'Ailbe's Vale' after St Ailbe of Emly, a 6th-century Irish bishop and patron saint of wolves who reputedly baptised St David. It was, after all, from St David's (*Din Dewydd*) that Cadog's monks came to destroy Arthur.

It is possible that the chapel established by the monks of Iona at Meigle, immediately to the south of Alyth, in about 606 was dedicated to Ailbe, for this was on the very spot where Arthur had been attacked by the monks from *Mynyw,* where St Ailbe is honoured as 'St Elvis'. It was also the burial place of Arthur's wife.

Gwenhwyfar (known locally as *Guanora*) was imprisoned in *Dum Bharraidhe,* the vitrified 'Fort of the Baron-Baillie' on the summit of Barry Hill, above Alyth. The 'cave' in which Arthur's men found her would therefore compare with the underground cavern which supposedly connected the hill-fort with the ruined Castle of Inverquiech in the Balloch below.

The *Culhwch and Olwen* legend indicates that the witch was cut in half: they 'made two vats of her'. Gwenhwyfar's blood was drained, probably beside the Alyth Burn or 'Water of Quiech', and then taken in the cauldron to Iona, where it was interred with Arthur's head. The Welsh version of the *Perceval* tale has Peredur of York (who died at Barry Hill) visiting the 'hidden retreat' of the Fisher King and seeing not a *graal* but a man's head in a serving dish surrounded by a profusion of blood.

Evidence of Gwenhwyfar's execution still exists in the area around Meigle.

In about 1120, Lambert of St Omer wrote:

> There is in Britain – in the land of the Picts – a palace of the warrior Artuir ... in which the history of all his exploits and wars is to be seen in sculpture.

The greatest concentrations of Pictish symbol stones occur in Aberdeenshire and Angus, both of which witnessed the clashes of Arthur's final campaign. Many of these carved stones depict battle scenes, with helmeted horsemen and cloaked, monkish foot-soldiers.

One of the most famous of these symbol stones is Vanora's Stone – Meigle 2 – which appears to show Arthur's queen being savaged by wild beasts, possibly after her bloodless body was abandoned in Meigle's boggy meadow.

Another of the Meigle stones was destroyed in 1869. Known as Meigle 10, it was unique in depicting a two-wheeled horse-drawn chariot bearing two passengers, with a crouching archer taking aim at the vehicle. The design of the chariot suggests that it was a Roman *carpentum* or processional wagon.

Among the Thirteen Treasures of Britain was *Car Morgan Mwynfawr*, the 'Chariot of Morgan the Wealthy', which might have borne Morgan and Gwenhwyfar to their final destination. It was one of the items, soon to be Arthur's grave-goods, which were gathered by Myrddin Wyllt and taken to the 'Glass Fort' on the hill above Alyth.

"Glamis Manse Pictish symbol stone – cauldron with human legs sticking out of it (left) and warriors above; two-handled cauldron symbol also on right. Reproduced by kind permission of RCAHMS."

Artus de Bretania

The Glamis Manse Stone displays the 'Triple Disc and Cross Bar' image which appears on no fewer than 14 Pictish stones and seemingly represents the two-handled cauldron. Also shown are two men fighting with axes and a cauldron with two pairs of human legs sticking out of it. A similar image can be seen on the St Vigeans 7 stone, where a human figure is being lowered headfirst into a bowl or vat. Both of these stones were found within a few miles of Meigle. Their comparable images recall the initiation tableau on one of the interior plates of the Gundestrup cauldron – the difference being that, while the Gundestrup cauldron represents the equestrian 'rebirth' of humble foot-

"Reconstructed sketch of St Vigeans 7 Pictish symbol stone, Angus, with figure (right) being held head downwards in cauldron. By kind permission of RCAHMS."

soldiers, the Pictish stones of Angus show the cauldron as an instrument of death, l ike the cauldron of Medea, which both gave and took the blood of life.

St Vigeans in Angus also boasts a stone inscription which names 'Drosten' (Drystan/Tristan). At nearby Invergowrie, a slab depicts a mounted warrior quaffing from a drinking horn, the end of which forms a bird's head, smirking quizzically, as if to remind us that the 'sweet' mead turned to 'poison' in the bellies of the Gododdin.

Other images found on the Pictish stones include the comb and shears which Arthur's heroes sought to seize from the head of the renegade Boar-King and such recognisably Druidic symbols as the salmon and the serpent, the latter often 'pierced' through its middle – as was Arthur (see endnotes).

In Brittany, Arthur's queen was remembered as *Wenlowen*, recalling St Luan and the 'Kerlouan' fort of Elouan, as the émigrés from Lothian thought of Alyth. Meanwhile, on a marble archivolt above the Porta della Pescheria in the Italian cathedral of Modena, Gwenhwyfar is identified as *Winlogee* – possibly from 'Lughaidh', a variant of Luan.

The Modena archivolt was completed between 1120 and 1140. At the centre of the carved relief stands a twin-towered fortress, labelled *Burmaltus* (a 'berm' is a ledge or embankment between a defensive ditch and a rampart – compare the Scots *barmkin*, the 'outermost fortification of a wall'; *Burmaltus* therefore signifies the 'High Fortress' or 'Hill-Fort of Alyth'). Two figures shown inside the *Burmaltus* castle are named *Winlogee* and *Mardoc*, the latter being reminiscent of St Cadog or 'Mádoc', who was almost certainly the foster-father of Gwenhwyfar.

Artus de Bretania – 'Arthur of Britain' – attacks the fortress from the left, along with *Isdernus* or Áedán, who was romanticised as 'Yder' or 'Edern' and Christianised as 'St Ethernan' (*Ithernanus* in 1219; *Ydarnasius* in 1220).

On the right-hand side of the hill-fort, *Carrado* (Caradog) fights with *Galvagin*, while *Che* (Cai) and *Galvariun* approach bearing lances.

Galvariun indicates a 'follower' of St Barre or Findbarr, who was honoured at Nevay, two miles east of Meigle. He was the inspiration for Geoffrey of Monmouth's 'Barinthus', the ferryman who transported Arthur to Avalon, who was also identified as Manannán (Brân's brother, Manawydan). As St Finbarr, he was originally known as Lóchán or Loan, and it is clear that Finbarr/Findbarr bears comparison with Findabair – the Irish form of Gwenhwyfar – just as 'Loan' recalls the Breton name for Arthur's wife. These names are preserved at Alyth (the only place with a church dedicated to 'Luan') and Meigle, where the farmstead of Glenluie/Glenlouie reminds us of the 'Luan Lake', *Llyn Llywan,* where Arthur finally confronted his boar-like nemesis.

What is portrayed on the archivolt over the Porta della Pescheria at Modena is the storming of the 'High Hill-Fort' above Alyth in the summer of 594 and the violent treachery of a 'follower of Fagan' – *Galvagin* – named after an obscure missionary who, like St Cadog, was associated with South Wales.

"Artus de Bretania *attacks* Burmaltus *fortress,* Isdernus *behind him. Detail of carved 12th-century archivolt over the Porta della Pischeria, Modena Cathedral, Italy."*

12

The Waste Land *ricorso*

They came for our land, for what grew or could be grown on it,
for the resources in it, and for our clean air and pure water.
They stole those things from us ... and now ... they've come
for the very last of our possessions; now they want our pride,
our history, our spiritual traditions.
They want to rewrite and remake these things,
to claim them for themselves.
Margo Thunderbird

OF COURSE the original Arthur had to be forgotten. How could it have been otherwise when the Church exercised an effective monopoly of the written word?

Something dreadful – momentous, cataclysmic – had happened: the Britons had lost Arthur, their 'shield against the Mordei', and with him had fallen that band of brothers who had fought for the lands of the Old North. Most of those territories were overrun, almost immediately, by the Germanic interlopers.

The very notion of Britain vanished for 1,000 years, eventually to be resurrected under a Scottish king who, when he was baptised at Stirling, was hailed as a new Arthur. But the Britain of old was gone forever.

St Columba outlived Arthur by three years. One of his last recorded acts was to stand on the large mound which housed Arthur's gory remains, the bodies of his comrades and the 'Treasures of Annwn', and to address his monks, declaiming:

> From this very moment poisonous reptiles shall in no way be able to hurt men or cattle in this island, so long as the inhabitants shall continue to observe the commandments of Christ.

A century later, Adomnán of Iona confirmed that, 'from that day to the present, the venomous reptiles with the three-forked tongues could do no manner of harm to man or beast.'

It was not snakes that Columba had banished from the sacred isle, but the 'serpents' of the old religion (see endnote).

Old magic

St Columba had brought the religious-aristocratic Heroic age to North Britain. His was an all-or-nothing creed. The presence of a time-honoured alternative to his doctrine was repugnant to him – as he had previously demonstrated in Ireland – and so it had to be eradicated.

The result was the Waste Land. The Grail was lost: both the practice, since no more warrior-poets were initiated, and the objects, for the cauldron and the horn were buried with Arthur.

Our investigation has come full circle. We opened with the Waste Land, that pervasive sense of moral and spiritual despair, and in this final chapter we shall examine the underlying causes of the Waste Land – and some possible solutions to the problem.

Curiously, the Waste Land was hinted at in the *Life of Columba*: it happened a few years before Adomnán settled down to write his hagiography of Arthur's nemesis.

A spring drought had desiccated the fields, imperilling the survival of the monastic community on Iona. The monks resolved to parade Columba's tunic around the cornfields on the west side of the island and then to climb the chambered burial cairn of *Sithean Mór* and read aloud from the books which St Columba had transcribed.

Suddenly, and with remarkable rapidity, clouds rose from the sea, 'copious rain fell day and night, and the parched earth being sufficiently moistened, produced its fruits in good season, and yielded the same year a most abundant harvest.'

The monks put the success of their rain-making gambit down to 'the invocation of the very name of the blessed man

[Columba]' – but it should not have escaped our notice that the strange ritual took place on Arthur's grave. When the barrenness and sterility of the Waste Land threatened, the monks resorted to a form of the old Druidic magic, though they clothed it in Columba's vestments.

The Once-and-Future King

Apart from the sparse references to Arthur in the *Life of Columba* and the Irish annals – all sources that originated on Iona – the Church pointedly forgot what had happened. Ordinary folk, though, didn't forget.

Arthur survived in the Divine age memory: in place-names and poetry, proverbs and folktales. Though the clergy forbade overt mentions of Arthur, they could do little to erase his alter egos – Lugh and Brân, to name but two. The popular tales could not be curtailed by censorship. The 'emperor' lived on in the cultural DNA of his people.

According to an account written by William of Malmesbury early in the 12th century, an English monk named Stephen Harding first went to Scotland and then travelled to France, where he founded the Cistercian Order. Before long, the Cistercians had established themselves in Arthur's former territory; they even had an abbey at Coupar Angus, a couple of miles from where Arthur made his last stand. The Arthurian romances they recounted made frequent references to Scotland.

But the sterile ignorance and self-interest of the Waste Land reasserted itself. First, the Benedictine rivals of the austere Cistercians claimed to have unearthed Arthur's remains at Glastonbury – a flagrant scam which has blighted Arthurian studies ever since.

The Cistercians themselves were actively engaged in the extermination of the Cathars, those 'perfect' ones whose morals were pure, but whose spirituality offended the materialistic papacy.

Whether or not the Cathars had inherited something of the *sant grathail* tradition, it seems likely that the Cistercians' brothers-in-arms, the Knights Templar, rediscovered and reintroduced the rituals practised by the Grail warriors. The Templars had preceded the Cistercians into Arthurian Scotland. Their eventual destruction was as treacherous and terrible as the betrayal of Arthur and his men.

RE-INVENTING THE GRAIL

The form taken by the Grail in the Divine age was a cauldron and a horn. Where Divine age thinking persisted – in medieval Scotland and Wales, for example – these crucial items retained their true forms. We find them in the legends of Canonbie Dick and the Lucken Hare (a stone's throw from the Cistercian abbey of Melrose) and Rosslyn Castle (close to the Templar settlement at Balantrodach and the Cistercians' Newbattle Abbey) as well as in such contemporary folktales as the *Romance of Horn* and *King Horn*. Robert Biket's *Lai du cor* took the magical horn as its focus, while the Hebridean *Sgeulachd air Sir Uallabh O'Còrn* personified the horn as the father of Sir Uallabh, whose uncle was 'Chief Arthur son of Iuthar', a 'King in Ireland'.

It might even be said that the 20th-century poet Edwin Morgan tuned into this ancient tradition when he had St Columba and St Kentigern debating the merits of '*le son du cor*'. St Columba found the sound of the horn 'sad'. St Kentigern loved it, and in response to Columba's dour remark that the sound 'dies', Kentigern averred that it '*renaît et se prolonge*'. As was noted in Chapter 3, the French *son du cor* could also be translated, 'bran of the horn'. So maybe it was Brân who was 'reborn and lives on'.

The horn also featured in the medieval *Roman de Fergus* and *Sone de Nausay*. The hero of the latter – whose name, Sone, relates him to Brân – visited an abbey and discovered the Grail in the shape of an ivory horn.

Under Cistercian influence, however, the Grail ineluctably

began to shift into its Heroic age form. This was the cup used by Christ at the Last Supper, in which his blood was collected as he was brought down from the Cross.

Inevitably, the Benedictines of Glastonbury proclaimed that this miraculous cup also belonged to their abbey.

The chalice
The depiction of the Grail as Christ's cup was both true and false:-

- *True* – in that the original horn was used as part of a Eucharistic meal shared by a chosen few; a *krater* filled with wine mixed with hemlock was present at the Crucifixion; and blood was collected in the cauldron after the sacrificial death of Arthur
- *False* – in that it took the items away from Arthur and his cult and bestowed them on Christ and his disciples, thereby helping to cement the central myth of Christianity: that only Jesus had ever undergone the initiatory death-and-rebirth ritual

The point was well and truly missed. The Grail knights had not sought Christ's mystical grace; rather, Jesus himself had belonged to the same age-old Mystery tradition from which the cauldron and its rituals had sprung. This was the 'hidden stream' of authentic spirituality which the Church repeatedly condemned and attacked.

One of the major contrasts between the earlier Divine age and the subsequent Heroic age is that the former is wary of the written word. It prefers memory.

The Heroic age, meanwhile, is founded on the written word, and the medieval Church was its record-keeper.

The first texts the Church created regarding Arthur portrayed him in a very bad light. Admittedly, churchmen also transcribed much of the native material (the tales of the *Mabinogion,* the verses of Taliesin and Aneirin, and so on). At the same time, though, the Church was peddling its own versions of the legends. In these elaborate fictions, Arthur became a Christian king and the 'Holy Grail' the ultimate Christian souvenir.

The Church foisted its anachronistic 'King Arthur' on a courtly audience so efficiently that – even today – many are seduced by the medieval flummery and cannot imagine the Grail as anything but a chalice.

The Island of Afallach

The Waste Land descended when Arthur was betrayed, his elite war-band annihilated, and Britain handed over to her enemies. Such would have been the viewpoint of the majority of Britons and Scots, and something of their anguish peeps through the medieval accounts.

Perceval (Peredur) rides through a devastated land which has suffered ever since his father was 'wounded through his thighs and his body maimed'; his uncle, the Fisher King, has been similarly incapacitated, and the mysterious Grail procession replays the fatal wounding of Arthur.

Insult was added to injury when the clergy began to retell the old tales. Having conspired to eliminate Arthur, the Church later went on to claim him for Christianity.

This was the Waste Land Mark II: the denial of popular memory and the misappropriation of cultural heritage. The Church killed Arthur and then tried to forget him. But he would not be forgotten. So the Church stole him.

The 13th-century praise poem for Raghnall son of Somerled sheds a powerful light on the period during which the Cistercians were altering the Grail to suit their Heroic age agenda. The clergy refused to allow anyone to remember that *Ioua insula* had ever been anything other than the Island of Columba of the Church – but the Norse king of the isles still knew that Iona was 'Emain Ablach of the yews'.

Arthur's burial mound, the poet declaimed, was a 'fort finer than all dwellings, where bright apple-trees abound':

Fair the place of the man of the mound
Who has drunk the honey's liquor:
To go to the burial cairn, the fair *sídh*,
Is to go to the fine mead-fort.

The clergy tore down the church that Raghnall built on Iona. Raghnall's sin was that he would not collude with the Church authorities in forgetting that Iona was once the 'Fresh place of the dark blackthorn, / Where Lugh the poet's son was raised' (see endnote).

SEEING/NOT-SEEING

It is essential to grasp the fact that the successive phases of society – the Divine, Heroic and Human ages – do not see things the same way. To illustrate, let us consider an experiment carried out by Dr Arthur J. Ellison, Professor of Electrical Engineering at City University, London.

Professor Ellison arranged for a bowl of flowers to rise up into the air in the middle of one of his lectures. He studiously ignored it when it happened. At the end of the lecture he invited questions from the audience.

Eventually, one of the students nervously asked if anybody else had noticed something peculiar happening to the bowl of flowers during the lecture. It transpired that several others had seen the bowl 'wobble' and some had observed it rising above the table, hovering, and then settling back down again.

A few students claimed to have seen 'spirit hands' raising the bowl.

They were all mocked by those in the theatre who had witnessed nothing out of the ordinary.

Overall, there were three different responses. Some students had seen something unusual going on and automatically ascribed it to some spiritual agency; they saw 'spirit hands' at work, when in fact the trick was performed through the clever use of electromagnetism.

Others saw nothing and rudely dismissed the experiences of their neighbours as imaginary. Their brains had filtered out the information. Bowls of flowers do not spontaneously levitate, and so it did not happen.

But some had seen the flowers move, and they were curious. Moreover, they were anxious to know if anybody else had shared their experience.

Here we see the different mindsets at work. Those who saw 'spirit hands' had Heroic age mentalities, which assume that the universe is God's plaything; the group that saw nothing were of the Human age mindset, which is conditioned to ignore the extra-ordinary; and those who witnessed something but were unwilling to impose a pat explanation (it was 'spirits', or it was all 'imagination') were Divine age thinkers, unimpeded by cultural indoctrination.

The brain block

The brain receives a constant stream of information from the outside world. Much of that information doesn't make it past the reticular activating system (RAS) in the brain stem. What does get through is then filtered by the 'palaeomammalian complex', otherwise known as the limbic system – the emotional core of the brain – which determines whether the information received is of relevance to the avoidance of pain or the achievement of pleasure.

Only when the 'older' parts of the brain have sifted the sensory input does that information reach the thinking neo-cortex or 'neomammalian complex' of the brain.

Before any of us gets to think about anything we see, hear,

touch, smell or taste, the reactive parts of our brains first decide whether or not that information is important enough to pass on to the neo-cortex. This means that the stimuli must first pass certain 'relevance' tests based on instinctive reflexes, subconscious emotional reactions and long-term memory. The brain has the ability to reject incoming information, or to interpret it as 'negative', before it even reaches the level of conscious awareness.

Some students failed to see the bowl of flowers rising up into the air because their brains had selectively filtered out that sensory input. The information was 'irrelevant'. It triggered a subconscious negative emotional reaction, which then caused the students' conscious minds to deny what their eyes had seen.

Others had been programmed to interpret inexplicable happenings as evidence of divine intervention. The disturbing possibility that demonic forces might have been involved was rejected by the emotional limbic system, which offered up the reassuring illusion of 'spirit hands' lifting the bowl.

Conditioned responses

Both reactions were wrong: there were no 'spirit hands', although the bowl really had risen into the air. But if we accept that these two erroneous responses to external stimuli were symptomatic, respectively, of the Heroic age mindset (which supposes that God is behind everything that happens) and the Human age mentality (which rationalises everything in strictly materialistic terms) then it becomes clear that we have been misinterpreting the world around us for centuries.

Our brains have identified divine intervention where it did not apply and then ignored phenomena that could not be accounted for. We have seen things which did not happen – and we have failed to see things that did!

The brain's tendency to filter information on the basis of hardwired paradigms and prejudices impacts on our understanding of Arthur and the Grail.

If you have been conditioned to think along Heroic age lines – 'God's in his heaven and the aristocracy are his appointed representatives on earth' – then your reactive brain will reject any evidence that points to Arthur having been a pagan prince of the North, and the Grail a magical device for the initiation of poets and warriors, *before that information reaches your conscious mind* – that is, before you even get a chance to think about it.

Much the same goes for Human age conditioning, which programmes the brain to perceive only the material and to neglect the mystical. The point being that both of these reactions – though ingrained to the point of being wholly subconscious and involuntary – are mistaken. They are not the results of thinking, but of kneejerk and/or temperamental responses to anything which challenges firmly implanted beliefs.

The issue of how we see things, and whether we see them, or we see things that are not there, has a bearing on why St Columba did what he did.

DEATH OF A RELIGION

Arthur's predecessors had noticed something unusual about Iona. Though separated from the Isle of Mull by no more than a mile of sea, it is composed of a very different kind of rock.

A tectonic fault-line runs along the eastern seaboard of Iona so that, to all intents and purposes, the little island exists on a different continent from the mainland and its larger, volcanic neighbour. Stretching westwards into the Atlantic, the older landmass could be thought of as the birthplace of the inhabitable world, its metamorphic bedrock having solidified more than 2.5 billion years ago.

Iona was *Ogygian*, in the sense of predating all known history. It was also the most accessible outcrop of this westerly edge of Europe. Beyond lay the Sea of Shadows, *Mare tenebrarum* – that great river of Ocean which encircled the known world like the

Ouroboros snake. The sun set on the far side of that oceanic River, taking with it the souls of the dead, ferried in the solar boat of Osiris. Iona was indeed a launch-pad for souls seeking entrance to the Otherworld. It was, as Taliesin remarked, the 'island of the strong door': the gateway to the beyond.

The Sanskrit word *duir* gave us both 'door' (Welsh *dôr*, Old Irish *dorus*) and the Celtic words for the 'oak' (Welsh *dâr*, Old Irish *daur*). The 'island of the strong door' was also the site of the World-Tree. And like the human spine, which joins the 'root' chakra, *Muladhara*, to the thousand-petalled 'crown' chakra, *Sahasrara*, at the top of the head, the World-Tree connected the Underworld with the Upperworld, the earth with the sky.

Whether it was the ash-tree (Gaelic *nuin*, whence 'Annwn'; also *nòin*, genitive *nòna*, 'evening'), where the mighty serpent slept coiled among the roots, or the oak with its ink-yielding golden apples, any such large sacred tree was considered a 'yew' (Irish *eo*). Iona was the 'Yewy' isle; the 'place of yews'.

Converting Avalon

St Columba set his heart on this place. A power centre of this eminence had perforce to be 'Christianised'.

On the metaphorical level, Columba did this by commandeering the Stone of Destiny (Chapter 5), which embodied the sovereignty of the Scottish colony. This stone was probably a bloc of Iona marble, shot through with veins of green serpentine, and so it was similar to the green Stone which, according to Wolfram von Eschenbach, had fallen earthwards from Lucifer's crown (Venus) and was nothing less than the 'Gral'.

Once Columba had seized the Stone of Destiny (using it for his pillow, like the biblical Jacob, or as the Holy Stone – *Moel-blatha* – which sustained Columba through famine, just as the 'Gral' nourished its 'warlike company') it became necessary for the Scottish kings to be 'ordained' by Columba on that sacred stone. But this did not make them Christian. As Geoffrey of

Monmouth would recall, the island remained home to a sisterhood of nine maidens whose leader, 'Morgen', was Arthur's sister.

How, then, was Columba to tear the pagans away from their time-honoured practices and impose his creed on the people?

With a strong king, Áedán, to rule them, and the inspiring 'emperor' Arthur to lead their British allies through the Mithraic brotherhood of the Grail, the Scots were seemingly unstoppable. They had no need of an alien Gospel.

If they were traumatised, though, they would have been much more susceptible to Columba's preaching.

Tuireadh Brighid

The death of Arthur was a cosmic tragedy. At the time, it would have felt as if the world had ended.

The shock of his death swept aside the old religion. Evidence for this comes in the form of a Gaelic elegy, preserved among the manuscripts of the Advocates' Library in Edinburgh and entitled, 'Death-song of Brighid'.

Brighid – otherwise Brìde, pronounced 'breed' – was the tutelary goddess of the Western Isles or *Eileana Brìde*, the 'Islands of Brighid'. The folk of the Hebrides were 'Brìde's People', *Aois-Bhrìghde*.

The classical world had noted the existence of the nymphs of the Hesperides, who tended their garden with its golden apples on the edge of the Atlantic Ocean. These 'Western Maidens' ('Sunset Goddesses', 'Daughters of Evening') were reputedly the offspring of Hesperus, the Evening Star – or Venus, as it is also known.

Brighid was the Celtic equivalent of Venus, the Romans also giving her the attributes of Victoria, whose winged statues inspired the Christian concept of angels. She was the goddess of light, wisdom, medicine, motherhood, poetry, artists and craftsmen, including blacksmiths.

An ancient tradition records that the virginal Bride was raised on Iona. The Christians would later claim that she had been transported by angels to Bethlehem, where she became midwife and foster-mother to the infant Christ. Thus, Brighid (Christianised as 'St Bridget') was considered the 'Mary of the Gael'. But her earlier associations were with the cauldron.

Chuir Brìghd' a làmh sa bhobhla, states a Gaelic proverb: 'Brìde put her hand into the bowl' (an old Welsh word, *chwyf*, preserved the same sense of a stirring motion and might explain the middle elements in the names of Gwenhwyfar and her smaller sister, Gwenhwyfach). As the personification of the planet Venus, Brighid represented the intended destination of the Grail initiate, her eight-pointed star corresponding to the eight outer plates of the cauldron.

When the cauldron's liquor turned to 'poison' in the bellies of Arthur's men, Brighid was blamed. Her burial under a stone – like that of Arthur's sister, 'Little Anna of the Poison' – prompted this bitter Gaelic lament:

TUIREADH BRIGHID
I call and pray to you, stone,
Do not release Brìde.
When she poisoned the drink,
To many a good warrior without fault
She brought death.
Your thirst now exceeds thirstiness;
An eternal thirst upon you, Brìde.

SHOCK TREATMENT

In 2007, the Canadian journalist Naomi Klein published *The Shock Doctrine*. Subtitled, 'The Rise of Disaster Capitalism', Klein's book revealed how catastrophic upheavals have been and continue to be rapidly and ruthlessly exploited by neoclassical economists.

The godfather of Disaster Capitalism was Milton Friedman (1912-2006). A leading evangelist of neoliberal ideology, Friedman fanatically opposed any form of state intervention in the free market – his mentor, Friedrich von Hayek, had branded any such intervention as 'The Road to Serfdom' – and transformed the Economics Department of the University of Chicago into a hot-bed of messianic capitalist radicalism.

Initially, Friedman was out-of-step with current thinking. The post-war consensus was built on the Keynesian model of a mixed economy, in which the role of government is to regulate markets and, where necessary, take steps to protect the weak from unbridled capitalism.

With governments everywhere anxious to insulate their citizens against the worst excesses of the free market, Friedman was a voice in the wilderness. He realised that 'only a crisis – actual or perceived – produces real change.' Until that crisis came, his Chicago School acolytes would be powerless to alter a nation's economy. But they had only to wait and prepare:

> When that crisis occurs, the actions that are taken depend on the ideas that are lying around. That, I believe [wrote Friedman], is our basic function: to develop alternatives to existing policies, to keep them alive and available until the politically impossible becomes politically inevitable.

In his own words, Friedman was 'an old-fashioned preacher delivering a Sunday sermon.' And although his followers sought to present themselves as dispassionate clinicians, operating on an economy like a surgeon on a patient, the reality is that their beliefs were *religious*. The free market was 'sacred'; any outside meddling with its workings was anathema.

The new Heroic age

The thinking was apocalyptic – as if the Heroic age mindset, frustrated by such Human age constraints as democracy and evidence-based science, was plotting to unleash its polarised, fundamentalist beliefs once again on an unsuspecting world.

Only a disaster, natural, man-made or imaginary, could produce the 'blank sheet' upon which the Chicago Boys could quickly rewrite the socio-economic rules.

Their first opportunities came in Latin America, where democratically-elected (i.e. Human age) leftist governments were toppled by Washington-backed military dictators. The peoples of Chile and Argentina were stunned by violent coups d'état. Then came the medicine – and it was harsh. Extreme reforms were implemented with bewildering speed. Markets were deregulated, state-owned assets privatised. Any opposition was crushed without mercy. Thousands were imprisoned, tortured and executed.

Friedman's radical theories actually required two shocks: the initial, destabilising crisis, followed immediately by brutal repression. His fundamentalist free-market ideology could only be imposed at gunpoint whilst the populace was still reeling from the trauma of a bloody revolution or civil war.

This was done in the name of *freedom*. 'Freedom' was the buzzword, but it did not mean what it appeared to mean.

It meant freedom for the rich to become much richer at the expense of those on lower incomes; the freedom for foreign firms to plunder natural resources at the expense of the environment; the freedom for the friends and families of the ruling elite to salt away fortunes in tax havens while the majority suffered in terrified silence.

Across the globe, the Heroic age struck back, one country, one economy, one crisis at a time. New aristocracies – from Russian oligarchs to China's 'little princes' – were established under the new Church of corporatism.

At the same time, wages fell, prices rose and people were 'disappeared'. Friedman's peculiar notion of 'freedom' came at an incalculable human cost.

"Milton Friedman (1912-2006), economic architect of the new Heroic age."

'Depatterning'

Naomi Klein opened her exposé of the methods employed by the new Heroic age to seize the wealth and restrict the liberties enjoyed by Human age societies with an examination of the work of Dr Ewen Cameron at McGill University in Montreal. Over a number of years, Dr Cameron received funding from the CIA to explore ways of 'depatterning' patients suffering from mental disorders. Through the liberal use of electroshock therapy, psychiatric drugs and long periods of isolation, Cameron endeavoured to unmake a patient's personality – to achieve that illusory 'blank sheet' which could then be remodelled along more socially desirable lines.

In fact, Ewen Cameron achieved nothing of the sort. Many

lives were ruined; not one was remade. But some lessons were learnt.

Like the economic shock therapy demanded by the Chicago School and its High Priest, Milton Friedman, Cameron's experiments had shown that immense trauma could wipe out the memory and reduce the patient to an infantile condition, after which they might never be restored to full health.

The Russian physiologist Ivan Petrovich Pavlov had discovered something similar in his experiments with dogs. By subjecting his canine subjects to stresses, up to and beyond the 'transmarginal' point at which the dogs' normal behaviour no longer produced relief from suffering, Pavlov noticed changes in the ways their brains functioned.

First, Pavlov noted an 'equivalent' phase, in which the dogs responded equally – or indifferently – to all stimuli, regardless of the strength or weakness of the stimulus.

Next came the 'paradoxical' phase, in which livelier responses were produced by weaker stimuli than by stronger ones.

Finally, there was the 'ultra-paradoxical' phase, in which the dog's original behaviour patterns were converted into their opposites: whatever it disliked before, it now liked, and what it had formerly shunned, it now sought.

Pavlov had proved that, under sufficient stress, a dog would reverse its previous conditioning. Like Winston Smith in George Orwell's *1984*, it could be made to love Big Brother.

THE CONTINUUM

Pavlov's study of 'transmarginal inhibition' in dogs demonstrates how dramatic religious and political conversions can be made to happen.

We know that the reticular activating system of the old 'reptilian' or 'R-complex' and the limbic system or 'paleomammalian complex' act as gatekeepers to our conscious minds, filtering sensory information before it reaches the neo-cortex.

The crocodile and the horse in our heads decide whether incoming data is important and relevant enough for us to think about, depending on whether it passes the tests of survival instinct and emotional memory.

When intolerable levels of stress are applied, however, the brain can reprogram itself – even to the extent of altering the conditioned responses of the older 'reptilian' and 'paleomammalian' parts of the brain. In such circumstances, the most strong-minded individual can be made to believe the very opposite of what she had held to be true, regardless of how irrational the new belief might be.

(Interestingly, Pavlov observed that his dogs fell into four temperamental categories, almost perfectly matching the four human personality types – sanguine, choleric, phlegmatic and melancholic – which made up the 'humours' theory advanced by Hippocrates in the 4th century BC. Pavlov found that the 'strong excitory' and 'weak inhibitory' dogs, whose behaviour compared with the 'choleric' and 'melancholic' personality types identified by Hippocrates, broke down more quickly under stress.)

To reprogram an individual – and, theoretically, a society – all that is needed is stress, and plenty of it. Evidence that Disaster Capitalism is ruining an economy simply provokes calls from the Chicago Boys for more of the same medicine. More shocks must be applied for the patient (the human brain, the body politic) to be reduced to the infantile 'blank sheet', that empty vessel which can then be refilled with new beliefs which are the polar opposites of what was previously believed.

Breakdown

Something like this happened long ago. In his seminal study of the *Origin of Consciousness in the Breakdown of the Bicameral Mind* (1977), Julian Jaynes argued that the gods had routinely spoken to Western man until about 3,000 years ago. Then some kind of catastrophe thrust us out of paradise and onto the historical stage. The gods retreated, and we have been hurting ever since.

It was not that we began to think (*Homo sapiens* is, by definition, a thinker) but that we began to think *exclusively with our left-brain hemispheres*. The 'intellectual' side of the brain started to dominate; the 'intuitive' side was suppressed. Patriarchy had arrived with a vengeance.

The result was civilisation: first in its religious-aristocratic Heroic age form, and latterly in the Human age guise of science and democracy. As we have seen, though, the Heroic age has been making a comeback lately.

Giambattista Vico predicted this – he dubbed it the *ricorso*. The advocates of Heroic age obsessions (religious extremism and socio-economic inequality) are effectively guaranteeing the collapse of civilisation and a return to the magical thinking of the Divine age.

The original crisis – which might have had something to do with the Babylonian exile of the Jews (see endnote) – propelled us into the Heroic age. The new Heroic age automatically exploits crises, natural or man-made, for its own ends.

So what can this tell us about the transition from prehistory to history, the looming *ricorso* that will hurl us back into the Divine age, and Columba's determined destruction of the Grail cult?

Paradise lost

Jean Liedloff was a New Yorker who left her studies at Cornell University to take part in a diamond-hunting expedition to Venezuela. She made further expeditions to the jungles of South America, spending time with the Yequana people, who were essentially a Stone Age tribe. Her observations of life among the Yequana informed her 1975 book, *The Continuum Concept*, which came to bear the suggestive subtitle, 'In Search of Happiness Lost'.

Concentrating especially on Yequana child-rearing practices, Liedloff concluded that millions of years of evolution have primed human infants to expect certain experiences. The child naturally knows how to develop, and if it is permitted to do so along the lines mapped out by our evolutionary heritage – the 'continuum', as Liedloff called it – a well-adjusted adult will emerge.

The 'continuum' requires the Yequana mother to spend most if not all of her time with her baby, denying it nothing but allowing it the freedom to explore. The child is never impeded and never denied the reassuring feel of the mother's hands and arms, her breast and her thigh.

In short, nature taught us how to raise children. But now, we think we know better. A multitude of 'experts' regale us with their theories (left-brain inventions) and pour scorn on the traditional Yequana methods, which have come to be known as 'Attachment Parenting'. Look at the evidence, though, and you'll see that modern child-rearing practices are a major disaster. We raise needy, greedy, frightened and contrary monsters, who then rear the next generation of maladjusted misfits.

We do not nurture them: we traumatise them, resisting their instinctive demands and expecting them to cry themselves to sleep.

When we forgot how to raise children, the Heroic age was born. Presumably, a section of society began to feel that it was too important constantly to attend its own offspring, or that its heirs had to be brutalised so that they would grow up to dominate and subjugate others.

We turned our backs on the 'continuum' – the paradise of our Divine age ancestors – and struggled to nurse the invisible wounds of the child within. Relying on our 'thinking' brains to fill the void left by neglectful parents, we learnt to snatch at everything. What could not be possessed, we destroyed.

FEAR AND LOATHING

Civilisation is built on fear.

Our children are traumatised, 'depatterned' through the stress of inconsistent and unnatural parenting, their inbuilt behaviour patterns bullied out of them. They are then conditioned to play society's destructive games – as Wordsworth put it, 'Getting and spending, we lay waste our powers' – and programmed to perpetuate the cycle of abuse.

The baby screams its lungs raw in the dark. And then it is terrorised. The nightmares it has begun to suffer in its lonely crib are converted into the terrors of religion.

'Heaven' and 'Hell' are the carrot-and-stick of the Church. They are Heroic age ideas: abstract concepts presented as if they were actual places. The fear of 'eternal damnation' is used to shock people into the 'ultra-paradoxical' phase of sudden conversion; John Wesley, the authoritarian founder of the Methodist movement, recorded many occasions on which his vivid descriptions of 'Hell' produced the same changes in behaviour as Ivan Pavlov achieved with his dogs.

The moment when the Heroic age, with its polarised notions of 'Heaven' and 'Hell', clashed with the Divine age – which did not recognise such things – was captured in the legend of St Oran (*ambran*/Brân/Arthur). St Columba had buried his friend. When he reopened the grave, Oran proclaimed:

> Heaven is not special,
> Nor is hell all darkness;
> The good are not transformed,
> And the bad are not punished.

Columba was horrified. The message he had brought to the Scots relied on an unwavering fear of 'Hell' and the conditional promise of 'Heaven'. Arthur, however, had seen the beyond – the death-and-rebirth ritual of the cauldron had taken him there – and he knew that 'Heaven' and 'Hell' were empty threats: psychological weapons used to bring about conversions and enforce conformity.

No wonder Columba insisted on shutting him up!

I nam ban bòidheach

The shock of Arthur's death broke down his people's defences. Like Pavlov's dogs, they had no readymade response to this level of stress.

Further pressure was applied – Columba's vision of 'Hell' matching the devastation caused by the resurgent Angles – and soon the 'ultra-paradoxical' phase was reached. The pagans were 'depatterned', reprogrammed, converted.

Muirgein's sisterhood of nine maidens was obliterated. A saying, recorded on Iona in the 19th century, vaguely remembered them:

> *Thiodhlaic mi mo naoi nighnean mar sheachdar an Cill mo Neachdáin ann an Í.*
>
> ['I buried my nine daughters as seven in the Chapel of my Nechtán on Iona.']

Never again would Iona be what it was – 'Iona of the beautiful women', those harmonious nymphs who worshipped the beautiful Brìde, *Brighid bhòidheach,* in their western garden. It was Columba's island now.

St Columba knew that the Angles would eventually succumb to his teachings: there were already 'Englishmen' serving in his community. The saint saw no evil in collaborating with Aethelfrith of Northumbria (the Britons called him 'Deceiver') to bring down Arthur and the warriors of the Grail. The sons of Aethelfrith were later given sanctuary at Columba's monastery, and it was probably during their time on the island that the magnificent cauldron disappeared from Arthur's burial mound.

The royal isle of the Scots became the graveyard of their enemies, the first authenticated burial on the island being that of an Anglian king, Egfrith, in 685. Arthur's father, Áedán mac Gabráin, was not buried on Iona.

And so the 'Navel of the sea' was secured for the Church of Columba, which then had to deny that Iona had ever been *Emain Ablach*, the Island of Apples. Eventually, the Angles showed their gratitude by attributing their victories over the Britons to Columba's spiritual intervention and inviting a missionary from Iona to establish a monastery at Lindisfarne – where Arthur had come so close to ridding Britain of the Anglian menace altogether.

The wound

Whether it comes in the form of an intolerant Church and a belligerent aristocracy or plutocratic corporations and a socio-pathic '1%', the Heroic age thrives on catastrophe. Damaged by cold, cruel parenting, educated to be exploitative and acquisitive, it profits from the enslavement of others.

The natural world is ransacked. Alternative voices are silenced. Science and democracy are sacrificed to the dark gods of entitlement, privilege and riches.

No lie is too outrageous, no outrage too atrocious. Evidence can be fabricated; history rewritten. Loud opinions trump quiet facts.

This all stems from a deep wound that splits the psyche. The inner child or 'low' self, *unihipili,* never recovers from its childhood traumas. It comes to see the Father as an unpredictable tyrant – 'our Protector/Persecutor', as Donald Kalsched put it in *The Inner World of Trauma* (1996). The Mother also undergoes a schizoid reclassification, becoming the idealised, desexualised Madonna and her dangerous opposite, the Wicked Stepmother. Brighid, the great mother-goddess of old – whose sacred animals (snake, cow, raven) reflected her threefold aspect of Maiden, Mother and Crone – is reduced to a cynical dichotomy: an impeccable virgin or an irredeemable whore.

The wounded inner child cannot see beyond its agony. Sigmund Freud noticed in the 1920s that some patients possessed a 'daimonic' force inside them that defied analysis. More recently, Donald Kalsched commented:

> Once the trauma defense is organized, all relations with the outer world are 'screened' by the self-care system. What was intended to be a defense against further trauma becomes a major resistance to all unguarded spontaneous expressions of self in the world. The person survives but cannot live creatively.

Such a person can hate but not love. He is a slave to his own demons and a 'Protector/Persecutor', whom he knows as 'God' and who authorises his assaults on anything associated with the right-brain virtues of integration and relatedness, any manifestation of completeness, all vestiges of natural joy. And, being no longer fully human, he is liable to snap and snarl like a dog – as a few minutes on the internet should quickly prove.

THE GRAIL

We are all Arthur: every one of us a Maimed King who can find no relief from his suffering until somebody asks the right question.

We are Perceval too, in that we have seen the anguish and wonder of the Grail procession.

The time to be silent has passed. As it reasserts itself in a whirlwind of bigotry and propaganda, the Heroic age threatens everything from the environment we live in to the rights we hold so dear. It once plunged us into a thousand-year reign of ignorance and prejudice – and it is doing so again. Only this time, the results will be worse than anything we can imagine.

Strange as it seems, the Grail may yet be our salvation. As an object, it is inconsequential; from the descriptions of the cauldron, and the depictions on the Pictish symbol stones near the scene of Arthur's last battle, we can reasonably assume that it now resides in the National Museum of Denmark, Copenhagen (see endnote) – although where the horn ended up is anyone's guess.

But only a mind fixated on the material would seek the Grail as a physical object. What matters is, *what was the Grail for?*

One of the clues available to us is the sword which was presented to Perceval by the Fisher King. If broken, this sword could repair itself. Peredur of York successfully repaired it twice, though it remained in pieces the third time (Arthur, we might recall, was released from three spells of ritual imprisonment by the 'Gilded' son of Constantine, the third of his cauldron-initiations leading ultimately to his fatal wounding beside the River Isla). Chrétien de Troyes, meanwhile, stated that the sword could only be 'rehammered, retempered, and repaired' at the lake beyond the River Forth, where the 'Smith' who wounded Arthur plied his trade.

The sword is life. It can be broken (death) and repaired (rebirth).

Energy and mass

The Cathars – who were associated with the Grail and destroyed by the Church – believed in two gods: the 'God of Love' and the 'King of the World'. The former was pure spirit, while the latter governed the material realm.

Matter ('mass') is essentially spirit ('energy') that has been slowed down and frozen solid. Most of the known chemical elements were created when stars exploded: as Carl Sagan said, 'We are made of star stuff.'

The atoms which make up a tree or a human being are fossilised fragments of energy – and energy, as Einstein realised, is 'mass' times the square of the speed of light. William Blake, meanwhile, remarked that 'Energy is Eternal Delight.'

The Cathars rejected the 'King of the World' in favour of the 'God of Love'. In other words, they sought to escape from the bonds of matter ('mass') into the state of pure spirit or cosmic energy. Their *Rex Mundi* was Lucifer, the 'Light-Bringer', who was also the Genetrix, 'Heavenly Venus', the 'Purifier'. The path described by Lucifer when he 'fell' was the condensation of star-energy into atomic matter.

A similar trajectory was followed by Mithras, the 'guide of souls', when he descended from the heavens to be born of a virgin in a rock. As C.G. Jung noted, 'The soul comes "from the stars" and returns to the stellar regions'. Light is solidified; spirit becomes matter. Eternal delight ('energy') is converted into substance ('mass') – and so we are born.

A green Stone fell from Lucifer's crown. This was the symbolic form of the Grail – a deposit from the green planet, Venus; a lump of condensed love. It could act as a bridge between the terrestrial and the celestial, or as a particle accelerator, transmuting the initiate from the primal ('green') state of mass into 'golden' energy and returning him to the stars where his bodily elements were made.

The end

It required a death. The 'liquor of science and inspiration' awakened the serpent power, sending it up through the spine and out through the 'heavenly doors' of the head. The soul ('low' self) and the spirit ('High' Self) were released. The initiate walked among the eternal family of gods, the 'Great Poe Aumakua'.

He returned enlightened – a 'Shining One' – and so, like Christ after his initiation, he gave off a sort of radioactive glow. He had been energised. Though reborn in a physical body, his experience had taken him across the threshold of death. He knew what lay beyond this world: that mass converts to energy and we return to our astral home, where matter was forged.

A recurring feature of Near-Death or Out-of-the-Body

Experiences is that the witness reports a changed attitude towards death – which they no longer fear – and life, which no longer feels like a desperate struggle for dominance. And herein lies the key to understanding the Waste Land.

When the Heroic age robbed us of that natural acquaintance with the universe which was part of our evolutionary heritage, it left us terrified of our unavoidable bodily demise and in dread of a 'jealous' God. No greater crime was ever perpetrated against mankind.

It may be that we cannot halt the slide into chaos as the new Heroic age undermines science and overthrows democracy. Perhaps we are not meant to. The *ricorso* will happen: civilisation will disintegrate. But out of the wreckage, a new Divine age will dawn.

We will rediscover how to raise our children without hatred and greet death as a beginning.

Or, in the words of John McGrath's *Song*:

When governments and industries
Lie choked by weeds in fertile rain
For sure the few who stay alive
Will laugh and grow to love again.

CAVTOPATES

Endnotes & Key Sources

CHAPTER 1

Ashley, M 2005 *The Mammoth Book of King Arthur*. London: Constable.

Guest, C 1877 *The Mabinogion*. London: Bernard Quaritch.

Hatto, AT 1980 *Wolfram von Eschenbach: Parzival*. London: Penguin.

Johnson, RA 1977 *He: Understanding Masculine Psychology*. New York: Harper & Row.

Kibler, WW 1991 *Chrétien de Troyes: Arthurian Romances*. London: Penguin.

Watson, D 1963 *Three Plays by Eugène Ionesco*. London: John Calder.

Williams, GA 1994 *Excalibur: The Search for King Arthur*. London: BBC Books.

CHAPTER 2

Baigent, M, R. Leigh & H. Lincoln 1996 *The Holy Blood and the Holy Grail*. London: Arrow.

Brown, D 2004 *The Da Vinci Code*. London: Corgi.

Gardner, L 2002 *Bloodline of the Holy Grail: The Hidden Lineage of Jesus Revealed*. London: Element.

Graddon, N 2008 *Otto Rahn & The Quest for the Holy Grail: The Amazing Life of the Real "Indiana Jones"*. Kempton: Adventures Unlimited Press.

Lupack, A 2007 *The Oxford Guide to Arthurian Literature and Legend*. Oxford: OUP.

Marsh, D 2001 *Giambattista Vico: New Science*. London: Penguin.

Morgan, G 2011 *A Brief History of the Holy Grail: History, Myth, Religion*. London: Constable & Robinson.

CHAPTER 3

Note: *Canonbie Dick*. The name of the horse-trader would suggest that he came from Canonbie, a small village which just happens to lie immediately to the north of the Moat of Liddel, the probable site of the 'Action of Arderydd' in AD 573. The localised legend of the Lucken Hare in the Eildon Hills, with all its Arthurian undertones, is therefore linked – via the figure of Canonbie Dick – with the place where 'Merlin went mad' at a battle which, as I argue in Chapter 7, was the start of Arthur's military career.

Jones, G & T. Jones 1949 *The Mabinogion*. London: Everyman's Library.

Loomis, RS 1967 *Celtic Myth and Arthurian Romance*. New York: Haskell House.

Matthews, J 1991 *Taliesin: Shamanism and the Bardic Mysteries in Britain and Ireland*. London: The Aquarian Press.

Mithen, S 1998 *The Prehistory of the Mind: A Search for the Origins of Art, Religion and Science*. London: Phoenix.

Morgan, E 2000 *New Selected Poems*. Manchester: Carcanet.

Oxbrow, M & I. Robertson 2005 *Rosslyn and the Grail*. Edinburgh: Mainstream.

Skene, WF 1868 *The Four Ancient Books of Wales: The Cymric Poems attributed to the Bards of The Sixth Century*. Edinburgh: Edmonston and Douglas.

Welsh texts retrieved from www.maryjones.us and translated by the author.

CHAPTER 4

Note: *Gogfrân Gawr*. The term 'Gog' is Welsh slang for a 'northerner' (a contraction of *gogledd*, 'North'), but that does not seem to be the meaning behind the 'Gog' element of *Gogfrân* or, indeed, of the *Gogyrwen* associated with the cauldron and its inspirational liquor (see Chapter 3). The fact that the Welsh *cog/y gog* is cognate with the Gaelic *cuach*, a two-handled drinking cup (also *gogan*, a 'wooden dish'), might explain the 'Gog' element in both

Gogyrwen ('Cup-of-inspiration'?) and *Gogfrân* ('Cup-of-Brân', i.e. the 'Raven's cup'). The term *cuach* also appears in the *Carmina Gadelica* collection of traditional Gaelic hymns and incantations: a woman would pluck nine roots of a plant called *am mòthan* – possibly the bog violet – and knot them together to form a *cuach* or 'ring' (Gaelic *cuach*, 'ringlet' or 'curl'). She would put this into the mouth of a girl, and if the girl then kissed her beloved while the *cuach* was in her mouth he would instantly become her eternal bondsman; this folk tradition recalls the role of the protective ring in the Sacred Marriage of the cauldron initiate and his female soul-partner (see Chapter 9).

There is also an old Welsh word, *gogof* (modern *ogof*), a 'cave' or 'lair', which offers a very plausible 'Lair of the Blessed' or 'Cave-of-Inspiration' (*gogof* + *awen*) or even a 'Cave of the Yew' (**gogof-yr-ywen*), anticipating the chambered burial cairn or Mithraic temple (*mithraeum*) on Iona, as discussed in later chapters. Other possibilities, however, exist.

The Old Irish *og* signifies an 'egg' (Welsh *wy*; Gaelic *ugh*, genitive *uighe*) or 'testicle', while *óg* in Old Irish indicated something 'whole' and 'pure', as in a virginal maiden. Similarly, the Old Irish *óc* meant 'youth' (Gaelic *òg*) – hence the legendary *Tír na nÓg* ('Land of the Young') or *Tír na nÓige* ('Land of Youth') of Irish tradition. This 'Land of the Ever-Young' compares with the 'Land of Promise' (*Tír Tairngire*) and *Emain Ablach*, both of which can be identified as the Isle of Iona, the original 'Isle of the Blessed'.

It can be posited, then, that Iona was once *Í-oighe*, the 'Isle of Youth' or *Tír na nÓg*, the natal, *Ogygian* 'egg' of the world and the womb/tomb of heroes and champions, associated with youthfulness and rebirth, in which case the Welsh construct [G]*ogyrwen* might imply 'Óg [Iona] of the Blessed' (*óg* + *yr* + [*g*]*wen*). [G]*ogfrân* might then be an attempt by Welsh-speaking Britons at an Irish term meaning 'Young-Raven' (Gaelic **ògbhran*) or 'Iona-Raven'.

The Welsh *wy* (Gaelic *ugh*, Old Irish *og*) is also recalled in the early Arthurian tales of *The Mabinogion*; *Culhwch and Olwen* features the Eagle of Gwernabwy ('Alder-son-of-Egg') while the *Dream of Rhonabwy* recounts a vision of Arthur before his last battle as dreamt by one 'Lance-son-of-Egg'. It is possible that Iona or *Ioua*, the island of 'Youth' (Old Welsh *iouenc*), was mistranslated by Welsh bards, becoming the 'Egg' isle (Welsh *wy*, pronounced 'oo-uh'), the Gaelic for which would be *Í-uighe* (pronounced 'ee-oo-uh'); the Middle English *ey*, 'egg', also meant 'island', raising the possibility that, to the Divine age mind, an 'egg' and an 'isle' were much the same thing. It is equally conceivable that the oak-apples, which incubate the larvae of gall wasps, were thought of as 'eggs' – Latin *ova*, which would appear as [*I*]*oua* in the 7th-century script used by Adomnán of Iona.

Mention should also be made of the biblical figures of 'Gog and Magog', or 'Gog, of the land of Magog', who is referred to in *Ezekiel* 38-39 as a 'chief prince' of some northern barbarian people with allies in Persia, Ethiopia and Libya, amongst other places. The Bible repeatedly treats Gog and Magog, or Gog from Magog, as an archetypal enemy of God's people. The Qu'ran also features Gog and Magog as a distant people who do 'great mischief on earth' [*The Cave* 18:95], while Og, son of Anak – apparently from Egypt – is the only giant permitted to survive the Flood. In Britain and Ireland, Gog and Madog are remembered as giants; they are associated with oak-trees and celebrated as the guardians of the City of London. One myth claims that the Roman Emperor, Diocletian (AD 245-311), who was famous for his persecution of Christians, had 33 wicked daughters, one of whom was named Alba [the Gaelic name for 'Scotland']. Led by Alba, the daughters of Diocletian murdered their husbands, for which crime they were set adrift on the sea, washing up on a windswept isle which they named 'Albion' [Britain]. There, they coupled with demons and gave birth to giants, two of their descendants being Gog and Magog (this myth is heavily indebted to a Greek myth, which recalls that the Egyptian king Belus – Bel, Belial, Ba'al – had two sons, Aegyptus and Danaus, and according to Diodorus Siculus, Belus founded a colony on the River Euphrates and appointed the Mesopotamian astrologer-priests known as the Chaldeans. Aegyptus decided to marry his fifty sons to the fifty daughters of his twin brother, Danaus. Danaus built the first-ever ship and escaped with his daughters to Greece, where they founded the city of Argos. Aegyptus caught up with them, so Danaus ordered his daughters to kill their husbands on their wedding night. One of the daughters – Hypermnestra – refused to do so, and thus the dynasty known to Homer as the 'Danaans' was established). It is possible that the 'Gog' of British and Irish tradition was related to *Ogma*, an Irish god of letters, words and wisdom [Gaulish *Ogmios*] who created the Druidic 'Ogham' alphabet, every letter of which was styled after a tree. Ogma, or Oghma, was one of the 'three gods of skill', along with Lugh and the Dagda (Ogma was the Dagda's brother and Lugh's half-brother; his grandsons – the 'Sons of Tuirenn' – killed Lugh's father, Cian; see Chapter 5). And so, once again, we find a tradition which appears to originate in Mesopotamia but which leads us back to Arthur and his circle.

Crane, E 1980 *A Book of Honey*. Oxford: OUP.
Crookall, R 1992 *Out-of-the-Body Experiences – A Fourth Analysis*. New York: Citadel Press.
De Martino, E 1972 *Magic Primitive and Modern*. London: Tom Stacey.
Hoffman, E 1981 *Huna: A Beginner's Guide*. Atglen: Whitford Press.
Hoffman, E 2012 *New Brain, New World*. London: Hay House.
Nicholson, S (ed.) 1987 *Shamanism*. Wheaton: Quest Books.
Wilson, C 1979 *The Occult*. St Albans: Granada.

CHAPTER 5

Note: *the Garden at the East of the World*. All other sources indicate that the apple-bearing place was in the west. However, the Gaelic word *domhan*, genitive *domhain* – 'the world' (Old Irish *domun* or *domain*) – derives from the Proto-Celtic **dubnos*, 'the deep' (Gaelic *domhain*). The Garden at the 'East of the Deep', or east of the 'Abyss', would in fact be on the edge of the Atlantic Ocean and therefore 'in the west' from a European mainland point of view. Conceivably, the Isle of Iona (or the 'Iouan' isle, as Adomnán called it) was originally *I-dhomhan*, the 'Isle of the Deep'; it is referred to as such in the 'Iona Boat Song' of Kenneth Macleod, and the largest bay on the western, Atlantic side of the island is known as the Bay at the Back of the Ocean (*Camus Cùl an taibh*; variant *Camus Cùl an t-Saimh*, the 'Bay at the Back of the Shoreline' or 'Bay at the Back of the God/Giant/Hero').

Note: *Iona*. Kenneth Macleod, a Scottish poet who is buried on Iona, referred to the island as 'Iona the blest, *I mo chridh thu*, / Isle of my heart, my grail' and as 'I-mo-chree, my Grail-lit isle'. Bessie J.B. MacArthur, meanwhile, declaimed:

O fair Iona,
Dream-girt Isle,
Guardian of saints and heroes, kings,
Thy ground is holy.

See: *An Iona Anthology*, edited by F. Marian McNeill (The New Iona Press, 1990).

Aitchison, N 2000 *Scotland's Stone of Destiny: Myth, History and Nationhood*. Stroud: Tempus.

Barber, R 1999 *Myths and Legends of the British Isles*. Woodbridge: Boydell Press.

Campbell, ME 1888 *Sgeulachd air Sir Uallabh O'Còrn*. Proceedings of the Gaelic Society of Inverness Vol. XIII 1886-87.

Clancy, TO (ed.) 1998 *The Triumph Tree: Scotland's Earliest Poetry AD 550-1350*. Edinburgh: Canongate Classics.

Ó Corráin, D, L. Breatnach, K. McCone (eds.) 1989 *Sages, Saints and Storytellers: Celtic Studies in Honour of Professor James Carney*. Maynooth: An Sagart.

Ritchie, A & E. Ritchie 1934 *Iona Past and Present with Maps*. Edinburgh: Geo. Stewart & Co.

Rutherford, W 1983 *The Druids: Magicians of the West*. Wellingborough: Aquarian Press.

CHAPTER 6

Beck, R 2006 *The Religion of the Mithras Cult in the Roman Empire: Mysteries of the Unconquered Sun*. Oxford: OUP.

Hutton, R 1991 *The Pagan Religions of the Ancient British Isles: Their Nature and Legacy*. London: BCA.

Lincoln, B 1991 *Death, War, And Sacrifice: Studies in Ideology and Practice*. Chicago: University of Chicago Press.

Macquarrie, A & E.M. MacArthur 1992 *Iona through the ages* (2nd Edition). Society of West Highland & Island Historical Research.

Matarasso, PM 1969 *The Quest of the Holy Grail*. London: Penguin.

Rieu, EV 2003 *Homer: The Odyssey* (Revised translation by DCH Rieu). London: Penguin.

Sandars, NK 1987 *The Epic of Gilgamesh*. London: Penguin.

CHAPTER 7

Jaynes, J 1990 *The Origins of Consciousness in the Breakdown of the Bicameral Mind*. London: Penguin.

Joseph, R 2011 *Right Hemisphere, Left Hemisphere, Consciousness & the Unconscious Brain and Mind* (3rd Edition). UniversityPress.info.

Koestler, A 1989 *The Sleepwalkers*. London: Arkana.

Laing, RD 1990 *The Divided Self*. London: Penguin.

Sherley-Price, L 1990 *Bede: Ecclesiastical History of the English People* (Revised by RE Latham). London: Penguin.

Thorpe, L 1966 *Geoffrey of Monmouth: The History of the Kings of Britain*. Harmondsworth: Penguin.

Tolstoy, N 1990 *The Quest for Merlin*. London: Sceptre.

CHAPTER 8

Note: *Clan Campbell*. The powerful Campbell clan emerged in the late-13th century as a sub-branch of the MacArthur dynasty, otherwise known as *Clann Artair* or Clan Arthur. The MacArthurs were renowned for the antiquity of their line and traced their ancestry back to Artúr mac Áedáin, the blazon of the chief's armorial shield (*Azure, three antique crowns Or*) corresponding to the supposed arms of the legendary 'King' Arthur. The MacArthurs were originally associated with the settlement of Strachur ('Vale of the Hero/Champion') on the shore of Loch Fyne, the lake of the 'vine' or the 'family', in Argyll; an old Gaelic proverb refers to *MacArtair Srath Churra o bhun an stoc fheàrna* – 'MacArthur of Strachur, from the root of the alder' – while early Scottish manuscripts cite a 'chief-hero' and 'powerful Lion' of Loch Fyne.

The Campbell branch of the family descended from Arthur preferred to trace their roots back to Diarmaid, the Fingalian hero – possibly because any mention of Arthur was inimical to the Church – and so they were often referred to as *Clan Diarmid*, their chief seat being at Inverary, across Loch Fyne from the Strachur of the MacArthurs. The fact that the Campbells chose the boar's head (Welsh *pen baedd*) as their emblem does seem to reflect the slaying of the Pictish 'Chief-Boar' Galam Cennaleth (recalled as Ysgithrywyn Penbaedd – 'White-tusk Chief-boar' – in the native British accounts) which established Arthur as the hero of the North. The Campbells also sported the bog myrtle (see Chapter 9) in their bonnets as a sort of clan badge, the MacArthurs favouring the wild myrtle or fir club moss.

Barber, R 1987 *The Arthurian Legends*. Woodford: Boydell Press.
Innes, M 1995 *Ovid: Metamorphoses*. London: Penguin.
Matthews, J (ed.) 1988 *An Arthurian Reader: Selections from Arthurian Legend, Scholarship and Story*. Wellingborough:

Aquarian Press.
North, A 1998 *The Supernatural: A Guide to Mysticism and the Occult*. London: Blandford.
Peat, FD 1996 *Blackfoot Physics: A Journey into the Native American Universe*. London: Fourth Estate.
Sagan, C 1997 *The Demon-Haunted World: Science as a Candle in the Dark*. London: Headline.
Watson, WJ 1993 *The History of the Celtic Place-Names of Scotland*. Edinburgh: Birlinn.

CHAPTER 9

Note: *Ea*. These various names – Aea, Ea, Ia – which refer either to the Isle of Iona or another 'remote' island of classical antiquity, also point us back to ancient Mesopotamia and the legends of the Flood. Several centuries before the biblical Hebrew story of the Flood legend was written down, cuneiform tablets recorded the Mesopotamian versions of the same story. In these, it was Enki, the Sumerian 'god of great understanding', who advised the 'exceedingly wise' Flood survivor, Atra-Hasis, to construct an Ark ('Destroy [your] house, build a boat; spurn property and save life!'). The Babylonian equivalent of Enki was Ea, an omniscient god of wisdom who lulled his own father to sleep and then stole his radiance (compare the Greek myth of Kronos, who was castrated and displaced by his son Zeus; Kronos was then imprisoned in a state of permanent sleep on an island off the west coast of Britain).

Both the Sumerian Enki and the Babylonian Ea were associated with the creation of life (it is possible that Ea derives from a West-Semitic root, **hyy*, which meant 'life' and reminds us that Iona was also known as *Hii*), as well as being the masters of craft, cunning, intelligence and the gifts of civilisation; like Apollo and the leontocephaline Mithras-Kronos, their image was the Caduceus or double-helix snake, associated with the arts of medicine. Ea and Enki were essentially water-gods, their temples being the 'house of waters' (Sumerian $E_2.A$; compare e_2-*anna*, the 'House of Heaven' held sacred to Inanna, the Sumerian Venus). Their animals were the goat and the fish, later combined into the half-goat, half-fish symbol of Capricorn, and the gods themselves were often depicted in human form but with the skin of a fish. This should instantly remind us of Oannes, the 'Fish-Man' who survived the Flood and taught the arts of civilisation to the people who lived by the River Euphrates (discussed in Chapter 6). Oannes was supposedly one of 'seven sages' who were all associated with Ea/Enki, the god of water and wisdom.

If Ea and Oannes remind us of the Isle of Iona – the 'Navel of the sea' – then the 'seven sages' who helped to civilise the people of Mesopotamia might correspond to the 'seven bishops of Hii'. These 'seven bishops' of Iona were mentioned by the 8th-century Irish monk, Óengus of Tallaght, in his *Félire Óengusso Céli Dé* ('Martyrology of Óengus the Culdee'). An account of St Columba's taking of Iona had him summarily dismissing two bishops from the island on the grounds that they were 'not true Bishops'. Presumably, they belonged to a Druidic order.

Adomnán, as we know, referred to the Isle of Iona as *Ioua insula*, the first part of which compares with various attempts throughout the last two millennia to render the Tetragrammaton (*YHWH*) in English, with *Iehováh*, *Iehoua*, *Ieoa* and *Jova* all having been offered as alternatives to the more familiar *Yahweh* or *Jehovah* (*Jova* would have been written 'Ioua' in Adomnán's day). It may be, then, that *Ioua* was an early version of 'Jehovah', while the later *Iona* corresponds to the Hebrew *Yonah* (biblical Jonah), a 'dove'. Closer still is the Levantine sea-god Yw or Yaw, who appears to be related to both the Canaanite Yahweh and the Mesopotamian Abzu (god of sacred waters). Yaw was a god of rivers and seas, of the oceanic abyss, and was equated with the Greek Poseidon; he was similar, then, to the Babylonian water-god, Ea.

Another point worth making is that the original form of the

Ark, in which creatures were saved from the devastating Flood, was a large, round coracle (see *The Ark Before Noah: Decoding the Story of the Flood* by Irving Finkel, Hodder & Stoughton, 2014). Not only was the Primary Chief Bard Taliesin set adrift in a coracle after his cauldron initiation, but similar ordeals were undergone by a pregnant princess of Lothian, who was probably the mother of Arthur, and the sister of St Cadog/Catán, who had reputedly been impregnated by Áedán mac Gabráin, the father of Artúr.

There are, then, a number of threads which suggest that some sort of primordial wisdom emanated from the Isle of Iona, replenishing the stock of human knowledge after the disruption caused by rising sea-levels or a sudden cataclysmic disaster. The identification of Iona as *Aea* or *Ea* indicates that the little isle was associated with wisdom and the healing arts – the gifts of those 'Wise Salmon' who survived the cauldron initiation. The use of the coracle (also thought of as a 'box' or 'hamper' of wickerwork) in the final stages of the initiation process can be seen as a recapitulation of the Flood and the survival of primal wisdom, embodied in the initiate, which was then disseminated throughout the world by the 'seven sages', who were both men and fish.

There is certainly a sense of things coming full circle, with the possibility that Oannes, the fish-like sage, brought antediluvian wisdom from Iona (Ia, Ea, Aea) to the people living between the Tigris and the Euphrates, and the fact that a Persian god, Mithra, worshipped around the headwaters of the Euphrates, was later venerated by Arthur and his warriors. This cyclical exchange of gods and learning is neatly symbolised by the Sword of Strange Hangings, the hilt of which combined the ribs of a Scottish 'serpent' and a 'fish' found only in the Euphrates, and by the 'lightning' spear of Lugh – the most 'famous yew of the wood', which could both wound and heal and was said to have belonged to Pisear, the 'King of Persia'.

Burckhardt, T 2006 *Alchemy: Science of the Cosmos, Science of the Soul*. Louisville: Fons Vitae.
Carmichael, A 1992 *Carmina Gadelica: Hymns and Incantations from the Gaelic*. Edinburgh: Floris.
Gregory, A 1905 *Gods and Fighting Men*. Kindle Edition.
Macleod, F 1982 *Iona*. Edinburgh: Floris.
Ramsay, JH 1915 *Bamff Charters A.D. 1232-1703*. London: OUP.
Rieu, EV 1971 *Apollonius of Rhodes: The Voyage of Argo*. London: Penguin.
Versluis, A 1986 *The Philosophy of Magic*. London: Arkana.

CHAPTER 10

Note: *Beltane*. This festival, the name of which meant 'fires of Bel', was probably the most significant event in the Celtic calendar. It celebrated the sacred marriage of the Sun (Bel/Beli Mawr/Belenos) and his lunar consort, Anna, and so the occasion was devoted to fertility (couples copulated 'anonymously' in the woods on Beltane night) and, it would appear, the conception of special – i.e. god-given – children. Significantly, the names of Bel ('Lord') and Anna (Sumerian *nin-anna*, 'queen of heaven') can both be traced back to ancient Mesopotamia, the sister and lover of Ba'al having been 'Anat or Anath.

Taliesin underwent his cauldron initiation at Beltane, and there is Beltane imagery in the *Sgeulachd air Sir Uallabh O'Còrn*, when Arthur's nephew is sentenced to be torn apart by horses between two fires (at Beltane, cattle were driven between fires as part of a purification ceremony). St Columba stormed the Isle of Iona on the 'eve of Whitsunday' in 563, rightly assuming that the resident Druids would be preoccupied with their Beltane festivities; these would have been celebrated at the 'Hill of Fires', otherwise known as *an Sithean Mór*, the burial mound on the west side of Iona in which the cauldron initiates were laid to rest for three days before they were released in their 'rebirth' ceremony.

It is probable that Beltane was not celebrated on a fixed date.

Like those other Moon festivals (Imbolc, Lughnasadh, Samhain) it seems likely that it was a moveable feast timed, perhaps, to coincide with the phases of the Moon. Beltane might then have taken place over the three-day period of the New Moon. Solar eclipses can only take place during the New Moon, and such total eclipses would supply the Beltane imagery of the lunar Anna sleeping in the arms of her solar lover, Bel. The same imagery might explain the slaying of the horned Moon bull by the solar hero, Mithras ('Sol Invictus'), and the magical ring with its precious stone which formed part of the Grail-related paraphernalia in the Arthurian legends and compares with the 'diamond ring effect' of the Moon being positioned directly in front of the Sun. Eclipse imagery can also be detected in Taliesin's accounts of Arthur's burial, suggesting that Arthur's head was interred in the chambered burial cairn on Iona at about six in the morning of Friday 23 July 594 (Artúr mac Áedáin, as we know, died in 594, his death later being celebrated in Ireland as *Bron trogain* or *Lughnasadh* at the beginning of August).

Giles, JA 1841 *The Works of Gildas and Nennius, Translated from the Latin*. London: James Bohn.

Green, CW 1998 *Jocelyn, a monk of Furness: The Life of Kentigern (Mungo)*. New York: Fordham University.

Headrick, J 1845 *'Parish of Dunnichen': New Statistical Account of Scotland, Vol XI*. Edinburgh: William Blackwood & Sons.

Morris, J 1973 *The Age of Arthur: A History of the British Isles from 350 to 650*. London: The History Book Club.

M'Pherson, JG 1885 *Strathmore: Past and Present*. Perth: S. Cowan & Co.

Stirling, R M'D 1894 *Inveresk Parish Lore from Pagan Times*. Musselburgh: T.C. Blair.

Warrack, A 1911 *A Scots Dialect Dictionary: The Words in Use from the Latter Part of the Seventeenth Century to the Present Day*. London: W & R Chambers.

CHAPTER 11

Note: *The Smith*. We have already seen that St Columba's smiths melted down the sacrificial knife belonging to 'Molua' or 'Luan', which the saint had blessed and then prevented Molua from using, and we might wonder whether this was the same knife as that with which Gúaire son of Áedáin fatally wounded his own knee. References to smiths are scattered throughout the Arthurian sources and their localised variants: in Chapter 5, we saw that 'Cian', the father of 'Lugh Long-Hand', was killed by the three Sons of Tuirenn, where 'Tuirenn' compares with the Irish *tuireann*, meaning 'sparks from a smith's anvil'; it was also noted of the Hebridean *Sgeulachd air Sir Uallabh O'Còrn*, which was recorded near the Isle of Iona, that the Irish king (who might have been Arthur) suspected that his wife had a lover and lost a battle with the 'Big Lad', son of the 'King of Innean', the Gaelic *innean* signifying a 'smith's anvil'. Finally, we might recall that Chrétien's Perceval was presented with a sword which was destined to break at a critical moment; the sword could only be repaired by the smith who made it, and who was based at the lake beyond the River Forth (presumably Loch Venachar, the source of the Cascade of the Smith, near Callander, where a fair was held in honour of 'St Kessog' of Luss).

Note: *St Constantine/Llwydog Gofynniad*. As discussed in Chapter 3, the cauldron was wrested by Arthur and his men from Ireland and left in the care of Llwyd ap Cil Coed at a place identified as Mesur-y-peir ('Measure-of-the-cauldron'). Elsewhere, Llwyd ap Cil Coed is described as the 'bishop' who prepared the mystical cauldron as a trap for 'Pryderi' and his mother (Pryderi – 'Anxiety' – and his mother Rhiannon, meaning 'Great Maiden' or 'Little Princess' – also **rhi-annwn*, 'Lord of Annwn' – can be identified as the historical Owain and his mother, Arthur's sister, Muirgein, the 'daughter of Afallach' and 'daughter to the King of Annwn'). The name of Llwyd ap Cil Coed signifies a 'Grey' or 'Holy' one, the 'son of the Hermitage of the Wood' or the 'Chapel of the Grove'. Llwyd was, apparently, a 'bishop' as well as being Arthur's 'chief huntsman', a term which could be rendered in Welsh as *cynydd* or 'master of hounds' (the dog-like nature of Columba's monks is discussed in Chapter 8).

If the 'Measure of the Cauldron' was the burial cairn of *Sithean Mór* on Iona, where the cauldron initiates were incubated during their ritual imprisonment, then the 'Chapel of the Grove' suggests a holy place on the island of the grove of sacred trees (Iona). The name of the treacherous Llwydog Gofynniad, meanwhile, could be interpreted as a 'Smith' who was associated with the grey/holy Llwyd of the 'Chapel of the Grove'. This would certainly make sense if Arthur's assassin was baptised by St Columba (the 'Grey/Holy' one of the church on the 'Yewy' isle) and subsequently sought refuge in the 'Vale of Yews', *Ystrad Yw*. St Constantine would therefore have been the creature of Columba, doing the bidding of his religious master when he slew Arthur in Strathmore and subsequently protected by Columba. His remains were later housed in a stone sarcophagus which recalled his fatal wounding of a horseman labelled 'A'.

Note: *Pictish symbol stones*. Norman J. Penny, an Inverness-born engineer, has spent a lifetime studying the Pictish stones across Scotland, and has formed the conclusion that they are the relics of a particularly insular form of Mithraic worship. His website – pictish-mithraism.com – discusses his theories about the recurring symbols carved into the stones and his belief that the Pictish stones constituted a form of 'outdoor mithraeum'. Whether or not this was indeed the case (the very concept of an 'outdoor' temple of Mithras seems like a contradiction in terms) it is notable that Penny has identified what he feels is Mithraic imagery on the symbol stones of Pictland.

Forbes, IWG 2012 *The Last of the Druids: The Mystery of the Pictish Symbol Stones*. Stroud: Amberley.

Laing, L and J. Laing 1993 *The Picts and the Scots*. Stroud: Alan Sutton.

MacArthur, EM 1995 *Columba's Island: Iona from Past to Present*. Edinburgh: Edinburgh University Press.
Maclean, C 1997 *The Isle of Mull: Placenames, Meanings and Stories*. Dumfries: Maclean Publications.
Senior, M 1979 *Myths of Britain*. London: Book Club Associates.
Sharpe, R 1995 *Adomnán of Iona: Life of St Columba*. London: Penguin.
Stirling, SA 2012 *The King Arthur Conspiracy: How a Scottish Prince Became a Mythical Hero*. Stroud: The History Press.

CHAPTER 12

Note: *the 'serpents' of the old religion*. Nothing better illustrates the ways that the different periods in the development of civilisation use language. The Divine age tends to see the snake as something mystical and worthy of reverence; more than anything, the serpent is associated with youth (its ability to slough its skin and reappear in a renewed form suggests rebirth and regeneration) and with earthly wisdom (snakes tend to vanish into holes in the ground just before earthquakes happen). Consequently, the great Celtic goddess Brighid or Brìde was symbolised in her youthful Maiden aspect by a snake, which was one of her three sacred animals. The Heroic age upends this view of snakes, probably because of the serpent's presence in the Garden of Eden story; they become emblematic of evil and untrustworthiness, even after the original meaning of the 'serpent' – a Druidic 'adder' or wise man – has long been forgotten. The Human age might note that neither Ireland nor Iona has ever hosted venomous snakes and conclude that the twin legends of St Patrick and St Columba banishing these creatures from their respective shores are nothing more than religious fables. The reality is that no actual snakes were banished by either saint, but the serpentine practitioners of the old traditions were.

Note: *Fresh place of the dark blackthorn*. The legend of Deirdre of the Sorrows forms part of the Ulster Cycle of mythological stories. The tale concerns a beautiful young priestess who escaped from Ireland with her Druidic lover, Naoise, and his two brothers. They settled first in Argyll, where the Scots first gained their foothold in western Scotland. In time, Deirdre and her Druidic friends decamped from Glen Etive and established a new base on an 'island in the sea'. Deirdre, in a touching lament known as her 'Farewell to Alba', referred to this island as *Draigen*:

> Beloved is Draigen,
> Dear the white sand beneath its waves ...

The Old Irish word *draigen* (Old Celtic *dragino-*) meant 'blackthorn'. The 'island in the sea', where Deirdre and her Druids made their home in exile, was therefore the 'Blackthorn' isle, and it remained so up until the 13th century, when Raghnall son of Somerled's praise poem referred to Iona as the 'Fresh place of the dark blackthorn'. The blackthorn was used as a protective hedge around shrines – especially those sacred to Brighid, the goddess of the hearth, whose Imbolc festival was celebrated during the 'Blackthorn winter' of early February. One tradition has Brighid growing up on the southern flank of Iona's highest hill. The existence of the blackthorn enclosure on Iona is revealed by place-names on the south-east flank of Dùn Í, the highest hill on the island, just west of St Columba's monastic settlement.

The reference to Iona as the 'Blackthorn' isle reminds us that Arthur's father, the 'Lord of Annwn' and the king who protected the Island of Apples, was also the *Pen Draigen* or 'Chief of Iona'.

Note: *Babylonian exile of the Jews*. Between *c* 597 and *c* 539 BC the most prominent Judeans were effectively held captive in Babylon. The biblical *Book of Daniel* reveals that the Babylonian king, Nebuchadnezzar, ordered the Judean intelligentsia to learn the language and literature of Mesopotamia: 'And the king spake unto Ashpenaz the master of his eunuchs, that he should bring certain of the children of Israel, and of the king's seed, and of the princes; Children in whom was no blemish, but well favoured, and skilful in all wisdom, and cunning in knowledge, and understanding science, and such as hand ability in them to stand in the king's palace, and whom they might teach the learning and the tongue of the Chaldeans' (*Daniel* 1: 3,4). The urge to preserve Judean history as an antidote to complete assimilation in Babylonian culture ultimately led to the writing of the Old Testament, which betrays so many Mesopotamian influences (not least of all in the story of the Flood) that it clearly grew out of the knowledge acquired by the Jewish exiles in Babylon. It was there that they learnt to read and write (cuneiform, initially) while suffering the traumatic identity crisis of the unwilling exile. The result was a religion which relied exclusively on the Book – the very hallmark of the Heroic age.

Note: *National Museum of Denmark, Copenhagen.* A replica of the cauldron is also on display at Trinity College, Dublin. The existence of a facsimile of the Gundestrup Cauldron in Ireland suggests that the artefact is of some relevance to Irish history (in 1979, Garrett S. Olmsted argued that the images on the cauldron illustrate a Gaulish version of that great myth of Ulster, the *Táin Bó Cuailnge*, thereby relating the cauldron's imagery to the cultural nexus of Arthur's people). The fact that there is no such replica in a Scottish museum reflects the later prejudices, largely imposed by the south, which refused to acknowledge that the original form of the 'Holy Grail' was a magnificent cauldron of 'rich workmanship', a 'vat' of gold and silver with a 'band around the rim'. It is surely time to turn our backs on the medieval nonsense and accept that the Gundestrup Cauldron is either the physical manifestation of the Grail itself or the closest thing to it, in which case there should be a high-quality copy of it (at least) in a British museum, and preferably in a Scottish one.

Horovitz, M (ed.) 1969 *Children of Albion*. Harmondsworth: Penguin.

James, O 2007 *Affluenza*. London: Vermilion.
Klein, N 2007 *The Shock Doctrine*. London: Penguin.
Liedloff, J 1976 *The Continuum Concept*. London: Futura.
Nicolson, A (ed.) 1996 *Gaelic Proverbs*. Edinburgh: Birlinn.
Perera, SB 1981 *Descent of the Goddess*. Toronto: Inner City Books.
Sargant, W 1959 *Battle for the Mind*. London: Pan.

MOON BOOKS

Moon Books invites you to begin or deepen your encounter with Paganism, in all its rich, creative, flourishing forms.